"Ready?" the Disciple asked Jade, grimacing and favoring his right leg. "Go."

Harmonious Jade drew her final arrow, sprinted to the roof's edge and hurled herself toward the next nearest safe vantage. The Disciple started firing immediately to knock down the climbing ghosts who had made it closest to where Jade intended to land, and the arrows whizzed all around her, dangerously close. Jade ignored these distractions, however, and focused all of her concentration on twisting just so, taking instant aim and drawing her final arrow back to her cheek. Power surged in her as she did so, and as the arrow left her bow, it roared _____ The dazzling flare flew faster and _____ rmal arrow, and it went str_____ The priestess flinch_____ error, but all she n_____ ing censer into the arrou_____ olt hit it, and both objects ex_____ hunderclap that sent the priestess flyin_____ ard into the mausoleum. At the same time, Harmonious Jade finished her slow roll through the air and landed in a three-point crouch.

As soon as Jade landed, the Disciple leapt into the air after her. The leering deathknight threw another long needle at him and missed, but the Disciple didn't even bother to return fire. He focused solely on clearing the distance, even sacrificing grace in his landing. His knees and forearms hit the roof first, and he slid to a rough halt well beyond where Jade had touched down. Jade rushed over to him and helped him laboriously to his feet.

Blood was running down his forehead and between his eyes.

EXALTED FICTION
FROM WHITE WOLF

THE TRILOGY OF THE SECOND AGE
Chosen of the Sun by Richard Dansky
Beloved of the Dead by Richard Dansky
Children of the Dragon by Richard Dansky

FORTHCOMING EXALTED NOVELS
Relic of the Dawn by David Niall Wilson
In Northern Twilight by Jess Hartley
Pillar of the Sun by Carl Bowen

ALSO BY CARL BOWEN
Predator & Prey: Vampire
Predator & Prey: Mage
"Silent Striders" in Tribe Novel #2: **Silent Striders & Black Furies**
"Silver Fangs" in Tribe Novel #6: **Silver Fangs & Glass Walkers**
"Thief's Mark" in **Champions of the Scarred Lands**
"A Legitimate Obligation" in **Demon: Lucifer's Shadow**

For all these titles and more, visit
www.white-wolf.com/fiction

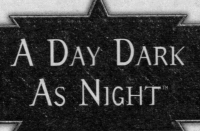

A Day Dark As Night™

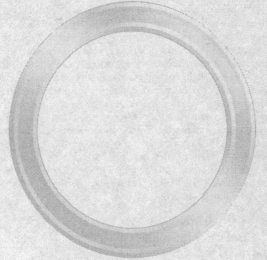

Carl Bowen

Cover art by UDON featuring Noi Sackda and Omar Dogan. Book design by Brian Glass. Art direction by Richard Thomas and Brian Glass. Copyedited by John Chambers.

ISBN 1-58846-859-3
First Edition: May 2004
Printed in Canada

White Wolf Publishing
1554 Litton Drive
Stone Mountain, GA 30083
www.white-wolf.com/fiction

It Is the Second Age of Man

Long ago, in the First Age, mortals became Exalted by the Unconquered Sun and other celestial gods. These demigods were Princes of the Earth and presided over a golden age of unparalleled wonder. But like all utopias, the age ended in tears and bloodshed.

The officials histories say that the Solar Exalted went mad and had to be put down lest they destroy all Creation. Those who had been enlightened rulers became despots and anathema. Some whisper the Sun-Children were betrayed by the very companions and lieutenants they had loved: the less powerful Exalts who traced their lineage to the Five Elemental Dragons. Either way, the First Age ended and gave way to an era of chaos and warfare, when the civilized world faced invasion by the mad Fair Folk and the devastation of the Great Contagion. This harsh time only ended with the rise of the Scarlet Empress, a powerful Dragon-Blood who fought back all enemies and founded a great empire.

For a time, all was well—at least for those who toed the Empress's line.

But times are changing again. The Scarlet Empress has either gone missing or retreated into seclusion. The dark forces of the undead and the Fair Folk are stirring again. And, most cataclysmic of all, the Solar Exalted have returned. Across Creation, men and women find themselves imbued with the power of the Unconquered Sun and awaken to memories from a long-ago golden age.

The Sun-Children, the Anathema, have been reborn.

This is their story.

PROLOGUE

One night's ride outside the city of Nexus, two old soldiers rode side by side through the mounting chill of early night. The land around them was quiet in hushed anticipation, disturbed only by the occasional trill of a cricket or screech of a bat taking wing. Before them, the solemn, hard-packed road was empty. Behind them, yeddim muttered, the wheels of wooden carts creaked, and fifty booted, lightly armored mercenaries marched in uneasy silence. Beyond that, came the metallic four-beat rhythm of a small unit of light cavalry. The soldiers surrounded a Guild caravan heading northeast from a trade outpost near the city of Mishaka, and they had been on the march for weeks. The caravan had been on the move most of this day already with little rest. The Guildsmen and soldiers weren't overly tired just yet, but the danger they had been promised on this trip had not yet appeared, and that made them edgy.

The two riders out in front of the caravan and company consisted of a man and a woman who were better armed and armored than most of the other mercenaries. The man was tall and grim, wearing fine lamellar armor that creaked as he moved. His mustache and beard were flecked with white, and his eyes had the determined set of a veteran of countless battles, but those were the only clues to his age. His body was hard and powerful, in the prime of health. If he bothered to mention it, his actual age would have come as a surprise.

One might have been even more surprised by the woman beside him. She rode on his right side, and she looked much younger than her captain. Her skin was smooth and flawless, with a vibrant green tint that was only apparent in direct sunlight. Thick auburn hair was woven into a ponytail and pinned into a bun at the base of her neck. She wore lighter armor than her captain, though just as fine, and she rode with a thick, black, jade-tipped spear at the ready by her side. At first glance, she appeared every bit the officer-sophisticate with little bloody experience, flanked by a tough, savvy sergeant at arms.

Such an impression was only an illusion, though, for the woman was actually a Terrestrial Exalt. She had been elevated above her peers into the rank of the divine nobility of Creation by the blessings of the Elemental Dragons. Her name was Risa, and she had been chosen by the Elemental Dragon of Wood to carry the standard of the Realm into the untamed places and shed on them the light of civilization. At least that was what her family had always tried to impress upon her. She recognized the power in her blood, but she had grown up feeling unworthy of it. Therefore, she had left the Imperial City of her birth and set out into the Threshold to grow into her power and responsibility. Since then, she had joined up with a mercenary company in the city of Nexus and risen high in its ranks.

The man to her left, Dace, was her commander. He respected Risa's Exalted station, but he still allowed her no authority in his company that did not originate with him. Where she had earned high marks in military theory and tactics in school, he had already been a leader of soldiers for fifteen years before she had joined her first company. Where she was a proud and capable soldier, he was a nigh-unbeaten veteran with decades of campaigns to his name. Where she inspired confidence in the mercenaries, he made them love him. And where Risa was Dragon-Blooded and Exalted above the masses, Dace was one of the Chosen of the Unconquered Sun.

The dogma of the Realm proclaimed that ones such as Dace were Anathema—power-mad blasphemies against nature, who would destroy civilization and break the whole of Creation to pieces—but Risa knew better. She knew Dace as well as any lieutenant knows her captain, and she had seen in him power and nobility and courage that defied any blandishment. She loved him as much as any of the mercenaries under his command did. She would follow him into the Yozi hell of Malfeas if he commanded her to, and she'd stay behind to cover his escape if he asked her to. She trusted him, and above all else, she respected him.

"So, are we almost home yet?" she groaned, breaking the silence between them at last. "How much *longer?*"

Dace just shook his head. "Damn it, Risa," he grumbled, "that wasn't funny on the way to Mishaka, and it's not funny now."

"Oh, how would you know, you gruff old bastard?" She never spoke to him thus around the men, but Dace tolerated it when they were alone.

"I'd say it's probably less funny now than it wasn't before," Dace continued. "The only thing worse than your bad jokes are your old bad jokes. Nothing gets funnier with age."

"Says the rule to the exception."

"What's that?"

"Nothing, sir." Risa looked away up the road. "It looks like the scouts are on their way back."

She nodded toward the road, and Dace looked ahead. Low mist occluded the distance, and shadows stretched up the path in their direction, but he could see that, indeed, a horse was coming toward them. On it rode Chassom Kestrel, one of the company's younger scouts. He wore a light buff jacket over his uniform, with a quiver of arrows sticking up over his right shoulder. He clung to the reins and rode hunched over, and his face was pale. Dace and Risa had ridden out ahead to hear their scouts' scheduled report, and from the look in Kestrel's dancing eyes, it was not going to be a good one. The fact that he was alone, although he'd been sent ahead with two others, didn't bode well either. Kestrel stopped short, and his horse danced in a nervous circle before he could bring it fully under control.

"Captain, Lieutenant," Kestrel gasped. "Something's wrong."

Risa stilled her mount as the scout's horse excited it. "Where are the others?"

"I'm not sure," the scout huffed. "I think… Ikari Village is up ahead… You know that, of course."

"Of course," Risa said. "Look, calm down, Kestrel. Catch your breath."

"Get it together, soldier," Dace said, glaring back the way Kestrel had come. "Report."

"Yes, sir," the scout said, taking a few quick deep breaths to calm himself. "Yes, sir. Sorry." Dace's eyes narrowed, and he motioned for the scout to continue. "Brand, Dust Fox and I rode ahead like you ordered, sir, to let the mayor know we were coming and to make arrangements for the caravan to set up there for the night. But no one came out to greet us as we arrived. We knocked on a couple of doors at some outlying houses, but no one answered. The same was true the closer we went to the town square. The place was quiet as a tomb. That's when we looked in the temple to the village's harvest spirit."

The scout paused and swallowed hard, as if to fight back nausea.

"What did you see?" Risa prompted.

"It was the villagers. They were in the temple. Dead. It looked like they'd all been hacked apart. Or chewed, maybe. I don't know. It was… I've seen worse in battle, but these were women and children too. And they'd been *arranged*. They were laid out like they were worshiping. I've never seen anything like that."

Risa looked at Dace. "Have you?"

"Similar things," Dace said. "How long had they been there like that?"

Kestrel shook his head. "The blood I saw was black and dried, and the stench was pretty powerful. I didn't see any wild dogs or other scavengers in the streets, though."

"So, probably not very long," Risa said. "Late last night possibly. Maybe even some time today."

Kestrel nodded. "Brand and Fox sent me back to report while they tried to put together what happened. I tried to get them to come back with me, but they told me they'd be right behind me as soon as they figured it all out."

"So you left them there?" Dace said.

"They ordered me to, sir," Kestrel answered. "I would have gone back, but the sun was almost down, and I started hearing…"

"What?"

The scout moaned, unable to look either officer in the eye. "First I heard the sound of wagons, then some kind of wailing, then the sounds of Fox's and Brand's horses galloping behind me. Then I heard them screaming… I couldn't go back then, Captain, I'm sorry. Not by myself."

"No," Dace said. "None of the three of you should have been there after nightfall in the first place."

"So, what do you think, happened, Captain?" Risa asked.

"Could be something wrong with the harvest spirit," Dace said. "It's getting close to Calibration, and that always makes the little gods kind of crazy. Could be another spirit got jealous and tried to move in. Could be Wyld barbarians. Might just be something in the water made the people go crazy and kill each other. Don't know."

"So what do we do?"

"First, I want you to get back to the others and stop the caravan where it is. We'll make camp right here. With the sun down and the villagers murdered, that place is probably crawling with hungry ghosts by now. I doubt our caravan master would enjoy spending the night there very much."

"Nelis will like losing his little trade outlet even less, I bet," Risa smirked. The Guildsman in charge of the caravan, Ourang Nelis, had paid Dace's company very well not to talk to any of his peers about this impractical detour from the beaten Mishaka-Nexus trade route.

"Next," Dace said to Kestrel, "I want you to get back to the cavalry and get me a detachment of good men on fresh horses. Then, get them back here double-time."

Kestrel nodded once and spurred his horse back toward the caravan. Risa turned her horse to follow the scout but hesitated a moment before leaving.

"Anything else, sir?" she asked.

"Yeah," Dace said. "Double the guard around the wagons tonight. This isn't a very tenable place to have to make camp."

"We'll see it suits."

"Good. Now, one more thing. I'm taking these riders to get Brand and Fox out, but we won't be coming right back. It's possible we won't actually get back here before dawn. Don't send anyone in looking for us until the sun's up."

"Yes, sir. Is that it?"

"Yeah. Head back and hustle up Kestrel and that detachment I ordered. We'll come back after dawn, and when we do, we're going to have to break camp and push on to Nexus fast. Make sure everyone's ready."

"Yes, sir. I'll take care of it." Risa then nudged her horse's flanks, snapped the reins and trotted back to carry out her orders.

When Dace and his detachment of cavalry entered the village, they found it every bit as eerie and deserted as Kestrel had made it sound. A waxy yellow fingernail moon shone in an ebony firmament set with diamonds, casting an unhealthy light over the empty place. No dog barked, no livestock made any noise, and even the rats and raitons seemed to have abandoned the place. The only sound around them was the unwholesome whispering of the wind, which carried a faint hint of decay and rot.

From the greasy dark grass lining the road to the skeletal emptiness of the buildings to the chalky ash mixed into the dirt of the market square, all the evidence pointed to the fact that something very bad had happened here. Many people had died here, likely all at once. Sometimes, when things like this happened, the shroud between the worlds of the living and the dead thinned, blending the two worlds together into a place called a shadowland. There the living could interact with the dead and even travel into the Underworld like a restless ghost. In fact, if someone tried to leave a shadowland before the sun came up, that very thing would happen. Dace didn't know if what had happened here was bad enough to breach the Shroud, but it certainly looked it.

"All right," he said, "spread out and start checking houses. Don't get out of earshot of each other, and whatever you do, don't leave town. I don't think I have to tell you why." The soldiers shook their heads and scanned the area warily. "Good. Whistle out if you find Brand or Dust Fox. Keep an eye out for hungry ghosts too. This place should probably be crawling with them, and I don't like that it isn't."

The men grunted assent and spread out to search. They checked both sides of the small village's main street and worked toward the center of town. Dace rode out ahead of them with one hand on his reins and the other hefting his sword—a reaver daiklave forged of purest orichalcum—which gleamed strangely in the faint moonlight. It did not surprise him when the search failed to turn up any immediate clues as to what had happened here. It was not until the riders drew close to the modest temple of the village's patron harvest god that they found anything. They saw a great many tracks and the whorls and divots of what could only have been a mounted man fighting for his life against foes on foot. A largish impression in the center was smeared with drying blood, and a deep set of parallel tracks showed where something heavy had been dragged away. The surrounding area, however, was a chaos of boot and hoof prints, so it was impossible to tell if one or both scouts had died there. Dace just hoped that, if either one of them had survived, they'd had to sense not to bolt off in a random direction out of this place.

"Captain, look," one of the men said, trotting up beside him as he tried to read the past in the turned earth. "By the temple."

Dace glanced up and saw something coming from around behind the mean stone building slowly and with obvious effort. It was a horse, Dace realized as the thing left the shadow of the temple, and it was in bad shape. Blood gleamed on its flanks, and it was favoring its back right leg. Its tail hung limp behind it, and the horse seemed to be dragging a heavy burden. Upon a moment's inspection, it was obvious that the burden was a limp body, dangling by one leg from the stirrup of a ripped and bloody saddle.

"Dust Fox," Dace growled, recognizing his mercenary company's brand on the horse's flank before he recognized the ruined scout's features. "Damn it."

The soldier beside him turned and whistled over his shoulder to the other cavalrymen, all of whom hurried to join their captain. While Dace was turning to tell them what he wanted done, though, the soldier beside him—Lugan—took it upon himself to ride over to Dust Fox's horse. The wounded animal stopped politely and cocked its head to gauge the soldier's approach. By the time Dace realized that Lugan had gone, it was too late to call him back. He cursed and spurred his horse ahead as well.

"Lugan, get back here," he called, but the soldier's fate was already inevitable.

Lugan gained the wounded mount's side and was reaching down to cut the stirrup that entangled his comrade's foot when he heard Dace's shout. He looked up just in time to see Fox's horse bow its head with a malicious gleam in its eyes and buck up on its front legs. It snapped out a kick that caught Lugan in the mouth and broke his neck. He flew backward out of the saddle to land beside Dust Fox, and his own horse bolted. It ran straight back toward Dace, who had to stem his own charge to keep the beast from plowing into him. He heard curses behind him as the rest of his men also had to break stride and formation to get out of the way.

Taking advantage of the momentary distraction, Dust Fox's horse turned toward Dace and bowed low as if it were mocking him. Its gesture proved purely practical, however, when Dust Fox himself sat up and grabbed its mane. The horse then scrambled back upright and Fox pulled himself into the saddle. Or, rather, what looked like Dust Fox did so. Considering the mortal wounds on its neck and chest, what looked like Dust Fox was actually a nemissary—a clever, immaterial ghost animating someone else's body. Another such ghost was animating the horse. With a wicked, un-earthly laugh, the pair charged at Dace.

Howling a battle cry, Dace barreled straight at the oncoming nemissary duo, expecting a rational warrior's reaction. A mortal horseman would have flinched and turned aside at the last second, giving Dace an opportunity for a broadside chop. That was not what happened. Instead, the Fox nemissary sprung up to a crouch in his saddle and the second nemissary fled its stolen equine body. The dead horse staggered and fell immediately, and the remaining nemissary leapt clear, flying toward Dace, knife in hand. Dace's horse collided with the tumbling dead one, and Dace had just enough time to get his daiklave in front of him before Dust Fox slammed into him. The four bodies spun and sprawled and crashed to the earth as the rest of Dace's cavalry detachment parted around him and thundered past to keep from trampling their captain. The nemissary that had fled Dust Fox's horse headed for Lugan's body.

Dace's head swam, and he saw stars, but the pain of being stabbed in the side brought him around instantly. The Fox nemissary had worked his knife under the edge of Dace's armor and scored a weak gash, and now, its free hand closed around his throat. The thing leered and hissed at him, dribbling Dust Fox's blood in his face. It grinned evilly, supremely confident that its trap had netted an-other handful of hapless victims. Dace almost smiled back at it through the pain of his wounds, for he knew something the nemissary didn't.

He sucked in a deep breath, and the power of the Unconquered Sun bloomed deep within him. A sunburst mark of energy began to glow on his forehead, and his eyes blazed with rage. His blade glowed too, and he hurled the nemissary back. He then kicked up to his feet to meet the nemissary's second rush. His weapon swept up from a low guard position trailing a fan of incandescent energy and caught the nemissary under its outstretched knife arm. Dust Fox's body spun sideways through the air and split cleanly in half, blinding Dace with a spray of blood. It hit the ground in two heaps, and the nemissary fled it.

Dace wiped blood out of his eyes with the back of his hand and felt a rush of icy air as the nemissary ghost brushed past him to take up another body. It settled in the tangled corpse of Dace's heavy war-horse, which lay nearby, and lurched forward to bite the back of Dace's leg. Hearing the animal moving behind him, Dace twisted around awkwardly and bashed the horse in the side of the head with a downward hilt strike. Then, he twisted all the way around the other way, surrounding himself in blazing contrails of energy, and chopped the animal's head off. The horse's body collapsed, and the ghost fled again. It feinted toward Dust Fox's horse then switched back and simply bolted, deciding not to take its chances.

Dace almost charged after it to finish it off, but it suddenly occurred to him to wonder why his men hadn't tried to help out at all. He didn't especially need their help to deal with one nemissary, but they were trained better than to just make assumptions about one another in dangerous unfamiliar territory. Dace turning back toward the temple and saw that Lugan's body was up on its feet once again, keeping a pair of cavalrymen at bay with his long spear. What's more, he was calling out in an old, almost-forgotten language, giving orders. At his command, the village temple's doors swung open, and the fully materialized hungry ghosts of the slain villagers poured out like packs of wild dogs. Those of Dace's soldiers who weren't busy with Lugan's nemissary turned to meet this new challenge, but they were now severely outnumbered. The look on their faces showed a hopeless realization as they calculated their odds. They were going to die here without divine intervention.

Fortunately, their captain represented just that. He raised his sword and bellowed his company's war cry once more, and his entire body began to glow. Turning the darkened square as bright as day, he ran toward the hungry ghosts' flank and started chopping into them.

About a hundred yards away in the Underworld proper, two figures watched what was going on in the town with distaste. One stood rigid at the top of an upthrust stone with his arms crossed. His long, drawn face was lined with faint shadows of disappointment beneath the rim of a broad hat. The other sat cross-legged on a lower stone, resting elbows on knees and chin on knuckles.

"How annoying!" the seated figure lamented. "Hardly anybody ever comes here in number with mercenary guards anymore. Deset said so!"

"It seems he was misinformed," the standing figure said. "Or he's a lying double-crosser."

"I doubt that. There's nothing to be gained from that kind of guile. Besides, Deset likes me. He wouldn't do that."

"Yet, here we stand, watching mercenaries ransack our tenderly cultivated shadowland."

"I know! How galling! At least we got what we came for already. We should really teach those louts a lesson."

"Some other time. We've got more work to do tonight, and the Walker in Darkness will need to be told about this. We can always catch up to this Sun-Child later in Nexus."

"Oh, fine," the seated figure said, rolling backward over one shoulder and standing up. "You're right, as usual. Let's go."

Meanwhile, a third figure crouched in a natural blind across the shadowland from the first two watchers but in the living world. He wore an outfit of leather and heavy black cloth, and he carried an ornate black longbow with a black arrow at the string. The blazing energy and the symphony of battle going on in the village interested him greatly.

Walker's agents must be responsible for this, he thought. *But why would they seed a shadowland all the way out here?*

Chapter One

The beautiful killer Harmonious Jade knelt on the stylized cornice of a building overlooking the sprawling Little Market of Nexus. The market was a patchwork of awnings, tents and crude bivouacs all in leather, canvas or wood. It thronged with people from all over the city and all over the greater River Province, of which Nexus was the center. They flitted from place to place with their ugly, graceless gaits, squawking at each other and waving their arms in consternation. It made Harmonious Jade think of angry, featherless raitons flocking for the sake of convenience but trying very hard not to get along. It was funny from a distance, and the base unrelenting humanity of it had a certain beautiful purity. The killer preferred to enjoy it from a distance just the same, though.

Jade had not been in Nexus very long, but already, she had decided that she preferred the Little Market over its neighbor, the Big Market, just a few blocks away. The Big Market was dominated by imposing warehouses and auction arenas, and the narrow streets were perpetually clogged with lines of yeddim-drawn carts and very serious merchants going about very serious business. Every place of business in the Big Market was a clearinghouse in which large-scale transactions took place from dawn to dusk. Miners sold iron to smiths. Smiths sold weapons, armor and horse tack to mercenary quartermasters. Successful farmers sold the fruits of their harvest wholesale to shop-owners. From wool and cotton to hemp and pine pitch, bulk quantities of all the raw materials around which this region's economy turned changed hands at auction in the Big Market. As a result, the place was packed with not only dour merchants who were anxious with the strain of constantly trying to rip one another off without being ripped off in return, but their grim and eagle-eyed bodyguards as well. These hired toughs ranged and strutted around their masters like trained dogs, glowering in every direction at once.

And, as if that weren't enough, the black-helmeted mercenaries of the Hooded Executioners company patrolled the streets looking to put a quick end to any trouble that might upset the busy, bustling peace. The Executioners made up just one of Nexus' many professional mercenary outfits, and both the city's ruling Council of Entities and the mercantile Guild paid such mercenaries well to run off troublemakers and loudmouths in the name of keeping the peace. The Executioners considered such work a singular honor, for Nexus had no standing army or professional police force. Nexus was a city with few laws. Local society revolved around six imperishable decrees (the Dogma) and a bewildering roster of ever-changing lesser proclamations (the Civilities). Harmonious Jade had no idea how the Council enforced (or even kept up with) all of the Civilities, but it was obvious that it hired mercenary units such as the Hooded Executioners to punish those who broke them. Nexus was no less a lawless snake pit of treachery for it, but those who pushed such acts too far and upset the working order of the city were just as likely to be caught and punished as to get away with them. One of the decrees of the Dogma was that none shall obstruct trade, and the mercenary peacekeepers hired to watch over the Big Market took their mandate very seriously.

As a result, the Big Market was a dangerous and inconvenient place for a killer to do her work.

Nexus' Little Market was more accommodating to both killer and citizen alike. Its pavilion of tents and stalls marketed household goods and items of small, but not insignificant, value to the masses. It welcomed and thrived on the common man, and the smaller scale of each pocket of activity fostered a more personal, intimate atmosphere. The merchants and vendors of the Little Market were no more gullible or charitable than their Big Market counterparts, but they conducted their business with a glaring sincerity that Harmonious Jade respected. The merchants knew how to get what they wanted, and their customers were under no illusions to the contrary, so even in the bustle and confusion, the nature of the place made itself apparent and held nothing back. Jade had grown up in a small, intimate community with a similar nature, and she enjoyed finding evidence of the same forthright ideals in this vast and uncaring world.

Even here, though, shadows of what made the Big Market so distasteful still loomed. When a merchant was leaving or approaching his stall, he always traveled with at least one bodyguard, if not a handful of thugs and leg breakers. Competition between businessmen was fierce and ugly. Mercenaries from small companies took on uncoordinated patrols, as well, making up in decisive brutality what they lacked in numbers and organization. The wealth at stake in the Little Market was small relative to that in the Big Market, but a significant disturbance could still obstruct trade, so the peace was still to be kept. For that reason, certain Guildsmen, unions of local merchants and rich businessmen with a vested interest in the area put up respectable amounts of silver for that added layer of security.

The inconvenience to Jade was less in the Little Market, but it was still not an ideal place for a killer to do her work. Therefore, Jade had waited until nightfall when the Big Market had shut down and the Little Market had shrunk to less than a quarter its daylight size. No one saw her as she watched and waited, changing position as necessity dictated.

From her high perch, she now looked down on the Night Market huddled in the westernmost quarter of the Nexus district. Numerous secondhand Civilities of varying obscurity prohibited the sale of certain items—such as weapons or tomatoes—once the sun went down, but the Night Market was still able to do a brisk business. It was a commercial reality that people could discover a need for certain things at any hour, and the Night Market catered to such needs while the rest of the city slept. It was nowhere near as loud or frenetic as either of the other markets was during the day, but it was still alive and busy enough to make it worth many shopkeepers' and craftsmen's time to have a presence there after dark.

In fact, the Night Market was relatively civil. A firefly swarm of candle lanterns on iron hooks illuminated the space, swaying in intermittent breezes. Perhaps it was just the time of year—the month of Descending Fire when temperatures were at their highest and even the nights were sweltering—but the denizens of the Night Market seemed more docile and relaxed. As a result, the mercenary presence was a token one at best. People were just less excitable and less inclined to cause trouble in this heat at day's end. It was almost an ideal time for a killer to do her work with a better-than-average chance of getting away clean afterward.

Harmonious Jade appreciated that, but still, she waited, just as she had done all day and for several days leading up to this one. She was here to kill someone, but she was under no obligation to hurry. She had tracked this person halfway up the coast of the Inland Sea from the stained-glass city of Chiaroscuro, then spent her first week in this bizarre new city figuring out where the person was. Once she'd located her target—a woman named Selaine Chaisa—she'd admitted to herself that, after so long in pursuit, another few hours or even days weren't going to make any noticeable difference. So, Jade had chosen to follow her victim around the city for a while to learn her routine and to take in a few sights at the same time.

The city was a fabulous example of a thriving metropolis. It blended base Second Age architecture with magically crafted structures that had endured since the First Age. The same was true back in Chiaroscuro as well, but most of the leftover buildings there were in various stages of disrepair as a result of some terrible tragedy long ago. The people who used those places were more or less squatting in beautiful ruins, with no appreciation for the times long past. Here in Nexus, however, the sky-piercing towers were in good repair, as were the bridges, canals, aqueducts, sewers and dams that bounded and connected the city's various districts.

Nexus was also much more cosmopolitan than Chiaroscuro. It housed, fed and employed almost one million people, all of whom enjoyed the same governmental non-interference so long as they abided by the Dogma and the Civilities. Just walking down random streets, Jade had mingled with people from every point on the compass, from every class and caste of Creation's most far-flung cultures. From the swarthy diamond merchants of Gem to the willowy seamen of Abalone to the diminutive black-and-white djala people of the East to even the rare snakemen or earthbound Fair Folk, Nexus took in all comers and challenged them to thrive or perish in its disorderly community. Jade had trouble feeling at home anywhere these days, but at least she did not feel unwelcome or unwanted here. If nothing else, she actually felt more mature and confident than she had in Chiaroscuro. She could survive here. She could thrive here. She could make this place a new home and even start a new life—one more like her past incarnation, which she remembered only in glimpses and fragments. That was the life she wanted. The one she had been given was far less pleasant.

Jade had been raised in the Southern desert by a cult called the Salmalin. The cult served and worshiped the undying Yozis, a race of demons imprisoned outside Creation at the dawn of the First Age, constantly seeking a way to free its infernal masters. Able to appear in this world only at the behest of rare sorcerers, the demons communicated with their followers in dreams and arcane portents, and they had demanded that the Salmalin raise and train a caste of killers to carry out their wishes.

Sold into slavery as an infant, Jade been chosen and trained by the cultists, and she had proven an apt and gifted pupil. She had forged her body into a beautiful and powerful weapon, then practiced relentlessly with the bow, the knife and an assortment of other weapons. Suffering ignominious punishments for her few failures and receiving only faint praise for her many achievements, she had become the most effective Salmalin killer in decades. The grace and efficiency with which she carried out her holy duties earned her cult vast sums of money and elevated her to the position of Janissary of the Faithful Elite—one held high in the cult's Yozi masters' esteem. Through her and the others like her, the Yozis would one day win their freedom and return to rule Creation.

Knowing no other existence and expecting no more from life than what the Salmalin provided, Harmonious Jade had been content. She killed who she was told to kill, then she returned to worship in the hidden temple beneath the sand. She wanted nothing more, for there was nothing else of importance in the whole of Creation. She was not happy as such, but neither was she *unhappy*, and that was good enough. Yet, times change, and one catastrophic night had obliterated Jade's perfect, unquestioning contentment.

It had happened for no reason Jade had ever been able to discern. She was working at the time—stalking a magistrate in the city of Paragon—when a blinding light had filled her mind's eye. A voice as old as Creation had spoken to her then of a secret destiny greater than she had ever dreamed possible. The voice was that of the Unconquered Sun, who had claimed her as His own, opened her mind and body to the hidden flows of essence all around her and gifted her with powerful magical abilities unseen for an Age. He had Exalted her in the truest possible sense, and the mark of that Exaltation was an empty ring mystically branded on her forehead. The ring symbolized night—that is, the shadow on Creation cast by the Unconquered Sun, in which His most subtle and cunning agents were to do their work—and it glowed when she used her power in certain ways. She had not understood what had happened to her at that time, but she had felt a surge of pride and trust welling within her upon her Exaltation, and the experience had felt strangely, inexplicably familiar. Energized and excited, she had returned home to share her good news with her elders and superiors.

Her homecoming was not pleasant.

The first person she told was a man named Sahan. He had been in charge of her training and of arranging her contract work with prospective employers, and he knew her better than anyone. He was the one who punished her when she learned something too slowly, and he was the one who rewarded her when she pleased the Yozis. It was through him that the Yozis expressed their love for the work she was doing. He was neither warm nor especially comforting, but he was proud of her, and he appreciated her victories. She'd felt close to Sahan, and she'd trusted him, and she'd assumed that, if anyone could explain what her Exaltation meant, Sahan would be the one.

He had not shared her joy or excitement when she'd told him what had happened. Instead, he'd actually gone pale and excused himself to confer with the elder priests. The look on his face when he did so was not one of scholarly confusion or academic intrigue, though, it was one she had seen many times in the course of her work—fear. Disturbed by this upset in her mentor, she'd followed him to the chamber where the Salmalin elders met and listened from the shadows by the door. When Sahan had related what Jade had told him, the elders reacted just as he had. They appeared to know exactly what she had experienced, and they began to argue among themselves in fear.

Jade had not understood everything they'd said about her, but their final decision came through clearly enough. They had ordered Sahan to return to the room where he had left her waiting and to distract her with a discussion on the implications of her new existence. The elders would then surprise her with the ancient weapons of their Yozi masters and put her down before she ever had a chance to realize what she had become. She'd held her breath then in abiding terror, her hope and her fate resting on what Sahan's response would be. And his response had been quick. This man—whom she'd trusted, respected and even come to love in her way—had given his word that he would do as the Salmalin elders commanded, without so much as a word in his pupil's defense.

Tears had burned Harmonious Jade's eyes then, and her heart nearly stopped as the shock dizzied and nauseated her. Yet, even then, her training and her will to survive had not failed her. She concealed herself in shadow as Sahan passed then followed him as he came to betray her. And when the two were alone, she had killed him. She'd then fled the temple in a dreamlike panic, wishing that she could die rather than go on living in this world where everyone she knew and could rely on suddenly feared her and wanted her dead. She had never been marked for death or hunted like a wild animal before. She had never been betrayed. It almost broke her spirit and her sanity.

What Jade had learned since then was that the Salmalin cultists and their Yozi masters had every reason to fear what she had become. According to a savant she had met in Chiaroscuro, the Solar Exalted had been born at the dawn of the First Age to fight a war for the fate of Creation. Wielding the power of the Unconquered Sun, they had cast down a race of demon tyrants and imprisoned them in an Elsewhere outside Creation. Once the masters of reality and the undisputed kings of all they perceived, those demons swore sacred oaths on their True Names to no longer torment Creation. They disappeared then into a hell of their own design to sire successively weaker offspring and to scheme eternally in hopes of one day winning their freedom.

Learning this had put her circumstances into perspective, but nothing softened the blow of her betrayal. At the time it had happened, she'd fought her way out of the temple as warning gongs had begun to ring in alarm, then she'd fled north, eventually winding up in Chiaroscuro. Chiaroscuro was not only an enormous city that was easy to hide and get lost in, but a thriving seaport as well. She would hide out there and make sure that the Salmalin were not in immediate pursuit, then she would get on a boat and see where the wind blew her. Yet, when she arrived in that city after weeks of hard travel and meager subsistence, she learned two harsh and ugly lessons. The first was practical and easy enough to solve, but the second was one she still had trouble with even today. In fact, it was part of the reason she was here in Nexus furtively following Selaine Chaisa with murder on her mind.

The first such lesson was simply that, without money, she wasn't going anywhere, on a boat or otherwise. Although her Exaltation had hardened her body, cleansed her of impurity, eradicated any concern she might have had about illness and even started to wear away the ugly dogma the Salmalin had brainwashed her with all her life, she still had to eat. A big city such as Chiaroscuro was no place to make a living as a hunter, and although it was indeed a port city, Harmonious Jade had no idea how to fish. And as she spent more time on her own, she realized that there was a world of experience that had been denied her and that not knowing how to fish was among the least of her worries. She didn't know where to look for work or how to find safe housing for little money. She didn't even know where to go to wash her clothes or to buy new ones. Despite her unique powers and abilities, she was once more the abandoned, frightened child she imagined she was before the Salmalin found her.

After a long night of much-needed sleep followed by a long walk in the sun's early light, though, Jade had realized that she was not without recourse. The Salmalin might not have taught her much of this world outside their own warped sphere of influence, but they had taught her the means of making her way in it. They had made of her a formidable killer with few compunctions about the sort of work she would take. The gifts given her by the Unconquered Sun made her work all that much easier, and the relatively hands-off approach the deity took with her after her Exaltation gave her latitude to do as she wished. Her one abortive discussion with Sahan about how much money her work earned for the cult—which had earned her a beating for the appearance of greed—had inspired her to believe that she could support herself handily doing what she had been raised to do. So, in that regard, solving her first major problem took little more than faith in herself and an application of skills that came easily to her. Despite count-less blunders and gaffes of inexperience, she had slowly established herself as a reputable killer for hire. She had even considered raising her modest rates.

That easy solution, then, had left only her second and much larger issue to deal with—that of her Exaltation. Much time passed, in which she cemented her reputation, secured a place to live and took precautions to see that the Salmalin had not caught up to her. Her original intention had been to get on a boat out of town as soon as she had enough money, but as more time passed, the idea began to daunt her more and more. She had lived most of her life cloistered and hidden from the world, and she had found comfort in the stability of her surroundings. Having then set up a similarly comforting and stable existence in Chiar-oscuro, she was reluctant to leave it all behind just to find out how much *else* of the world she knew nothing about.

Plus, she had heard nothing more from the Uncon-quered Sun since her Exaltation regarding what exactly He wanted her to do. It was not her style to strike out on her own and just expect events to draw her in. She much preferred to have objectives set out for her so that she could methodi-cally pursue them one by one. Without some sort of guiding influence, she felt uncomfortable and pointless. Not to mention the fact that she had a very real fear of disappoint-ing the Unconquered Sun without even realizing it. If the Yozis could exact brutal punishments through the Salmalin for failure, how much worse would be the hand of the one who had raised an army to cast them down?

So, with that subtle unease growing, she'd set out to learn more about what she had become and to thrash out her station in this world. In her search, she'd traveled from Chiaroscuro repeatedly (though never far or for very long) to speak with historians and savants of all stripes. She'd broken into the libraries of the rich and traveled into First Age ruins that others feared to even approach. In so doing, she eventually discovered enough to learn that she had lived before, in the First Age. She had been a man then, chosen by the Sun, and she relived his memories in sporadic flashes. That warrior had fought the tyrants who had later surrendered and become the Yozis, using a gleaming orichalcum powerbow that had been buried with him. Not long ago, Jade had pieced together the whereabouts of that warrior's tomb and crept into it late in the night. Outwitting traps and sneaking past undying guardians, she had found and reclaimed that peerless weapon, feeling that much more complete for having done so.

Her search taught her one unexpected and valuable lesson, however, through which the nature of her second major problem was revealed. Namely, there was no place in this world for the Chosen of the Unconquered Sun. It seemed that the average, everyday people of Creation hated and feared the Solar Exalted as much as the Yozi masters of the Salmalin did. According to history, the Solar Exalted had grown extremely powerful in the First Age and had turned that power on their subjects, just as had the demon tyrants whom they had cast down. If not for the forces of the Dragon-Blooded dynasts who now ruled from the Imperial City, the Solar Exalted would have eventually enslaved and destroyed the entire world. Now, whenever it was revealed that a Solar Exalt had been reborn, the Dragon-Blooded sent an armed force called the Wyld Hunt to kill him or her, lest history repeat itself.

Jade discovered this aspect of Second Age life by accident and had had to cut short her research on more than one occasion for fear of attracting undue notice. It was bad enough to know that the Salmalin were out there somewhere hunting her, she'd figured, without inviting the armed forces of the Realm to take up the chase as well. For the time being, Jade had decided, she would just have to content herself with doing the work she'd been trained for and waiting for a sign that the Unconquered Sun wanted something more.

That sign had eventually come in the form of Selaine Chaisa, whom Jade had recently followed all this way to Nexus. The woman was an elder in the Salmalin cult, and Jade had known her since infancy. Chaisa had baptized Harmonious Jade into the cult, drawing the lines of lamb's blood on her forehead and speaking words of promise to her demon masters. Chaisa had led the prayers and orgiastic revels at the cult's annual holidays, and she had presided over the five-day festival of Calibration at the end of every year. Chaisa had taught Jade about the Yozis and what a paradise they would make for their loyal servants when they finally broke free of their prison. Chaisa traveled extensively throughout the South and up into the East searching for extant relics of the First Age, and she had returned them to the fortress, weaving tales of heroism and tragedy from a time when demons had ruled the world. Chaisa had even punctured the barrier between realities on more than one occasion and summoned lowly demons of the First Circle to serve the cult for a year and a day. Growing up, Jade had wanted nothing more than to be a woman just like Selaine Chaisa some day.

Therefore, Jade had been crushed to overhear Chaisa's voice calling first and loudest for her blood after her Exaltation. She and Chaisa were not as close as she and Sahan had been, but the condemnation from her admired hero had struck just as deeply as the betrayal of her trusted mentor. All Jade's years of dedication and hard work had made no impression on this woman she worshiped, but one unwanted circumstance thrust on her was enough to convince Chaisa to sign her death warrant. Even now that she better understood the evils the Salmalin had done in the Yozis' service, that last unfairness still stung.

After her escape from the cult, Jade had been prepared to live her days in Chiaroscuro and just be content to keep her distance from the Salmalin, but Chaisa had not allowed her even that. Not long ago, Chaisa had stopped briefly in Chiaroscuro with a mercantile Guild caravan on its way to Nexus, and word had gotten to her that Harmonious Jade was living in the city too. Adding cavalier insult to past betrayal, Chaisa had summoned a subtly clever demon into this world and commanded it to lie in wait for Harmonious Jade and then kill her. An agent of Chaisa's had then arranged a phony contract killing and sent Jade into the demon's trap. They had underestimated her, though, and Jade had escaped and come back for the contact who had set her up. She'd killed him slowly, and before he'd expired, he'd given her Chaisa's name and revealed where Jade could find her. Chaisa had left for Nexus to meet contacts there, he'd said, so Harmonious Jade had made a decision. If the Salmalin weren't content to leave her alone in this world that already considered her Anathema, she would return their attention in kind. If ones such as Chaisa and Sahan considered her their enemy, she would not disappoint them. She would take the power that the Unconquered Sun had granted her and teach the Salmalin—and others like them—to fear it in earnest. She'd finally received the direction she'd been waiting for, and she had set out that very night in pursuit of the caravan that had taken Chaisa away.

And now, here she waited, taking her time before putting an end to Selaine Chaisa and choosing her next Salmalin target. She'd been following Chaisa around for several days, and her target's pattern was uninterestingly consistent. Chaisa began her day in the Big Market with the drover of the caravan that had brought her to Nexus. They sold loads of adamantine glass that Guild slaves and local peasants had scrounged for them from the ruins of Chiaroscuro. Scraps of it ranged in size from miniscule arrowhead chips to spear point slivers to shards the size of daggers to broader panes that could be incorporated into shields or makeshift armor plates. The material held an edge indefinitely, and few forces anyone remembered in this Age could break it. The glass was not a huge moneymaker for the Guild—especially in bulk at the Big Market—but Chaisa took a percentage of what sales it garnered and seemed happy enough with the sum.

When that day's bulk shipments had more or less sold through, Chaisa then collected scraps and castoffs, hiked up the per-unit price dramatically and hawked it in the Little Market to the individual consumer from a rented booth. Before day's end, she closed up the booth to do her own shopping until it was time to head back to the Night Market. She had two porters carry a large, flat case between them, and she entered the tented-off private section of the same secluded stall every night. The stall advertised curiosities from all over Creation, and subtle up-close reconnaissance had revealed that Chaisa sold and traded the items of lesser value that she found on her journeys, haggling endlessly like a Guildsman.

Chaisa's routine had not changed since Harmonious Jade had started following her, so it was just a simple matter of choosing when and where to track her down and kill her. With Jade's gifts and abilities, she could likely have done the deed at any point during the day or night. She could render herself completely unnoticeable to any human sense, she was a crack shot with her powerbow out to a range of almost three hundred yards, and she was as agile and careful a stalker as any hunting cat. She could pick Chaisa off from the shadows and disappear before anyone realized where the shot had come from. She could simply wait down the length of an alley, call Chaisa's name and put an arrow in her throat the moment their eyes locked. If she wanted, she could even make her way to Chaisa's Little Market booth and slit her throat in plain view of all her customers and take off into the back streets in the confusion. She had not yet mastered the intricacies of Nexus' design, but she was confident that she could lose any pursuers and disappear before anyone laid a hand on her.

The practical side of her knew that she should just take her shot from the shadows and disappear. That way, the thing would be done, and she could move on. The other two options introduced elements of risk that increased her chances of being spotted and identified, and they complicated her escape. Either one had serious potential for disastrous complications that could slow her down or even result in her capture. If nothing else, a large enough disturbance would be seen as an obstruction of trade, which could earn her the attention of the Council of Entities. The Council was not as feared or renowned as the Wyld Hunt—which would also come into play if she had to use her supernal abilities ostentatiously to make her escape—but in Nexus, it was not to be trifled with.

The substantial risks of doing otherwise could not convince Jade to kill Chaisa anonymously, though. Chaisa had condemned her to death with a sort of impersonal cruelty, not caring if Jade understood her fate or not. It was a heartless, evil thing to do, and it had almost broken Jade's spirit. Now, as much as she might hate Chaisa and all the rest of the Salmalin, she still respected her erstwhile hero enough to spare her that indignity. That meant a personal kill somewhere she could get close to Chaisa, but far enough out of sight of everyone else that she didn't start a panic. Jade had been thinking along those very lines for days now, and last night, she had chosen just the place to bring everything together. All she needed now was for Chaisa to emerge from her business within the curiosity-seller's private tent and make her way to the ratchet-and-pulley transit cart at the edge of the Nexus district.

The night was only some four hours old when Chaisa at last began to make her way home. She had her porters in tow with their cumbersome burden, and she met up with a handful of waiting mercenaries who casually fell in around her after an exchange of hand signs and a small clinking pouch. That was a little unusual for Chaisa, who normally eschewed having more than one guard with her at a time. The slight change in routine troubled Jade, but she rationalized it in only a moment of hesitation. Chaisa had been doing business for days now, so perhaps she was transporting the proceeds of that activity. That would warrant the extra security, Jade allowed. Granted, it was possible that some contact or spy of Chaisa's had somehow noticed Jade watching and trailing her these last several days and tipped the woman off, but that wasn't a significant worry. If Chaisa thought these five toughs would be sufficient to protect her, she had underestimated the danger she was in. So, as this formation made its way up Wander Street toward the cable-cart station, Jade stood and began to shadow them along the edge of the rooftop from which she had been watching.

Harmonious Jade trailed the troupe thus until everyone boarded a waiting cable cart, then she lit out at a sprint, leaving the slow-moving transit vehicle behind. She knew that the cart traveled from the Nexus district to cramped Sentinel's Hill and into the Firewander district and that Chaisa rode it all the way to the end. Firewander was not the safest part of Nexus—much of it was still tainted by Wyld energy that undermined its fundamental stability—but the outskirts of it were still livable, and it was to those parts that Chaisa headed at the end of every day. After she debarked and unloaded her belongings, the cart's operator would switch the vehicle to an outbound cable and retreat with all due haste, leaving Chaisa all alone in a sparsely populated corner of Nexus. It was there that Jade would confront her and kill her.

The addition of bodyguards changed things, however, so Jade had to adjust her plan and get into Firewander quickly. The slow cart made several stops for other passengers, but Jade wanted to move into position early enough to get a few moments of rest before her targets arrived. She needed a spot with a clear field of view that also offered several different points from which to pick off Chaisa's entourage. She had to be able to move around so as to not only conceal her firing position, but also give the illusion of a larger number of killers and hopefully paralyze Chaisa with indecision as the woman tried to figure out which way to run. That pause would give Jade time to get to the ground and deal with Chaisa personally.

She needed to hurry to find the best such position, though, so she sprinted off ahead of the cart, guiding on a tall watchtower and a pillar of incandescent Wyld phantasma-goria that marred the night skyline from deep within Firewander. The steep hills on which Nexus had been built made the going tough, but not so tough that she couldn't make decent time ahead of her quarry. She sprung from rooftop to rooftop across wide streets, darted across thin footbridges between towers when she could and even bounced on a wire holding up a banner announcing the advent of Calibration to cross one particularly wide road. She made no sound as she ran; she did not so much as tear a shingle or dislodge a tile. She might have been a ghost for all her passage disturbed the world around her. From the heart of the Nexus district, across the huddled tenements of Sentinel's Hill and over Sentinel's Wall beneath the mercenary-staffed watchtowers overlooking Firewander she made her silent progress undetected.

She slowed a little in Firewander itself because the buildings were farther apart and more shabbily constructed, but she knew that she was still ahead of her prey. Her progress to the end of the cable-cart line was more cautious and circumspect, as she took a few minutes to stake out the perfect place for her ambush. She had no sooner chosen just the spot, however, when she heard the hiss of a tile sliding out of place two rooftops back. She glanced back just in time to see a figure lazily somersaulting through the air to land on a roof less than one hundred yards away and disappear into the shadow of a taller building. Jade could make out few details in that instant, but she did not like what she saw. The figure was male, broad-shouldered, tall and dressed in an outfit of black wool and leather. A black hood obscured his features, and he carried a jet-black longbow in his left hand with an arrow to the string. And he was coming right toward her as she moved toward her first chosen ambush vantage.

Jade didn't know if the man had seen her or not, or even what he was doing out here, but she decided to assume the worst. More than likely, her initial assessment that Selaine Chaisa had been tipped off was correct, and this man was a bodyguard sent ahead of the cart to scout for trouble. That, or he was a Salmalin killer who'd made this trip with Chaisa and was *acting* as a bodyguard. Either way, Jade could hear the cable-cart approaching in the distance, and she realized that whoever this man was, he was about to complicate everything. Cursing the inconvenience of it all, Jade put an arrow to her powerbow's string and ran sideways looking back the way she had come. She waited until her mystery pursuer made his next leap before she took to the air herself to deal with him.

Her timing was impeccable, and the man had no-where to go when she sprung her impromptu trap. As he leapt into the air, easily at a high enough angle to clear the alley beneath him, Jade emerged from the shadows and jumped toward a high wall to her left. The man's face jerked in her direction instantly, but it was already too late. Twisting gracefully as she flew, she fired one arrow and then another back in the man's direction while he had no leverage to dodge. The arrows flew true, and he flipped over backward in an ungainly tumble to disappear beneath the edge of the roof he'd been leaping for, missing it by almost a foot. At the same time, Jade's feet connected with the wall she'd been leaping for, and she twisted and sprung out away from it. Her momentum carried her up over the ledge of the next roof ahead of her, and she landed on her knees with her feet together. Soot and bird shit on the roof provided little traction, but she slid to a graceful halt nonetheless, twisting around to cover her back-trail with her powerbow.

Jade counted backward and forward to thirty, and her pursuer did not reappear. When she was certain that the coast was clear, she crossed to the opposite side of the roof and swung over the edge onto an empty balcony below. Half of this building had been carved away by fire, and the rest was abandoned, so she had only to step through a broken window to gain full access. Inside, she could move from window to window and floor to floor without sacrificing visibility. She could make her way to the ground floor in almost perfect concealment—her mystical powers of stealth notwithstanding—and eliminate Chaisa's bodyguards in short order. Then, it would be short work to run Chaisa to ground and show her what it felt like to be condemned and hunted.

As the cart drew near, Harmonious Jade went inside and forced herself to wait patiently. It was all but over now, yet that was no reason to let herself rush. She still had to plan for contingencies, take calm and precise shots and conserve arrows. Planning and reconnaissance were well enough, but as she had learned in Paragon, the unexpected could ruin even the best-laid plan.

She could not let errant thoughts distract her now. Her waiting was about to pay off at last, and the idea filled her with grim satisfaction as she crouched and watched the almost empty cable cart clatter to a stop below her. Chaisa's guards debarked, then her porters, then she stepped down herself. When it had been unloaded, the cart immediately reversed direction, and Harmonious Jade drew back her first arrow.

Before she could fire, something dropped next to her feet and distracted her. She glanced over and saw two of her arrows lying on the dirty floor, and someone she hadn't even realized was there was standing beside them. That someone was the black-clad pursuer she had sworn she'd killed moments ago, and as she looked in his direction, he seemed to be materializing from ephemeral shadow that rained down around his leather-thong sandals. More importantly, however, he was pointing an obsidian arrow at her from less than two yards away while her own weapon was more than ninety degrees out of position.

"I believe those are yours," the man said softly. "I think, however, you should explain what you think you're doing with that bow, grave robber. It belonged to someone very dear to me."

Chapter Two

The black-clad stranger's weapon was a gruesome, evil-looking thing. It was a six-foot length of bone and metal, lacquered the sinister black of dried blood seen on a moon-less night. At its center, a leering black skull with runes carved into its forehead and a wan light flickering in its eyes protected the archer's hand. Above that lay the point of an obsidian arrow that was aimed at the center of Jade's throat, right above the orichalcum flange of her armor breastplate. At this range, Jade realized, an arrow would go all the way through her and into the floor behind her.

"That's right, grave robber," the black archer whis-pered. "Lay the bow aside, then lament to me how you found it."

Jade calculated her odds of turning and firing before the black archer got a shot off. She was fast, and she already had an arrow drawn… all she had to do was throw herself backward, twist and loose in one motion. She'd practiced that sort of thing plenty of times. But no… she'd never make it. The slightest twitch in her shoulder produced a parallel motion in the archer's string fingers that told her all she needed to know. He'd kill her and just take the bow, and the strange, intriguing thing he'd said would remain a mystery. Rather than foolishly trying her luck, she slacked her arrow as he commanded and lay it with the other two she'd shot at him earlier.

"At least that much common sense," the black archer said. "Now lay it down. Slowly. You may forestall the inevitable as long as you must, but make no sudden move."

Jade turned on her heel but did not stand up or immediately hand the bow over. Instead, she leaned back slightly on her haunches, raised the toe of her right boot and held the bow in front of her. She held the bow by the ends, and the string came to rest against her upraised toe. She then pushed her hands toward the ground as steadily and casually as she could. In the dim light, the archer didn't seem to realize what she was doing.

"I don't know who you are," she said, trying to find the stranger's eyes in the shadows of his hood, "but this bow is mine. Come and take it if you want it."

"If I were so rude, grave robber, I would alr—"

Jade let go of the ends of her bow, and the string tension across her boot shot the weapon upward into the skull face leering down at her. The archer flinched as the impact drove his aim straight up, and his arrow stuck deep in the ceiling. Her bow bounced away into dust and shadow, and Jade kicked at her opponent's ankles. The black archer jumped over the sweep, but by the time he landed, Jade was already back on her feet. She snap kicked the bow out of his hand and then tried to close the distance with a knuckle strike to the throat. The archer barely blocked it with his elbow and backed off a step to regain his footing and composure.

Jade flowed forward with him, and the two of them traded lightning-fast jabs and open-palm blocks. Each tried to maneuver the other into an over-extension that could turn a simple block into a disabling joint lock, but neither fighter fell for it. The tangle finally ended when the black archer backed away in a quick quarter-circle and snaked his ankle around the leg of a wooden stool. He swept it around his body toward Jade's knees then kicked it at her, and she had to twist sharply to avoid a crippling blow. She did manage to catch the stool by one leg as it flew toward her, though, and set it down without a clatter behind her. Even as she fought this immediate opponent, she did not want to make so much noise that her intended quarry outside heard the commotion.

Yet, her care almost cost her, as her opponent came after her with a sweeping left cross, a high kick and three quick jabs. She ducked the cross, shoulder-rolled across the top of the stool to avoid the kick, then lifted the stool between her and her attacker to block the jabs. With the last block, she stepped in and twisted the stool to trap the black archer's wrist between its legs. Stepping around him and keeping a firm grip on the stool, she pulled him in a large circle by his outstretched arm. The archer countered by twisting his trapped arm brutally at the shoulder, then spinning backward into Jade's path with his free arm outstretched. The sword-edge of his outstretched hand hit Jade in the cheek, and she lost her grip on the stool. She stumbled into a table, and the black archer caught the stool before it could crash to the floor.

He set it aside just as carefully as Jade had done, but unlike her, he actually paid for his care. As soon as the stool left his hand, Jade jumped forward and hit him with an open-palm strike to the side of the face. He reeled, almost falling, and then a strange thing happened. Jade remembered something...

The spy's face stung, and he put his fingers to what would be a bright red spot in a few seconds. His lover, the beautiful brown-skinned assassin, glared at him with a fury that rivaled the intensity of the sea that was hurling itself on the rocks all around them.

"You think I didn't see you with that Wyld-touched bitch?" the assassin hissed. "I saw everything!"

"I was doing my job," the spy protested, taking his lover by the shoulders. "That woman is feeding information to the Fair Folk. I have to get close to her to find out how much she's told them. Look, would it help if I admitted I was thinking of you the whole time?"

Harmonious Jade recovered first, and she buried her knuckles deep in the center of her opponent's black hood. She didn't understand exactly what had just happened, but a hot tear burned in the corner of her eye, and her next punch was more savage and wild than the first. Staggering away, her opponent crossed his arms and blocked the blow more by lucky timing than skill. He skipped back almost a yard before he found his footing again. Retreating back all the way to the wall, he blocked punch after punch as Jade's style sharpened back into focus once more.

"You look embarrassed," he whispered with faint amusement. "Did something distract you?"

In answer, Jade feinted a low punch then spun around with devastating kick to the head. The black archer dropped forward and out of the way but had to reach back up at the last moment and catch Jade's heel with the backs of his fingers to keep her from smashing out the window right behind him. The deflection pulled Jade's leg out to full extension much higher than she'd intended, and she over-balanced. She bent back and planted her hands behind her, hoping to salvage the attack and turn it into a back hand-spring kick, but her opponent saw the move coming.

Holding one leg aloft, he sidestepped the kick and trapped it under his free armpit. He then reached out, planted his hand right on the decorative golden lion's head on the front of Jade's cuirass, took a single step forward and shoved her flat onto her back on the ground. Jade let herself fall, reaching for the knife sheathed at the back of her belt as her opponent came down on top of her. He saw what she was doing, and his hand followed hers back toward her knife. They both got two fingers on the hilt and started wrestling for leverage. As they did, it happened to Jade again…

The spy rolled on his back with hardly a protest, letting his lover pin him. Black clouds were beginning to roll in from the west as the city's storm conductor made ready for this evening's performance, and a light rain had already begun to fall. The spy laughed and put up a half-hearted struggle as the beautiful assassin straddled his chest.

"We ought to get back to the Manse soon, you weakling," the assassin said, eyes smoldering with mirth and rising passion. "My Circlemates will start saying I've killed you if we don't."

"They know you're more selective about your prey than that," the spy said. "If they're too polite to state the obvious, they'll tell each other you're off crying because I've left you again."

"If they thought that," the assassin said, leaning down to kiss the spy's earlobe, cheek and neck between words, "they'd know I'd killed you." The assassin nipped the spy's neck possessively to punctuate the thought.

"Ouch, you raiton," the spy chuckled. "At least wait 'til I'm dead to pick my carcass clean."

"Quiet, you romantic," the assassin said, kissing the spy's neck where the playful nip had drawn a spot of blood. "There, I'm sorry. Now, keep your opinions to yourself—I've got plans for your carcass."

"Ah, a fellow romantic, I see. What about your Circle back at the Manse?"

"They can wait."

Hands behind her head, Harmonious Jade rose into a striking cobra position over the black archer, kneeling and straddling his waist. Still somewhat disoriented, the archer reached up and put his hands on her thighs, sliding his palms up toward her hips. Jade unconsciously writhed against him, losing herself in the eerily familiar sensation before remembering the knife clutched in her fist. She wasn't certain when she'd come up with it—or how she'd wound up in this position to begin with—but her mind cleared quickly enough. Coiling forward, she brought the knife down hard, aimed at the black archer's throat. He caught her hands between his upraised crossed wrists, and the sound of a laugh came from within his shadowed hood.

"I guess you've decided to wait too," he teased. "But your eyes are still dancing."

Jade flinched, and in that moment, the black archer threw her aside. She rolled away a few feet, and the knife thumped point-down into the floor between them. Jade kicked up from flat on her back to a low crouch, and the black archer kicked his feet over his head to roll backward over a shoulder. The archer feinted toward the knife, and Jade kicked it away, but that was exactly what he wanted her to do. Without even having to shift his weight, he swung an almost lazy leg sweep at a point just below her knees. Jade jumped over it, of course, which was, again, exactly what he wanted her to do. His lazy sweep coiled him up like a jungle cat, and he released his energy in a fierce pounce that drove his fist forward like a battering ram. Ideally, this punch would have connected with Jade's solar plexus when she landed, folding her in half and driving her across the room into a three-point crouch. Then, with one last leap and an elbow strike to the head, the fight would be over.

Jade did not come back down, however, which broke the black archer's rhythm and froze him in confusion. He looked up comically slowly and saw his intended victim clinging to his own black arrow that she had made him shoot into the ceiling. The thing couldn't hold her weight for more than a second, but that was all she needed. As it came free with a sharp crack, Jade dropped down on the black archer and drove a crushing ax-kick into his temple. The kick tore his black mask aside, and he crumpled with a shocked grunt. A second later, Jade was on her knees beside him, pressing his chin back with her left hand and preparing to plunge the rigid fingers of her right hand down into his exposed throat.

Yet, before she could kill him, it happened again. This time, the memory was so strong and sudden that Jade had no idea which life was real and which was the remembered dream. In both, she knelt beside a strong, lithe, beautiful man with pale skin and spiky, shock-white hair. The man had the fine features of a bored aristocrat, but his eyes were wide with shock and dulling pain. He had blood in his hair, which ran toward his eye, and Jade wiped it away, whispering nonsense to calm him. She thought she loved him… sort of. There was something about a fight… Either she had been fighting with him, or something she had said had made him leave her looking for a fight. It had happened before, but he had always returned to her unscathed to mock her sardonically for worrying about him. This time, though, he wasn't smiling.

"Look at me," she whispered. "Look at me, damn you. What's the meaning of this? Get up at once, you weakling."

"You raiton," the black archer breathed. "I should have known… all this blood… maybe you were right… They didn't even let me surrender… One of them was laughing at me…"

Jade wiped the man's forehead again, trying not to smell the carnage all around her or hear the sounds of battle receding into the distance. Poisonous smoke was rising into the sky to blot out the sun. Blood was welling on her lover's forehead, forming an empty crimson ring in blasphemous mockery of the glowing violet circle his caste mark should have been. She wet a strip of cloth in the river where her lover lay and tried to wipe the blood off, but the ring just formed again and refused to fade. A tear fell in the center of that ring, and Jade gathered her lover up into her arms.

"I'm sorry," she moaned. "I should have been with you. I'm sorry."

And with one last kiss, her gravely wounded lover…

…opened his eyes wide and slipped a hand around the back of her neck to hold her to him. Shocked back to her senses, Jade's own eyes popped open, and she shoved herself away from the black archer. To his credit, he looked almost as surprised as she did, but he did not look anywhere near as embarrassed. He heaved himself up to a sitting position, scrubbed his hand through his white hair and leered at her like they two were old friends. Rage boiled in Jade, heating her cheeks and turning her breath into invisible steam, yet she sat very still, holding one knee to her chest. How dare he? Who did he think he was?

She'd never seen him before in her life, except this very night and... and in half-remembered dreams of another life an Age ago. But how *dare* he?

"I remember you now," the man said, at least sounding as confused as Jade felt right then. "You always apologized when you kissed me. Why was that?"

"Be quiet!" Jade snapped. "What do you want from me?"

"Nothing," the man said. "Well... no. Not 'nothing,' but... Ah, how impertinent! I don't want anything from you."

"Who are you? Why do I—"

"Don't bother asking my name," the man said. "I gave it up a long time ago. I've taken the title Disciple of the Seven Forbidden Wisdoms, and that suffices. But you... somehow I remember *your* name. Isn't that peculiar?"

"You're a liar," Jade said. "You're a Salmalin killer trying to—"

"I'm not. I'll prove it."

Before Jade could stop him, he looked in her eyes and spoke. When he did, his words proved that he wasn't lying, for what he said was actually her name. Yet, he did not say Harmonious Jade. He said a word that Jade had once seen etched in stone over a hidden sarcophagus, inside which she had found her ancient orichalcum powerbow.

"You see," the Disciple said. "I do recognize you, after a fashion. It's been a long time. I guess you aren't a grave robber after all."

"...and that's how I found it," Jade said, looking down at her powerbow, which now lay unstrung across her lap. Her long fingers traced the ornate eagle motif that decorated the weapon, and she studiously avoided looking at the Disciple for more than a few seconds at a time. They had been sitting cross-legged on the floor talking for quite some time, not three feet apart, yet Jade could still barely bring herself to look up into his cold, eerily familiar eyes.

"It was right where Zeroun suspected it would be," she went on. "It was lying in my coffin on the remains of a body that used to be mine in a tomb guarded by servile demons sentries that had been there since the First Age. It was so strange being there, looking down at that corpse. I knew it was mine, yet I hardly remember that life at all. Only in certain circumstances—" the Disciple smiled slightly at that "—can I recapture the slightest shade of what it was like. But I know I lived it. I feel the certainty of it in my soul."

The Disciple did not respond. He just stared at her with a thin glaze of obvious attraction on top of something older and deeper. Jade remembered so little about who he had been in the First Age—only as much as they two had shared earlier—but the way he looked at her suggested that he remembered more. And he clearly wanted to relive whatever it was he was thinking about. Jade dropped her gaze.

"I think this weapon felt some of that certainty when I found it," she said. "It was a part of me once, and I think I carried that part forward into this incarnation. I'm not sure, but that feels right. I'm afraid there's still much I don't know. It hasn't been very long since… everything changed."

The Disciple gave a faint nod, but he still didn't seem to have anything to say. He only tilted his head slightly to the right and continued to peer at her as a cobra would peer at a young bird. She could feel him lean another degree closer to her, and her heart hammered in her chest. Was he *doing* something to her? Had he cast some sort of spell on her that was making her act like a little girl? Probably not, but she sort of wished he had. That she could at least explain without embarrassment. She lifted the end of her powerbow and reached across the space between them to touch the Disciple's black bow.

"So, what about this?" she asked, looking down at the wicked thing in the failing moonlight that came in through the window. The weapon's skull seemed to be leering at her worse than the Disciple was. "Where did it come from?"

"Who's Zeroun?"

Jade blinked. "Pardon? I mentioned him, I thought. He's an Exalted savant I met in Chiaroscuro. He helped me. He's… a friend."

"A lover?"

Jade scoffed. "I'm sure it was on his mind, but…"

"But what?"

"But that's none of your business," Jade snapped, trying desperately to rein in her thoughts. "I can't believe you even asked me that. I can't believe I *answered*."

"Old habits die hard," he said. He then stood up, leaving Jade to ponder that statement. She flinched at the sudden movement, and the Disciple crossed to the window behind him. It was the same aperture through which Jade had intended to start firing down at Selaine Chaisa what now seemed like an awfully long time ago. The Disciple scanned the street in silence for more than a minute before Jade stood up and walked over to him.

"I'm afraid they're gone," the Disciple said, inclining his head to regard her slantwise. "It seems they slipped away while we were… distracted."

Jade glanced outside herself to confirm what the Disciple said. She had already suspected as much. "You're right," she said. "But it's only one night. They'll be back tomorrow, just like all the nights before."

"I see. So, you've been watching these people?"

"I have," Jade said. "Now, is there some reason you're avoiding my question so studiously?"

"Your question?"

"Well, I asked you mostly to make you stop looking at me the way you were, but the way you changed the subject makes me curious."

"Ever curious… I guess I don't remember your question. I *do* seem to remember something you once—"

"You're doing it again," Jade said. "And you most certainly do remember my question. I asked about this bow and where it came from. It's odd that you—"

"There's nothing odd," the Disciple said, no longer meeting Jade's eyes. "I just don't want to talk about it. It's an uncomfortable fable best left untold."

"I don't understand. I told you—"

"You told me you braved demons and Age-old traps set by servants you don't remember. You told me you had to desecrate your own tomb, break into your own coffin, look yourself in your own dead eyes and pry that tool from your own dead fingers so that it could kill for you once more."

Jade frowned at that ugly rendition of the story she had shared with him.

"My own story isn't that pleasant," the Disciple said. "I don't intend to tell it to anyone. Ever."

Silence settled in the room at that, and the distance of Ages that made them strangers in this lifetime lay heavy between them. Jade stepped away from the window and bent down to pick up the three discarded arrows that lay nearby. The Disciple turned around and leaned against the window frame. He scowled at the darkness for a few seconds before looking back at Jade.

"Listen, if I were going to tell anyone, you would be—"

"Don't bother," Jade said, standing back up and stuffing her arrows back into her quiver. Her features softened after another moment, but the casual, distracted air was gone from her. Her senses seemed to be returning, if somewhat belatedly. "I apologize for being so forward. It wasn't my place to ask. Things are confusing right now."

"Very much so," the Disciple agreed. "Something about you makes me not myself. It's quite disturbing."

Jade nodded. "Quite."

"Perhaps a change of subject was not altogether inappropriate, then?"

"Perhaps," Jade admitted, and the look in her eyes softened just that fraction more. She looked back out the window at the street below, and a less tense, more comfortable silence passed between herself and the familiar stranger beside her. In the calm that followed, she spoke again.

"So, why were you following me?"

"Well, if it isn't my lady, the Elemental Pole of Earth," the Disciple chuckled. "Sorry to disappoint, but I wasn't following you."

"Of course you were," Jade said, stung. "Unless you pulled those arrows you dropped at my feet out of your twin brother. And washed the blood off them."

"Ah, I apologize again. It *was* I you were shooting at. In fact, I'm ashamed to say you very nearly hit me. Nonetheless, I wasn't following you. It was merest coincidence that our paths happened to cross as they did. Or possibly fate." He looked up at the night sky that he couldn't see and added with a faint smirk, "A sufficiently amused fate, I hope."

"So, what were you doing?"

"The same, I suspect, as you were doing. I was following a transit cart full of undesirables not native to Nexus. Considering how I found you, though, I think our goals diverged somewhat."

"Unless you were coming here to take a life, you're right. But what do you want with Selaine Chaisa if not to kill her?"

"Is that her name?"

"Of course it is," Jade said, frowning in confusion. "Didn't you know that? Why were you following her if you don't even know who she is?"

"Any number of perfectly reasonable lascivious intentions could account for that," the Disciple replied. Jade was not amused. "But in truth, she's an acquaintance of acquaintances. And oddly, it seems that your Miss Selaine festers with the corruption of a Yozi's touch."

"Oh," Jade said, nodding. "*That.* Of course. Was that the only reason?"

"'Of course'? You aren't surprised? Maybe you don't know what I mean by the word Yozi. You said you have not long been—"

"I know what a Yozi is," Jade snapped, "and if only *one* has defiled Selaine Chaisa with its touch, I'm the City Father of Chiaroscuro. It was she who taught me what the Yozis are. I came here to kill her because of that festering corruption."

"Oh," the Disciple said. "Of course." He paused awkwardly, unsure how to proceed, then asked, "So, you know her well? Answer this, then. Has she always had nemissaries acting as her bodyguards?"

Jade frowned. "Nemissaries? You mean neomah?"

"No."

"Sesseljae, then? Or do you mean amphelisiae?"

"No, I don't."

"I suppose you could have misheard the word tomescu. Regardless, it's not unheard of for a priestess of Selaine's stature to be able—"

"No," the Disciple said, also frowning. "I mean nemissaries, and I'm sure I've never heard of a demon-priestess employing so much as one. Are you sure you know what a nemissary is?"

"I thought… No, judging by the look on your face, apparently not."

"I see. Then you wouldn't understand why I find it so strange." The Disciple paused then and scratched the back of his neck. "I wonder if talking to you was always so frustrating."

"I think we're doing well, considering the fact we've each tried to kill the other more than once since we met. This evening."

"It is quite remarkable," the Disciple said. "Another argument in favor of fate. But perhaps what we need now is rest and meditation to clear our heads and refocus our oddly similar efforts. Dawn is coming, but ironically, the morning casts me in an unflattering light."

"That's not so ironic, considering—"

"Trust me. I must leave soon to attend to a spiritual matter, but I believe you and I have more to discuss. Tomorrow, we should talk—without trying to kill one another, preferably. I know just the place you should meet me tomorrow evening when the Big Market closes."

"Wait," Jade said, "things are happening very quickly. I shouldn't—"

"It's a squalid Age in which it seems patience is rarely a virtue," the Disciple said, stepping onto the window sill and leaning halfway out. "We've wasted much time tonight, but we can make up for it by starting early tomorrow. Be at the pit arena—the largest one—before sundown tomorrow, and I'll find you. We'll discuss everything then. Now, I apologize, but I must go. I can wait no longer."

Jade stepped toward him to grab his arm, but she was too slow. Before she could say a word of protest, the Disciple of the Seven Forbidden Wisdoms leapt into the night and disappeared.

Curse it all, Harmonious Jade thought. *What did I just let happen? I'm smarter than this. What is it about that man that steals my wits? I don't even know him.*

Except in those moments when I do…

After she returned to her rented room to sleep, Jade dreamed of her life in the First Age. It was one of the clearest dreams she had ever had of that period, even though she experienced it as her current self rather than her prior self. The Disciple figured prominently as well, but she recognized him only by the cast of his eyes and the language of carriage and posture she recognized in his body. His actual appearance was unfamiliar, but she recognized him nonetheless. In the dream, she felt that she would know him anywhere. Strangely, though, his name would not come to her.

Jade had come to visit her lover, whom she had not seen or heard from in some months. He had left her sleeping one morning and disappeared on some mission he had only hinted at the night before. Jade had raged at first, but that reaction was merely rote. Her lover had slipped away thus many times before, but he had always found his way back. Her second reaction was one of icy dread, but it passed just as quickly. Her lover spent much of his time far from his home and allies, surrounded by enemies of every stripe, but he was also one of the Solar Exalted. Regardless of what danger he threw himself into, he always came back to her with no less than contempt for her worry. He certainly never expressed the least concern when she told him that she and her Circle were going on some protracted mission at the behest of the

Deliberative. She just had to content herself with waiting to see him next and thinking of new and entertaining ways to welcome him when they could find time alone.

This time had seemed no different. An informant had told her that her lover had returned home, so she had taken leave of her Circle and gone to visit him. He wasn't in the castle Manse that dominated his property, and his servants had all told her that the master wanted only to be left alone for the rest of the day. Such a request was not uncommon after a long journey, but his exclusion of company never applied to her. She left his Manse and walked into his gardens to the reflecting pool, where she always found him when he wanted time alone to think.

He was there, of course, sitting up at the highest point over his pool and looking away to the west. Below him was a wonderland of pearl, silver and adamant glass, crafted to resemble a place he remembered fondly from his youth. In the center was an enormous pool of clear water through which enormous clockwork goldfish went about their bizarre business. Floating on the water and towering over it were giant-sized crystalline replicas of perfectly ordinary freshwater lilies. Some were in full bloom, others had only begun to bud on thin stalks, and a few were nothing more than broad pads lying on the water's surface. A series of the pads still balanced atop strong stalks high above the water, and it was on the highest of these that her lover perched. Jade walked out onto the closest pad and leapt from it to the next highest out of the water and to the next and so on. As she bounded up this irregular staircase, the crystal chimed softly and sent ripples through the water below, which rewound the internal mechanisms of the clockwork fish.

"I see you've found me," her lover said as Jade alighted on the pad behind him. He didn't look at her, even when she came over and sat down beside him. "Didn't the servants tell you I wanted to be alone?"

"So, what if they did?" Jade said. "It's me. I was worried about you."

Her lover only sighed, rather than mocking her, and the light smile Jade had worn faded away.

"Should I have been worried?" she asked, putting a hand on his shoulder. His muscles were rigid. "Has something happened?"

"Nothing's happened," her lover snapped. "I'm perfectly fine. I'm whole and unharmed, so let the Unconquered Sun be praised."

Jade flinched and pulled her hand back. "What's the matter with you?"

Her lover growled and jumped to his feet. He stalked to the opposite edge of the crystal pad, and Jade rose and caught up to him before he could leap down. She took hold of his elbow, and he spun around to face her at last. When he did, Jade fell back a step in horror with a hand to her mouth. What stood before her was not her lover at all, but a desiccated corpse in her lover's clothes. Hateful, demonic fire burned in its eyes, and black blood seeped from its forehead from a ring where his caste mark should have burned.

"I'm dead!" the vile thing howled, coming toward her now. "I, my Circle and all the rest of our kind. Even you. We're all shambling and rotting, with no place left for us in this festering, diseased Creation! We're all dead!

"The ones we loved have made it so!"

Jade sat up in her bed, covered in icy perspiration, and for a moment, she did not remember where she was or how she'd gotten there. She remembered as soon as sunlight hit her eyes, and as she came fully awake, the fragments of the dream evaporated like mist. All that remained was a vague unease, a whisper of paranoia in the back of her mind and the feeling that she had just been betrayed all over again.

CHAPTER THREE

There were five men in the pit, each armed with spears and wrapped in leather armor that shone in the fading sunlight. Each of these men had come into the pit with throwing nets in addition to their spears, but bad casts had rendered them useless. Now the men were circling and darting in and out of their deadly ring with their spears, thrusting and sweeping the weapons with the efficiency of a team of experienced hunters. They knew what they were doing, for they had been working the tournament circuit together for years. Their tactics here in Nexus' largest pit arena were legendary. No other force in this challenge division had beaten this team or even killed so much as a single member. These men were the Leather Sharks, and an announcement that they would be fighting in the pit almost always filled the stands at the arena.

The Sharks were five good fighting men, well trained and in top physical condition, but their opponent today was a living legend. He was all but a god here in Nexus, and the merest *rumor* that he would even be attending a pit fight was enough to fill the seats to capacity and clog traffic around the arena for blocks in every direction. He had no name but Panther—which he'd earned as much for his lethal power and grace as for his gleaming ebony skin—and he had made himself rich killing opponents for the joy of the crowd. He had never lost a match, but more than that, he was an exceptional showman. No matter the odds or the fighting conditions, his pride, charisma and style left the audience howling in adoration. Even now, he let the Leather Sharks close in and dance around him, occasionally knocking a spearpoint away with one of his spiked gauntlets. Every clang of a parry elicited a scream from the fans. Nonetheless, this Panther was only letting the audience cool down and catch its breath after the show he had put on escaping and countering the Sharks' efforts to snare him in their nets.

Personally, Harmonious Jade didn't see the attraction. Did these caterwauling simpletons truly believe that real people fought this way when their lives were really at stake? If this Panther were a true warrior who was actually fighting for his life against five better-armed men, he would have held onto one of the nets that had failed to trap him and used it to defend himself. He could have trapped some of those spears or at least taken one of his opponents out of the action by now. Not to mention the fact that he wasn't making any effort to take away any of the spears the Sharks kept waving at him. If he were smart, he would have grabbed one and either snapped the haft over his knee or used it as a lever to smash some of his enemies together. The man was fighting like he was on a stage, and he was just lucky his opponents were doing the same. Otherwise, they would have killed him five times over by now. Provided, of course, any of the action going on in the pit wasn't just staged and choreographed beforehand.

Jade couldn't say for certain because she hadn't been here long enough to see anyone actually lose a fight. She had slipped away from the Big Market and made her way here as the Disciple of the Seven Forbidden Wisdoms had asked, but the crowds had slowed her down. Her intention had been to arrive hours earlier than the Disciple had asked and to lay out a plan in case it turned out that he *had* cast a malicious spell on her, but the logjam of bodies all clamoring to be allowed in had ruined it. She hadn't been able to take to the rooftops and sneak in either because all the closest rooftops, bridges and balconies that overlooked the ring were thronging with paying spectators, and mercenaries guarded all points of access. Jade hadn't understood why people would be so anxious to see what was happening, and even now that she was witnessing the spectacle, she still wasn't sure she did. She was no fan of thronging, screaming, stinking crowds to begin with, but even on a purely academic level, she didn't get why watching people trying to kill each other was supposed to be so entertaining.

The masses around her did not share her opinion, however. People elbowed her in the ribs as encouragement to cheer with them. People tried to get her to bet on the outcome of the fight. People were constantly walking up and trying to sell her food and trinkets—they'd been doing so ever since she'd come within two blocks of the arena. Worse, people kept ogling her lasciviously with eyes flush with vicarious excitement. With the mass and press of people all over the place, she wondered how the Disciple was ever going to find her. She wondered why he had chosen this place for them to meet at all.

Fortunately, he did not keep her in suspense for long. The hulking lone warrior down in the pit had just succeeded in disarming two of his opponents and was finally going on the offensive, when the Disciple appeared as if from nowhere and sat down at Jade's right. "Good fight?" he asked. "Who's winning?"

"The one in the middle," Jade said, feeling a light heat in her cheeks that intensified with embarrassment a second later. "But he's just making them angry, and angry fighters can be more dangerous than skilled ones sometimes. One of them is going to get lucky and get one of those spears under his ribs in a minute."

"That would be an unlikely turn of events," the Disciple said. "What kept you so long?"

"I've been watching the show. What took you so long to come join me?"

"Only self-control. Spotting you was easy."

"Even in this mob?"

"What mob?" the Disciple answered after a thunderous roar rose from the crowd as Panther felled the first of his five opponents. Jade blinked and half smiled, a little uncertain just what the Disciple meant by that. "It looks like the sun's going down. Perhaps we should go somewhere we can talk. And possibly get a snack. Are you hungry?"

"I… I could eat."

"Good. Let's get out of here. I know a place with some privacy and a nice view." He stood, and Jade followed him toward the nearest exit.

By dusk, they sat side by side on a roof in the Sentinel's Hill district with a small bag of sugared dates balanced between them. A warm breeze blew around them as they alternated taking dates out of the bag and watching the road beneath them. The wind held at bay the foundry stink and redirected the rolling clouds of sulfurous fog and coal ash endlessly pumped out by the factories of the Nighthammer district. Their high vantage improved the air quality as well, and it offered them a spectacular view of the colors the sunset painted on the broad river that ran through the center of the city. From this far away, they could not hear the curses of the barge captains or smell the river pollutants that the wind picked up and carried in the evening mists. At this distance, Nexus looked like a beautiful metropolis, rather than the urban cesspit it was trying so hard to become.

"Let's start simply," Jade said after a while, dragging her gaze away from the deceptive beauty below. "What's a nemissary?"

"It's a ghost puppeteer operating a dead body," the Disciple replied. "Nemissaries are strong, tough and often quite troublesome. The bodies they choose aren't viable for very long in the living world, but they're able to serve as temporary spies and shock troops for the Deathlords. I assume you know what a Deathlord is."

"More or less. They're the monarchs of the Underworld."

"Right."

"So, why is it so strange, then, that nemissaries might keep company with Selaine Chaisa?"

"It could be nothing unusual at all," the Disciple said. "They might be spying on her, I suppose. It's also possible she simply isn't what she seems. I haven't been following her long enough to figure that out, and of course, I don't know anything else about her. Maybe there's something you could tell me that would illuminate the mystery. You seem to know her fairly well."

"Well enough," Jade said. "I grew up with her. I looked up to her as a hero."

"I see. Do you hope to assassinate all your heroes? That has a certain warped nobility. Death would preserve them and elevate their legends to—"

"Maybe you should let me finish," Jade said, angered partly by the Disciple's irreverence but mostly by her own memory of her feelings for Chaisa. "I spoke in the past tense for a reason."

"Then, please finish. Forgive my rudeness."

Jade looked away from the Disciple's bemused eyes and did as he asked, dividing her attention between her tale and the bag of dates between them. Being abashedly careful not to reach into the bag at the same time the Disciple did, she recounted for him her memory of the first time she had met Selaine Chaisa, and the next, and every other after that. But although her story began as a simple profile of the woman she had come to Nexus to kill, it gradually became something else. With subtle urging and careful questioning from the Disciple, the story became that of her own life, from the first man she had killed to the first demon she had seen summoned to her last assassination for and her subsequent betrayal by the Salmalin. She told him about learning what her newly Exalted body could do, about how the Unconquered Sun's influence had helped her break through her Salmalin brainwashing and about what steps she had taken to learn about what it meant to be Chosen of the Sun in this turbulent age. Her story ended with her long trek to Nexus in pursuit of Chaisa. When she finished speaking, the sun had disappeared completely, and the sliver moon that presaged the coming of Calibration at year's end had risen.

"That's more than I meant to say," Jade said, looking down at her feet. "I hope I at least answered your questions about Chaisa."

"That and more," the Disciple replied. "Have you ever told anyone any of that before?"

"I told Zeroun some of it, but not nearly as much as I just told you. It's not something I've been eager to discuss."

"I gathered. Do you feel any different now, having told me?"

Jade thought about that for a moment. "Not especially. It's just what happened. It's the past. The oddest part is that I actually told it to you at all. Why do you suppose I keep doing that?"

The Disciple shrugged. "We used to know each other, even if we don't anymore. We're familiar strangers. Some people find comfort in that sort of relationship." He shrugged again. "It isn't really important why, I suppose. Some cornerstone of common sense would have silenced you if that story were full of truly sensitive and damning secrets. As it is… like you said, it's just the past."

"Were any of the parts about Chaisa helpful?"

"Unfortunately, no. From what you've said, she sounds like a devoted, zealous, talented priestess of the Yozis."

Jade nodded. "I don't understand why that makes the situation so confusing for you."

"It's a simple matter of fealty," the Disciple growled, unaware of the sudden intensity of his words. He sounded almost offended. "Ultimately, every nemissary—every denizen of the Underworld—serves the Deathlords. In time, *all* things that die serve the Deathlords. But in the time before time, the Yozis chose surrender and banishment after their war with the Exalted, rather than risking death. They made cowardly bargains with their enemies. They let their siblings and lovers die just to save themselves. What Deathlord could abide such disrespect?"

"I see," Jade murmured, staring down at the road.

The Disciple sighed, and his tense body relaxed. "I apologize for that outburst. It's just that thinking about that conflict reminds me of an unpleasant memory from the First Age. It reminds me of having no choice but to fight to the death because surrender was out of the question."

A long, uncomfortable silence passed, and the Disciple finished the last of the dates from the bag at his side. The wind caught the bag as soon as it was empty and blew it away behind them. Harmonious Jade started to speak a couple of times, only to stop short before making a sound. Instead, she busied her hands by binding up her hair in a short scarf. She wore her hair in dozens of long, thin, beaded braids, so she had to wrap it up tightly to keep it from clacking while she was working. It also took several minutes, so the silence gave her and the Disciple some time for quiet reflection. When that time had passed, the Disciple shifted his weight on his thin perch so that he was facing Jade directly.

"I don't like it," he said. Jade tried to conceal a flush of embarrassment and disappointment. "This situation with Chaisa simply doesn't add up."

"Oh… right. Because demon cultists and vassals of the Deathlords don't usually work together."

"Never, in my experience. It just shouldn't be done."

"Except, now it is."

"Correct. And if I'm not able to figure out why it is that things should be different in this case… Let us just say that my resulting disappointment and shame would be most acute."

"Okay," Jade replied. "In that case, since it's so important to you, I am prepared to wait."

"Pardon? Wait for what?"

"To kill Chaisa. Your influence has made me curious, so I'll help you find the answers you're looking for. I'll wait to kill Chaisa until you are satisfied."

The Disciple blinked once and then leaned back on his hands laughing out loud. Jade flinched and looked around to see if anyone had noticed the noise.

"Stop that," she hissed, scandalized. "Keep it down."

"I'm sorry," the Disciple chuckled. "I'm sorry. You just made that sound so very noble." That got him laughing again, and he almost lost his balance on the rooftop. "I am prepared to wait… until you are satisfied."

"I don't sound like that," Jade said, erecting a stony façade of dignity. "And you shouldn't laugh at me. I was trying to be nice. I thought I offended you."

"I know, and I truly apologize," the Disciple said with dubious sincerity. "It's just that my work doesn't necessarily hinge on keeping this Chaisa woman alive. She's one of several interconnected locals I'm investigating. A mercenary captain, a Guild master artisan, even some prodigy scavengers from outside Firewander. I more than a little suspect she's heading a cell of fanatics somewhere in the city. You can kill this nemesis of yours any time you please. I really don't mind. But if you must wait… until I am satisfied…"

"All right, that's enough," Jade said, trying not to smile back at the Disciple. "I understand. And besides, it's just possible that I have reasons of my own to want to know more about what Chaisa is up doing now."

"Of course."

"Because I'm Exalted now."

"Yes, you are."

"I have a duty to look into these sorts of things."

"Naturally."

"It's what the Unconquered Sun expects of us."

"I couldn't agree more."

"Good."

"Very well." The Disciple smiled and peered down the street. "With that, then, it appears it's time for us to get ready. The cart's coming. Perhaps we should move to the end of the line and find out where our quarry goes when she debarks."

"Good idea. Lead the way."

He rose and dusted off the seat of his pants, then offered Jade a hand up. She took it and caught a fleeting memory of sitting with her lover in a floating chair high above the docks of Chiaroscuro, listening to the music of the wind in the city's skyline flutes. When the image faded, the two of them hopped from their high perch and slid down the steeply pitched face of the tile roof on their soles. At the edge, they sprang out through the open space between this roof and the next. As they flew, the Disciple turned to her over his shoulder.

"By the way," he whispered over the rush of wind in her ears, "I like what you've done with your hair."

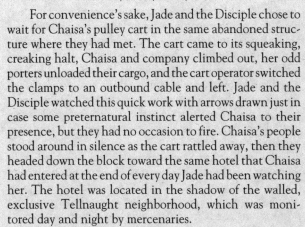

For convenience's sake, Jade and the Disciple chose to wait for Chaisa's pulley cart in the same abandoned structure where they had met. The cart came to its squeaking, creaking halt, Chaisa and company climbed out, her odd porters unloaded their cargo, and the cart operator switched the clamps to an outbound cable and left. Jade and the Disciple watched this quick work with arrows drawn just in case some preternatural instinct alerted Chaisa to their presence, but they had no occasion to fire. Chaisa's people stood around in silence as the cart rattled away, then they headed down the block toward the same hotel that Chaisa had entered at the end of every day Jade had been watching her. The hotel was located in the shadow of the walled, exclusive Tellnaught neighborhood, which was monitored day and night by mercenaries.

"Let's get ready to move," the Disciple breathed into Jade's ear as quietly as the wind.

Jade tried not to shiver. "Why?"

"Chaisa will be moving soon. The other night, she didn't stay here long before she took off deeper into Firewander. I lost her before I could figure out where she was going because I didn't realize she'd left until her trail had gone cold. I intended to tail her a little more closely last night, but circumstances didn't permit."

"I'd been assuming that she just came in and went right to bed at day's end," Jade replied. "She's been coming to and leaving from this place every night and morning on a set schedule. I didn't realize she was sneaking out."

"Ah. Well, she didn't wait long the other night before she skipped. We should move quickly so we don't lose her."

Jade agreed, and she and the Disciple took to the rooftops again, trying to ignore the fluctuating Wyld energy coming from the heart of the district. The buildings in this neighborhood were a little farther apart and in considerably poorer repair, so the going took a few minutes in order to maintain absolute stealth. The two of them could have simply vanished from all mortal senses, but neither did so just yet. Mostly, they did not want to lose sight of each other, but Jade had other reasons as well. She worried that Chaisa might have some talisman or other blessing from her Yozi masters that would alert her if a Solar Exalt were to use his divine power nearby. Considering how much the Yozis hated and feared the Solars, such a thing wouldn't be out of the question. Fortunately, the Disciple seemed of a similar mind, so the two of them made their way undetected simply by sticking to the shadows and stepping lightly on only the sturdiest of structures.

When they arrived at a vantage overlooking the hotel's rear exit, they found the door already open but no sign of Chaisa. They waited a minute, hoping that their quarry was only just now making ready to leave, but time passed and nothing happened. Proof of their bad timing arrived another moment later as a scullery servant came out in annoyance, looked around, then closed and locked the door, grumbling, "Damnation, the rats don't need any help."

The Disciple scowled and motioned for Jade to follow him as he leapt down into the alley behind the hotel. He landed without a sound, and Jade alighted right behind him just as quietly. He scoured the area, then lowered his head and raised his hands in a meditative posture. He murmured something as he concentrated, and the air around him seemed to flex and grow clear of obscuring haze as if Jade were looking at him through a convex lens. The distortion lasted only a moment, but when it passed, the Disciple looked down the alley and pointed with confidence.

Effecting a technique similar to the one the Disciple had used, Jade meditated briefly to hone her own senses to supernal levels. When she opened her eyes, the shadows that filled the alley became hollow to her, and she could see a fresh footprint in a puddle of cast-off cooking grease that someone had dumped near a sewer drain several yards away. The print was small enough to be one of Chaisa's, and it tracked the grease away into the night for several more yards, giving the two of them an idea of which way their quarry was going. They nodded mutual understanding of the clue and hurried away in that direction, keeping to the shadows themselves, but watching their steps more carefully.

Following the trail through the stinking back alleys of Firewander took several more minutes, but it was not hard work. They were able to follow the minute signs of Chaisa's recent passing without having to backtrack or even pause for more than a few seconds to navigate a turn or switchback. They stopped only to hide in shadows from locals who happened by too closely or to distract roving dogs before the mongrels could start barking. They kept their bows in hands and an arrow to each string in case Chaisa was deliberately leaving clues to lead them into an ambush, but they encountered no Salmalin resistance whatsoever. By the time they had to actually stop for more than a few minutes, Jade was somewhat disappointed in her former hero's lack of caution. Granted, Chaisa probably didn't expect trackers with such exceptional senses to be on her trail, but there was only so much that night shadows could conceal if she wasn't watching what she was stepping in.

When Jade and the Disciple had to pause for a moment, it wasn't because they had lost the trail, but because more caution was required. Chaisa's path had led them through a ruined, abandoned neighborhood dangerously close to Firewander's perilous heart, dodging occupied buildings and staying away from what passed for main streets in this district. At last, it had come to a dilapidated tunnel entrance in the shadow of a bridge that had long since collapsed.

Boards and rubble obscured the entrance, and some childish vandal had scrawled, "Fall away, ashes, fall away, skin," onto it in several places with a piece of chalk. Smears on the graffiti and a minute smudge of grease on the first visible step leading down suggested that Chaisa had come through here recently and disappeared into the darkness.

"What do you think?" the Disciple whispered.

"She went in. But where does this go?"

"The Undercity," the Disciple replied. When Jade just looked at him blankly, he explained. "It's the guts of the old city of Hollow that the new founders of Nexus built over when they resettled this area. A lot of it's been in ruins since the Great Contagion. Some of it's still thick with Wyld energy left over from when the Fair Folk ransacked this place. Many structures down there are still perfectly sound and in use, though. Whole communities of people live and work in the Undercity, never having to see the sun if they don't want to."

"That sounds like something Chaisa would like," Jade said. "But she's got a room at the hotel back there. Does she have contacts down here or something?"

"Not that I know of," the Disciple shrugged. "In fact, this isn't a section I'd ever heard was open. Most of the usable parts are miles away in that direction, closer to Sentinel's Hill or Nighthammer."

"So, whatever she's got set up inside, it hasn't been widely publicized."

"As evidenced by the state of the entrance," the Disciple said dryly. "We ought to be more circumspect in our pursuit now. We'll stay hidden from here on in but keep to the trail. I'll take the lead and drop an arrow if we need to regroup. If you find one on the path, follow where it's pointing."

Jade nodded, taking the Disciple's orders just as she'd taken Sahan's and Chaisa's in the past. His voice was so confident and direct—even at a bare whisper—that she followed it by rote, just as she had done all her life with others in authority over her.

"Ready?"

She nodded again and took a deep breath to center herself. The Disciple coiled into a defensive stance then swept his arms in a series of long, graceful arcs, and a cloak of shadow enveloped him. Harmonious Jade simply stood very still with her palms pressed together in front of her, and her body began to shimmer as if she were emitting a great heat. The hazy distortion intensified until her body was all but invisible, blending into the background. Only the grossest physical display would reveal either of them to watchful mortal eyes now. In fact, even standing right beside him on the street and using her refined senses, Jade had trouble making the Disciple out. She caught a hint of him disappearing into the tunnel, but she knew she'd never find him again with just her eyes and ears to rely on. She understood their tentative plan, though, so without any more stalling, she made her way into the ruins of Nexus' Undercity.

Chapter Four

The darkness swallowed Harmonious Jade, but it made little difference. She picked her way through the rubble, finding the path downward to be unimaginatively uncomplicated. Debris had been cleared in a zigzagging and coiling way so as to keep any light shining within from getting out and to confound casual trespassers, but as long as she could see where she was going, following along was no trouble. Furthermore, there were no guards or even mantraps along the way. As long as she didn't dislodge any of the stacked rubble or simply panic in the darkness, getting down to wherever Chaisa was going would be easy.

After several long minutes of careful descent, she found what appeared to be the bottom of the stairs. The rubble here had been cleared into something of an alcove, and she found a rack of hooks, on which hung glass oil lanterns. The smell of lantern oil was fresh and strong in this alcove, obliterating any trace of Selaine Chaisa's scent trail, but that proved no setback. As she exited the alcove, Jade could smell a faint hint of oil from farther inside. Someone who had passed this way recently had been carrying a lantern that leaked. Jade assumed that Chaisa was the one who had been so careless. She was sure that the Disciple would have known better than to take a lantern in the first place, just as she was sure that he had picked up on the new trail himself.

Outside the antechamber alcove, she found herself at the threshold of a buried thoroughfare between tumbled-down and debris-congested buildings. All around her, abandoned Second Age façades and the bones of even older subterranean buildings rose into the darkness, seeming to tower hundreds of feet into black infinity. Jade took a slow, calming breath and fought down a momentary disorientation as the sensation that she was a fish exploring some sunken tomb full of benthonic predators washed over her. When she was calm again, she crouched with bow in hand and followed the meager trail that led into the forbidding darkness.

A short time later, Jade realized that a wan light was shining in the ruins ahead of her and that she could hear the sound of many figures moving around. As she came closer to the source and the light grew stronger, she also realized that the path she'd been walking on was marred by ruts as far apart as the tracks of a wagon. They were fairly fresh, and whatever had made them had apparently swept away isolated pockets of debris from the path. The way ahead was clear and straight now, leading right into the middle of whatever activity Jade could hear in the distance. Jade was left uneasy by this strange development, and she was quite relieved when she noticed one of the Disciple's arrows by the side of the path.

The arrow pointed at a relatively sturdy structure of concrete slabs, so Jade picked up the thick shaft and headed in that direction. At the base of the structure, she found another arrow balanced on end and pointing straight up. She took this arrow as well and made her way to the roof in only a few short hops between her intended destination and the neighboring building. All that was left of her destination's actual roof was the top of its outer wall and a crude parapet that hadn't completely fallen in yet. A final arrow on this precarious ledge pointed toward the shadow of an overhanging rock ledge a few dozen yards away toward the source of the mysterious light, so Jade took it and headed that way. When she made it into the protective shadow, she found the Disciple there.

"Were you lost?" the Disciple breathed, nearly silent.

"I was sightseeing," Jade replied. "This is my first visit to this wonderful Sun-forsaken pit, and I've misplaced my map."

"Of course. I've found a striking point of interest ahead if you'd care to continue your tour."

"I'm most interested in where all that light and noise is coming from," Jade said.

"Then, you're in luck. Follow me. My fee is three black arrows."

Jade handed over the three shafts she had collected finding this place, and one of the shadows in this hiding place detached itself from the rest. The arrows disappeared into the cloaked mass, then the Disciple breezed past her. She followed mostly by watching where his footsteps disturbed the dust, keeping low and moving quickly between points of concealment. In a few moments' time, she found herself crouched beside the high guard rail of the remains of a bridge that had long ago been severed by falling rock. From this point, they looked down on a scene of mysterious industry.

The area below them was not as it had been designed in the First Age, and it bore many hallmarks of Second Age practicality. Oil lanterns hung on stout wooden poles, casting the area in a yellowish light. The poles stood at the corners of roughly three and a half square blocks of paved streets from which old rubble had been swept aside into neat piles. A few sturdy buildings stood between these streets, and as far as Jade could tell, they had once been temples. The doors of the one nearest her had carved on them an image of a living tree pouring water into the mouths of a family of foxes. The lintel above the door of the next nearest one sported an ageless emblem of the Elemental Dragon of Earth. It might have been a temple, Jade figured, but it could just as easily have once been the mansion of a Dragon-Blood. Each door had an ornate seal made of black jade in the center.

What made this place a striking point of interest was that every building that lay exposed below them had long since fallen into ruin and was now a hive of bizarre ghosts.

These atavisms wore the rough shapes of men and women, but their clothes were centuries old and their skin was mottled and discolored yellowish-green. They thronged the cleared streets and climbed up into the rubble, snapping at each other or otherwise going about their insane business. The scene was like that of a colony of ants whose hill had just been kicked over, except for the lingering throwback behavior of what had obviously been once-rational souls. Some of the ghosts were singing, others were laughing uncontrollably, and still others shrieked and tore at their corpora for no evident reason.

"What is this place?" Jade whispered. Like any decent woman, she respected the proper cycle of reincarnation. To see the cycle so clearly broken down offended her. Even when she'd blithely killed people for the Salmalin, she had wished her victims' souls an uneventful round trip back to Creation.

"Look there," the Disciple said, leaning close to her and motioning toward what had been the main street of this partially excavated refuge. His breath brushed her cheek and elicited in her a reaction that was wholly inappropriate to the situation. "That might answer your question."

Set into the tumbled stones as if a landslide or earthquake had once buried it was the grim façade of a large mausoleum. Although huge boulders had fallen on this stately construct an Age ago and had sat there ever since, it had never crumbled. Now, the stones that had presumably sealed off the front door once had been cleared away and the enormous marble doors hung askew just enough to permit passage.

"I don't understand," Jade whispered. "Is that a tomb? Is that where all those… troubled ghosts came from?"

"Well, yes," the Disciple replied, "but it's the doors that are significant. Look at the broken seal across the front. Can you read what's inscribed there?"

Jade focused all of her attention on the door. She could see that the black seal that had been affixed to the marble doors as others had on the other buildings was broken into two pieces. It was interesting in an academic way, but Jade didn't see the significance.

"Those are sorcerous glyphs," the Disciple explained. "Old, powerful ones. I'm not a savant of the arcane, but they look like warding signs."

"To ward off what?"

"What's been etched across the face of both doors," the Disciple replied. "Look above and below the broken seal. It says hullufv."

"I don't understand. Hollow's the old name of what's now Nexus, but—"

"I'm not saying Hollow, I'm saying *hul-lufv*. It's a word that dates back to the end of the First Age. It means creeping sickness or wasting illness."

"Then, these people were trying to keep some sort of plague out."

"No," the Disciple said. "Look at the way those wards are arranged. They were put up to keep the plague *in*. These people were herded into these buildings and sealed away down here to keep the infection from spreading. That's what I think happened. Their bodies were preserved in these airless crypts, and their souls could never escape."

Jade was unable to say anything for a long time. When she finally spoke, she did so in a barely audible hissing whisper through gritted teeth.

"Is there anywhere else Selaine Chaisa could have gone other than down there?"

"No," the Disciple said. "I saw her come out of that door myself and then disappear back inside. But what was really strange was that the wraiths didn't even seem to notice her."

"Then let's hope my luck is as good," Jade said, rising from her hiding place and putting an arrow to bowstring. "I'll go in and finish her off, then I'm leaving. I want out of this place as soon as possible."

"No," the Disciple said. "You can't go in there. Not before dawn."

"I've dealt with worse than ghosts," Jade began to protest. "You haven't seen—"

"No, don't you feel it?" the Disciple said, anxious now. "Those aren't just buried ruins with a bad history down there. Cruel, torturous death has ruled this place for centuries as those ghosts have slowly gone insane and degenerate to this state. I don't know about any of the other structures buried here, but whatever those spirits went through in that mausoleum has torn a festering hole in Creation. Somewhere within that place lies a gateway into the Underworld. I can feel it, even from up here with you."

Jade was familiar with the concept of shadowlands from the time she had lived in Chiaroscuro, but this revelation only served to distress and confuse her.

"I think I understand your confusion over all this better now," she said. "Chaisa never mentioned any such exploit as this to me. I would have remembered."

"And here's a stranger thing," the Disciple said, looking down at the mausoleum now instead of at Harmonious Jade. "Your Chaisa is no longer alone. In fact, she's in company I recognize."

Jade peered down in that direction and saw that, indeed, Chaisa had reemerged from the mausoleum flanked by two strangers. One was a short, slim, pretty young woman with ashen skin and hair of both raiton black and chalk white. She wore coal-black leather armor that was accented in crimson, and she held no weapon in her delicate hands. A sinister black brand glowed on her forehead in the shape of a circle, filled in with black on top but only an empty ring on the bottom half. It was similar to Zeroun's holy mark of the Twilight Caste, Jade thought, but it radiated an unholy essence. At her approach, the mad plague ghosts adopted crude postures of reverence or abject fear.

On this woman's left, a tall, emaciated figure towered over her, wearing a wide hat of woven reeds—or possibly bone—that obscured his face above the chin. No mark radiated visibly on him, but his skin had the same starkly pallid cast as the woman's, and he stood at her side unflinchingly awash in her energy. He and his diminutive partner stood without fear in this place, dwarfing Selaine Chaisa with their dread presence.

"You recognize them?" Jade asked. "Who are they?"

"The woman's called the Witness of Lingering Shadows," the Disciple said. "The man beside her is known as the Visitor in the Hall of Obsidian Mirrors. They're deathknights in the service of the Walker in Darkness."

"Deathknights," Jade said, awed by the sound of the word. She had never heard of such a thing. "Where do you recognize them from?"

"I came to Nexus to spy on them. I've been hung up trying to find out why they suffer your priestess to associate with them."

As the Disciple said this, it was to Selaine Chaisa that the deathknights both turned now with at least a veneer of respect. The priestess was walking around in front of the mausoleum, dangling a fist-sized glowing censer that emitted a bilious green light and a heavy white mist. Even the most violent of the mad ghosts that clogged the street made way for this threesome as Chaisa walked an erratic path back and forth, chanting something softly to herself.

"What's she doing?" the Disciple whispered.

Jade wasn't certain, but the answer became readily apparent soon enough. All of a sudden, the censer let out a blinding flash, and the Salmalin instantly looked up to where Jade and the Disciple were hiding. She shouted and pointed in that direction, and the censer flashed a second time. When it did, the two deathknights also knew where their observers hid. With a third flash, followed by a shouted command from the female deathknight, the plague ghosts looked up at them as well with insane hatred in their eyes. The power that concealed Jade and the Disciple unraveled in a spray of bent light and ragged shadow.

The Disciple jumped up, as did Jade. He only had time to say, "Let's go!" before a storm of chaos broke loose.

The deathknight in the reed hat was the first to act. Holding up his right hand, he extruded a long bone needle from the tip of each of his longest three fingers. He then lashed out and hurled the three slivers at Jade and the Disciple. Already running along the ruined bridge that had been their hiding place, Jade dodged one of the needles with a jumping twist, and the second skipped off the side of her powerbow as it flew by. She sent two arrows winging back toward the Visitor, but neither did any damage. The first sailed over his head, and he plucked the second out of the air inches from his heart. Jade was at the edge of the bridge then, and she leapt to a small stone outcropping high up on the wall almost a dozen yards away. She planted her feet on the wall and leapt away again, aiming for the building that was either a temple to the Earth Dragon or a Dragon-Blood's mansion. As soon as she was clear of the wall, she heard three more needles ricochet off the stones behind her. She landed and paused to let the Disciple catch up.

For his part, the Disciple was airborne as well. Yet, where Jade had jumped at an angle to cover the distance, the Disciple sprang straight from the edge of the bridge to where Jade had landed. As he arced through the air, he fired a stream of arrows, hoping to send his foes diving for cover. The Visitor snatched away the shafts intended for him and for Chaisa, and a pair of plague ghosts put themselves in front of the Witness of Lingering Shadows. Here in this sunless place that was so rife with necrotic energy, the ghosts were fully material, so the arrows lodged in their bodies and stuck deep. The Disciple hit the roof heavily and staggered two steps past Jade. Jade put a hand on his shoulder to steady him.

"I'm alright," he said, picking a bone needle out of the back of his left arm, then another out of his right calf. "We should keep moving."

At the same time, the Visitor was first taking aim at Jade, the Witness had begun barking out a series of orders in a language seldom spoken by the living in the Second Age. Bleak, necrotic essence inflated her words, and energy began to wash from her in inky tendrils that were bright enough to read by. Enslaved by her power, many of the mad plague ghosts were now scuttling up the walls of the nearest buildings and rock ledges, trying to surround the two intruding Exalts and cut off any easy escape.

Jade and the Disciple only realized this fact after they had landed on the Terrestrial temple's roof and started trying to decide where to go. The Disciple had pointed back the way they had originally come when the first wave of hungry ghosts appeared at the roof's edges and came toward them like a pack of ravenous animals. Without hesitation, Jade and the Disciple took opposing stances back to back and opened fire with their bows. Their strings hummed in eerie concordance, and no ghost could approach within five yards of them. At this distance, the range and strength of their powerbows was far in excess of what was necessary, so Jade chose her shots carefully to conserve ammunition. She waited until two ghosts were close together, then she put a single shaft through both of their necks. She waited until several came at her in a cluster then she let her arrow fly at the leader. The shaft burst into flames in mid-flight and rocked the ghost back hard enough to carry two of his partners over the edge of the roof with him.

Only once did her concentration slip as she glanced back to check on the Disciple. His broad shoulders were a blur of motion as he drew arrow after arrow from his quiver and winnowed the ranks of the ghosts who came toward him. That quick glance cost Jade a precious second, however, and four wraiths rushed her. Ever cool under fire, however, she did not panic. She drew and fired on the closest one, hitting him high in the left shoulder and spinning him into his next closest ally. She then spun around and ducked, whipping her powerbow in a tight arc that crushed the next ghost's distended lower jaw and sent him careening into a pair of wraiths charging the Disciple's off side. In the same motion, Jade whipped her knife out of the sheath at her back and flung it into the third attacker's throat. As that one fell, Jade completed her descending spin and cleared her next arrow. She had just enough time to draw and fire as her fourth ghost closed to arm's length with her. The arrow passed all the way through its stomach and out its back, and it staggered past Jade and into a knot of ghosts that was just climbing up. All of them disappeared over the edge.

Jade had only one arrow left at that point, but there were no more hungry ghosts on the roof to worry about. The Disciple had laid waste to the rest, and he was hunched over slightly, breathing hard. Oddly, though, his quiver still seemed full. Jade envied him the Charm that made that possible, and she hoped the Disciple would teach it to her some time.

"Let's go before more of them reach us," she said, taking the Disciple by the elbow. His sleeve was wet with blood from where the bone projectile had hit him. "That ledge is in reach, and we can make it into the top floor of that building before the dead climbing it do."

"You first," the Disciple said woodenly. "I'll cover you."

Jade nodded then stuck her head out over the edge of the roof to gauge the situation below, and in that brief glimpse, she marked her opponents' positions. The Visitor was striding down the main thoroughfare, slipping between the ghosts like a dancer. The shape of an ebon ring with a smaller black circle in the center had begun to glow on his forehead, visible even through the weave of his hat. The Witness had climbed onto a reposing lion statue by the mausoleum and was still giving orders to the ghosts. Chaisa had retreated back into the mausoleum and was watching from just inside the door with her glowing censer held out before her. As soon as Jade took all this in, she had to jerk her head back out of the way of three more bone needles the Visitor hurled at her.

"Ready?" the Disciple asked, grimacing and favoring his right leg. "Go."

Jade drew her final arrow, sprinted to the roof's edge and hurled herself toward the next nearest safe vantage. The Disciple started firing immediately to knock down the climbing ghosts who had made it closest to where Jade intended to land, and the arrows whizzed all around Jade, dangerously close. Jade ignored these distractions, however, and focused all of her concentration on twisting just so, taking instant aim and drawing her final arrow back to her cheek. Power surged in her as she did it—making her caste mark blaze—and as the arrow left her bow, it roared and flashed. The dazzling flare flew faster and straighter than any normal arrow, and it went straight for Selaine Chaisa's heart. The priestess flinched and tried to raise her hands in terror, but all she managed to do was lift her glowing censer into the arrow's path. The blazing bolt hit it, and both objects exploded with a thunderclap that sent Chaisa flying backward into the mausoleum. At the same time, Harmonious Jade finished her slow roll through the air and landed in a three-point crouch.

As soon as Jade landed, the Disciple leapt into the air after her. The Visitor threw another long needle at him and missed, but the Disciple didn't even bother to return fire. He focused solely on clearing the distance, even sacrificing grace in his landing. His knees and forearms hit the roof first, and he slid to a rough halt well beyond where Jade had touched down. Jade rushed over to him and helped him laboriously to his feet. Blood was running down his forehead and between his eyes.

"It looks worse than it is," he said, reading Jade's expression. "That bastard got me with a couple of those darts, and there was some kind of poison on them. I can feel it working."

"How bad is it?"

"Bad enough to mortally offend my dignity. Are you out of arrows?" Jade nodded. "I see. Then, we need a new strategy."

"I'm listening. What do you have in mind?"

"We should split up. I can't keep up with you like this, and if I tried, those two would easily catch up to us both. Instead, I'll provide you a distraction while you go back the way we came."

"That sounds good to me," Jade said, charting a path across the remaining rooftops back toward the hidden tunnel that led to Firewander. "Ready?"

The Disciple frowned. "I expected something of an argument over that actually…"

"Well I didn't think you were just going to noisily hand yourself over to them while I ran away," Jade said. "You do have a plan to get yourself to safety, don't you?"

"I do," the Disciple said. "It might not be a great one…"

"Let's just go before it's too late," Jade said. "I can hear the dead clawing their way up the walls."

"Right," the Disciple said, working a persistent stiffness out of his left elbow and shoulder. "Of course. You get ready to move, and don't stop until you're out on the street. Don't even look back for me."

"I won't," Jade said, which elicited another small frown from the Disciple. "Where should I meet you once we're away to safety?"

"There's a place called Ikari Village outside of Nexus about a day's ride west by southwest off the Mishaka trade route. I'll meet you by a set of large granite boulders overlooking the place from the north after dawn two days from now. If I can. If I'm not there…"

"I'll see you there," Jade said, "and we can decide then how to proceed." She then began to unwind the scarf that bound the beaded braids of her hair. She used a corner of it to wipe the blood from the Disciple's face, then she tied it off around his head to keep the wound from blinding him at an inopportune moment. The odd injury immediately started soaking through the material, and the Disciple turned away.

"All right," he said. "No time left. As soon as I'm over the side, you start moving. One… two… now!"

❖　❖　❖

On that cue, the Disciple ran to the edge of the temporarily safe vantage and jumped over, meeting a cluster of hungry ghosts that had been inches away from gaining the roof. He shot each one in the throat with an arrow then landed ungracefully on the one nearest him. The wraith collapsed under his weight, but he balanced on its disintegrating corpus and rode it as it slid down the pitch of the roof and came apart. He descended at a breakneck pace, firing at two more plague ghosts on the way and letting the mass beneath his feet take out a handful more. When the body came apart entirely, he hurled himself out into space toward where the Visitor in the Hall of Obsidian Mirrors appeared to be waiting. The Disciple hadn't expected him to be so close already, but he was committed to the action he'd taken. Though his sight was beginning to blur and his muscles burned with poison, his anima flared all around him, and he sailed toward his foe firing one last arrow. The Visitor extruded, aimed and hurled one last needle at the same time, and the two projectiles passed each other in midair. The Disciple rejoiced to see his shaft punch through the center of the Visitor's outstretched throwing hand, but his victory was short-lived. Though he tried to twist out of the way, the Visitor's needle twisted in midair and punched into his stomach. The projectile was poisoned like the others, and the toxin had finally done its work. His limbs cramped up like those of a dying spider, and he crashed to the ground at the Visitor's feet. There was no way he was going to make it out of this, he realized. If he didn't come up with something else quick, he was going to die here at this deathknight's feet.

The Visitor pulled the Disciple's arrow through the back of his hand and tossed the shaft on the ground next to where the black-clad man had fallen. He then kicked the Disciple's bow out of arm's reach and rolled the faintly glowing man over. The Disciple's arms and legs were still twitching as his body fought the poison that had infected it. A trickle of blood seeped out from beneath his ring-stained headband and ran down his cheek like a tear.

"It seems the priestess was right," the Visitor said, kneeling beside the Disciple and gripping the end of the needle that protruded from his stomach. "Spies did follow her this evening."

He twisted the needle, making it a spindle for the Disciple's guts. The Disciple cried out and tried to writhe away, but the Visitor held him down.

"How very interesting," the Visitor continued. "You're not one of Walker's agents. Who are you working for? Or is that a foregone conclusion?" He waited for an answer that wouldn't come, then asked again with another twist of the needle. The Disciple screamed and tried to defend himself with useless limbs, but he still only shook his head. The Visitor sighed, pulled the needle out of his victim's stomach and held it up where the Disciple could see it. "Very well. If you can't say who your master is, you're better served returning to him. Pray the Malfeans treat your soul with respect and allow it to return quickly."

The Visitor held the bone needle over the Disciple's eye and brought it down slowly, intent on driving it up into his brain and killing him. The Disciple tried to turn his head and close his eyes, but the Visitor grabbed his forehead and peeled back his eyelid with a thumb. The Disciple tried one last time to get free, but he was hopelessly trapped. Finally, as he blinked and the gore-stained needle touched his eyelash, he cried out.

"Wait! Please, wait. I'm not here to stop whatever you're doing. I'm just a spy. I'm not ready to face the darkness of Oblivion, please… I'll do anything you ask if you spare me. I swear."

That got the Visitor's attention, and he stopped the needle's slow progress less than an eyelash's length from the Disciple's eyeball. The ring-and-circle caste mark on his head flashed, and a ribbon of ancient characters swirled in the air around him, sanctifying the spoken oath.

"You must be young yet to be so desperate," he said, sitting back on his heels. "A better man would have more faith in his destiny. But I'm intrigued. Maybe we'll find a use that suits you. A watchdog, perhaps…"

The Visitor began to laugh then, but the Disciple said nothing. He merely turned his head to look back the way he'd come, hoping at least that Harmonious Jade had escaped. All things being equal, he'd rather she died than see him like this.

Meanwhile, Harmonious Jade was not wasting time. She jumped out into space in the opposite direction, just barely missing the talons of a ghost beneath her. She darted back the way she had come just an hour or so earlier, relying on her sharpened senses and the fortune of the Unconquered Sun to guide her safely. She made it to the hidden tunnel without incident or any immediate pursuers, and several long minutes later, she was back on the street looking up at the smog-filtered sky. As the Disciple had told her, she did not pause there to wait for him to effect his own escape. She bolted toward the industrial wasteland of Nighthammer, thinking of nothing but stealthy, steady flight. If she couldn't lose pursuers in that noisy, wretched place, she never would. She did not allow herself to feel the fear that she had had to keep hidden from the Disciple when Chaisa had revealed their hiding place. Nor did she allow herself to even acknowledge the guilt and worry that wanted to overwhelm her for leaving the Disciple alone. Her only thoughts were of minding the path she was taking and deciding what to do in two days' time when she and the Disciple of the Seven Forbidden Wisdoms were reunited.

If fate had such a reunion in mind for them at all…

CHAPTER FIVE

Harmonious Jade's first priority after she left the Undercity was to get back to her rented room and get some rest. She hadn't gotten much over the past few nights, and with things developing so rapidly, she needed to clear her head and go over everything with a fresh mind. Peaceful, dreamless sleep was just the thing to cure that unease, but considering what had been happening, she was too jittery and out of sorts to sleep. So, first, she meditated, centering herself and pushing every clamoring distraction out of her mind. She pushed away the face of the Disciple—familiar, yet strange and intimidating at the same time. She pushed away the dread, malevolent image of the deathknights. She pushed away Nexus and Chaisa and the Salmalin until her thoughts were still and her body was relaxed and temporarily at peace.

When she woke refreshed, she practiced her regular morning exercise regimen and then ate a late breakfast at her inn's dining room. She sat alone, discreetly listening to the other patrons' hushed conversations and wondering how they could seem so interested in such commonplace things as their jobs and their families when the world was so much more complicated and dangerous than they seemed to realize. Jade didn't understand this seemingly willful ignorance, but she welcomed the distraction of thinking about it. Without it, she would find herself obsessing over the last two days' events with the nauseating mixture of fear and wonder that was creeping up on her even now.

After she finished her breakfast, Jade went out into Nexus to set her mind at ease about at least one of her lingering worries. Before she left town for the next few days, she had to know that Chaisa was dead. Her first stop in checking up on that was to visit the hotel in Firewander where Chaisa was supposedly staying. She watched the place for about an hour, then made her way into the building itself. She subtly checked the manager's ledger to find out what room was Chaisa's, and she was heartened to discover that Chaisa had not checked out. Hopefully, that meant she was dead and rotting in the Undercity, rather than erecting wards on her door and window and summoning guardian demons from the realm of the Yozis.

Fortunately (and expectedly), the latter turned out not to be the case. Jade found Chaisa's room empty, even though it still showed signs of life. The bed had not been slept in, but Chaisa's clothes were still in the drawers, and her makeup and other beauty accoutrements lay in disordered piles on a vanity dresser in front of an old, dingy mirror. Chaisa owned combs of wood, bone and jade, as well as a selection of pins that she sometimes wrapped her long, curly black hair around. Also on display were pots of cream, powder and various dyes, which Chaisa wore in seemingly endless variety. Jade had never been allowed to wear makeup among the Salmalin—which Sahan had said was to keep her from tempting her more righteous fellows—but she had always seen Chaisa wearing it. The only decorations Jade had ever been allowed were the beads in her hair.

Standing in Chaisa's room now, Jade touched several of the bottles and pots arrayed before her, then turned and double-checked the lock on the door. She then returned to the mirror, opening every vial and container in front of her. For the next hour or so, she touched her fingertips to various admixtures and experimentally tried them out on her own face. She mostly made herself look ridiculous, but the experiment wasn't a total disaster. One or two of Chaisa's perfumes was subtle and a little exciting, and Jade decided to take a small bottle of the one she liked best. She left everything else as she had found it, but the temptation to take *something* was irresistible. If Chaisa came back and found it missing, she would realize that, even here, she was not safe. If she didn't come back, she wouldn't miss it anyway. Jade also found the money Chaisa had been transporting yesterday, and she took as much as she thought she might need over the next few days. Filled with a somewhat peevish satisfaction, she then washed her face and slipped unseen out of the hotel.

Her next stop was the loud and crowded Big Market, and she watched Chaisa's regular auction block from a collapsing orbit of high vantages. As she approached, she saw that the remainder of Chaisa's lot of scavenged Chiaroscuro glass had shrunk to a collection of castoffs no larger than a spearhead and was being packaged for shipment to the Little Market. Jade followed the wares, but at no point did she see or hear from Selaine Chaisa. In fact, several of the people with whom Chaisa had been doing business were forced to wonder if perhaps she had left town unexpectedly. One or two even speculated that she had met an ignominious fate on her way to gods-forsaken Firewander. Such ill fortune was all too common in Nexus, as the metropolis thrived with no official peacekeeping force. The worst infractions of the laws were punished by the Council of Entities or its mysterious but insanely powerful Emissary, but a possible robbery turned homicide was hardly even worthy of notice. Not unless one's friends were well connected.

Jade haunted the markets for a few more hours of reconnaissance, then she did a little shopping of her own. She bought trail rations, a boot repair kit, a new knife and more arrows, then headed along the noisome waterfront facing the polluted Gray River. At the Coffleblock Market, she bought a decent horse and led it to the head of the Mishaka trade route. She knew at this point that she couldn't reasonably stall much longer, so she finally made up her mind to ride out to meet the Disciple of the Seven

Forbidden Wisdoms. She just hoped that he understood how much effort she was going to on his behalf. This was quite an overture of trust and good nature she was extending his way. She hoped he appreciated it.

The rest of that day, night and following morning passed uneventfully as Jade made her slow way out to her rendezvous. She had only her thoughts to entertain her, but at least she wasn't set upon by bandits, Wyld barbarians or evil spirits en route. She wasn't especially worried for her safety, even with Calibration fast approaching, but she was concerned with conserving ammunition on the off chance that a trap was waiting for her beyond the plantations that lay closest to Nexus' borders.

What she found when she finally located the town the Disciple had spoken of was no trap, but it ruined any hope she might have had of a pleasant reunion. Even at a distance Jade could smell ugly odors blowing out of town toward her. When she caught the scent, she also noticed that no one appeared to be working in any of the fields that lined the largely overgrown road. Birds flocked and chattered at each other like happy children, and fat rodents skittered around in brazen defiance of any human presence. Yet, as she approached, the animal presence dropped off sharply, and even her horse started trying to make her turn back. Jade tied the animal to a crooked fence post and continued on foot.

What greeted her in Ikari Village was a scene of carnage and slaughter on a scale unlike anything she had ever seen before in this life. She had killed plenty of people—likely more than had met their fate here. She had seen plenty of dead bodies. Yet, never had she seen so many who had been killed so savagely and grouped in one place.

She found the bodies laid out in attitudes of worship and reverence at the local temple shrine, bearing countless wounds. The wounds ranged from clean slices to blunt trauma to ragged, brutal lacerations, and some even appeared to be wicked, human-shaped bite marks. Jade couldn't think of any single entity that could have committed such violence, but she wouldn't have put it past an enraged spirit patron. The villagers might have offended their god somehow, or the thing might simply have somehow lost its senses as Calibration neared.

That initial theory seemed unlikely, however, the more Jade looked around. Dozens of sets of horse tracks and footprints marred the area, and the doors and windows of the nearby homes were all broken in or left ajar. Yet, the places hadn't been visibly robbed or vandalized inside. The evidence of disturbances indicated that the townspeople had been rousted from their beds, dragged into the street and murdered there. Then, whoever had committed this atrocity had ridden on out of town back toward Nexus, apparently with at least two heavy wagons in tow.

The senseless brutality of the scene didn't make sense to Jade. It was just violence for violence's sake. What's more, none of the dead in the temple had been given anything resembling proper funerary rites, which was going to make this place a hornet's nest of hungry ghosts, not unlike the one she had so recently escaped in the Undercity. Jade was keenly aware of this fact as the sun sank toward the horizon, and she decided to get out of the village before sundown found her surrounded once more by the dead. She returned to her horse and rode to the rock formation where the Disciple had told her to wait for him. The vial of perfume she had stolen from Chaisa's room for that rendezvous lay forgotten in the bottom of her saddlebag.

Along the way, she found something that piqued her morbid curiosity. It was a row of freshly dug graves set off the side of the road about a hundred yards outside of town. Wooden plaques with names and military ranks carved on them had been laid at the head of each. What was more, the hilt of a broken three-edged dagger lay atop each grave, and the base of each hilt had a snarling wolf's head embossed on it. Jade didn't recognize the symbol, but she understood its significance well enough. The bodies in these graves were either organized bandits or professional mercenaries who had been killed in their raid on this village. Although they hadn't paid the villagers the same respect, the survivors had at least had the warped decency to bury their own dead. Then, they had packed up and continued back toward Nexus. Expansive fertile fields, thick forests and an enormous freshwater lake provided the town with a relative isolation that had concealed the murderers' deeds, and they had blithely carried on with their travels, likely hoping to blend into the human morass that was Nexus and escape the punishment they deserved.

The callous cruelty of it sickened Jade and ignited a passion in her that had not been there before her Exaltation. She wanted to see justice done for this wanton cruelty, and the price for that justice would be these wolf-soldiers' blood.

First, though, Jade still intended to meet up with the Disciple once again and share her outrage with him. If he didn't already know what had happened, she planned to show him, and the two of them would set aside some time to put right the evil that had been done. She would show him the evidence she had found, and the two of them would punish whoever had done this. This carnage offended her on a spiritual level, and she intended to make sure that she did right by the massacred villagers' souls, even though the villagers' nearest neighbors were too afraid or apathetic to do so. It was what the Unconquered Sun wanted.

Unfortunately, the Disciple never showed up. She waited for the rest of the day and night, and through most of the next day as well, but he never appeared. As evening came on the second day and Calibration loomed, Jade realized that he probably wasn't coming. It was possible he was three days dead in the bowels of Nexus, having sacrificed his life for a woman he barely knew. A woman who hadn't even tried to talk him out of it. This admission shamed Jade, but another more chilling possibility occurred to her. The Disciple had told her that, although Chaisa was not a native to the city, the priestess wasn't working alone there.

A mercenary captain, a Guild master artisan, even some prodigy scavengers from outside Firewander. *I more than a little suspect she's heading a cell of fanatics somewhere in the city,* he had said. Judging by the rough age of the wagon tracks through the village and the time she had wasted getting out here, Jade guessed it was possible that Chaisa's mercenary contact had been sent here at about the same time the Disciple should have arrived. If Chaisa *had* survived and had made contact with the mercenaries, they could have arranged a trap for the Disciple—one that had somehow ensnared all the villagers as well. The villains could then have returned before Jade had left, missing out on ensnaring her too because she had dragged her feet. It would be just like Chaisa to have such a contingency in the works, and the more Jade thought about it, the more sure she became. By the time she finally admitted to herself that her waiting was pointless, she was absolutely convinced.

Selaine Chaisa awoke in pain surrounded by darkness, lying in a coach moving through what sounded like forbidding territory. The wind moaned, thunder snapped at high altitudes, and the ground beneath the coach's wheels cracked and scratched as if the road were paved with bones.

"Where am I?" she whispered, barely able to raise her voice higher. Her face burned as she tried to speak, and something wet and sticky covered it.

"She lives," a female voice cooed in the darkness. "Hope swells."

"They all resist the inevitable," a male voice replied. "It's what they call courage. She would have been better off a coward."

"We wouldn't," the female voice said. Despite her pain and confusion, Chaisa recognized the voice as that of the Witness of Lingering Shadows. "Her partners would think we'd killed her and disposed of her body. It would be enough to break the deal you made with them."

The man—the Visitor in the Hall of Obsidian Mirrors—grunted in disdain.

"Where am I?" Chaisa whispered again. "I can't see." She reached up toward her face, but the Witness gently restrained her hands.

"You shouldn't touch," the Witness chided. "You'll reopen your wounds. You might even pull out an eye."

"I've never seen anyone do that to herself," the Visitor said, intrigued.

"Don't tease her," the Witness said. "Chaisa, do you remember what happened?"

The memory came forward for the asking. She remembered inspecting the newly converted Salmalin temple, then exploring the nearby tomb the Visitor had found so fascinating. The warning of intruders, using the Lantern of Ligier's True Light, seeing Harmonious Jade... That Anathema was still alive and here in Nexus with only one possible purpose.

"She was there to kill me."

"She almost did," the Witness said. "The arrow went right by me, higher than your curious armor could have intercepted. How lucky you were to have that artifact in front of you. It's gone now, by the way. The pieces we couldn't pull out of your skin melted away."

"Where is Jade?" Chaisa wheezed, feeling a blister on her jaw split and soak into her bandages. "Tell me you killed her."

"No," the Visitor said.

"What about the other?"

"Yes, let's discuss him," the Witness said, patting Chaisa's hand like a dear girlfriend. "You told us that you had arranged the certain death of your former pupil back in Chiaroscuro. Now, she's here hunting you in most peculiar company. How do you account for this galling inconvenience?"

"I underestimated her. At least tell me you dealt with her partner."

"I dealt with him," the Visitor said.

"Don't be so modest," the Witness said. "He actually begged for his life. That's no small accomplishment, considering..."

The Visitor only shrugged.

"Well, anyway," the Witness continued, "I don't suppose you know who he is or how he came to be involved in this, do you?"

"No. Didn't he tell you who he was?"

"He didn't have a name to tell me, obviously," the Visitor said. "And he's sworn to greater oaths than I could force him to break not to reveal his master's name."

"Not that that isn't obvious," the Witness said.

"So, what's he doing with Jade?" Chaisa asked.

"When I asked, he swore to me that he was only sent here to find out what we were doing, not to get in our way."

"He was very sincere," the Witness added.

"Still, Jade's out there," Chaisa moaned. "She's changed so much. She'll kill me. Maybe I should get out of Nexus and postpone the ritual until the next Calibration."

"That's not possible," the Visitor said.

"But—"

"No, he's right," the Witness said. "We have to move very quickly now, and having you disappear would make our dealings with your masters very... tedious. Besides, your comrades in worship would think the most awful things about us."

"Anyway, where do you think you'll be safer?" the Visitor said. "Out there on your own or with us?"

"You're right—where is my faith?" Chaisa sighed, ashamed of herself. "So, where are you taking me?"

"To a friend's estate in Bastion," the Witness said. "Haven't you always wanted to live there? It'll be perfectly safe. So safe you might even come to resent your host's hospitality."

"Provided you survive your wounds," the Visitor grumbled.

"Oh, you needn't worry about that. She'll survive as long as she must to see her life's greatest work complete. Won't you, Chaisa?"

"I will."

"There, very good. How life-affirming!"

CHAPTER SIX

Investigation wasn't Harmonious Jade's strong suit, but the Salmalin had taught her the rudiments of the craft. A killer needed certain skills to track down a prospective victim, to punch holes in his defenses and to get to know him well enough from afar to be able to predict his behavior. A killer had to be a talented stalker of human prey first, or all the martial skill in the world would go to waste. Without that talent, a killer was nothing but a bumbling leg breaker. Jade knew this well, so it was with much care and circumspect deliberation that she set out looking for Selaine Chaisa's mercenary contact.

Her first idea was to return to the Little Market and visit a contact-broker she had seen Chaisa visit once or twice. This broker acted as a middleman for small-time businessmen or visiting nobility who wanted temporary bodyguard service but had no contacts in Nexus' mercenary district, Cinnabar. Jade visited his booth, waited her turn among the broker's sweaty clientele, then finally sat down with him to ask what business he'd done with a woman named Selaine Chaisa. Jade asked if Chaisa had requested bodyguards from any particular company or if he had randomly put Chaisa in contact with the captain of a company. Jade doubted that Chaisa would have been so careless, but one of the first rules of investigating anything was to rule out the most obvious possibilities first.

The contact-broker—a hairy man named Ibex—was eager to answer Jade's questions, although he hardly looked at her eyes once. He touched her hands or her arms when he said something funny, and he squeezed her knee more than once in the short while they spent together. He didn't have much to say about Chaisa, but he went on at length about how he had once been a mercenary himself and had won numerous honors in many glorious battles. Of course, he had tired of that life and decided to make his fortune here instead, so now he earned a comfortable living and rented a house just a short ride down the hill from the affluent Bastion neighborhood. (Well above the sulfuric clouds of "poor man's breath" that Nighthammer's foundries belched out, he assured her.) His eyes were wide with excitement as he spoke of all these things, and he seemed to believe that Jade would be equally fascinated.

She wasn't. She only wanted information, not a new friend. To make this clear, she disengaged herself from his grasping hands and disappeared back into the crowd. She heard him calling her a serpent, a vixen and a mongrel bitch, but she was more frustrated with the encounter than he was. Now, she was going to have to go into Cinnabar and poke around. As she wasn't familiar with that neighborhood, her investigation seemed more likely to stand out there. There was nothing for it but to try, though, so she made her way uphill and across town to what she'd heard others call the mercenary district.

She found Cinnabar to be a clean, orderly, relatively civil community that seemed far less crowded than the Nexus district. The river smelled and looked better too for being upstream from Nighthammer, though the property nearest it was still the cheapest, owing to how frequently the river flooded. The streets on the outskirts wove between barracks and walled compounds that ran the gamut from imposing fortresses to squat erstwhile hotels. Watchtowers dotted the district at random, having been subsidized by public funds and now made available for rent by any mercenary organization with an eye toward public safety. Banners

hung from most of them displaying the grim insignia of the
Hooded Executioners, the mercenary outfit of choice of the
Council of Entities. Beneath each so-occupied watchtower
lay an awning-covered recruitment stall staffed by masked
or hooded men who directed prospective applicants to the
recruitment offices on Glory Street. Several other prominent companies had bought real estate along this street, so
it was there that Jade started her investigation.

Her first goal was simply to look for a mercenary
company logo that matched the ones she had seen on the
broken daggers of the buried murderers outside the massacred village. She remembered that snarling wolf's-head
image very well, but none of the recruitment offices displayed that insignia. She found the Iron Wolves, the Steel
Fangs and even a company called the Two-Tailed Wolf
Brothers, but none of those companies' icons matched the
one she was looking for. She spent hours roaming from one
military compound to another, but none she saw looked
like the one she wanted. As dusk came and night fell, she
hid herself away and began spying on neighborhood patrols to see if she could find the insignia on any soldiers'
uniforms, but that proved useless. The patrols were too
numerous and too widely spread out for her to check out
effectively and quickly.

She kept up her investigation for another couple of
hours that night, then started again in a different section of
town the next morning. Her luck feinted in a positive
direction when she discovered a better funded contact-
broker with a directory of all the mercenary outfits operating
in Cinnabar, but even that didn't pan out. Several hours of
searching (at a price of three silver dinars) revealed no mon,
crest, seal or insignia that matched the one she had found.
That meant either that the soldiers had recently changed
their symbol or that they weren't headquartered in Nexus to
begin with. Regardless, passive observation no longer seemed
adequate to the task. She would have to start actually
mingling and making inquiries with the mercenaries themselves if she expected to make any progress.

This idea did not appeal to Jade, as she was fairly inept at interviewing people for information. She knew the physical fundamentals of torture, but the psychology of interrogation escaped her. More often than not, she had trouble getting people who weren't predisposed toward cooperation to give her what she wanted. A series of failed negotiations over her skills in Chiaroscuro testified to that fact, and she was in no hurry to frustrate and embarrass herself the same way again. Of course, if she wanted to find out what had become of the Disciple and root out the rest of Chaisa's Salmalin conspirators, she didn't have much choice. So, as the first night of Calibration fell, she started visiting taverns and restaurants in Cinnabar to ask the locals questions.

Like much of Nexus, Cinnabar was an addition to the ruins of old Hollow rather than a renovation, and it consisted entirely of Second Age buildings. Much of the district lay on a flood plain, so those buildings closest to the waterfront were sturdy and watertight, making them seem squat outside and claustrophobic inside. The abundance of citizens who came out to celebrate the five-day year's-end Calibration period intensified that impression, making Jade feel even more uncomfortable. (To say nothing of the acute embarrassment that impaled her every time some drunkard watching her from a balcony or a publicly maintained pavilion wandered her way slopping cheap beer on her boots to ask if she was looking for company.) She could feel the various taverns' and restaurants' customers sizing her up like she were a harlot, and she almost cringed any time someone scowled or laughed at her for asking her questions.

Not even her money seemed to help. She paid one bartender an entire jade obol before she'd even asked a question, and he just laughed in her face and had her thrown out by mercenaries hired to guard the door. Elsewhere, she offered a server a much smaller amount just to get him to talk to her, and he told her to meet him out back in an alley with more money twenty minutes later. She did as he asked, but when she got there, the server was nowhere to be found. The manager later told her that the server had left for a party in Sentinel's Hill. Still another potential informant led her on with vague answers to her questions as she paid out dinar after dinar to refresh his memory. Finally, he grew tired of taking Jade's money and excused himself to the bathroom. He never came back.

Each of these humiliations exasperated Jade, but she learned from them. She slowly refined her method until she felt she could finally discern truth from lies and honest cooperation from simple tricks. By the time she had decided to return to her room for the night, she was confident enough to try again after she got some sleep.

The next day, her persistence was rewarded. She visited a few more places—some of which she had been to the night before but made no impression in—until she came to a sparsely decorated and very dim bar called the Lathe and Chain. The bartender was whittling, and he barely looked up at her as she described the snarling wolf's-head insignia that she had asked about dozens of times already in the last twenty-four hours. He grunted and waved her off, but the grossly hung-over young man sweeping up evidence of the previous night's revels waved her over, introduced himself as Winter Birch and asked her to repeat her description. She did so warily, as this seemed to be the favorite lead-in of Cinnabar's most opportunistic con men.

"And you say this icon was on a dagger hilt?" Birch asked when Jade was finished. She nodded. "And was the blade whole or broken?"

The way he asked implied a significance that intrigued Jade, especially since she hadn't mentioned that detail yet.

"The ones I saw were broken," she said, taking heart.

Birch leaned on his broom and nodded, saying, "Ayuh, I recognize the symbol. It belongs to a company called the Ravenous Wolves. Don't operate out of Nexus."

"Still, it sounds appropriate."

"Ayuh," Birch continued, "the Wolves've got a decent reputation for honorable work and fair prices.

Only a few sound defeats in its history, and most of those probably fated from the start anyway. You thinking of joining up?"

"Not likely," Jade said. "Tell me about the daggers."

"Sure," Birch said. "Their called 'wolf fangs.' Time was, the company commanders issued a dagger with a wolf on the hilt to any soldier who completed the probationary service period. While they're on duty, they're supposed to wear them on their belts."

Jade was about to ask where these Ravenous Wolves' headquarters were, when Birch went on to explain that a broken wolf fang was an entirely different matter.

"Few months ago, the captain of the Ravenous Wolves disgraced him- or herself somehow—can't remember—and had to leave the company. I might remember it better, but last night's echoing in my head."

"Of course," Jade said, noting the red spider webs in his eyes.

"Anyhow, a fifth of the soldiers stayed loyal to their captain despite the resignation. They didn't think the captain did whatever the rest of the command staff wanted him or her to quit for. They split off from Wolves and came to Nexus to form their own company. When they did it, they all broke their wolf fangs and started carrying the hilts as a symbol of their broken trust. That's how I heard it."

"I see."

"None of the mercenaries of this new company wear their broken fangs where people can see 'em—the Council of Entities says you can't wear broken weapons in public—but all the former Wolves have them. Rumor has it they're even buried with them."

Jade asked with growing excitement what the name of the new splinter-company was called and where she could find it. Birch told her the company called itself the Bronze Tigers, and he gave her its address. He couldn't remember the captain's name just then, but he gave her the name of a cousin of his who had recently joined up and told her to ask for him.

When the man had nothing else to say, he asked Jade why she wanted to know so much about the Bronze Tigers. She answered vaguely and uncomfortably that she had discovered a small burial plot on her way into town, then tried ungracefully to change the subject. She asked him how much money he wanted for the information, and he tried to deflect her offer with casual charm. Jade turned down his offer to buy her a drink or dinner or a stay in a nearby hotel and eventually had to force him to settle for a vague implication that she would meet him here later when his work shift was over. With that, the interview was over, and Jade left to perform a little reconnaissance before night fell and the Calibration revelers came back out.

That night found Harmonious Jade atop a concrete wall overlooking the Bronze Tigers' compound. She remembered passing the place before she'd known who she was looking for, and then, as now, she had been unimpressed. It squatted at the bottom of a hill near the waterfront, surrounded by a wall high and thick enough to hold back the water should the river exceed its bank. A grimy line high up on the wall's outer surface indicated that the place was no stranger to spring flooding. Uniformed guards marched the ledge behind the parapet, keeping an eye on the poorly lit streets below. None of them could see Jade, even though she crouched atop the parapet wall more or less at the soldiers' eye level.

Inside the wall were several squat buildings—from stables to barracks to storage facilities to an administrative structure—all arrayed around two pavilions and a tramped-down parade ground. Like most of the structures in this part of Cinnabar, the buildings were all functional and made of poured concrete and had been constructed during the Second Age. None of them demonstrated a sense of the architectural aesthetics of the imperishable First Age structures that dotted Nexus as a reminder of old Hollow.

A few soldiers marched around half-heartedly on internal guard duty within the compound, and others on leave to celebrate the holiday came and went, but Jade paid them little attention. If she'd had her bow with her, she could've picked off each one of them and still taken out the sentries along the walls before anyone in any of the buildings knew she was there. In fact, if these mercenaries kept a significant amount of grain or kerosene or any other inflammable material in with its supplies, she could cause a significant distraction and pick off even more soldiers at her leisure in the confusion. It would probably serve the Tigers right for the evil they had done, but that wasn't Harmonious Jade's goal this evening. It was tempting, but tonight, she had to be very particular.

In fact, she was not even carrying her bow right now. She had felt exposed without her ancient weapon all morning, but she had thought she ought to leave it behind during her earlier investigation so as not to put off potential informants. Now that she had that information, she did not want to wait even as long as it would take her to retrieve the bow and come back. Besides, she still wore her new knife, and that weapon was more conducive to what she had to do right now.

She had to find the Tigers' captain and make him admit what he had done. Then, she would make him (or her, if that were the case) tell her what had happened to the Disciple. Provided, of course, there was anything to tell and the Disciple hadn't simply perished in the Undercity. Then, if she still had the time, she would pry the names of Selaine Chaisa's other conspirators from the mercenary captain's throat. A knife made such operations more personal, more effective and more subtle. Her bow could accomplish the same goals more expediently, but now that she was here, she felt she could spare enough time to do things right before going back for it.

First, she had to find out who and where the mercenary captain was. She was burned out on interviewing informants, so her first idea had been to watch the compound and listen for the unwitting soldiers to let their captain's name slip. These Bronze Tigers—at least the sentries along the wall—were too well trained to distract themselves with idle chit-chat, though, so that hadn't panned out. She now had to slip in and check out the administrative building. Unless the officers all slept in the barracks with the rank and file, it was a good bet that they all had quarters there. Jade waited until the sentries nearest her were gone, then she ran toward that building across the merlons atop the wall.

When she reached it, she jumped from the battlements and slid down the administrative building's slightly angled outer wall to the ground without making a noise. Then, she drew her new knife from its sheath and began to look for a way in. Unfortunately, the building was designed to protect against rising floodwaters that either surmounted the walls or found their way in through some breach, so there was only one door and no windows on the lowest level. Other doors with depth-gauge floaters had been cut into the sheer walls at higher floors, but they were, no doubt, locked and designed to only open outward. So, with a silent sigh, Jade headed around the building toward the front door.

The Unconquered Sun was with her, though, and He granted her luck for her daring. No sooner had she rounded the corner, when six people came outside and headed for one of the pavilions aside the parade ground. Five of them were men, wearing uniforms of black, brown and gold, and the sixth was a woman in the plate-and-chain of a heavy cavalry rider with a tiger embossed on the front and back plates. Two of the men were trading tablets and rolls of paper between themselves and the armored woman, and the other three were carrying a heavy burden that Jade couldn't make out. The woman, whose auburn hair was twisted into a thick braid and pinned up, checked the items her two flankers kept shoving at her and either signed them or handed them back. The men around her deferred to her and called her "ma'am" on more than one occasion. She responded with clipped orders and officious-sounding grunts. Jade followed this woman at a discreet distance.

The party of Bronze Tigers stopped under an expansive, leather-topped pavilion, the ground under which had been covered with a deep layer of sand. The two clerks got the last of what they needed from their superior and left, then the armored woman turned to the three encumbered men. She held out a hand, and the three men hefted an enormous spear up on end before her. The haft of the spear was lacquered a glossy black, and it looked thick enough to turn a strike from an ax blade. A polished steel shoe covered its foot. The head of the spear was two feet long and almost a foot wide, and it was made of a slick, shiny jade alloy that was either black or a deep forest green. The soldiers struggled with the impressive weapon's weight, but their commander snatched the thing away from them with one hand and wielded it as easily as if it were made of balsa. She then ordered the attendants to light the lanterns that hung on the poles supporting the pavilion. They did as she asked, then departed, and the light they had provided clinched Harmonious Jade's assumption that she had found who she was looking for.

The final clue was the woman's skin. It had the beginning of a lush green tint that indicated an affinity for the natural element of wood. The ease with which this woman handled her unwieldy jade weapon bespoke a spiritual attunement that was beyond mere mortals. It was clear now to Jade that this woman was a Dragon-Blooded Exalt, not unlike a soldier of the Wyld Hunt or an officer in the imperial military. The fact that she was here in this second-rate mercenary compound instead of at some outpost of the Realm or further west in the legendary city of Lookshy only helped to confirm Jade's suspicions. This Dragon-Blood had to be the disgraced Ravenous Wolf who had formed her own mercenary outfit in hopes of earning new glory and erasing the stains of her past. Or at least hiding them, as her soldiers had failed to do in the doomed town one day's ride away.

As the Dragon-Blood began to weave her spear through a pattern of offensive and defensive stances, Jade thought about those slaughtered villagers this woman's soldiers had left behind. She thought about the wounds on their bodies and wondered how many had been delivered by this very weapon. As the Dragon-Blood's exercises increased in speed and intensity, Jade's temper rose. She thought of villagers running for their lives but being cut down like wheat. She thought of children crying and receiving no mercy. She thought of the Disciple, weak and wounded but thinking he had escaped to safety, only to run into this woman and her thugs. And somewhere in the deep recesses of her soul, her ancient self remembered the betrayal of the Terrestrial Exalted as they hunted their once-masters to the ends of Creation out of bitter jealousy. Her ancient self remembered the sound of arrows in the wind all around her as blood-thirsty usurpers—once her servants and lieutenants—harried her deep into a cave away from the comforting, empowering light of the Unconquered Sun...

Finally, Jade could take no more. She circled the Dragon-Blood and crept up behind her, timing the sweeps and thrusts of her enormous spear. Then, when the Dragon-Blood was over-extended and leaning awkwardly, Jade made her move. In a spray of unraveling light, Jade appeared directly behind the Dragon-Blood, stepped in between her wide-spaced feet, pulled her head back and shoved the edge of her knife against the Dragon-Blood's throat. The Dragon-Blood froze, and Jade whispered in her ear.

"Drop the spear," she hissed. The woman quickly complied. "I know the evil you've committed in Ikari Village, and you'll die for it, but first you'll answer two questions. Who else is working with you and Selaine Chaisa? And what have you done to the Disciple of the Seven Forbidden Wisdoms?"

Despite the torque Jade was putting on her neck, the Dragon-Blood's answer was very clear. "Go ahead and cut my head off, killer," she said. "May my blood sear your eyes."

Before Jade could react to the woman's audacity, the Dragon-Blood clenched her fists and took a deep breath, then a glowing green flare surrounded her. The flare surprised Jade and enveloped her in scathing energy that felt like a thousand thorny lashes tearing at her skin. She jumped clear, more surprised than wounded, but the adjustment cost her the advantage. The Dragon-Blood kicked her spear up to her hand, bellowed an alarum and charged across the sand at Jade, who was armed only with a knife.

An ordinary soldier would have panicked and bolted. An exceptional assassin would have fled—even a superbly trained Salmalin janissary. No mortal fighter could have withstood the might of an armed and armored Dragon-Blooded warrior. Jade, however, did not panic. When the Terrestrial charged forward with two quick jabs and an overhand sweep of her spear, Jade held her ground and dodged every attack. She curled inside the spear's effective range, letting the black staff skate off her form-fitted cuirass and went for the Dragon-Blood's throat with her knife. The mercenary knocked the blade aside with an armored bracer and spun her spear around one-handed to brush Jade back. The Dragon-Blood then followed the motion through and twirled the staff over her shoulder into a low-guard ready position.

When she closed on Jade again, her weapon began to hum audibly, and it stirred up loose sand around her into tiny dust devils. Inch-long thorns sprouted from the weapon's striking surface, and the Exalt's anima stood out in even sharper relief, waving like tall grass in a breeze. Even worse, mercenaries were running toward the exercise area now. Jade could hear them drawing blades and putting arrows to strings as they ran, and she knew that she was in it deep now. If she had her powerbow ready, she wouldn't have worried at all. She could have simply cut the soldiers down in one sweep and still had time to pick off their leader. Since she only had her knife out, though, she would only be able to deal with the leader before she had to make a break for it.

The Dragon-Blood put Harmonious Jade on the defensive at first, slashing at her and driving her back with the thorny spear. The attack pushed Jade into the open briefly, and she only barely managed to dodge the feathered shafts of the archers covering the scene. The sword-wielding mortal soldiers whom the Dragon-Blood's alarum had drawn to the scene were more than willing to let the archers finish Jade off, but although Jade could probably have dodged her way to safety, she had no intention of dancing for their amusement. Instead, she sprang toward the closest knot of foot soldiers, ducking and twisting unharmed between their blades and forcing the archers to hold their fire.

Without even pausing to attack, she dodged and twisted her way back through the startled mercenaries toward their commander without giving the archers another chance to fire at her. When she was under cover again, she kicked out and slashed with her long knife to give herself some more room—blinding one man with a slash across the eyes, breaking another's knee with a kick and crippling another's sword arm with a wicked slash from wrist to biceps. For her part, the captain waited until Jade's back was turned before she attacked with her spear again. She slashed at an upward angle to catch Jade low in the spine while the woman was ducking an overhand sword slash.

Yet, once again, Jade's grace and training preserved her from harm. She back flipped and twisted, impossibly graceful, and the spear swished beneath her. The Terrestrial barely managed to twist the weapon at the last second and catch the two nearest soldiers, for whom Jade had cleared the way, with the flat of the blade rather than the edge. They flew through the air, taking out more of their comrades, as Jade turned her flip into a back handspring up the spear's shaft. She kicked the Terrestrial square in the chest, and the two of them crashed to the sand. The Terrestrial scrambled to get up, but Jade was faster. She pinned the Terrestrial's chest with her knees and held her knife up to drive it into the mercenary's exposed throat. The woman's green anima still stung and scratched her, but Jade was ready for it this time, and she forced herself to ignore the pain. An intense violet ring of power burned on her forehead, and the Terrestrial's eyes were wide with shock. All around them, the sound of running feet died down as the men froze.

"What's the matter, butcher?" Jade couldn't resist the urge to ask. "Never seen one of the Anathema before?"

"It isn't that," the Dragon-Blood said. "It's just that I've never seen two in the same place."

A furious golden light fell over Jade from behind, and she tried to get up out of the way. But even as she shifted her balance to leap aside, something hit her from behind and plunged her into darkness.

Guild artisan Kerrek Deset was expecting company, but not exactly the company he received. He had just sent his last clerk on her way to the Guild headquarters in the Nexus district, and his seneschal had retired for the day to his cottage at the rear of the property. The servants were all under strict orders to go to the old man with any problems before bothering their master with them. The seneschal was under even stricter orders not to bother Kerrek unless the manor was currently on fire and the blaze couldn't be contained in a separate wing. Kerrek had been assured that his delivery from the harlotry in the Nexus district had arrived almost an hour ago. His bedroom staff had seen to it that his delivery was provided liqueur, qat tea or bright morning from his private stock, and he had stayed downstairs working for an extra hour so that he could sleep in tomorrow morning.

His delivery from the harlotry was to consist of a handful of beautiful women—at least one from each elemental region of Creation—and two flawless teenage boys. In celebration of Calibration, he was going to play his favorite game, in which the boys took turns whispering fantastically lascivious desires in his ears, which he would then act out with the women. The boys would then wash him in a bath of herb-infused hot water and aromatic salts, and the game would continue. Kerrek could feel himself stiffening as he hurried now to his bedroom. Yet, as he pushed aside the double doors, he found not at all who he expected.

"How galling," the black-and-white-haired woman in his room said. "We've been waiting for almost an hour, Deset." Her eyes flicked down the front of his robe, and she added, "At least you aren't entirely displeased we're here."

To his credit, Kerrek did not blanch as he greeted his unexpected guests. He knew the one who had spoken to him, the Witness, from past business dealings and his frequent dreams of unrequited passion. A man in a broad hat sat by the bed, and Kerrek recognized him as the Witness's partner, the Visitor in the Hall of Obsidian Mirrors. He even knew the woman who now lay motionless on his bed, her face wrapped in blotchy bandages. She was his sister in faith and a legendary priestess among his Salmalin brothers and sisters.

"Do come in," the Witness said, pulling him into the room by the open hem of his silk robe. "We must talk."

"Of course," Kerrek said. "But my other guests…"

"They're deep in illuminative dreams," the Witness said with a coy smile. Kerrek saw that several people were sprawled across his couches, floor pillows and even a tea table by the bay window. A couple of them were snoring. "They have no head for the ghost-flower tea we made them."

Kerrek knew well the soporific properties of ghost-flower tea, and he was also aware of its less pleasant qualities. Part of the business he did with the Witness was to import it from various shadowlands in the Scavenger Lands to high-paying clients with refined palates. He did not envy these harlots their dreams tonight.

"So, what did you want to talk about?" Kerrek asked, walking to the bed and looking down at Chaisa. "What happened to her?"

"Complications," the Visitor answered. "We need to leave her here with you."

"I beg your pardon?"

"She's injured, you see," the Witness said, laying a hand on Kerrek's shoulder. "Someone tried to kill her. We can't take her back to her hotel—it's compromised. We couldn't exactly take her to Stalwart Mastiff's compound either."

"He hasn't been exposed too, has he?"

"Possibly," the Visitor said. "We aren't certain."

"What about me?"

"Your connection to Chaisa remains a mystery in reputable circles," the Witness said. "However, you must keep her here until we come back for her, and you must make no effort to contact Stalwart Mastiff henceforth."

"But what about the Undercity salvage and the temple restoration? Mastiff and I haven't finished working out—"

"That project is over," the Visitor said. "You've done enough to make the site suitable."

Kerrek looked at the Witness who shrugged and nodded. "I was going to tell you about that. How irresponsible of me. Yes, your machines worked wonderfully well. The temple has been almost fully converted. It's been a fine week for both our masters."

"But Mastiff and I were supposed to put together expeditionary outfits to scavenge the ruins before the ritual gets underway. We have so much work ahead of us, and we've already established reliable secrecy measures to protect our contact with one another. How can I—"

"Figure something out," the Visitor snapped, standing up. "That isn't your priority anymore."

"Deset, you're very clever and ambitious," the Witness said more gently, stroking his cheek with a delicate finger. "Now, you must also be patient. Calibration only lasts so long, and you must take care of your priestess. This should be a time of great veneration of your Yozi masters, not an opportunity to fill your pockets. We'll be back for Chaisa tomorrow night to take her to the appointed place your money helped to excavate. We've placed nemissaries among your staff and posted an independent watchdog to help with security. Just keep her safe until then, and don't let anyone know she's here. If you do this, I promise that, by Calibration's end, your Yozi masters will know how you love them above all else. The rewards will be immeasurable."

"What if Chaisa dies before you return? How bad is she?"

"Her wounds are more shocking than serious," the Witness said. "It was touch and go for several days, and we couldn't move her around much, but she's much better now. She'll be disfigured, but she'll live a while longer. By sunrise, she should feel much better."

"So, why couldn't you just keep her with you? It's only three more days until—"

"We have preparations to make," the Visitor said. "We have to go somewhere she isn't willing to follow. You're welcome to take her place if you want."

"Now, now," the Witness chided her partner. "Deset, I think you would prefer to stay here and do as we ask. Besides, we're in something of a hurry. Can't you do us this favor?"

"I suppose," Kerrek said, sighing in resignation as the Witness stared into his eyes. "I'll do what you want, just as I always do. But perhaps, when this is finished, you can find some way to reward me yourself on your master's behalf."

The Witness leaned very close to him. Her chill breath tickled his ear and rippled his spine as she said, "Perhaps, but that all depends on what my master whispers in my ear." She glanced at one of the teenage boys sleeping nearby and then withdrew, leaving Kerrek alone to make his own conclusions.

"See?" the Witness said as she and the Visitor exited Kerrek's Bastion manor and set off down the hill. "I told you he likes me."

"He's a vulgar dilettante," the Visitor replied. "I should have oath-bound him just to reinforce how serious what we're doing is."

"That isn't necessary," the Witness said. "He'll never be a priest of his faith, but he's loyal enough. He'll suit for the time remaining. After all, he wouldn't let me down. How disappointing that would be."

The Visitor sighed. "It's shameful, the way you encourage him. He'll betray you if you keep leading him on indefinitely."

"Here now," the Witness chided. "Why do you think I wouldn't consummate my insinuations? You above all should recognize the power of a promise unspoken."

The Visitor only shook his head.

Chapter Seven

"Damn it, Risa," Captain Dace of the Bronze Tigers growled, "How in Creation did she even get in here?"

"I have no idea, sir," Dace's Dragon-Blooded lieutenant answered. "Sergeant Krislan's questioning the sentries and the patrolmen, but nobody I talked to noticed anything. Not until Beads here jumped on me."

The two of them were in the stockade under their compound, standing outside its only occupied cell. Their prisoner lay on the floor inside, still unconscious. Dace wore his full uniform (minus some armor) and held his square-edged daiklave loosely in one hand. Their prisoner, it seemed, was Exalted like him, so he didn't want to take chances that she would escape before he had a chance to interrogate her.

"You're lucky she attacked you out there and didn't have the sense to just follow you back to your bedroom. Why was she so hot to kill you? Did she say anything?"

"Mostly nonsense, it sounded like," Risa said. She leaned against the wall opposite the cell door, holding her jade spear across her chest. "She asked me about some woman and some kind of disciple of something or other. Then, she called me a butcher and tried to kill me."

"A butcher?"

"Yeah, because of that town we found on our way back from Mishaka with the Guild caravan. Ikari. She seems to think we're responsible for that."

"I wonder why," Dace said. "You think she's from there, maybe?"

"She looks like a Southerner to me. Sounded like one too. And, of course, there was the other bit…"

"About her being Exalted," Dace said, nodding. "That was an ugly little surprise. Oh, but thanks for referring to her and me as Anathema, by the way. I appreciated that from my senior lieutenant."

"Sorry, sir. Habit. Besides, she started it."

"What is this?" the prisoner suddenly murmured inside her cell. She was on her feet a second later, looking out the small, barred window in the door. When she laid eyes on Risa, she glared with murderous intent. "You! You can try to do with me what you want, Dragon-Blood, but you're going to have to come in here and get me first."

Risa tried not to flinch, and Dace scowled at the prisoner's bravado. He stepped in front of Risa so the prisoner could see him, and Risa stepped discreetly out of the prisoner's field of view.

"Settle down and be quiet, little girl," he said with the rumbling menace of faraway thunder. "You've made enough threats tonight. Now, it's time to start answering some questions. And whatever you've got to say, you say it to me. I'm in charge here."

"Don't try to intimidate me," the prisoner said. "I've killed men twice your size and half your age. Men in their prime. I don't care who's in charge, you're all going to die for what you've—"

"I said be quiet!" Dace roared. The thunder of his voice was accompanied by a lightning flash from within him that made his caste mark burn, and the authority of the Unconquered Sun shone through him. For a moment, he seemed broader and taller, and unearthly ferocity blazed in his eyes. The effect lasted only a moment, but the prisoner gasped and fell back a step in awe.

"That's better," Dace said. "Now, listen to me, girl. I think you're under a misunderstanding that it behooves you to straighten out before you get yourself in even more trouble. You've come into my compound and taken a knife to my officers. The only reason you're still alive is that you seemed to think you were doing righteous work. The will of the Unconquered Sun. Right?"

The prisoner glared defiantly, but confusion clouded her eyes. She backed up against the far wall of her cell and crossed her arms.

"I know what you are, girl," Dace continued. "Nobody else could have done that to my people so quickly and easily. You're Exalted, like I am."

"Not like you," the prisoner snapped. "I saw what you did to those villagers. Don't you ever say I'm like you."

"That wasn't us," Dace said. "We found that scene more than a week ago just like you did. We were too late to do anything about it, or we would have put a stop to that slaughter. I'm more like you than you want to think. That carnage infuriates me."

"But I saw it," the prisoner said. "The tracks… the blood. I even saw the graves you tried to hide."

"They aren't hidden," Risa piped up. "They're off the road so they won't be disturbed or casually desecrated."

"Those graves you saw belong to my scouts," Dace said. "They were the first to find the carnage. They were ambushed by nemissaries and the walking dead when they came to that village, just as we all were. The ones who did that were trying to drill a hole into the Underworld. We just happened through there at the wrong time."

"So, instead of fixing things, you ran and left the villagers' bodies to rot in their temple?" the prisoner said.

"We did *not* just abandon their bodies," Risa interjected.

"We had to move on at daybreak," Dace said. "We were guarding civilians, and we had to get them back here safely. It would have taken us more than all day to undo that sacrilege, and by nightfall, the hungry ghosts would have been back, possibly with more nemissaries."

"So, you just let the problem lie."

"No. That's what I'm trying to tell you. When we got back here, we informed our peacekeeper contact with the

Hooded Executioners, just like we're bound to. He assured me the Council would be told and the village would be dealt with that same night."

A shadow fell over Dace's features as he said that last bit, and his voice became more pensive.

"So, how long ago was that?" the prisoner asked.

"More than a week, which disturbs me now. It either means you've discovered something I've been lied to about, or you're a liar out to kill my men and cover something up."

"If I were trying to cover something up," the prisoner said, "why would I even bother lying? I'd just kill you one by one."

"That's a good point," Risa admitted, rubbing her neck.

"It goes for us, too," Dace said. "If we were like you think we are, we would have killed you outside. You know I could have. Regardless, we certainly wouldn't have bothered to let you regain consciousness."

The prisoner remained silent, but the hate and anger was gone from her.

"I'll tell you what," Dace said. "I'm inclined to let you out of there and to give you back the gear we took off you, but I don't think I want you to leave just yet. I think we should talk about what you've found. But I don't want to do that here—it's more comfortable in my offices upstairs. Consider this an overture of trust... unless you still think the Bronze Tigers are nothing but lying butchers."

The prisoner narrowed her eyes, but she nodded warily. "All right. I don't know if you're lying anymore, but I'm willing to let you convince me you're not. Just be warned: My mind is clear now, and the two of you won't catch me up in any more tricks."

"Of course," Dace said. "And in the spirit of honesty, we're keeping the money we found on you. You wounded several of my men, so your jade's going into medical supplies and treatment. Or compensation to their families if they can't fight anymore."

"Fine," the prisoner said. "It wasn't really mine to begin with. Can you let me out of here now?"

"Sure. On one condition." The prisoner raised an eyebrow. "Tell me your name."

"It's Jade," the prisoner said. "Harmonious Jade."

"I'm Dace, Captain of the Bronze Tigers. This is Lieutenant Risa." Risa nodded, scowling. "We'll let you know if it's nice to meet you."

Jade followed Dace and his lieutenant into a planning room on the third level of the administrative building of his compound. An oval table sat in the middle of the room, surrounded by plain wooden chairs. A larger chair upholstered in leather with bronze studs stood at the head of the table, and Dace went straight to it. Jade remained standing.

"Risa," Dace said, "I want you to go check on Sergeant Krislan's progress while Jade and I have a talk."

"Sir?" Risa asked.

"Go ahead," Dace said. "Start collecting reports, and drum up a tactical advisory for compound security. I want it on my desk tomorrow afternoon."

"Sir, shouldn't I—"

"You heard me, Lieutenant."

Risa hesitated a moment, then hid her confusion under a dutiful mask. She left and closed the door behind her, leaving Jade and Dace alone.

"She probably saved your life tonight," Dace said when his lieutenant was gone. "I was ready to kill you. Even after I knocked you out, I didn't notice your caste mark. Risa stayed my hand. You owe her for that."

Jade made a noncommittal gesture that was either a nod or a shrug, then turned away from Dace. She found the décor of the room oppressively masculine, with animal heads, notched weapons, a shield and even an exotic suit of armor mounted on the walls. One such trophy caught her eye in particular. It was the head of what had once been a simple yeddim, but its mouth was open in a feral snarl that bared predatory fangs, and its forward-set eyes were overshadowed by four spiny horns. Jade touched the end of the beast's nose tentatively, as if it might bite her, then she scratched the red fur under its chin.

"So, I'll start," Dace said. "Tell me what you were doing in Ikari Village."

"I was looking for someone," Jade said. She didn't want to say more, but she felt compelled to add, "Someone special to me."

"I see. Risa mentioned you asked her about someone. Are you from that village?"

"No. I'm from the South. Chiaroscuro."

"What drew you toward Nexus?"

"I was looking for somebody else. Somebody who tried to kill me in Chiaroscuro."

"I can't imagine why somebody'd want to do that. But from Chiaroscuro to here is an awful long way to go just for revenge."

"There's more to it than that," Jade snapped, coming away from the wall and standing at the opposite end of the table. "I'm not so petty. I'm doing a job. I'm doing what the Unconquered Sun wants."

"I see. And how's that?"

Jade looked at him but didn't answer.

"Okay," Dace said. "Maybe that's not my business. So, tell me who these people you're looking for are, instead. If you're not a local, I might know something about them you don't."

"I doubt it," Jade said. "I don't think either one of them is from here."

"It couldn't hurt to tell me," Dace said. "Besides, the fact that their paths and yours and mine have all crossed in some farming and fishing village a day's ride from here can't be entirely accidental. Maybe you could just start there. What made you choose that particular village to meet your friend?"

Jade frowned, but she had to admit that the mercenary had a point. He knew *something* about what had happened there, and he might be able to shed some light on what had happened to the Disciple. Plus, he was a living, thriving

Solar Exalt, a partner in duty beneath the Unconquered Sun. In such a squalid and dangerous Age, could she really afford to shut him out completely?

"I didn't choose it," Jade said after a long hesitation. "My 'friend' did. He calls himself the Disciple of the Seven Forbidden Wisdoms, and he's Exalted like me. Like… us. We were in trouble and about to be separated, so he told me to meet him there. I'd never even heard of the place."

"I see," Dace said. "Another Exalt in the city—I wonder how many more there are. Anyway, you said trouble. What kind?"

"That's complicated," Jade said. "It's a long story."

"Complications come part and parcel with our station," Dace said. "And if there's one thing I've learned from years of walking spoiled Guild tradesmen up and down the byways of the River Province, it's how to appreciate a long story. What say we take a shot at trusting each other here?"

Jade looked Dace in the eye, and tension that she hadn't felt building up slowly melted away. At last, she sat down.

"All right," she said.

She didn't intend to tell him as much as she'd told the Disciple, but once she started speaking, the words came almost unbidden. The tale came out in reverse as she described the investigation that led her to this compound, then her experience at the village, then her last contact with the Disciple. Dace sat up and listened quite intently when Jade told him about what she and the Disciple had discovered in the Undercity. His countenance clouded when she mentioned the ghosts and recounted the Disciple's assessment of what must have happened there so long ago.

"That's an interesting theory," Dace said, "but you'd best keep it to yourself outside this room. The Council of Entities doesn't like people suggesting what you're suggesting."

"I know what I saw," Jade said, confused. "There were plague-dead in that buried place. Possibly from the Contagion era. It might be *true* that this city, or old Hollow, was a plague city."

"That doesn't matter," Dace said. "The Council isn't always interested in the whole truth of how things were. The Contagion decimated this place and opened the door for the Fair Folk to lay it waste, and nobody wants to be reminded of that—even with the wreckage of Firewander right there plain to see. The Council doesn't want anything being said about its city that could make people shy away from coming here. That could severely obstruct trade, and that's against the second decree of the Dogma."

"But it's either true or it's just speculation," Jade said. "If it's true, it's just true, and there's nothing the Council can do about it. If it's only speculation, who cares what people think?"

Dace laughed and shook his head. "The *Council* cares, and that's enough. If you do what it doesn't like, it is within its power to punish you for it. If you're lucky, you'll just get a knife across the throat while you're sleeping. If not, you'll get a visit from the Emissary. I've heard about some of the things he's done, and apparently, you don't want to tangle with him. He's an old god or god-blooded or something. Maybe even a bound demon. Anyway, he's dangerous enough to make you want to watch what you say."

"Fine," Jade said. "If it's like that."

"But I distracted you," Dace said. "How was it you and this Disciple ended up in the Undercity?"

Jade put her reverse tale back on track and continued. She told Dace about meeting the Disciple in Firewander and confronting him, only to find out that the two had a similar goal in following Selaine Chaisa on her secretive business in Nexus. She diverged at that point to explain that Chaisa was a high-ranking priestess in the Salmalin Yozi-worshiping cult, who had tried to kill her while passing through Chiaroscuro. When Dace interrupted to ask why Chaisa had done that, Jade hesitated and said only that she had a history of antagonism with the Salmalin, before going back to her original story thread. She explained that, even though she wasn't exactly sure now why the Disciple had been following Chaisa, he had convinced her to join up with him to find out what she was up to. It had also been the Disciple, Jade revealed, who had pointed out how strange it was that at least two nemissaries were among Chaisa's company and seemed to be helping her go about her work.

"Nemissaries?" Dace interrupted again. "Are you sure?"

"I didn't recognize that's what they were, myself," Jade said. "Many people came and went around Selaine Chaisa. It did strike me as odd once the Disciple pointed them out, though. It was even stranger to find Chaisa in the company of two deathknights, once the Disciple explained to me what *those* were."

"Deathknights?" Dace exclaimed. "Where did you see this demon-worshiper in the company of deathknights?"

"In the Undercity. Didn't I mention that? They were the reason the Disciple and I had to split up."

"No," Dace said, incredulous, "you didn't mention that part. For the Sun's sake, girl, don't you realize how serious this is? Are you sure that was what you saw?"

"The Disciple was sure," Jade said, embarrassed and defensive. "He had no reason to lie. He said the two we saw with Chaisa were deathknights serving the Walking Darkness."

"You mean the Walker *in* Darkness?"

"That might be it. Yes, that sounds right."

Dace put his hands to his temples. "Oh gods above and below. Why didn't you tell me any of this?"

"I am telling you."

"No, I meant before. Don't you know anything about anything?" Jade flinched, and Dace stood up abruptly to start rounding the table toward her. "Walker in Darkness is a Deathlord, and his agents are creeping around the Undercity looking for gods' know what. They're probably responsible for what happened to Ikari Village, too. This can't all just be coincidence. It's providence that's thrown us together. Is there anything else you've neglected to tell me? Like maybe you're a Yozi-worshiper yourself, or this Disciple friend of yours is actually a Fair Folk cataphract or something?"

"I've told you everything just like you wanted," Jade said, standing up. "I'll thank you not to insult me for it."

Dace's eyes danced with frustration and outrage for a second before he got himself under control enough not to shout. He took a big deep breath, then said, "I'm sorry, but like I said, this is very serious. More serious than I realized. I've got to go tell someone about this, and I need you to come with me."

"Who? Where?"

"The headquarters of the Hooded Executioners. My contract liaison to the Council of Entities, Stalwart Mastiff, is there, and we need to get this news to him right now."

"Why?" Jade asked. "If you think this needs to be addressed right now, why don't we just handle it ourselves? Get that Dragon-Blood to get your men together, and let's get down into the Undercity and clean the place out."

"No," Dace said. "That isn't the way things are done here. If I go marching my men out of this district toward Firewander, the Emissary is going to be on our asses before we even get half way. After I was Exalted, I came here with my men and made a deal with the Council of Entities. They'd let me stay and work here despite what I'd become, but I had to report to them through certain peacekeeping channels. Right now, that means the Hooded Executioners. If I take on 'Nexus business' without going through them, I'm just asking for trouble. You don't move troops around like that without the Council's permission."

"I think this is a little more important, don't you?" Jade said. "Can't we just do this then explain—"

"No, this is the way things work," Dace said, "so it's the way things have to be done for now. It's stupid, but I'm not in a position to change it. Besides, if all this activity is what it looks like, we might just need the resources Mastiff's position can provide. But we can't just stand around here arguing. Let's get you your things back out of lockup and get moving. I want to be ready to act on this as soon as Stalwart Mastiff gives us the go-ahead."

He took Jade by the elbow and led her out of the room. Jade followed as if by rote, allowing her will to be directed by her newfound Solar acquaintance's aura of command. And as she fell into step beside him, she recognized an odd sensation of familiarity, as if this were not the first time she had followed this man's lead in doing the work of the Unconquered Sun.

CHAPTER EIGHT

Hours later, with dawn coming, Dace and Jade sat in a small private room in the headquarters of the Hooded Executioners with Captain Stalwart Mastiff. The man reminded Jade more of a baboon or a bulldog than any kind of a canine, and in her present mood, she was close to pointing that out. The man was a squat plug of muscle with broad shoulders, longish arms and somewhat short legs. His face was haggard with age and stress, and his hair was black and gray.

He hadn't enjoyed being rousted from bed so early, and he looked even unhappier now. Dace had introduced Jade, and Jade had recounted the basics of her discoveries for Stalwart Mastiff. She'd left out specific names and implications but revealed enough to make the situation clear. Mastiff had listened with a frown at first, then he had scowled, and now, he was practically glowering. Nonetheless, he listened patiently until Jade finished.

"So, you understand why I'm so concerned," Dace said. "This girl and I are talking about the same village I told you about when I last got back to Nexus. The one you told me your men were taking care of."

"What exactly are you trying to accuse me of, Captain?" Mastiff grumbled.

"No accusations," Dace said. "I'm just concerned. There's not only this village—"

"I told you that was being taken care of," Mastiff broke in. "It's done. It was done the day after you reported it. Just like I told you. I've arranged to have squads of men quartered in Ikari's nearest neighbors for protection, and a burial detail has been fixing it up while the sun's in the sky ever since they got there."

"But she's a witness," Dace said, looking back and forth between Jade and Mastiff. "She's seen things haven't changed since you gave me your assur—"

"And who's she supposed to be?" Mastiff said, glaring at Jade. "Some koku's-worth of beaded harlot you've never met before? She's just some foreigner stringing coincidences together and spreading heresies about old Hollow. How much did she charge you for her so-called information?"

"It wasn't like that," Dace growled. Jade only sat stunned. "She's uncovered something that could be—"

"It's lies," Mastiff said, thumping his fists on the desk. "My men sorted that village, and anyone who says otherwise is lying or up to something. None of the mayors of the nearest surrounding towns have reported any trouble since your return to Nexus. The nearest plantation owners haven't either. As for this Undercity business, do you have anyone's word other than this girl's that *anything* she's saying is actually happening? I bet you don't."

Dace didn't say anything, but Jade sat up and spoke. "I've come miles without count, leaving my home to see my work here done. I've lost someone important to me unraveling a mystery you're too blind to even recognize. I've navigated this maze of chaos you call a city, when all I ever had to do was turn around and disappear into the Scavenger Lands. Why in Creation would I even bother to lie about any of this?"

"Your false anger is just liar's passion, girl," Mastiff said, standing. "You can't back up anything you're saying with one shred of proof. You're wasting time, spouting lies and trying to drum up a panic."

"There is proof," Jade said. "The ruins in the Undercity are still there. Carcasses still litter Ikari Village."

"Lies!" Mastiff roared, bashing his desk again. "My men sorted that. If you say one more word to the contrary, I'll have you locked away for subversion of the Council's will."

"I'd be happy to see you—"

"All right, look," Dace said, standing up between Jade and Mastiff. "Obviously, there's some sort of misunderstanding here. You're right, Mastiff, about us not having any proof of any of this. Maybe I came to you too quickly without substantiating this girl's claims. What can I say? You see how she is. She excited me and stirred me to act without thinking. Young women can be like that." Jade flinched and looked at Dace as if he'd just turned into a viper. "So, I'll tell you what. I'll take my men out to Ikari Village and make this girl show me what she thinks she's found."

"You'd be wasting your time," Mastiff said, mollified somewhat, but still glaring.

"Probably," Dace said. "But it would be worth it to make this girl face the truth if she is lying. Especially considering I've come all this way stirring up trouble for you." Mastiff nodded at that and grunted a haughty affirmation. "But while I'm doing that, how about you take some men down into the Undercity? Jade can even tell you how to find—"

"Sorry, Dace," Mastiff said. "I don't have the time or the manpower for that. The Council keeps this company busy with too many *real* assignments. Especially with Calibration parties ramping up all over town and drunken revelry so often getting out of hand."

"I understand," Dace said, still apparently upbeat. "Thanks for your time, and I'll get back to you once we get back from—"

"Right, right," Mastiff said. "Now, if you don't mind, I've got a full schedule ahead of me."

He gestured toward the door, and Dace turned to go. He put a hand on Jade's arm to lead her, but she knocked it away. She brushed past him, yanked the door open and stormed out. Dace gave Stalwart Mastiff a shrug and a quick salute and followed her out. When they were gone, Mastiff closed his door.

Out in the main arched and colonnaded hallway, Dace hurried to catch up with Jade before she hit the street and disappeared on him. He jogged up beside her and glanced down to gauge how angry she was. She was walking with her arms crossed, staring stonily ahead.

"I'm sorry about that," he murmured, "but I thought it best we get out of there quickly."

"Of course," Jade hissed. "So sorry for embarrassing you, Captain."

"Look, I'm sorry for those things I said, but it was what Mastiff wanted to hear. I didn't want him to realize I knew he was lying."

"You think?" she snapped. "What makes you so sure I'm not the liar?"

"One, I don't change my mind about people just because somebody gets upset with me. Two, I know Mastiff. Nothing you said came as a surprise to him. Not even the possibility that deathknights might be digging in his city's guts. We all but told him the Walker in Darkness has his eye on the city, and Mastiff didn't even blink.

"Plus, there was the way he just blew you off. He should have ordered some men to check out your story, no matter how implausible he thought it was. Even if it was just a scout or a runner, he'd normally have sent somebody. He would have at least asked *me* to check into it. He loves making me prove myself wrong, and he jumps at every chance he can get. He didn't even try this time. He just wants me to back off and stay out of this. It isn't his style."

The two of them passed through the main gate and out into the street, pausing their conversation for a moment as they passed a line of gate guards. They walked another block before Jade spoke.

"So, what do you think it means?" she asked.

"The optimist in me says he's only just now getting around to alerting the Council and he doesn't want me to move first and embarrass him. The realist, though, says he already knows what's going on and he's covering it up."

"So, let's go back in," Jade said, looking back. "If you hold him and ask the questions, I can make him answer."

"I hope you're kidding. Did you see how big that compound was and how many people were in there? A lot of the captains and lieutenants are Dragon-Bloods, and they've each got more than fifty men under them."

"So?"

"So, we wouldn't stand a chance, even as powerful as we are. Plus, it would just be the word of two Anathema against the honor of the Hooded Executioners. The Council would be on us so fast we'd both wish we'd never come to Nexus to begin with."

"I already wish that," Jade grumbled. Dace couldn't tell if she was kidding or not. "So, are we supposed to just let Chaisa and these deathknights get away with whatever they're doing? They killed someone close to me. They slaughtered those villagers, and Mastiff's men are keeping word of it from getting back here. Chaisa's caused the deaths of countless others, and there's no telling what those deathknights have done. I don't care how things are done in this city, I won't let this go."

"Don't worry," Dace said, putting a hand on Jade's shoulder. "I won't either. But we've got to have some kind of proof to justify what we're doing before the Council. I need to talk to some people about Mastiff and about that village. People better connected than me. After I do, I want you to take me into the Undercity and show me what you and your friend found. If what we find is too much for us to handle, we'll at least know enough to force Mastiff to take action. We'll sort your demon priestess out then."

"If she's even still alive," Jade said.

"Right. Of course, if we're lucky, you actually killed her a week ago like you thought and ruined whatever she was planning, and everything's all fine now."

"That would be an unlikely turn of events," Jade said. "Chaisa's a survivor like her Yozi masters."

"I gathered. But we'll deal with that when we come to it. For now, I have schedules to interrupt and hard questions to ask of men I still owe favors to. You're welcome to stay at my compound for the next few hours if you like. You look like you could use some sleep. Real sleep, that is. Not the kind that comes out of a daiklave pommel."

"No thank you," Jade scowled, embarrassed. "I'll meet you there later. I've left some things back in my room, and I have some work to do too."

"All right," Dace said. "You know where to find me. Just one more thing: Be careful. Don't take any worthless chances, and don't go back to the Executioners' compound without me."

"I won't. Goodbye, Captain. I'll see you again soon."

Dace nodded, and the two Solars parted ways to do their separate work.

When they were both gone, a nondescript man named Pelsen with a wave of blond hair stepped out of the shadows of a vender's stall nearby. He was dressed in the simple tunic, trousers and domino mask of a clerk of the Hooded Executioners' support staff. He had been following Dace and Jade since they had left the Executioners' headquarters—catching some of what they were saying over the general murmur of Nexus' early morning traffic—and he had heard plenty to pique his interest. Still possessed of little more than suspicion and unfounded allegations, he turned around and headed unseen back toward the mercenary compound.

Stalwart Mastiff leaned against the door of his office for a long time with his hands in his hair, wondering what he was supposed to do now. He was still exhausted and disoriented from being awakened too soon after being out far too late the previous night, and he'd completely lost his composure with Dace and that Southern girl.

It was too late to bemoan fate on that front. Now, he had to make sure Dace and that girl didn't mess things up. He had to find out how much they knew. He had to find out who they had talked to. He had to make sure that the spies the Council had slipped in among the Executioners were either distracted or paid off. Then, he had to get a message to Kerrek and Chaisa and warn them.

He had to move fast, though, because Calibration was rapidly coming to a close, and he didn't want to have to wait another whole year before they could try this again. He knew the cult's Abyssal partners wouldn't enjoy being put off that long. Whatever it was their master expected to get out of his cooperation with the Salmalin, it wouldn't please him to have to wait while his agents seemed so anxious to move ahead quickly.

And frankly, Mastiff was plenty impatient himself. He'd been promised a generalship in the first free Yozi's army, and the longer he had to wait for it, the less satisfying the rank of captain became.

CHAPTER NINE

For the rest of that day, Harmonious Jade, Dace, Stalwart Mastiff and the blond spy named Pelsen were very busy.

Mastiff was engaged with keeping these unforeseen developments from blowing up in his face. The first thing he did was to compose a coded note to Kerrek Deset and another to Selaine Chaisa. In each, he wrote that one of the mercenary captains under his supervision and a brown-skinned Southern girl had caught wind of what the three had planned and had begun to ask questions. He assured his readers that no proof connected any of them to any wrong-doings but warned them not to come to him or congregate with each other in public until the ritual was at hand. A trustworthy illiterate runner took the note to Chaisa's rented room in Firewander, then Mastiff sent the other note to Kerrek's estate via pigeon. The rest of the morning passed quickly as Mastiff busied himself with breakfast, morning inspections, a daunting stack of paperwork and overseeing the drilling and training of his company of soldiers.

He kept one eye open and one ear cocked the whole time for signs that anyone was talking about this morning's visit from Dace or his own disturbed behavior after the fact. A couple of the guards who had been on duty at the time talked about having heard Mastiff shouting and making a ruckus, but they hadn't heard anything specific. All they remembered was Dace and some pretty girl who was young enough to be his daughter leaving in a huff. The handlers and watchers from the Council of Entities seemed to be minding their own business, at least in regard to that subject, so that was something of a relief. He made a mental note not to argue as hard the next time those parasites came looking to increase the size of their monthly bribe. On the whole, it appeared that his ill-timed morning meeting hadn't stood out or drawn too much attention to itself, which helped Mastiff relax.

That relaxation was nearly shattered when he received responses to his two early missives late in the afternoon. The first to arrive came from the illiterate runner he'd sent to deliver his note to Chaisa. The boy was waiting in Mastiff's office when Mastiff returned from a trip to the lavatory, practically cringing behind the thick wooden door. He still clutched the slim leather message tube Mastiff had given him, and he held it out to Mastiff now apologetically. Withering under Mastiff's glare, the boy said he'd found Chaisa's room empty and unlocked despite the fact that her belongings were all still inside. Dust on the furniture suggested that no one had been in the room for days, and an inquiry at the rental desk confirmed that suspicion. Chaisa hadn't checked out. She had simply disappeared. The only good news was that none of the staff remembered any unsavory characters asking after Chaisa or lurking around her room.

Mastiff paid his runner a handful of dinars to keep quiet about the whole thing and dismissed him. He then sat behind his desk for a long time quietly panicking and wondering what had happened to his priestess. Had she gone too deep into the Undercity and been attacked by something? Had Kerrek's Underworld associates betrayed them all and laid some trap? Had Chaisa somehow displeased her Yozi masters and incurred their wrath? Had Dace and that Southern girl been busier than they'd let on and actually done something to Chaisa? How much did they know? How much had been exposed?

A few answers came later when a message arrived from Kerrek by pigeon in the early afternoon. It said simply that

Chaisa was in Bastion with him, that she had been attacked but not gravely injured, that the ritual was still on and that contact was all but forbidden until then. Finally, it advised him to be wary, as the potential for exposure was higher than ever. The note was authentic—as Mastiff could tell from the smell of the paper and Kerrek's peculiar cipher—but it only set his mind at ease a little bit. He was glad things hadn't been called off, but the necessity of tightening their already-excessive secrecy measures didn't sit well with him. It made the situation seem too precarious, and he didn't like to operate in those kinds of conditions. He preferred a greater assurance of success and victory, such as when his Hooded Executioners quelled street riots inside the city. He didn't much fancy the thought of finding himself on the wrong side of such a conflict.

As a safety precaution, he sent one last round of messages to the heads of the Salmalin cells hidden among the unsuspecting citizens of Nexus. None of the other cell leaders knew each other—though they knew *of* each other—but Mastiff knew them all. He distributed messages by pigeon, runner and innocuous personal signal that each cell leader was to cease all recruitment practices and stifle all illicit contact between cell members until the day of the service. Secrecy was the utmost concern now as the day of Nexus' destiny drew near. No one must take any chances or commit any acts that could even potentially expose the cult. Everyone had worked too hard for too many years to see everything come apart now.

Having done everything he could for his brothers in faith for one day without drawing undue attention to himself, Mastiff kept to himself in his office and tried to force himself to act normally. He planned to lose himself in strictly official work for the rest of the day, in hopes that the meditative tedium would clear his mind and give him some idea how to deal with Dace. With the handlers from the Council of Entities nicely distracted and other mundane authorities still blessedly ignorant, that gruff old Bronze Tiger bastard was really his only worry.

Despite his self-assurance to the contrary, Stalwart Mastiff was wrong on that last count, for while he recognized most of the spies the Council had inserted among the Hooded Executioners, he did not know them all. In fact, some of the more obvious and greedy ones had been placed near him just to distract him from the more subtle and dangerous ones. He was too canny and perceptive to be entirely taken in by this subterfuge—which was part of the reason Chaisa had recruited him into the cult so many years ago—but at least one crucial figure slipped beneath his notice. That figure was Pelsen, who had overheard his conversation with Dace and Harmonious Jade early that morning.

This spy had been emplaced among the Hooded Executioners only recently to investigate Stalwart Mastiff's finances. He'd found no evidence of skimming, but something about Mastiff's record-keeping practices still seemed suspicious. The only serious outside expense the spy had been able to uncover, though, was a small fund that helped subsidize expeditions into the Wyld-riddled ruins of Firewander that hoped to push back the chaos and make that region livable again. None of the activities the money supported were explicitly illegal, yet obvious care had been taken to conceal the originators of the various transactions.

Pelsen might have been willing to overlook the expenses as flights of fancy had it not been for what he'd overheard this morning. It seemed to him now that Mastiff must have been looking for something specific beneath the Firewander ruins. Stories abounded of explorers finding caches of First Age artifacts in the most unlikely places as the Wyld tides ebbed and flowed throughout that district. Most of the inhabitable sections of the district had been long since picked clean, but it was possible Stalwart Mastiff had unearthed some long-hidden cache of weapons and figured out how to use them. If that were true, then Ikari Village could have been a testing ground for one of them, rather than the site of a naturally occurring pinhole shadowland Mastiff had claimed it was (and claimed he had taken care of).

Pelsen reported that supposition to his superiors and asked that a contingent of investigators be sent out to confirm it. They agreed and dispatched a group immediately. While that team was on its way out of town, it fell to the spy to try to locate where such a hidden cache might be. While he went about collecting this information, he made time for a trip across the Cinnabar district to the mean headquarters of the Bronze Tigers under the guise of a standard-procedure weekly audit. While there, he met a fellow spy among the mercenaries and learned the odd circumstances of the captain's introduction to the Southern girl. After telling him that story, the spy promised to notify him if anything further developed, and Pelsen returned to the Hooded Executioners' compound.

For their parts, both Dace and Harmonious Jade's independent investigations went well. After a brief stop at his compound to inform Risa what he would be up to, Dace took a trip to the hive-like Guild headquarters in the Nexus's eponymous central district. Once there, he threw some money around and arranged a visit with the master of the caravan that he and his men had last escorted to and from Mishaka, Ourang Nelis. Having let the mystery simmer and go unchecked because of his grudging trust in Stalwart Mastiff, he was now resolved to find some answers for himself.

Nelis was initially reluctant to discuss the matter at all—much as he had been when he'd first proposed the detour from the main trade route on the way back to Nexus. He tried to buy Dace's silence, first with a handful of jade obols, then with an exclusive service contract that would be worth far more. Yet, although both offers were tempting, Dace held his ground and refused to take no for an answer. He had already let himself be led by Mastiff, so he wasn't about to let the same thing happen again. That wasn't why he had been Exalted. Sensing Dace's stubborn resolve, Nelis eventually broke down and told Dace what he wanted to hear.

"Growing up," he began, "I was just a wheelwright's apprentice traveling the Mishaka route with the caravan that employed my master. When I was a young man, bandits attacked that caravan during a terrible storm, and most of the people with me were captured or killed. The rest of us were scattered, and we wound up at that village, which none of the bandits seemed to realize was there. We stayed a while, waiting for the storm to pass and our strength to return, then we made our way back home."

"Why don't you skip ahead," Dace suggested.

Nelis nodded and began again. "Over time, the other survivors and I grew up and rose in the ranks of the Guild until we could support our own caravans and travel the Scavenger Lands in search of profit. None of us forgot that community that had sheltered us, and we saw in it what any savvy Guildsman would—a potential profit resource. So, without each other's knowledge, we each arranged small side trips to stop by Ikari Village briefly on the way to or from Nexus. Yet, it was small and poor, subsisting on the lands it farmed and making a minor show of trade in livestock and fish with its distant neighbors. The villagers had very little surplus, so after one Guild caravan came and went, they were reduced to trading what goods they had acquired from the first with the next one to come along. While the first full caravan each season was able to turn a tiny profit, the others actually lost money just by showing up.

"Finally, we survivors of that long-ago raid met to discuss our patronage of that village. We worked out a schedule for how often we could reasonably visit Ikari without cannibalizing each other's profit share, and we agreed to send only a small retinue of carts that could do business on a scale more comfortable to the villagers. But even that effort was still a bit much, considering the small profits we could capture there after the villagers paid their taxes. Eventually, we just decided to stick to the larger routes and let younger Guildsmen with smaller loads of wares go to the trouble."

This part of the story did not please Dace at all.

"Wait a minute," he said. "Are you telling me we trudged dozens of miles out of our way and got up to our elbows in nemissaries and hungry ghosts for nothing? I lost good men in that village! If we'd come by later, we might have lost the whole caravan!"

A shadow of shame darkened the caravan master's face at that accusation, but a darker cloud of outright grief overpowered it. His eyes misted and his lip began to tremble as he spoke.

"Your loss is grievous, Captain," he said, no longer looking Dace in the eye, "but it is nothing next to mine. I had a son in that village. A son who was murdered alongside his mother and all his neighbors."

"What?" Dace gasped.

"I told you we decided to stop visiting the village once our caravans grew too large to make it worth our while," Nelis said, choking back a sob. "But I continued to make trips regardless. I knew the profit in it was negligible, but I enjoyed the sidetrack immensely. I got along with the locals famously, and I even fell in love with one of the young girls there—Mara. In time, I fathered a child by her named Timon. I made it a routine thereafter to return to the village every year on Timon's birthday and shower him with the gifts and praise I couldn't bestow the rest of the year."

"Why not?" Dace asked. "If you were married, why didn't you bring your family to Nexus?

"*Because* I'm married," Nelis said, "but never to Mara. My wife and family here know nothing about Mara or Timon. But nonetheless, I saw that Timon never wanted for anything. I remember he wanted to become the village's mayor one day, or its peacekeeper or priest-intercessor with its local harvest god, and he would have been good at it. Now, of course, that won't ever be."

As he said those words, Nelis began to cry in earnest.

Dace let the man endure his grief in silence, and when the tears dried up, he concluded his inquiry. The last thing he wanted to know were the names of the other survivors from the decades'-gone bandit raid that had driven them to the small village in the first place. The man gave Dace the names he asked for—none of which Dace recognized—then asked Dace to leave him alone.

Dace did as Nelis asked, surprised by the old Guildsman's charity. He'd grown up orphaned among the Ravenous Wolves, and he'd seen plenty of men leave behind bastard children in small villages all over the Threshold. He'd probably sired a few bastards of his own before his Exaltation, for that matter. Among the Wolves, men either retired to marry their children's mothers or dismissed the whole business out of hand and never looked back. Yet, Nelis had taken great pains to make his illegitimate child's life the best it could be while taking nothing away from his true family. It was a far sight better than any of the Wolves had ever done—Dace included. The realization left Dace a little ashamed of himself, and he returned to his compound in a bad mood. He told Risa what information he'd uncovered and had her follow up on it, then he disappeared into his office to brood.

Harmonious Jade had a much more uplifting experience. Like the captain, she earned her information from a caravan master of the Guild, but her methods were far less genteel than his were.

Her first order of business in setting to this work was to return to her rented room and retrieve her orichalcum powerbow, her arrows and her other personal effects. She pulled a cloak on awkwardly over the bow and quiver, then she hit the streets again. Despite its light weight and loose weave, wearing the cloak might have been a bad choice in this, the month of Descending Fire, but the temperature didn't bother Jade. She welcomed the heat and power of the Unconquered Sun just on principle, and besides, she was from deep in the South, near the Elemental Pole of Fire. She knew all about scorching, unforgiving heat. These sweat-soaked, lethargic sons of the Scavenger Lands didn't know from hot. They had a right to dread the seasonal advent of the omnipresent sweltering humidity the city's waterways gave birth to, but the annoyance of it was still nothing compared to the punishing climate Jade was used to.

Regardless, the cloak served the singular purpose of allowing Jade to conduct her affairs in comfortable obscurity. (Not that her odd clothing and the hints of orichalcum that stood out from beneath her cloak attracted less attention from the people on the streets, but the hood blocked out the sight of the odd looks people gave her as she passed them.) The first thing she did was to sneak back to Firewander and check out Selaine Chaisa's hotel room again. The room was still uninhabited, and the strewn effects were only as disturbed as Jade had last left them. She skimmed off another healthy helping of Chaisa's money then slipped back downstairs and into the main lobby. On her way out, she noticed a nervous young man with a capped leather tube stuffed into his belt sash asking after Chaisa's whereabouts. Unfortunately, the clerk at the desk had nothing more to tell him than Jade had already read in the clerk's ledger earlier. She thought about following the messenger back to whoever had sent him here, but he accidentally let it slip that he was working for Stalwart Mastiff of the Hooded Executioners, so she didn't even bother. She already knew that mercenary was dirty, but she'd promised not to go back after him until later.

So, instead, she decided to go after the Guild caravan master who had transported Chaisa to Nexus from Chiaroscuro. From her early reconnaissance in the city, Jade knew that that Guildsman had a fiscal partnership with Chaisa, so she thought she would see what he knew about the priestess and how deep his association with her went. As the day was still young, she hurried to the spot in the Big Market where she had watched Chaisa for several days and found herself just ahead of the man she was looking for. She shadowed him for a few hours, then mystically concealed herself and slipped down to street level as he headed to the privies. The man walked with two bodyguards even to the stalls, but Jade did not let that dissuade her. As the three men approached, she leapt on an awning and over the heads of milling pedestrians to alight atop the long row of wooden booths at the end of the pavement beside the river. No one saw or heard a thing. Then, when the Guildsman had chosen his stall, Jade positioned herself right above him and made her move in a razor-thin moment between when the man folded open the door and his guards turned away from him to watch the crowd and talk among themselves. In that instant, she snatched the man off the ground, pulled him right over the top of the stall and jumped into the river with him under her arm before he even realized what was happening to him. A spring on the hinge pulled the door shut, and the ambient crowd noise and the rush of water muffled the sound of the two of them splashing into the dirty river. The Guildsman's guards remained oblivious, and if anyone else noticed the abduction, no one dared get involved by speaking up.

The slimy water's fast current didn't carry the two people very far before Jade snagged an outcropping of stone in the retaining wall of the river and hauled her burden to land. She pulled the choking, sputtering Guildsman into a long, half-flooded access tunnel that led to a dark chamber with a standing wooden crank in the center. This room had at one time been manned by petty criminals who had been impressed into civil service by the Council of Entities. The crank once operated a series of cables and pulleys that provided the motive force for a water-based version of Nexus' pulley cart system. The system had been abandoned because the knowledge required to work the First Age technology that managed the speed and depth of the river had been lost, but Jade had seen potential in this chamber. She had discovered it shortly after her arrival in the city, and she'd considered bringing Chaisa here.

Old, dirty water stood a foot deep here, and Jade wondered if the Guildsman was making the water around him just a little warmer right now. As he came to his senses from the shock of being snatched off the street, he spat up a lung's worth of water, then he began looking and splashing around wildly to get his bearings. Jade stood over him in silence enjoying his panic, then she pushed him face first into the water with a boot to the back. When he came up for air and rolled belly up, he found her standing over him holding her bow and pointing a drawn frog crotch arrow at his throat. Drops of water fell from the sinister Y-shaped arrowhead and splashed on the pale flesh of his neck.

As is typical of such encounters, the man and woman exchanged the formal pleasantries that were to be expected. He plaintively demanded an introduction, while she politely refused and instead educated him on the futility and inadvisability of rejecting her hospitality. She proposed that he should cooperate with the height of funereal dignity, and he grudgingly accepted with every modicum available to one in his position. He even retained the good grace not to point out how limited his options were in that regard. She silently commended that grace under these pressing circumstances and brought the formalities to a close in favor of more significant business.

The interrogation proceeded quickly and with a minimum of obstreperous recalcitrance. Its subject told Jade that he was unfamiliar with the goals and methods of the Salmalin cult, as he was not an adherent of the faith himself. He was nothing more than a businessman with many associates from the South, and he had garnered a long camaraderie and working relationship with Chaisa through many mutually profitable arrangements. He had been unaware of the priestess's attempt on Jade's life in Chiaroscuro, and he had no idea what agenda the woman might be pursuing here in Nexus.

When the conversation changed tacks slightly, the Guildsman became somewhat more informative. The next thing Jade asked him was what, if anything, Chaisa might have said or asked him about the village that had been so horribly abused between here and Mishaka. In response, the merchant gave her much the same story as Dace heard from Ourang Nelis. It seemed that this Guildsman had also been one of the survivors of that fateful bandit raid years ago, and he had risen in station considerably since then. He vaguely remembered discussing with Chaisa the village that had sheltered him once a long time ago, but she hadn't shown much interest then or ever brought the subject up again.

Finding that particular bit of trivia intriguing if not especially illuminative, Jade then took a gamble and asked the Guildsman what he knew about Stalwart Mastiff, whom she assumed was materially connected to Chaisa. The man recognized the mercenary as a prominent Hooded Executioner, of course, but he also knew Mastiff from earlier in his career. Apparently, Mastiff had begun his martial service as a freelance caravan guard, and one of his most frequent employers had been the very Guildsman Jade was now interrogating. Mastiff had been around for the last few trips the Guildsman took to the village, and he had been around when the Guildsman had met and first entered a partnership with Selaine Chaisa. He had been a good fighter and a trustworthy associate, and he had even gotten along with Chaisa when many of the mercenary guards had not. He had eventually taken a job with a more influential Guildsman whom the one Jade was interrogating knew well, before eventually hiring on with the nascent Hooded Executioners. That intermediary Guildsman was another of the survivors who knew about the village, though he had been the first to recognize how costly and unprofitable the side trip actually was for a large caravan. That man's name was Kerrek Deset, and the Guildsman heartily suggested that Jade speak to him if she wanted to know more about Stalwart Mastiff.

Jade tested her luck farther by asking her captive what he knew about other Salmalin priests and priestesses she hadn't seen or heard from in years, but he didn't recognize any of the names she gave him. After another hour of questioning, she realized that he knew nothing more that would be of immediate help. She pressed the issue a little longer just to be safe, but the well of his usefulness had run dry. The Guildsman recognized this realization in her as it came upon her, and with renewed dread, he began to beg for his life. Jade could not grant his requests, however, not only as a simple matter of practical expediency, but also as a result of his long support of Selaine Chaisa. The Guildsman's influence, money and other resources had aided Chaisa and the greater Salmalin cult immeasurably over the years, and as the power of the Unconquered Sun stirred in her, Jade could not abide even that tacit support of evil. She explained her position to her victim, then hardened her heart to his piteous counterarguments.

In gratitude for his cooperation and honesty thus far, she respectfully endured his threats of vengeance from beyond the grave and graciously ignored his shameful subsequent outburst of cowardice and self-pity. She allowed him to compose himself and screw up his courage, then she indulged him in a brief hand-to-hand scuffle. Putting away her bow and arrow, she fended off his clumsy attempts to knock her down and strangle her. She twisted one flailing arm behind him in a powerful joint lock and held him down in the shallow water.

The man thrashed at first, but soon his body could only jerk spasmodically while his limbs trailed weakly in the water. In his diminishing struggle, his free hand landed on top of one of hers and squeezed with no more strength than a child. The contact startled Jade, who had already closed her mind to the man's struggles, and her thoughts betrayed her in the man's final moments. She asked herself what grave wrong this man had done to earn a death sentence. Was it enough that he subsidized the activities of the Salmalin, albeit unwittingly? Did his ignorant collaboration justify his sacrifice on the altar of expediency? Would anything justify killing this man who had knowingly done no wrong? This man… Jade realized that she didn't even know his name. Aside from his association with Chaisa, she didn't know anything about him. Who was she to punish him—especially for someone else's crime? Jade looked up, silently begging the Unconquered Sun to tell her unequivocally if what she was doing was wrong.

No answer came, but Jade had already made up her mind. With a curse, she hauled the Guildsman out of the water. The man hacked up twice as much water as he'd done before and collapsed to his knees, crying and retching. Jade reached out to slap him on the back and get him coughing, but he shrunk back from her and cowered against the wall. She took a step toward him, but he drew his knees up to his chest and sat rocking in the shallow water, still certain that he was about to die but now convinced more than ever of the cruelty of his killer. Jade knelt down to look him in the eye, but he just moaned and refused to engage her. Finally, Jade stood back up and backed away, swallowing down shame for what she had just put the man through.

"Listen to me," she said, "I'm not going to kill you. But if you tell anyone about this, I'll be back. I'll know you talked, and I'll come hunting you. And if you keep doing business with the Salmalin, I'll be back. You know I can find you. You'd better change your ways, or next time, you'll wish I'd finished the job here."

The man didn't respond or even seem to have heard what Jade said, but just saying it was enough for Jade. She headed back toward the river, eager to return to Dace's compound with what she had discovered. Once she'd done that, she could put her crisis of judgment behind her.

Dace emerged from his office as late afternoon slid into early evening, and he called Risa in to speak with him. He'd given up brooding and immersed himself in some mundane business, and in so doing, he'd realized that the course of action he had set for himself had the potential to annoy the Council of Entities. Should that prove true, he foresaw a tighter budget and a short-term reduction in reputable work for the company, as an annoyed Council of Entities could prove a formidable obstacle between the Bronze Tigers and future clients. Dace's men didn't work exclusively for the Council, but jobs the Council arranged provided the company's most lucrative work and helped to generate the word of mouth that made it easier to win outside contracts. Should Dace's recent independent actions estrange him from the Council, the entire financial dynamic of his company would change, and he wanted to prepare Risa for that possibility so that she could prepare the rest of the men for it.

True to her professional demeanor, Risa digested the reality of the situation as Dace explained it, and she accepted it without question. She told him she understood that he was doing the right thing and that any rules that sought to keep him from doing so weren't worth following in the first place. Then, she sat down across the desk from her captain and looked for ways to save the Bronze Tigers money without sacrificing pay or those funds that had been set aside for upkeep and replacement of weapons and armor. The figures they were working with were especially fresh in Risa's mind as she had sat through the weekly audit the company had been subjected to earlier that afternoon. In a few hours' time, the two of them made some progress, but the economic forecast did not look good should the Council withdraw its support. The future looked bleak indeed if the Council decided to actively hinder and disparage the company. The Bronze Tigers might have to leave Nexus altogether and reestablish themselves elsewhere if that happened. Provided the Council would let them.

After the financial discussion wrapped up and the uncomfortable discussion on how to broach the subject with the men came and went, a young member of the auxiliary staff opened the door and inquired about what the two officers wanted for dinner. Dace declined, but Risa took that opportunity to make her exit. She wanted to discuss her and Dace's assessment of the Bronze Tigers' future with the rest of the senior command staff, but not on an empty stomach. Before she could get away, Dace stopped her for one last question.

"Say, Lieutenant," he asked, "where's that report I asked you for?"

"Sir?" Risa asked, stepping back into the room. "Which one was that again?"

"The security report. The one I asked for last night in the planning room. You remember."

"You mean when Beads was here with you?"

"Yes. I wanted it on my desk by this afternoon."

"You were serious about that?"

"Of course I was. We had a major security breach last night, and the guards' response was a complete disaster."

"I thought you were just trying to get rid of me," Risa said, putting on a slightly diffident and wounded air.

"What are you, kidding me, Lieutenant? Did you even do it?"

"Did you really want me to?"

"*Yes.* It sounded like an order, didn't it?"

"No, sir. Well, I suppose it could have."

"Risa…"

Risa cracked a thin smile that wouldn't have been visible across a larger room. "Of course I drew up the report, sir," she said. "As ordered."

"Then, when were you planning on handing it over?"

"Actually, I was planning to wait another hour or so, sir," Risa said. "I thought I'd shame you into an apology for brushing me off by bringing it by later after you'd forgotten all about it."

"I see. You were that offended?"

"Mortally, sir."

Dace nodded. "Fine. I'll tell you what, Lieutenant. You go get that report, and when you bring it to me, I'll give you your job back."

"Fair enough, sir. Apology accepted. I can just give you the gist of it now if you want."

"That'd be great," Dace said. "Let's hear it."

Before Risa could answer, a soft knock sounded at the half-open door to the office, interrupting her. She expected the same auxiliary staffer who'd offered dinner to be there, but when she turned around, she found Harmonious Jade standing right behind her instead. The girl was wearing a shabby gray cloak over loose pants, a long-sleeved shirt and a metal cuirass in bizarre defiance of the seasonal heat, and she was poorly hiding an enormous golden bow and a fancy quiver of arrows on her back.

"Well, sir," Risa said to Dace over her shoulder, "it looks like security could use a little more tightening."

"Hello, Dragon-Blood," Jade said with a stiff nod. "Can I come in?"

"So, we're asking for permission now?" Risa replied. "That's a leap in the right direction. You didn't litter our practice field with wounded soldiers this time, did you?"

"You did as much damage to your men as I did. You and that spear of yours."

"That's an… interesting point. Why do you smell like the Gray River?"

"I don't really want to get into that."

"I see. Won't you come in? That is if the Captain's not on his way to dinner."

"Let her in, Risa," Dace said, standing up behind his desk. "And go on ahead to dinner. I want to talk to Jade alone."

"Yes, sir."

"And don't forget to bring that report to me later."

"Yes, sir."

Risa left, and Dace offered Jade a chair.

"Did I keep you waiting, Captain?" the girl asked, taking off her cloak and setting her weapons beside the chair he indicated.

"No," he said. "And you can call me Dace. You're probably young enough to be my daughter, but we're both equals under the Sun."

"Thank you."

Jade sat down and rested one hand on the lip of her quiver, saying nothing more as she looked down at the curves of the stylized aquiline motif of her powerbow. Dace sat down too and tapped his thumb on his desk, waiting for Jade to meet his eyes again.

"So," he finally had to say, "that's quite a piece of hardware you have there." Jade nodded. "What's its range?"

"Three hundred yards. A little more if it's not windy."

"Not bad. You any good with it?"

"Better than anybody you've seen, I'd bet."

"Maybe. It's certainly a nicer than any bow I've seen. Is it orichalcum?"

"Yes. I owned it once... before. In the First Age."

Dace nodded his understanding. The sword he carried had belonged to him in his last life too. The day he'd recovered it from his ancient self's tomb, he'd felt like his Exaltation in this Age was finally complete. He started to relate the story to Jade, but she interrupted him.

"This isn't why I'm here, Captain," she said. "It's interesting, but right now, there's work to be done. Can we talk about that first?"

"Sure, sure," Dace said, plastering on a more business-like façade immediately. "You're right, of course." He paused to gather his thoughts, then said, "Well, I talked to my contact like I said, and I found out something interesting about Ikari Village."

With quick, clipped precision, he recounted his discussion with Nelis. He diverged briefly to describe the events of the fateful night they had discovered the fate of Ikari Village, then used that backdrop to describe the caravan master's reaction to the scene of carnage the following morning. At that point, he told Jade the story the Guildsman had told him about finding the village originally and finding excuses thereafter to visit it.

About halfway through the recitation, Jade began to nod and voice affirmative-sounding non-words, as if what Dace was saying was confirming what she already knew. He asked her about it when he was finished, and she told him what she'd learned from her own Guild "contact." She filled in what details Dace's story had left blank, including the connection from Stalwart Mastiff to the two Guildsmen who knew about the village and knew how to find it. She then extended that connection to Chaisa and the Salmalin cult and went on to extrapolate it into including the master artisan Kerrek Deset. Dace recognized that name from the story his own contact had told him, but he didn't know Kerrek and was unwilling to accuse him of any wrongdoing on the sole basis of unlikely coincidence.

"Wait a minute," Jade said. "I thought you didn't believe this was all just coincidence. You said it was providence that threw us together. That wasn't even twenty-four hours ago."

Dace winced. "I did say that, didn't I? I ought to be more careful. The problem is, I just don't want to believe any of this. Nexus may be rough and ugly, but it's *civilized*."

"What, so nothing bad ever happens here?"

"No, there's plenty. It isn't that. It's just... Yozi cultists, deathknights, conspiracies, a slaughter of innocents... How does something like this go unchecked and undiscovered in a place like this?"

"I don't claim to know everything about your city, but I know what can be done and what can't be done. I know how the Salmalin operate, Captain. They're slow and subtle and infinitely patient. They take their time and do whatever they have to do to gain influence and manipulate the people who have the power they want. They're grains of desert sand carried in the wind—in time, there's no place you won't find them. Even here."

"Damn this Age," Dace said, and there was a centuries'-old bitterness buried in his voice. "But you're right. Whatever this is, it's happening whether I want to believe it or not. And it's looking like Mastiff's definitely involved."

"Right," Jade said. She stood up and grabbed her bow and arrows off the floor. "So, let's go take him out."

"Wait, no. Hang on, girl! I told you before that isn't how we do things here. What's wrong with you?"

"Nothing. He's a Yozi-worshiper. I don't see the problem."

"He's *probably* a Yozi-worshiper," Dace allowed, "but he's just one link in this chain. He's a *lead*. We can't just kill him."

"Sure we can," Jade said, just as plainly as if she were discussing map routes between Threshold kingdoms. "We've still got this Kerrek we can get answers from. Then, if he somehow doesn't turn out to be connected, you and I can go into the Undercity where the Disciple and I…" She had to pause there to blink back a sudden irritation in her eyes and swallow a nascent lump in her throat. "Where he and I were separated."

"No," Dace said. "Mastiff is a respected man in this city, and for good reason. He's been a warrior and a peacekeeper and a lawman for years."

"A Yozi-worshiping one."

"He's connected to those people—it's hard to deny that—but that's all we know."

"He might be the one who butchered those villagers. Him or his men. I saw some of them out in the neighboring villages when I was on my way out there."

"It doesn't matter if he's responsible for those villagers' deaths. No, wait, I take that back. It does matter, but it wouldn't matter to the Council or the Emissary because that didn't happen in Nexus proper. They wouldn't consider it a crime, but they *would* call our punishing him for it a crime. That's how things work here."

"I don't care how things work here. This is—"

"I do care! I've made agreements to abide by certain laws, and while I'm willing to ignore some of them, I'm not going to throw them all out with the bedpans."

"So, what do you want to do?" Jade sneered, unimpressed. "Tattle on him to this Emissary?"

"No, I'm going to talk to Mastiff," Dace said. "Man to man, soldier to soldier, captain to captain. I'm going to tell him what we know and give him a chance to come clean. I'll give him a chance to tell me what he's wrapped up in and to expose his conspirators before it's too late. Then, I'm going to let him turn himself in."

"Are you serious?"

"That's the way it's going to be. Mastiff's service to the city over the years has earned him that much."

"And what are you going to do when he laughs in your face and tries to have you thrown out, or worse? Because unless he's completely insane, that's exactly—"

"If I can't convince him to do the right thing," Dace sighed, "then I'll deal with him. I'll take care of it myself. Man to man, soldier to soldier, captain to captain. He's earned that much."

"You respect your enemies too much," Jade muttered. She could tell the mercenary's mind was made up, though, and that she would have to take overly drastic steps to change it at this point. "So, what do you expect me to do while you're busy overcomplicating things? I guess I could cover your escape when Mastiff calls the guards on you."

"That won't be necessary," Dace said without conviction. "In fact, I don't want you there at all." Jade's eyes blazed. "Hold on, calm down. I don't want you sitting around here tapping your toes either. I think you ought to check out this Kerrek Deset's place to see how connected he really is to what Mastiff's wrapped up in. Risa's got connections, so she can help you find him. If nothing else, this Deset might be able to shed some light on Mastiff that'll make good proof against him when the official Council inquiry begins."

"Or that'll exonerate you posthumously after they pull your body out from under every Hooded Executioner in that compound."

"However it works out," Dace said with a bleak half-smile. "But I doubt it'll come to that. Just check out Kerrek Deset, and meet me back here when you're done. One way or another, I'll have definitive news about Stalwart Mastiff to share, and we can figure out where to go from there."

"Fine," Jade said. "But when this blows up in your face, I won't feel sorry for you. Just be ready to do things my way."

"If," Dace corrected half-heartedly as Jade slung her bow and quiver over her shoulder. "And we'll see about doing things your way. This is still my compound, and I've got a few more years experience in this world than you do."

"Only in this life, Captain."

Dace just shook his head. "Good luck, girl. I'll see you back here tonight."

"Yeah," Jade said. "For what it's worth, I hope you're right about your man. I just don't think you are."

She left then, nearly knocking over an auxiliary staffer who was right outside the door just about to come in. It was the same girl who had come by earlier about dinner, and Dace acknowledged her with a curt nod. Jade took the staffer by the elbow and led her away asking for directions on where to find Risa. Dace watched them go and hung his head, feeling every one of his many years, Exaltation or no.

Jade was right about Mastiff, of course, but he had gone too far convincing her not just to sneak out and assassinate the man. In his shock at hearing such a pretty young girl talk like a hardened amoral killer, he'd slipped too far toward the opposite extreme on the scale, and now, he had to make good on his word. He had to walk into the headquarters of the Council of Entities' favorite peacekeepers, accuse a respected veteran of consorting with Yozis and Yozi-worshiping cultists, then somehow convince him to submit himself gracefully to his peers and subordinates in the name of justice. It wasn't going to be pretty, and it wasn't going to end well.

Nonetheless, Dace had committed himself to this course of action. There was no turning back now. He rose and made his way to his personal stores in the armory. His formal dress uniform and armor was there, and he wanted to be wearing it on what would likely be the last night he was welcome in Nexus.

Chapter Ten

"Is she going to kill me?" Kerrek Deset asked over a mug of qat tea—his third since lunch. "She is, isn't she?"

"What?" Selaine Chaisa snapped at her disconsolate host. She had been cooped up with him all day, and every time she tried to doze off for a few minutes, he started chattering at her inanely. Despite repeated requests for him to just leave her alone, she had been forced to endure Kerrek's company almost without pause. He'd left the room only twice all day, and that was just to compose a few messages and cancel his appointments for the rest of the week. Now, as night came, she had grown quite sick of him.

"That girl you told me about," Kerrek went on, staring at his untouched tea. "The one who did this to you."

"You mean Harmonious Jade, the traitor," Chaisa said, speaking slowly. It hurt her face to do much else.

"Yes. She's going to kill me, isn't she?"

"Why would she? She doesn't know where you are or even who you are. That's why I was brought to you."

"But she's looking for you. She followed you all the way here from Chiaroscuro. What if she comes here looking for you but finds me first?"

"She won't. This is the last place she would look. Our association is secret. This place is safe."

"It's *supposed* to be," Kerrek agreed, though his hands had started shaking. "But things aren't how they're supposed to be anymore, are they? That girl was supposed to be dead in Chiaroscuro. Everything we've been working on is supposed to be a secret. The masters were supposed to protect you against all enemies. Now, we're supposed to be safe here, but…"

"Do you really have so little faith, Kerrek?" Chaisa said, sitting up straight. "Don't you put your trust in our masters at all anymore?"

"Of course I do," Kerrek murmured. "It's just—"

"It's just that things aren't as they should be," Chaisa sneered. The expression opened blisters under her bandages. "But things have not been as they should since before the First Age. Not since Creation's rightful masters were last free have things been as they should. This world is a ruin because of the blasphemy of the gods and the Anathema, yet all you can think about is your personal safety?"

"I only—"

"Where is your faith?"

"I have faith," Kerrek stammered, unable to look at Chaisa. "My faith awarded me my position, my wealth, everything I have. The influence of the Yozis has blessed my entire life."

"Yet, you fear that now they've forsaken you."

"Yes." Kerrek began to tremble. "It shames me, but I'm afraid. The Yozis are powerful and eternal—blessed be their names—but in the end, they were beaten. Many died. Many more surrendered. As powerful as they were, they still lost their war to the Anathema. Now, here, the Anathema are born again, and one is right here in Nexus trying to find you."

"That doesn't matter, you mewling coward," Chaisa barked. Blood began to seep into the linen covering her face, and she winced. Irritated, she began to unwind the dirty bandages and pile them on a table beside the bed. "Do you think the Yozis are unaware of their own history? Do you think they don't know the Anathema have been reborn? How ignorant do you think your masters are?"

"I don't… I'm sure they know…"

"Of course they know. They know, and they are un-afraid. Our masters are eternal, and though things are not as they should be, they will be once again. We must only do as they command and never question what they desire of us. If we give our souls and devote our bodies to them, they will provide for us and protect us as befits our submission to their will. To do otherwise is base betrayal and blasphemy. Do you understand that?"

"I do," Kerrek mumbled. "I worship our masters. I just don't know how not to be afraid."

"Pray," Chaisa said. She pulled the last bandage free and dropped it on top of the others. The chill air in the room soothed her ruined skin, and she paused to enjoy the sensation. Another moment later, she found a washcloth and dipped it into a pot of salve on the table by the bed.

"Yes, Kerrek," she began again, "pray that the Yozis take your fear from you. Pray that they give you the strength to do as they command. Everything you ask for in our masters' name will be given if you are found worthy. You must only pray that you are."

"Just pray," Kerrek said, sounding no more confident or brave than he had moments ago. His gaze lingered on the burns and blisters that Chaisa's faith and devotion had earned her.

"Yes," Chaisa said. "Often and fervently. You should start now while you still have time."

"All right," Kerrek murmured. "I will." He set his teacup down with a clumsy rattle and knelt on the floor with his forehead between his knees and his arms splayed out in supplication. He began to recite the ancient words of veneration, but Chaisa cleared her throat and interrupted him.

"Wait, Kerrek," she said. "You shouldn't do that *here*. You must abase yourself in isolation, communing solely with the masters without distraction. Go someplace private and truly offer up your bare soul. Remember what the scripture teaches: 'Those hypocrites who pray before one another are only performing a dumb show to exalt themselves. True faith is silent and secret. Public lamentations of obeisance serve only the slave and insult the master.' You must not insult our masters, Kerrek."

"You're right, of course," Kerrek said, hauling himself to his feet.

"Do you have somewhere else you can go to pray? A different room?"

"I do. I'll go. But I'll return shortly so you don't have to be alone for very long."

"Take your time," Chaisa said, sinking back into her pillows. "You must hold nothing back in your devotions. Go tend to your soul, and don't worry about me."

"I will. Thank you, Priestess."

Chaisa waved him off, then lay back on the luxuriant bed. *Finally,* she thought as he exited the room and closed the door behind him. *Maybe now I can get some sleep.*

Despite the immense power and youthful vigor with which the Unconquered Sun had Exalted him, Dace's heart was heavy as he made his way across the Cinnabar district from his compound to the headquarters of the Hooded Executioners. His polished, creaking armor hung heavy across his shoulders. His crimson and midnight blue dress uniform bound and constricted him. His square-edged orichalcum daiklave pulled at his belt, trying to drag the ground like the tail of a haggard old wolf. The way Dace carried himself did not betray these illusory sensations, but the feelings were real enough in his mind. One who knew him could read them in his eyes. As he had left his compound, several of his men had noticed the sensations there and offered to accompany him to wherever he was going. He'd only turned them down and told them to report to Risa until he returned.

None of them had actually asked where he was going or why—they were better trained than that. They had the heart to look concerned, even worried in some cases, but they had enough respect not to press the issue. Dace appreciated that, not only because he didn't want to get them involved in his business tonight and because they couldn't have helped him anyway, but also because he wasn't sure why he was dragging his feet now that he had made up his mind. He had left his compound on foot rather than horseback, and he'd taken an indirect route uphill to the Executioners' base when a straight walk up two main streets would have had him at his destination in less than an hour. As it was, the trip took more than an hour and a half, and darkness had fallen in earnest by the time the Executioners' headquarters was even in sight.

He'd had plenty of time to think, and as he turned his last corner and made his final approach, he realized what it was that was making this so difficult for him. He was neither afraid of punishment nor intimidated by the danger that might lie before him, he simply didn't want to change the status quo. The life he had made for himself and his soldiers here was steady and comfortable, and he didn't want to jeopardize that. Here, he was relatively safe from the Wyld Hunt and more or less accepted despite his status as Anathema out in the rest of Creation. His position here allowed him to carry on the work he had been doing all his life, yet now, he could do it even better than before. Where his knee had been stiffening up and his eyesight had started to fade with age, his Exaltation gave him the power and energy of a dozen young men in their prime. He'd been given a new life, and Nexus had seemed like the only place where he could actually live it. That was why he had acquiesced to all the Council's demands and restrictions for so long, and it was why he was hesitant to risk changing the situation.

Simply put, he had grown set in his ways like an old man, rather than devoting all his newfound energy to the service of the Unconquered Sun. How had he let himself come to this? What must the Unconquered Sun think of this sloth? How long would he have let himself go on thus had Harmonious Jade not come into his life and lit a fire under him? The only answers to these questions he could conceive of shamed him, and he vowed to change his ways from this moment forward. He picked up his pace and marched into the Hooded Executioners' compound with renewed conviction.

The blank faceplates of the guards' black helmets followed him as he passed, but no one made a move to stop him. He was known here, and no one considered him a threat. Two guards armed with long poleaxes crossed their weapons in front of him at the pedestrian gate and asked him to state his business, but they did so strictly pro forma and let him pass without a hassle. He left them behind and strode out into the parade ground, heading toward the main entranceway. Troops were out drilling in full armor even at this hour, and the clockwork precision of how they moved together and practiced formation maneuvering impressed Dace distantly. This whole place had always impressed him. His own compound would fit neatly in the parade ground of this one, and each building that made up this complex was as big as a Bastion manor house. The size of the place and the authority it represented had always been intimidating, but tonight, he set that aside.

The guards at the inner complex's front entrance hardly gave him a look as he passed, and he entered the long, colonnaded main hallway without any problem. The place was still bustling with activity as troops came and went, surrounded by minor robed functionaries and auxiliary personnel. The soldiers' grim helmets concealed their facial expressions, but Dace could still read surprise and a little confusion in their body language when they noticed him in his full ceremonial regalia. The civilian staff was easier to read behind the color-coded domino masks they wore to display their station and responsibilities. They looked at him, then each other, then started whispering excitedly behind their hands and giving him plenty of room. He did his best to ignore them and walked up the center of the hallway toward the administrators' plaza.

He had made it only about halfway when he noticed Stalwart Mastiff coming up a side hallway in the midst of a group of staff sergeants and civilian clerks. He turned toward the pack of them, and the bureaucrats stopped and fell silent. Mastiff looked up from an inventory scroll and affected deadpan neutrality when he saw who was standing in front of him.

"We need to talk again," Dace said. His words carried in this enormous chamber, as a result of both simple acoustics and curious onlookers' word of mouth.

"Dace," Mastiff said in a monotone. "You're not supposed to be here. I thought you were looking into something outside of town."

"We should talk privately, Mastiff," Dace said.

"What's this about?" Mastiff said, rooting himself to the spot and standing up as tall as he could. He still had to look up to meet Dace's eyes. "And why are you dressed like that? Are you swearing in new officers this evening? That's bad luck on Calibration. Besides, I told you before that all promotions have to be approved by—"

"It's a courtesy to you, Captain," Dace said. "As is asking you to talk to me privately."

"No, it'll have to wait," Mastiff said. His eyes had started dancing now, and Dace could see a subtle tic lifting the corner of his mouth. "I'm very busy."

"I'm not giving you another chance," Dace said, casually hooking a thumb into his belt near where his daiklave hung. "Courtesy only goes so far."

Dace's gesture was not lost on the functionaries who surrounded Mastiff. They fell back from their commander and began to murmur. Others within earshot began looking at each other quizzically and sidling in for a closer look. Mastiff blanched at Dace's audacity, and he grabbed the sheath of his own sword with his off hand.

"That's farther than my patience goes, Captain," he said a little too loud. "If you have a report, you deliver it through the proper channels. And make an appointment if you want to talk to me. Now get out of the way! I'm busy."

Having said that, the captain set off and tried to avoid eye contact with Dace. The functionaries he had just abandoned looked at each other, then at Dace, then at their captain and milled about indecisively. Dace stood silently for a moment to rein in his temper, then he turned and called out again.

"It's about the slaughtered souls of Ikari Village, Stalwart Mastiff," he said, his voice echoing over a sudden stillness that was overtaking the room. "And the lies you've told. And about the Yozi-worshipers and deathknights you've been conspiring with."

That stopped Mastiff cold as a wave of exclamatory gasps radiated out through the listening assemblage. He turned around immediately and strode back toward Dace with his hand on the hilt of his weapon. Only sheer force of will kept him from drawing it. "What did you say?" he demanded.

"I said you get one chance," Dace replied, matching Mastiff's volume but making no move to draw his sword yet. "Now, I want to know about those people you let lay slaughtered after telling me you'd see to their burial rights personally."

"What are you talking about?"

"I want to know how long you've been conspiring with deathknights of the Walker in Darkness and how long they've been rooting around in the Undercity."

"Deathknights? You're crazy!"

"How long have you been allowing demon-worshipers to find haven in this city? How long have you been one of them?"

Dace was simply fishing now with what thin evidence he had, but the look of shame and desperate terror that flashed on Mastiff's face was enough to confirm the allegation. The room was positively buzzing now, and Mastiff had to raise his voice just to be heard.

"This is all preposterous!" he cried. He jabbed a finger into Dace's chest and thumped it hard with every sentence. "Who do you think you are? This is outrageous! You can't just come in here slandering an officer of this company! I work for the Council of Entities! I'll *hang* you for this!"

Dace knocked Mastiff's hand aside and shoved him backward. "That's enough," he barked. "I don't care who you work for. I answer to a higher authority, and in His name, your lies are exposed! Now, I want some answers!"

Mastiff's eyes rolled like those of a frightened horse as Dace came near him, and he drew his sword in a shaking hand. The entire chamber had fallen silent, and people were actually coming in from branching hallways to see what the noise was all about.

"Who are you working with?" Dace said, closing in. "What are you planning? What are you hiding in the Undercity?"

"Stay away from me!" Mastiff warned, holding his weapon out in front of him. "Stay away from me, Anathema!"

That declaration caused a sensation in the chamber, which almost erupted into a terrified riot on the spot. Although many people knew that Dace was a mercenary captain who was relatively new to Nexus, no Hooded Executioner below the rank of captain knew that he was a Solar Exalt. Certainly, no member of the civilian auxiliary knew. They might have been willing to excuse Dace's impropriety in claiming to favor a force higher than the Council, but the idea that he might be one of the Anathema removed any such charity from them. Some cried out in terror, others ran, a brave few drew weapons of their own, and a handful froze in place.

Dace's eyes blazed, and rage contorted his face as he came within striking distance of his target, and that expression of fury broke the last of Mastiff's restraint. Lashing out in pure animal terror, he wailed incoherently and aimed a clumsy overhand chop at Dace's head. Acting on years of training and age-old instinct, Dace drew his own blade one-handed at exactly the same moment. The flat of Dace's blade intercepted the steel broadsword easily and tore it out of the Hooded Executioner's hand. The weapon flew away and crashed through a stained-glass window high up the wall. As Mastiff gaped in shock, Dace grabbed him by the front of his armor, spun around and hurled him to the ground. The Executioner skidded on his back and fetched up against one of the columns in the center of the chamber.

Dace turned to face him, looking every bit the monstrous Anathema Mastiff had just named him. His sword trailed fiery red energy, the sunburst on his forehead glowed golden white, and his face was a mask of rage. More of the stunned onlookers in the chamber fled—or dropped their weapons, *then* fled. None of them had seen one of the Anathema before.

"That is enough!" Dace roared, pointing his sword at Mastiff, who only lay there gaping. "I gave you a chance to face this with dignity, but you didn't take it. Now, get on your feet and start talking before you really piss me off."

Thus far, the night had been the most memorable one of any Calibration any of the onlookers had ever experienced. If nothing else had happened, it would still have grown into a legendary tale of how a Hooded Executioner had faced an Anathema in single combat in the main hall of his own home, right in the middle of Nexus. The decision of who was protagonist and who villainous antagonist would depend on the veracity of the Anathema's accusations against Mastiff, but either way, the story so far would likely outlive anyone who actually experienced it firsthand. Something happened at that moment, however, that changed the nature of the tale completely—not to mention the lives of those who managed to survive it.

"Now, Mastiff!" Dace roared, coming to stand over the defeated captain like a god in judgment. "On your feet. I want answers!"

"As do I," a new voice breathed, silencing every other sound in the chamber as quickly as blowing out a candle.

The voice came from a dozen yards from where Mastiff lay, emanating from a floating disk of silver light. The disk elongated into an oval, then filled out into the solid, three-dimensional shape of a mask, as if an invisible being were stepping into a malleable membrane from behind. A silver light shone in the chamber, and in a flash of brilliance, a radiant being stood where none had been a moment ago. It wore flawless white robes of ancient design and hid its face behind a perfect silver mask. As it swept its gaze once around the room, people forgot about the Anathema in their midst. Abandoning decorum and forgoing their curiosity, most of them dropped whatever they were holding and ran as soon as they realized who it was that had just spoken.

The rest understood quickly enough. This being was none other than the Council of Entities' mysterious and implacable enforcer—the Emissary.

Several hours after his conversation with Chaisa, Kerrek finally felt a little better. He had prayed and abased himself and offered praises upon praises to the Yozis until his anxiety subsided, then he'd meditated in a bath with sea salt and lavender oil mixed in, while he sipped from delicate cups of qat tea. The Yozis had not deigned to speak with him directly as they did with servants of greater faith, but they had eased his mind and taken the greater part of his fears away from him. He emerged now clean and refreshed and in a much better state of mind.

His mood had improved so much, in fact, that he thought he might catch up on some work he had neglected while he was taking care of Chaisa. So, once his bath servants had patted him dry and wrapped him in a silk house robe, he made his way downstairs to his private office. The servants he passed smiled and whispered vague pleasantries, and he returned the gestures. He pulled one of them aside to order more tea, but he mostly ignored the rest. They knew not to trouble him with their base trifles when he'd been indulging in qat, and he repaid their respect with aloof good humor. None of them except the select few that the lovely Witness of Lingering Shadows had replaced with nemissaries knew about Chaisa, and Kerrek enjoyed their blissful ignorance vicariously. Yes, how wonderful it must be to be a common house servant. He sighed, relishing the simple purity of such a life.

His good humor carried Kerrek down a flight of steps to his private office. He pushed the door open, worked a small wooden slide on the wall that opened the valves on the room's gas lanterns and crossed halfway to his desk before the careless mood he had cultivated withered on the vine. Half-lidded and dimmed by qat, his eyes still shot open when he found a brown-skinned girl with a cuirass on her chest and wooden beads in her hair standing behind his desk looking through a sheaf of papers. The armor she wore was black with orichalcum edges, and a golden lion's head had been embossed in the center between her breasts. For a moment, Kerrek found this animal intensely fascinating. Then, the girl lifted her eyes to meet his, and he remembered that he didn't know her.

"What are you doing in here?" he asked her, enunciating his words carefully. The tone of his own voice made him want to giggle.

"I'm investigating," the girl said, matter-of-factly. "*Again*, if you can believe it. I didn't expect anyone to be coming down here after dark."

The answer sounded so perfectly reasonable that Kerrek just nodded. "What are you looking for?"

"I wasn't really sure when I got here," the girl said, "but these sketches are very interesting." She held up some papers covered in technical schematics drawn from various angles with a meticulous grasp of fine detail. The object represented looked like nothing less than a Wyld mutation that combined the most useful aspects of a beaver, a scorpion and a wooden wagon.

"Do you like them?" Kerrek asked, mimicking nonchalance.

"I don't understand all the mechanical details," the girl replied, "but the concept is very clever. If I understand correctly, a counterweight on the tail section activates this clockwork section in the center and moves these arms."

"And it multiplies the work you put in several times over," Kerrek said, beaming. "I designed that."

"It looks like you designed it to come apart and go back together very easily, too," the girl said.

"Oh, yes," Kerrek said, coming to the desk to speak to the girl. She sounded so very interested in the subject, and

it wasn't very often pretty young women showed any spon-
taneous interest in the work that had earned him his money.
"Each individual piece is light enough to be carried between
two strong men, or the whole thing can be transported in
two medium-sized wagons. It can be broken down and
reassembled in just under an hour. It's wonderful for clearing
fallen rocks or storm-felled trees from a trade road, and I've
sold several to the fire brigades for tearing down burnt-out
frames of buildings they couldn't save."

"I bet it's great for clearing rubble out of the ruined
sections of this city too, isn't it?" the girl asked.

Something in the girl's tone cut through Kerrek's qat
euphoria, and he stiffened. "I suppose it would be," he said.

"Especially down in the Undercity. You could carry the
machine pieces down one by one, put them together and
start excavating right out of an air pocket or an old sewer
confluence. Nobody would even know you were doing it, if
you were careful."

"I wouldn't know about that," Kerrek said, taking a
wary step backward.

"So, you've got no interest in excavation?" the girl
asked with that same peculiar tone in her voice. Was she
mocking him? Kerrek thought maybe she was. "That's
strange, because you have an awful lot of maps here with
possible entrances into unexplored sections of the Undercity
marked very clearly. You've got even more over there."

She glanced to her left, and Kerrek followed her gaze
to the hiding place of his wall safe. The panel it had been
hidden in was lying flat on the floor, and the door was ajar.
Not even his accountant or seneschal knew about that
safe. His sluggish wits were starting to put things together,
and he realized he wasn't at all happy with what he had
walked in on.

"I know what this is," he said, standing up straight and
looking the girl in her beautiful brown eyes. "You're a spy
sent to steal my designs. Who do you work for? Did Hierarch
Shen send you here? Or was it Gol Durgo? That bastard."

"No," the girl said. "I don't know them."

"It couldn't have been Gavin Bast. His money subsidizes my research and development. Though if he thinks I'm working too slowly…"

"I'm not a Guild spy, rich man."

Kerrek's eyes widened. "Then, you work for the Council, don't you? I can explain about those maps. You see, it's all very—"

"I don't work for the Council," the girl said. "Think harder."

Kerrek did, but the qat and his overall state of mind had left him a little too strung out to put everything together on command.

"Surely, it isn't that hard," the girl said, frowning in consternation. "Or maybe you actually don't know. I would have thought Chaisa at least described me."

Kerrek blinked once in confusion, then in a flash of understanding, he realized just what danger he was in. His eyelids peeled back, and he gasped, "You're *her*!"

"Enlightenment," Jade said, smiling with the malicious contentment of a cat staring at a broken-winged bird.

Kerrek turned to bolt for the half-open door behind him, but before he'd even made it two steps in that direction, something zipped past his ear and slammed the door shut. A thick yellow and black feathered shaft was lodged in the oak panel, quivering with the force of its impact. Kerrek turned around, cringing in mounting horror, and saw the girl holding an enormous orichalcum bow and aiming a second arrow at him.

"You're still alone down here," Jade warned him, aiming to sever his windpipe if he didn't take her meaning. Kerrek nodded rapidly, as if he were having a seizure. "Now, come over here, and sit down on the desk."

Kerrek did as Jade commanded, trying hard not to wet himself or cry out involuntarily. He sat down as Jade took a new position in the center of the room. She let the tension out of her bow as she did but kept her aim steady and her arrow to the string. The gleaming frog crotch arrowhead was the most sinister, vicious-looking implement Kerrek had ever seen in his life.

"Good," Jade said when Kerrek had settled himself. "You've already been more accommodating than the last people I've talked to. I was bluffing about Chaisa, by the way. I wasn't completely sure you'd know who I was talking about." Kerrek only blinked, still unable to trust his voice. "But you do know her, and that's good for you right now. I wonder, do you also know Stalwart Mastiff?"

"I do," Kerrek croaked, clenching the muscles around his bladder as tight as he could. "He introduced me to Chaisa while I was trying to sell my earthmovers to a man from Chiaroscuro."

"How long ago was that?"

"Years. I don't… I'm sorry. I don't remember how many. I'm really sorry."

"Relax. So, you do business with Selaine Chaisa. Are you Salmalin?"

Kerrek only nodded, squeezing his eyes shut. Based on the horror stories Chaisa had told him, he expected this girl to kill him for that admission alone.

"I see," she said instead. "How many more of you are there in Nexus?"

"I only know Mastiff and Chaisa," Kerrek said. "I swear. They know the heads of the other cells. I'm just a useful convenience to them. All I have is money. Lots of it. If I could… What I mean is… Would it be okay if I bribed you? Can I do that?"

"I'm afraid not. But as long as you keep being honest, you've got nothing to fear from me." Unfortunately, the girl's words were only cold comfort to Kerrek. "So, tell me this: How did your priestess get involved with deathknights of the Walker in Darkness?"

Kerrek's face somehow went a shade paler, and he gulped painfully. "I'm responsible for that," he wheezed. "They were my contacts long before I met Chaisa. I met one of them in Sijan, and we made arrangements to import ghost flowers. About six months ago, she had me introduce her and a friend of hers to Chaisa. They've been working with her off and on ever since."

"Interesting. Especially since demon cultists and vassals of the Deathlords don't usually work together. Never, in my experience."

Kerrek shook his head. "It's true, I promise. They seem to be working together very well."

"Is that so?" Jade said. "So, what are they doing? Does it have to do with what they were looking for down in the Undercity? Don't dam the river now, rich man. You wouldn't die quickly enough to make it worthwhile."

Kerrek gulped again and still hesitated, until Jade drew back her arrow and aimed for his navel. At this range, the shot would pin him to the desk, and even if he cried out for help then, he'd spend the rest of Calibration dying in agony. Then, his soul would have the Walker in Darkness to contend with over this miserable display. Unless Salmalin souls found their way to the demon-realm for the Yozis' pleasure...

"Okay," he whined, covering himself with his hands. "I'm sorry. I just really don't want to have to tell. And the truth is, I don't know enough."

"Extrapolate," Jade said, aiming lower by several degrees.

"They were looking for hidden shadowlands primarily," Kerrek said in a rush. "I don't know why. They wanted shadowlands and a temple to dedicate to the Yozis. And Chaisa keeps talking about some ritual she's going to do when the time comes before Calibration's over."

"What kind of ritual?" Jade asked, though she already had a decent idea.

"She wouldn't tell me," Kerrek replied. "But it's a big one. It's something she admitted she needed the deathknights' help with. I don't understand it. I'm no sorcerer, I'm sorry. I don't know what else I can say to help you."

"You've probably said more than enough already in every sense of the phrase," Jade said. "Yet, there is one more thing. I want to know where Chaisa is. Is she even still alive?"

Kerrek began to waver as if he was going to pass out from hyperventilation, and although he opened his mouth to speak, no words came out. Through the man's distress, Jade couldn't decide if he was trying harder to answer her question or to keep the answer to himself.

"Choose your course wisely," Jade said. She exhaled some of the essence inside her in a faintly luminous mist. The mist ignited the head of her arrow in ethereal flame, and an empty violet circle began to glow on her forehead. "Things might not go well."

Kerrek couldn't help himself any longer. The muscles around his bladder shuddered, and the next thing he knew, wet heat was running down his legs to pool on the floor in front of his desk. He sniveled uncontrollably and hung his head as a great sob wracked his entire body. He'd never known shame like this, even counting the night he'd first lain with a harlot and failed to achieve his goal. He almost wished this girl would just kill him now and get it over with.

"Tell me," she said instead. "Tell me, and it's over."

"She's alive," Kerrek groaned. "Upstairs. She's been here two days recuperating, and she looks a horrid fright, but she's still very much alive." He closed his eyes tight at the end of that admission, waiting for the judgment of this Anathema girl who'd broken into his home, exposed his sins, shamed him and ruined everything he and his brothers in faith had been planning, all in one swift stroke. Instead, however, he heard her slack the tension off her bow once more, and when he looked up, she was staring at him in rigidly controlled shock.

"She's here?" she whispered, barely louder than the crackling of the flame at the tip of her arrow. "She's alive, and she's in this house right now?" Kerrek nodded, dumbstruck by the change that had come over the girl. "Which room?"

Kerrek told her the truth without her even having to draw her weapon on him again, then the girl did a most peculiar thing. Rather than murdering him where he sat, she turned her back on him and headed for the door. While

Kerrek sat there with his mouth agape and urine running onto his feet, Jade opened the door then warned him over her shoulder to stay right where he was until she came back for him. Then, just like that, she was gone, running up the steps toward where Chaisa lay sleeping and unaware of her mortal peril. Kerrek sat paralyzed for another moment until finally the last vestige of his courage and dignity returned to him. He stood and crossed the room on wet, shaky legs until he was right inside the door of his private office. Then, he took a deep breath, squeezed his eyes tight and let out a bloodcurdling howl of alarm.

"Guards!" he bellowed, an octave or two higher than a man should scream. "Nemissaries! Chaisa! Wake up! Intruder! Assassin! Help!"

A commotion broke out upstairs immediately, and Kerrek decided not to take any more chances. He slammed the door, locked it, snapped off the lock lever and then started shoving his heavy oak desk across his warm, stained carpet to brace it against the door. He only hoped it would be enough.

CHAPTER ELEVEN

"One of you would do well to explain this," the Emissary said, looking from Stalwart Mastiff to Dace. His form-fitting silver mask didn't so much as twitch as he spoke, but neither did it distort his voice. The words sounded in Dace's head. "And quickly. I'm not often given to conversational indulgence."

That's true, Dace thought. *People say he almost never talks. Maybe Calibration makes him garrulous.* But as Dace paused in thought, Stalwart Mastiff tried to seize the initiative from him.

"It's the Anathema!" the Hooded Executioner cried, pointing at Dace. "He charged in here blaspheming and bearing false witness against me. He even attacked me and started tearing the place up. He's gone crazy!"

The Emissary looked up at the window Mastiff's airborne sword had shattered then looked down at Dace. He cocked his head.

"He's lying," Dace said, suddenly self-conscious about the light radiating from his forehead. He wondered if the Emissary recognized the symbol there or had reason to be afraid of it.

"Yes, of course," the Emissary replied. "He has been lying. But never yet to me." He directed his attention back to Mastiff. "Unless I count omission and misdirection. Tell me now you're a righteous man, Captain Mastiff."

"Dace is the one lying," Mastiff said without the slightest flare of credibility. "I've done nothing but serve this city and the Council of Entities faithfully for—"

"Then, the deed is done," the Emissary said, raising a hand that his sleeve concealed. "Stalwart Mastiff, for the crime of falsely claiming the Council's name or sanction by abusing the trust placed in you by the Council of Entities, you are hereby found guilty and sentenced to death."

"But I've done nothing wrong!" Mastiff shouted, trying to slide away on his rear end. "This Anathema has—"

"The sentence is to be carried out immediately," the Emissary finished. A bright stream of quicksilver tinged with unearthly green then began to pour from within the sleeve of his outstretched arm. When the stream hit the ground, it ran toward where Mastiff lay, forking and branching randomly like a silver bolt of lightning. Mastiff tried to scurry away, but the silver streak moved faster. It touched his leg and coiled around his entire body as the disgraced mercenary batted at it. A moment later, an arc of luminous green energy ran down the length of the stream from within the Emissary's sleeve, making a sound like a swarm of wasps.

Dace took half a step forward and reached out uncertainly toward Mastiff as the green energy coiled around the Hooded Executioner's body and began to fry him. Mastiff convulsed and tried to scream, and the smell of burning flesh and hair filled the chamber. The Emissary's punishment went on for more than a minute until the energy finally dissipated and the conductive strand dried up and blew away like so much silver dust. Stalwart Mastiff's blackened, desiccated body at last lay rigidly splayed on the floor in his smoking armor. Dace was sure he'd seen worse ways for men to die, but he couldn't think of any of them at the moment. He could barely bring himself to look away from the ruined corpse when the Emissary turned around.

"That was unsatisfying," the eerie, masked figure said.

"He didn't deserve that," Dace said, having difficulty finding his voice after what he'd just witnessed. "I was handling this."

"But slowly, Sun-Child," the Emissary said. "I understand you were here just this morning. The restraint you've showed this traitor is unbecoming."

"Evidence. I had no proof of what I suspected."

"But you gathered it. And quickly, once you knew what to look for. What's more, you enabled my agents to do the same—and uncover yet more information as a result. If it weren't already your duty as a free citizen of Nexus, the Council would reward you for the lengths you've gone to. On another day, I might reprimand you for interfering in my work, but today, I'm impressed you chose to come here to mete out justice on your own."

"It wasn't like that," Dace said. "I came to give him a chance to do the right thing. He would have submitted himself to the Council. He might have even exposed his secret accomplices if you hadn't… done that without questioning him."

"Unnecessary," the Emissary said. "The Council's agents are investigating the information you and your second uncovered. There was no need to forestall this one's punishment by so much as a moment. Nonetheless, you've just witnessed my generosity. I allowed him to lie to me in person and seal his fate officially. On another day, I would not have been so lenient."

Then, thank the gods it's Calibration, Dace thought bitterly.

"But my leniency goes only so far. Stalwart Mastiff was highly placed, and he almost achieved a great deal, despite the safeguards against that very thing. This cannot be allowed, and it will not go unpunished."

"What does that mean?" Dace tightened his fist around the hilt of his weapon.

The Emissary chose to demonstrate rather than answer. He raised both arms out to his sides, and a multitude of silver streams like the one that had killed Mastiff shot out from him. The streams arced out and hit the ground all around him, then zigzagged all across the floor and out of the chamber. Dace froze, and the silver lines avoided him.

"What are you doing?" he demanded, raising his daiklave.

"Mastiff is not the only traitor here," the Emissary replied as the silver lines he was creating raced about the mercenary compound. "He never existed in isolation, and he should never have been able to keep his aims a secret. Yet, no one in this entire compound ever caught on to his treachery. None of his men. None of his closest associates. Not even any of the spies I placed here. None save *one*, but he only caught on because of you. Their laxity and inattentiveness is unacceptable, and it must be punished." Green energy began to arc out from within the Emissary and trace the countless paths out of the chamber across the floor. "Relate that decree to the survivors, Sun-Child. When this company rebuilds its number, make sure it does so with more motivated, proactive citizens."

Dace's eyes widened as the implication of the Emissary's words hit him, and anger boiled in his guts. This bastard was going to kill gods knew how many people with no warning and for no better reason than the fact that they hadn't realized Stalwart Mastiff was up to something. Was the Emissary deranged, drunk on the fey essence of Calibration, or was he just that heartless? As the sound of screams and commotion broke out, Dace realized that it didn't matter. Even in Nexus, men had limits of how much injustice they were willing to abide in silence. Dace had just reached his.

"These people don't deserve this!"

As he spoke, his heart raced, and his weapon began to growl like a wolf and glow. He ran toward the Emissary, dodging between jagged lines of green electricity, then leapt the last ten feet through the air. His daiklave scythed through all the silver streams coming from one of the Emissary's sleeves, and his steel-toed boot connected with the Emissary's exposed side an instant later. The arcing energy ceased to flow, and all the silver paths it had been following dissipated, but the Emissary didn't crash to the ground or even so much as double over. Instead, the enforcer offered no resistance whatsoever to Dace's kick and slid away across the floor standing upright like an ivory figurine mounted on a block of ice. Dace landed awkwardly and had to shoulder roll in his armor, but he came up instantly ready to fight. He found the Emissary standing some fifteen yards away by the central array of columns that held up the chamber's tiled ceiling.

"I didn't expect such compassion from a Sun-Child," the Emissary said. "Or such foolhardy contempt for his station in my city."

"No more talk," Dace said, striding toward the Emissary without fear. His entire body had begun to glow. "You've done what you came for, now it's time to leave."

The Emissary only shook his head and raised an arm in Dace's direction. Rather than a quicksilver strand, however, what emerged from it was a spinning scythe of green energy. It sliced toward Dace's chest almost too fast to see, but the Exalt blocked it one-handed with his glowing daiklave. He slammed the green projectile away from him and straight up into the ceiling, which rained dust and tile back down on him. Dace didn't even notice. He just kept coming. The Emissary cocked his head but didn't lower his arm. Instead, he fired two more glowing scythes, both of which Dace parried and sent crashing into columns on either side of the large chamber. He had to stop walking for that, at least.

"You shouldn't bother going to this effort," the Emissary said. "Distracting me too much could have consequences."

"Leave now," Dace said, resuming his pace once again. "I won't let you punish innocent people for the crimes of one traitor."

"That isn't up to you," the Emissary said. A hint of green flared in his eyes behind his mask, and he raised his other arm to join the first. Putting his wrists together and forming a corona of ancient symbols around them, he opened fire.

Dace had already started moving more quickly, and he met the Emissary's attack with a determination that mounted as he gained ground. Now, rather than one or two scythes of energy at a time, the Emissary unleashed dozens of them. Dace met the onrushing projectiles with his orichalcum blade, knocking them all away. He deflected them at all angles, withstanding the attack like a stone turning aside a stream of water, and the green bolts peppered the floor, columns, walls and ceiling all around him. Dust and masonry fell like rain at each explosive impact, but Dace didn't even sacrifice any of his forward momentum. In fact, he sped up and jumped toward his foe with a roar when he had crossed more than half the distance. He leapt out of the stream of the Emissary's attack and came down swinging his blazing blade at an angle that would have split his enemy from left shoulder to right hip. Yet, the Council's enforcer stopped firing, threw his arms back for balance and slid safely out of range like a ghost. Dace's swing gouged a divot out of the floor.

"You've made your point, Sun-Child," the Emissary said in the moment it took Dace to regain his balance. "On another day, I would have dispensed with you already for having such audacity. But today, I intend to teach you a lesson. *I* enforce the laws here. *I* mete out the punishment. *I* decide who's guilty."

"Come on then," Dace said. Blazing energy rolled off him in waves. "We'll see who teaches what."

The Emissary lifted his arms, and his sleeves slid back from his white-gloved hands. He gestured, and a glowing green sword appeared in each one. Each weapon was as big as Dace's daiklave, but neither had a fixed form. They pulsed and flickered like flames or water reflections, which distracted Dace as the Emissary rushed toward him. Dace was forced to retreat and parry almost as fast as he could, with no opportunity to counterattack or take the offensive. The Emissary's blades pounded his defenses like a hammer ringing out against a shield, and they moved as fast as vipers could strike. Eventually, Dace had to retreat and parry the attacks as best he could, hoping to force the Emissary to attack into a series of quick stop-thrusts.

The reaver daiklave wasn't designed or balanced to accommodate that tactic, however, so the Emissary insinuated himself inside Dace's sloppy guard and cut the mercenary across the chest and the left leg. Dace's armor took most of the force out of the first slash, but the cut on his leg was deep and nearly debilitating. It burned with green fire, and everything below his knee turned numb. He brushed the Emissary back with a wild one-handed swing (which actually scratched the filigree that covered the silver mask) and tried to retreat, but the pain betrayed him. He staggered in an ugly arc, fending off attack after attack in a diminishing margin, but now the Emissary was just playing with him. The entity feinted a high attack then disappeared as Dace tried to block. He reappeared an instant later, but now, he was standing to Dace's left, and he nicked Dace's left arm by the elbow. The wound hissed, and Dace jerked the arm up close to his body, losing the steadying hand on his sword. He tried to adjust for the Emissary's new position, but as soon as he oriented in the right direction, the enforcer disappeared again and reappeared on the other side.

The Emissary kept this up for another few beats, harrying Dace back toward the center of the room. Dace barely managed to block a few of the worst slashes, but enough nicks and cuts slipped through his defenses that he knew he couldn't keep this fight going much longer. He couldn't work his left hand anymore, and his left foot felt like a sack of mud dangling from a rope. When he finally fetched up against a column in the center of the room, it was all he could do to keep his back against it and stay upright. Seeing this, the Emissary ceased his onslaught and stood still.

"What now, Sun-Child?" he asked, lowering his weapons and unraveling the energy that held them together. "I haven't changed my mind yet. Have you?"

"Not yet," Dace said through clenched teeth. He levered himself around so that he was leaning on the column with his right shoulder rather than his back. "But I feel better knowing there's something there I can actually cut into." He looked at the damage he'd done to the Emissary's mask, and the enforcer cocked his head quizzically.

"Indeed," the Emissary said, touching the shallow slash with a finger. "I hadn't realized. As a courtesy, I'll say this: It behooves you not to cut any deeper. Now, are you ready to go home while you can still walk?" Dace only glared and shook his head. "Fine. I'll have someone take you after I've gone."

He strode toward Dace, unarmed this time, and Dace hoisted himself up straight. His balance was precarious on his numbed leg, and his body wavered as the numerous shallow wounds he'd taken alternately cramped and burned, but there was no fear in his eyes. In fact, he smiled as his anima grew brighter and his sword began to throb with crimson fire. The light he radiated filled the chamber, and the totemic image of an enormous wolf appeared in the air above him, howling in elation.

"You might be stronger than me, you arrogant bastard," he growled as the Emissary came toward him, "but not what I represent. My power is unconquered. Invincible. You're not, and one day, you're going to answer for every unjust act you've committed."

"Another day, perhaps," the Emissary said, shaking his head in amusement.

He kept coming forward, and Dace put almost everything he had in a wide, backhand strike that was aimed at his foe's silver mask. The Emissary stopped in his tracks, bent back at the waist impossibly far and just managed to duck under the swing. He popped back up straight to find Dace holding his sword up high behind him and balancing unsteadily on his right foot. Yet, despite the Emissary's acrobatics, he had gained another shallow scratch across his mask. Dace saw it and smiled through his pain.

"I warned you against that," the Emissary said. "Believe me when I tell you how lucky you are that you cut no deeper."

"I cut deeply enough," Dace said. "Now, let this be a lesson to you."

The Emissary began to speak, but Dace's eyes darted to the right and distracted him. The enforcer glanced that way and saw only too late what it was that the mercenary was looking at. The central column against which Dace had been leaning was now marred by a crack that encircled it at an angle some five feet off the ground where Dace's back-swing had cut through it. Scorched dust hung in the air, and the column groaned where its two cleavage planes grated. Dace brought his arm down again, and this time, the flat of his daiklave struck the column rather than the edge, knocking the severed top section off the base. The top of the pillar slid down and struck the Emissary in the chest before the Council's enforcer could get out of the way. Ruined marble crashed to the floor, and the ceiling (which Dace and the Emissary's confrontation had already damaged significantly) began to crack and crumble. Dace was already hobbling away as fast as he could with one useless leg, and he had to leap the last twenty feet out the front door to keep from being buried as the roof collapsed. Behind him, the Emissary's robes fell flat like an empty sack and disappeared beneath a hail of falling rubble.

Dace hit the ground hard just outside the building, bounced another couple of yards in an ugly flopping roll, then came to a stop in a parade ground full of running soldiers, wounded soldiers and panicking civilians. He could see scorch marks on the ground from where the Emissary's green lightning had come this way, seeking victims. As he was a bonfire of essence visible for quite some distance, none of the non-wounded men or women was in a particular hurry to come check on him. In fact, most of them forgot about their comrades and made a break for it. They probably assumed he'd been the one who'd tried to kill them rather than the Emissary. Dace hoisted himself up to his knees and turned around to survey the damage he and the Council's enforcer had done. It was slow going, and he knew well that what little headway he was making against his pain and fatigue would be temporary at best.

He really wanted to be surprised by what he saw when he finally turned around, but in his heart, he had expected as much. Standing between him and the ruined building from which he'd just exited was the Emissary, glowing faintly in the light of Dace's anima and coming toward him.

The entity had not so much as a speck of dust on him, and even the scratches were gone from his mask. He walked right up to where Dace knelt, shaking his head.

"You do my work as effectively as I do, Sun-Child," the Emissary said, "but not as efficiently. I urge you to remember your station from now on. Another day, you would share the punishment these others are about to receive. Today, I think the knowledge that you couldn't stay me from my course serves as punishment enough."

Dace gathered the last of his strength, but it wasn't enough. He rose to his feet but could only stay upright for a couple of seconds. His knees gave out first, and he pitched forward. The last thing he heard was the sound of amused chuckling, followed by the quiet whisper of streams of quicksilver zigzagging through the grass all around him.

Harmonious Jade was not two steps across Kerrek Deset's lavish foyer when the shrill warning echoed up the steps and electrified the bravest members of the staff. Many of the lower-order servants—the scullery maids and hall boys and such—scattered, but the seneschal, a few cooks and even a handful of gardeners came running at their master's call. Jade had already incapacitated the actual guards posted at the gates and on the property's walls on her way in, but this response from the menial staff surprised her. That surprise annoyed her so much that she considered going back downstairs to kill Kerrek then shooting her way back up the steps as these would-be saviors rushed her one by one. Of course, if she did that, she'd only be giving Chaisa time to escape yet again in the commotion.

There was nothing for it, then, but to hurry, so Jade ran for the main staircase, drawing back the flaming arrow she still held to her string. The shaft caught Kerrek's seneschal right under the chin and set his hair and clothes on fire, tumbling him into a wooden display case with a glass front beside the main stairway. Jade passed him by and reached for another arrow as three knife- and cleaver-wielding cooks tried to pile on her from the left. She shot the middle one in the shoulder as he raised his weapon then blocked an overhand chop from the left one with the sturdy orichalcum edge of her bow. The one on the right tried to cut her throat with a backhand slash as his two partners dropped their weapons, but he was equally unsuccessful. Jade dropped below the wild attack, then tripped all three of them with a low spinning back kick. When they were down, she cartwheeled over them and pulled the arrow out of the middle cook's shoulder. When she was on her feet again, she put the bloody arrow back to the string and aimed into the midst of the handful of gardeners who were coming her way wielding the long-handled implements of their profession. She sighted on one in the front and shot him in the foot, pinning it to the ground. The impact tripped him up, and he flailed as he fell, taking down the rest of his cohorts. Jade gained the curved stairway while everyone was still down.

She took the broad, carpeted steps two at a time, watching for more brave servants. By the time she was halfway up, she thought she was in the clear, but such was not to be. A flash of crackling, snapping orange shot into the air on her right from the lower level, and she had just enough time to check her ascent before the thing crashed into the stairs in front of her. As it gained its balance, she realized what she was looking at, as well as what she was up against. It was the flaming, bleeding body of Kerrek's seneschal, still sporting the charred shaft of an arrow through its neck but standing ready to fight as if nothing were wrong. The actual seneschal must be dead, then, and this was a nemissary moving its body, just like the Disciple had told her about. Maybe all of these active guardians were nemissaries, while the rest of the serving staff had chosen to run and hide. That, at least, would explain why the gardeners were still hanging around after dark.

The carpet began to smolder as the burning seneschal came toward Jade with a long shard of glass in one hand, and the killer found herself on the defensive. The man slashed at her, and Jade knocked his flaming arm aside with her bow, careful not to let the string get too close to his burning sleeves. She then hopped up onto the banister rail and ran up it a few steps to avoid the seneschal's grasping arms. The man reached for her and missed again, and she dropped down behind him and kicked him in the small of the back. He toppled and rolled down the steps in a jumble of arms and legs. The three cooks Jade had passed to get here were just coming up the stairs at that moment, and they had to step lively to avoid what was headed for them. Two managed to jump over the man, but the third was already off balance and had no time to dodge. He caught the seneschal chest to chest and fell backward burning. Jade drew an arrow and put it through the back of the seneschal's neck, pinning him to the man who'd caught him. They stayed down this time, and both of their bodies shuddered as the fell spirits that were hiding inside them went in search of more suitable hosts. That left only the two on the stairs as immediate threats, and Jade took care of them with one arrow. She twisted as she ran and shot the closest one to her—the one she'd shot in the shoulder already—in the center of the chest with a frog-crotch arrow. The Y-shaped arrowhead was designed to disembowel an unarmored foe or to devastate thick muscles in an arm or leg, but it wasn't designed to penetrate deeply into bone. When Jade hit her pursuer with it in the sternum, however, she was counting more on impact than damage. The force knocked her target off his feet and into the arms of the man behind him, and they both rolled backward and down in a bone-shattering tangle. Jade took the rest of the steps in one bound.

Kerrek's master bedroom was more or less right where he'd said it would be, but Jade would have had no trouble finding it had he lied. Once she'd reached the upper level and taken the hall doorway, it was a simple matter of following the main hallway through two turns to its opposite end. An enormous and ornate set of double doors stood there, and all the other doors in the hall were subtly angled toward it. Jade dashed that way past a parlor, a game room, a study, a library and a bathing room before she heard the sound of running feet behind her. She grabbed the hall boy's chair from beside a foldaway wall bed and slipped into the room at the end of the hallway as her pursuers rounded the last corner behind her.

She slammed the doors shut, clicked the lock and stuffed the purloined chair under the handles to brace them, all before she turned around to find out she was not alone in the room. She wasn't even alone with Chaisa. Chaisa was there, of course, but she was not in bed. The priestess was standing by the room's open bay window pulling on a robe in a hurry. Her head was swathed in bandages, though hair puffed out between them irregularly in back, and her eyes were wide. She froze as Jade crept into the room. Jade would have drawn an arrow and fired right then, except that she was distracted herself by the other two people in the room with Chaisa. She had last seen them at a distance, but she recognized them perfectly in these close quarters. They were the deathknights she and the Disciple had faced in the Undercity.

The Witness of Lingering Shadows was standing by the bay window on the opposite side of Chaisa, holding a black blade out in front of her. She was chanting something, and as she spoke, a mote of black energy radiated from the tip of her blade. She flinched when Jade entered but kept up her chanting. The Visitor in the Hall of Obsidian Mirrors was leaning against the canopy post by the foot of Kerrek's enormous bed, halfway across the room between Jade and Chaisa, and he bolted upright at Jade's intrusion. A look flashed between the two deathknights, and Chaisa began to back up.

"I told you it was her," the priestess said in the eerie dead calm of mortal fear. "That's what Kerrek was shouting about. She's come for me."

"Finish," the Visitor said to the Witness at the same time. "I'll handle this." The Witness nodded and continued chanting, never missing a beat. Her blade glowed brighter.

Jade ignored this chatter and began to immediately draw and fire arrows. She didn't have a clear shot at the

Witness, but Chaisa and the Visitor were both open targets. As the Visitor came toward her, she fired one shot at Chaisa and two at him, then tried to move away from him for a clearer shot at the Witness. The first arrow hit Chaisa dead center in the chest, but the priestess only staggered and clutched the protruding shaft in annoyance. She pulled it free, and the skin under her robes rippled and wailed like a rabbit in a claw trap. A milky white eye peered through the hole from within, then a tendril of flesh with a thin mouth on the end rose up to whisper its panic in Chaisa's ear.

As for the Visitor, he came toward Jade without fear of her arrows. He sidestepped her first shot, which lodged in his broad hat parallel to his temple, and snatched the second away from his heart with a heavily bandaged hand. Before Jade could draw another arrow, the man interposed himself between her and Chaisa and kept himself there regardless of where Jade tried to go for a better firing angle. That didn't stop her from firing at him, of course, but black necrotic essence began to spark in the air around him, and he either dodged or caught the next three arrows she sent winging his way. Worse, he did so with only one hand as he extruded a bone needle from the index finger of the other. He hit Jade in the hand with it as she reached back for another arrow, and her fingers immediately curled up into useless numb hooks. He came too close to shoot at then anyway, so Jade stopped trying to circle around him and just stood to face him.

They came together like wild animals, each lashing out with vicious punches and kicks intended to kill, blind or cripple. Jade was at a decided disadvantage, however, with one hand practically useless and numbness spreading slowly up her arm. The poison on the needle stuck in her hand was very effective, and loss of that extremity was a serious distraction. The Visitor was taller and stronger, and although she'd been trained to fight adversaries with those advantages, she preferred to be at her full capacity when she did so.

She tried to even out the reach advantage by using her bow as a lever when she got in close, but the Visitor knocked it out of her hand and sent her sprawling with a roundhouse kick. She rolled with the blow and came up with her knife in hand, then sprang back into close range. Her first few slashes caught him off guard, but he changed the nature of the fight by dodging away from her and making a break for the doors she'd blocked off with the chair. They could both hear people pounding on the door and trying to force their way in, so the Visitor's new tactic was to knock the brace out of the way and let them join the fray. Jade caught his intention half a beat later and moved to cut him off. As he made his move, she flipped all the way over his head and landed in the chair itself. She kicked at him then lashed out with her knife, stopping him in his tracks.

Meanwhile, the Witness's chant had reached its climax, and the light at the end of her blade shone its brightest. She said one final commanding word then slashed the blade savagely through the air. The black energy left a jagged, glowing streamer floating where the blade had passed, which then split open as if the Witness had sheared the fabric of Creation itself. That assessment was not entirely inaccurate, as the space revealed on the other side was a black, howling expanse of tunnel that no mortal eye should ever behold. A wind of screams and anguished moans blew out into the room.

Needless to say, this distracted Jade, who was trying to stab the Visitor's elbow and cripple his arm. Her eyes flicked away from her opponent to see what the Witness had done, and the Visitor seized the opportunity. He deflected her knife blow with a vicious chop to the wrist then punched her in the face twice with his bandaged hand. The jabs stunned her and drove her back as her knife fell to the floor, and she tripped back into the chair blocking the door. She sat down hard and bashed the back of her head against the brass doorknob, which stunned her even further. At the same time, the Witness grabbed Chaisa by the wrist and pulled her toward the rent she had made. Chaisa resisted in horror—shouting, "*That's* what you were doing?"—but her struggle was for naught. The Witness scooped her off her feet and dove with her through the unnatural aperture. The Visitor left as well, departing only reluctantly. He obviously wanted to finish Jade off, but he knew that the howling gash in Creation wouldn't last long now that the Witness had already gone through it. So, with only a tip of his hat, he crossed the room and leaped into the blackness. As it was, his hesitation almost cost him his chance as the breach stitched itself shut right on his heels. Jade shook off her grogginess and picked up her knife just in time for the moaning wind to subside and the air to return to normal.

"Damn it," she hissed, trying to shake some feeling back into her wounded. "That's twice, Chaisa."

Yet, that concern was not foremost in importance, as the pounding on the door reminded her. The chair she'd put there was starting to come apart, and Kerrek's nemissary guards were about to come flooding in. They hadn't proved much of a problem thus far, but Jade was wounded and shaken up now, plus she was running low on arrows. Not only that, but she'd also caused more commotion here tonight than was typically prudent for an assassin to allow. She hadn't caused this much of a stir on the job since the night of her Exaltation when she'd been chased through the alleys of Paragon glowing like a lighthouse beacon. Perhaps now was not the time to cut a bloody swath back out the door, down the steps and away through the streets of the Bastion district.

Instead, Jade grabbed her bow and opened the bay window. She paused there long enough to see a brilliant golden glare lighting up the sky from somewhere off in Cinnabar, then leapt out into the night as the doors busted in behind her. She hit the ground, dashed for the property's boundary and sprang to the top of the wall. No one heard her land or saw which way she went, so she was able to disappear into the night unhindered.

Tomorrow morning she would check back up with Dace and find out how bad things had gone with Stalwart

Mastiff, but until then, she wanted to go somewhere and be alone with her frustration for a while. She had let Chaisa get away again, and once again, she owed her failure to those same two deathknights. First they'd taken the Disciple away from her, then they'd robbed her of her vengeance against her Salmalin enemy. Worse, she'd thus far proved completely powerless to stop them. Despite all her training and her Exaltation on top of that, she was nothing more now than a nineteen-year-old girl with no friends, family or even followers to turn to when she needed help. It was at times like this when her soul longed for the acceptance and worship her kind had been subject to in her dreams of the First Age.

And it was times such as this when she most regretted the Unconquered Sun's decision to alienate her from the only family and community she had ever known, without ever deigning to tell her why.

I didn't see that, the shadow-cloaked Exalt thought as he watched Jade's hasty exit from Kerrek Deset's manor. *You caused a disturbance on the other side of the house to confuse the guards. I thought I saw you, and I searched everywhere outside, but by the time I thought to check* inside*, you were already long gone. I underestimated your guile. Now there's nothing I can do but go to ground before the authorities and their inspectors arrive.*

No, not a thing, he thought, smiling as he watched the door of Kerrek's bay window sway in the light breeze. *If only I'd seen where you went running off to. Alas, what an unfortunate turn of events.*

CHAPTER TWELVE

"Is she alive?" the Visitor in the Hall of Obsidian Mirrors asked as he, his partner and Selaine Chaisa emerged from the mausoleum buried in the Undercity ruins of Nexus. Mist, wisps of shadow and the faintest sound of moaning wind followed the three of them out into the lamp-lit cave. The mad plague ghosts they had left wandering the cavern became attentive at their approach and began to converge on them as the Witness of Lingering Shadows stepped up to the Visitor's side, supporting an inconsolable, murmuring Selaine Chaisa. She passed her burden over to her partner, then held up a hand and murmured a word in a long-dead language. A sigil burned in the air in front of her palm, and the ghosts stopped and stood still. She said something else to them, and they retreated into the shadows to await her next command. After that, she took Selaine in her arms again and eased her onto a cracked stone bench.

"Well?" the Visitor asked, tightening the bandages around his hand and straightening his hat.

"She's fine," the Witness said, gazing deep into Selaine's eyes. "She's very resilient, it turns out. I think it's a byproduct of her unwavering fanaticism. Just the same, I doubt she enjoyed her trip through the Labyrinth and the Underworld very much."

"I remember my first experience in the Labyrinth," the Visitor said. "I wasn't impressed until I reached the Well of the Void. The higher levels had no effect on me."

"Yes, darling," the Witness said, "but you thought you were already dead. It made you hard to please."

The Visitor shrugged, spread his hands and bowed his head. "True. So, how is she? Will she still be able to participate in the ceremony?"

"She's only in shock," the Witness said, rubbing Selaine's upper arms to keep the woman warm, then sitting down next to her on the bench and putting an arm around her. Selaine clung to her instinctively, like a child. "She'll be fine by tonight. More than fine. I've found that touching and escaping our world makes the living appreciate the lives they have all the more."

"One would think it would resign them to the inevitable."

The Witness smiled. "Not even we are so universally enlightened. You remember how our reluctant watchdog all but foreswore his Exaltation begging for his life. I find it charming to see common mortals express such sentiments."

"Yes, but you're very strange," the Visitor teased in a flat voice. "You bring up a good point, though. I left our watchdog posted outside Kerrek's estate. I should probably contact him and have him spirit your doting dilettante here before we start making preparations for the summoning."

"No," the Witness sighed. "It's too risky to bring Deset here now. The inopportune arrival of Chaisa's young friend last night probably caused quite a commotion in Bastion, and I suspect the Council's mercenaries will be poring over the area very soon. They won't let Deset out of their sight, and the more they talk to him, the more likely he'll come to reveal our goals here. I can't express how galling it would be for him to draw that much attention to us now."

"I suppose you're right," the Visitor said. "The local Salmalin will be here soon. It wouldn't do to have them bringing Stalwart Mastiff's former compatriots with them because of something the Guildsman said."

"Indeed. I'm afraid poor Deset is too much of a liability now. We need to make sure he doesn't have the chance to expose us. He needs to be silenced, and his records relating to this project need to be destroyed. Do you think our reluctant watchdog can handle that? Is he clever enough, and willing?"

The Visitor nodded. "He and that girl found us before we knew they were looking. I think he can handle this. I'll go to him and see that he's willing."

"Good. Then have him come back here. I want him near us but out of the way when the ritual begins."

"Fine," the Visitor said, turning to leave. "And while I'm gone, you take care of that piteous wretch. Shock or not, if something happens to her now…"

The Witness smiled. "Yes, how unfortunate that would be. Don't worry, I'll take care of her and have her ready before the sun goes down. By midnight, she'll be ready to help us welcome the new year and change the lives of every breathing soul in Nexus."

"Not just Nexus," the Visitor said over his shoulder as he walked away. "We're going to shake the entire River Province to its bedrock. First here and Mishaka, then Sijan and Lookshy. Soon, our master's shadowlands will stretch from the Ebon Spires of Pyrron to the Inland Sea, unbroken."

"Of course," the Witness said. "But until then, we operate one night at a time. The Walker in Darkness rewards foresight, not farsightedness."

Slipping into the shadows in the distance, the Visitor only bowed his head, shrugged and spread his hands.

Harmonious Jade did not return to the Bronze Tigers' compound until late the next afternoon—the fourth day of Calibration. She had spent most of the previous night looping around and switching back through the celebrant-crowded streets of Nexus to convince herself she had not been followed downhill from the Bastion district after she'd left Kerrek Deset's manor. As dawn approached, she'd needed food and time at rest to work the Visitor's needle-poison out of her system, and as she went about procuring these things, she worked herself into a meditative trance to center and calm herself. Only when she was sure she was safe had she drifted off to sleep, and she'd slept much longer than she'd intended. She was fully refreshed when she finally woke up, though, so she'd replaced her lost arrows, eaten a late breakfast and headed across town to meet Dace.

When she arrived, she found the place to be a hive of activity. Annoyed Tigers went about daily exercises and security patrols, glaring at a host of outsiders who scurried back and forth across the compound's parade ground between buildings. Those outsiders ranged from curious civilians to auxiliary personnel from other mercenary companies all over Cinnabar to actual mercenaries in full uniform. They seemed civil enough, but they were constantly underfoot and seemed to be a distracting nuisance to the Bronze Tigers. Jade wondered why the Tigers didn't just shove everybody out and lock the gates rather than putting up with all of this.

For the moment, though, all the confused activity worked in Jade's favor, and she slipped in among a group of noisy bravos as they approached the Bronze Tigers' main gate. She stayed near the back among the stragglers, doing her best not to draw attention to herself. When the guards at the gate stopped the leader of the group—a blond-haired boulder of a man who looked like he should be wrestling demitaurs in the frozen North—Jade stopped with them then followed them in as if she were one of the group. When she was past the guards, she broke off from the others and poked around on her own for a few minutes to find out what all the fuss was about.

By discreetly listening to a few conversations, Jade found out that most of the civilians were accountants and appraisers working on behalf of both the Council of Entities and the Guild. They were recording the dimensions of the compound and taking notes on the condition of its walls and various standing structures. A few were taking soil samples for reasons that defied Jade's powers of deduction. The rest of the civilians were conducting what appeared to be a detailed inventory of the Bronze Tigers' armory and supply stores. A handful of men and women were even scurrying around in the cavalry stables, inspecting the horses with all the care and circumspection of professional livestock breeders. Approximately half of the members of the disparate groups of mercenary auxiliary personnel were following these investigating civilians around, acting as consultants.

Jade knew from prior conversations with Dace that his company had to put up with certain strictures and curtailments that the Council had imposed, but all this obstructive bureaucracy seemed like a bit much nonetheless. She found it strange that Dace would allow it to go on. She found even stranger the presence of so many mercenaries from so many rival companies. They weren't talking to Dace's men or helping their auxiliary consultants pester the civilian inspectors. Mostly, the soldiers were just wandering around the Bronze Tigers' compound and looking it over like real estate speculators. In a way that touched the most ancient part of Jade's soul, it was sad to see a fellow Exalt forced to put up with such a hassle just to find a place in this deteriorated world. And not just sad, but galling as well. This world had belonged to the Solars once, and they had made it a paradise. What right did anyone have to usurp and tear down the legacy the Chosen of the Unconquered Sun had created?

Jade closed her eyes and took a deep breath to clear her head. These moments of outrage and betrayal came upon her sometimes when she least expected them. They rose like bubbles from the sunken depths of her First Age soul and grew by accretion as she dwelled on similar circumstances in her present life. She found them to be increasingly common distractions when she was not focusing on some piece of business, which was probably the second most unfortunate side effect of her Exaltation. They were easy enough to deal with, though. All she usually had to do, as she did now, was clear her mind and remind herself who she was in this life and what she was supposed to be doing. The only times when that didn't work was when she was lying down to rest or she was bored and had nothing with which to take her mind off those persistent distractions. Fortunately, now was not such a time. She had plenty of actual work to do, and she was running late.

Having partially satisfied her curiosity about the activity at the compound and now forced herself to concentrate on the task at hand, Jade set about trying to find either Dace or his Dragon-Blooded snob of a lieutenant. She didn't see either officer out on the parade ground itself, so she slipped over to the exercise pavilion and stood next to the soldier who looked the oldest. Some twenty-five of Dace's men were exercising at the moment, either sparring with rattan weapons or training in unarmed combat, and the activity had drawn a small crowd of eager spectators. Jade had to squeeze and elbow her way between several loud, obnoxious mercenary onlookers until she'd reached the edge of the sandpit and found the soldier who appeared to be nominally in charge of this training session. He was watching two men fighting with blunted short swords and long, curved shields— more specifically, he was yelling at them for sloppy defense and footwork—and he didn't even turn around when Jade approached and asked where Dace and Risa were.

"Cap'n Dace ain't available," the man growled. "If you want the Lieutenant… Wait, hang on a minute. Hawk, I told you a hun'red times! When his blade gets between your shields, trap it and hack his shoulder! Now get it right!" He glanced back toward Jade as the soldiers went after each other again. "Sorry. What'd you want? Lieutenant Risa? She's in the meetin' already."

"The meeting?"

"Yeah, over in Admin'," the soldier said. Then, "Damn it, Hawk, what'd I *just* say? Since you don't wanna use your shield right, jus' put it down and go a round without it! And if you don't score first hit, it's twenty laps 'round the wall!"

"So, she's in a meeting?" Jade asked.

"Yeah, lady, the meetin'," the soldier barked. "Can't you see I'm busy here? Plannin' room, admin' buildin'. But if you're invited you're already late, so run along and get outta my— Hey, ha-ha! Good one, Tarsus! Didn't like that, did you, Hawk? D'you learn somethin'? Good! Now get up and gimme your laps!"

As onlookers cheered or jeered the outcome of the fight like bettors at the pit arena downtown, Jade drifted away. She headed for the administration building in the center of the compound, dodging a few pushy inspectors and stepping aside for a work detail of Bronze Tigers. Inside, she found even more civilian aides and busybodies milling around in the halls, most of whom were scribbling on notepads about what was happening all around them. She asked one of them where "the meeting" was, and the man she asked pointed her toward the same planning room where she'd spoken alone to Dace her first night here. At just about the same time, those doors opened and more than a dozen people came out, gathering up their aides and talking excitedly on their way back outside. Several of them were mercenary captains, others were either Council clerks or Guildsmen, and the rest were Hooded Executioners of fairly high rank. Risa was not among those leaving, though, so Jade forced her way upstream against them and entered the planning room. Risa was just dismissing one of her own sergeants as Jade entered. The sergeant stopped Jade at the door, but Risa told him to let her in. Jade then closed the door behind the enlisted man so she could talk to Dace's lieutenant alone.

"Where's Dace?" she asked.

"Well hi there," Risa said, not bothering to rise from her chair at the end of the room's long table. "It's great to see you too. Me? Oh, I'm fine, but let's not get into that right now. Let's just get straightaway to business."

Jade only looked at the Dragon-Blood without saying a word.

"Okay, fine," Risa said with a deep sigh. "Captain Dace can't talk right now. Why don't you take a seat? Maybe there's something I can help you with."

Jade sat down opposite Risa and laid her powerbow in front of her on the table. In the lamplight, she could see that the Dragon-Blood had a surprising haggard roughness around the edges. She wore no armor, and her uniform was wrinkled as if she'd slept in it. Her long hair hung loose all around her shoulders rather than being bound up in the tight braid it was usually in, and it had a slightly oily sheen as if she'd been combing her fingers through it for hours. Her skin retained the flawless, ageless quality that came with being a Terrestrial Exalt, but her fatigue and frustration were plain to see in her eyes and the set of her mouth. Even the way Risa sat in her chair all hunched over with her arms on the table signaled an overbearing weariness in her. She looked as if she'd been up all night with a stomach flu.

"So, what's the matter?" Jade asked. "Why can't Dace talk now?"

"He isn't available," Risa said.

"Why not?"

"No, it's my turn now. How'd you get in?"

Jade shrugged. "You mean through your watertight security? I just walked through the front gate. You've got quite a thriving mess out there. Do those raitons always start circling when a rival captain isn't available to scare them off?"

"Not usually," Risa said wearily. "These are special circumstances. They're here at the Council's invitation. It seems we're being shut down and asked to leave the city. And since we haven't finished paying off what we owe on this property, the Council's filed a lien. They're putting it up for auction in the Big Market the day after Calibration's over."

"Why? What happened?"

"The Captain caused a little bit of a disturbance last night looking into this conspiracy you brought to his attention. Maybe you noticed if you were outside. He turned the night bright as day for a while there."

Jade nodded, remembering the brilliance she'd seen rising from within Cinnabar as she'd left Kerrek Deset's estate. "So, how'd it go? How many of Stalwart Mastiff's men did he have to kill?"

"It was nothing like that," Risa said. "Apparently, the Emissary himself showed up for the same reason the Captain was there. *He* killed Mastiff and most of his men. The survivors say the Captain was actually trying to stop him, and that's when things turned ugly."

Harmonious Jade just shook her head, trying not to roll her eyes.

"To hear witnesses tell it," Risa continued, not sharing in Jade's comical exasperation, "the two of them knocked half the Hooded Executioners' compound down fighting about it. Finally, at about dawn, a detachment of Executioners brought Dace's body back here on a litter and informed me the Captain's been charged with 'willful obstruction of the enforcement of the Incunabulum.' As punishment, the Council's decided to 'ask' us to leave the city, and it's calling in all our debts at once. Once we're out, it's quartering those Hooded Executioners here who were displaced when their barracks were damaged in the confusion. And it's calling that a merciful verdict based on extenuating circumstances." She slammed a fist down on the table. "Bastards!"

"Did you say they brought Dace's *body* back?" Jade asked.

"What?" Risa said, trying to get herself back under control. "Yes. No—his *unconscious* body, I meant. Sorry. Apparently, the Emissary decided just to let him off with a horsewhipping for getting in the way. He's resting now and putting himself back together."

"Is he going to be all right?"

"It's the fastest I've ever seen anyone recover from the state he was in, but it's still going to be days, maybe a week, before he's one-hundred percent again."

"Is he conscious?" Jade asked. "I really need to discuss this situation with him."

"I told you he's recovering," Risa said. "And frankly, I don't think there's anything left for you two to discuss. You've gotten him in deep enough manure already, don't you think?"

"I'm sure he wouldn't mind," Jade said, matching the steady rise in Risa's tone. "We've still got more Salmalin to round up before the end of tomorrow. Just in case."

"No," Risa said, half standing out of her chair. "The Council's aware of what's going on now, and it's handling it. It knows as much as you and Dace ever figured out, and probably more by now. This is its problem. Dace isn't getting back in it. He's got his soldiers to take care of and resettle. He's got to clean up the fallout from this mess you got him into."

"I got him into?" Jade said. "He should thank me for pointing all this out to him before it got out of hand."

Risa's eyes widened. "Meet the herald, Jade: It's already out of hand! All we have to thank you for is jumping to all the wrong conclusions and forcing Dace to take a bad road so you wouldn't take an even worse one."

"At least my way would have worked," Jade said, louder now. "Mastiff would be dead, Kerrek would be dead, Chaisa would be dead, and Dace and I both could have dealt with Walker's deathknights together. If he'd just listened to me—"

"You arrogant little brat!" Risa shouted. Her volume rose with every sentence, and she crossed the room now to shout down in Harmonious Jade's face. "Dace nearly got himself killed because he listened to you! He's sacrificed this entire company's reputation and position by listening to you! What do you want from him? Would you rather he just threw his honor out with the bedpans too? Would you rather the Emissary came here and slaughtered all of *us* because he thought Dace had had a rival mercenary captain assassinated? Maybe you'd rather the Emissary killed him for defending his own men here at this compound? That would have been just great!"

Jade had jumped to her feet and knocked her chair over as Risa came toward her, and she had a hand on her knife before she even realized she was reaching for it. How dare this woman—this *Dragon-Blood*—talk to her this way? She came within a hair's breadth of lashing out with all the ancient power inside her and striking the impudent Terrestrial down, but a last-moment impulse stayed her hand. Despite all her anger, it was a feeling of shame and self-doubt, the kind that had been beaten into her over all her years of training with the Salmalin. The kind that lay buried deep within her thanks to almost two decades of abuse. It made her flinch in the face of Risa's commanding anger and second-guess the judgment that had led her to this compound and entangled Dace in the pursuit of her personal vendetta.

The flash of doubt did not subsume her anger, but instead redirected it inward, and she backed down. She took a step away and snatched her powerbow from the table, making ready to leave.

"Fine," she sneered, no longer looking Risa in the eyes. "I hear what you're saying. When Dace recovers, tell him I'll take it from here myself. Tell him I already talked to Kerrek Deset like he wanted, so the only loose end left is the demon priestess I was looking for. I'll just deal with her and her deathknight partners on my own. I won't be back to trouble him anymore. Or you."

She slung her bow over her shoulder then and shoved past Risa on her way to the door. Still seething, Risa didn't try to stop her. She did speak up one last time before Jade disappeared, though, saying, "So, that's it? You're just going to walk out and do whatever you were already going to do anyway."

"I don't see why not," Jade said. "But before I go, there's something else I want you to tell Dace. Tell him I said thanks for his help and for taking what I told him seriously. Maybe I shouldn't have expected him to, but I'm glad he did. Tell him I'm sorry it didn't work out better."

"He's probably sorrier," Risa snapped. "But I'll pass your heartfelt gratitude along when he wakes up."

"Good." Jade put her hand on the doorknob to leave but hesitated one last time. "And one more thing, Dragon-Blood. Was it really you who stopped Dace from killing me when I first came here? Even after I attacked you."

Risa frowned and said, "Yes, it was."

"All right, just checking," Jade said, opening the door. "That's what Dace told me, but I didn't believe him."

Before Risa could say anything more, Jade left and closed the door behind her. Risa scowled and scrubbed her fingers through her hair, scratching her itchy scalp.

"All right," she said to the empty room. "I guess you're welcome."

A few minutes later, once the gate guards had confirmed that Harmonious Jade had stormed off to sulk somewhere, Risa made her way to Dace's private chambers to check on her captain. She found him sitting up on a mound of pillows in bed with the golden sunburst on his forehead glinting in the light that came in through the high, thin window. His armor and weapon were laid out within arm's reach of him on a wooden stand by the bed. He looked up when she came in and started to get out of bed, scowling in dull pain.

"What is it, Risa?" he grunted. "Something going on?"

"The usual, sir," she replied. "Just hold your horses, and stay in that bed. I only came in to check on you."

"I'm fine, and I want to know how things are going out there."

"Well enough, sir. I just held that conference you ordered. I rounded up the most likely prospective buyers for this place and gave them the official story about the Council's judgment. They'll put the blood in the water, and we ought to have quite a frenzy over the place once Calibration's through. We might just break even."

"How are the men taking the news?"

"They don't like it, but they're not complaining around the gadflies and speculators. They're carrying on as usual for the time being."

"Anybody wishing they hadn't broken their fang?"

"Not yet, sir," Risa said, trying to smile.

"How about you, Lieutenant? How are you holding up? You look like ten miles of bad road."

"Says the standard to the example. I've got it all under control for now, Captain. Don't worry about me."

"Even still," Dace said, pausing to cough up something and spit it in a pan by the bed. "You look like something's bothering you. Go on, and tell me what it is. I'd rather you have it out now than your attitude get out and infect the men."

"Yes, sir," Risa said with a sigh. "It's Beads. She was here a few minutes ago."

"Jade was here?" Dace asked, sitting up again. The motion made him wince and put a hand over his tightly wrapped ribs. "Did you tell her what happened?"

"I did."

"Was she upset?"

"Upset? No sir, not until I yelled at her and told her to get lost. After that, yes."

"I see. You realize that wasn't terribly—"

"I know, sir. I know. It was her bad timing plus my irritation. I think she deserved it, though."

"Surely," Dace said, unconvinced. "Where is she now?"

"Sulking? I'm not sure."

Dace sighed. "Did she leave? When's she going to report back?"

"She said she had some things she wanted to check out on her own. I figured she needed some time to settle down."

"How long? It's going to be nightfall soon."

"Probably another few hours, sir. It's not like she really has anywhere else to go or anybody else to contact in the city, right?"

"Did she at least say what she found out at our man's estate in Bastion last night?"

"Oh, that. She said she talked to him, but she made it sound like she killed him. I can ask around and see if anybody's heard anything specific. If she made a big enough mess there, somebody's bound to know."

"Sure. Do that, and let me know. And if Jade shows back up, bring her to see me this time. Provided I'm not up and around already by then."

"I'll bring her, sir," Risa said. "You heal fast, but you're still going to need a couple of days of straight rest. Better the men don't see or hear from you at all in this commotion than see you hobbling around and grimacing every time you take a deep breath."

"I know, Lieutenant. You don't have to remind me. I'll rest until my body's mended. You just keep everything in order out there and bring Jade in here when she shows back up."

"Yes, sir. I will."

Risa turned to leave then, but Dace stopped her at the door.

"Lieutenant," he said. "I know we're both what you'd call Anathema, Jade and me, but even still… She's a pretty damn strange girl, isn't she?"

"I wouldn't say that, sir," Risa said. "That's not the exact word I'd choose."

"Not strange?"

"Not *girl*."

Chapter Thirteen

True to Risa's prediction, Harmonious Jade did spend a few hours by herself on the streets of Nexus, more or less sulking as the sun sank in the west. She walked alone through Cinnabar from the mercenary neighborhoods to a block of art galleries and even onto the campus of a moderately sized college that she hadn't even realized shared the district with the likes of Dace or Stalwart Mastiff's compounds. Within the space of a few minutes strolling uphill, she was suddenly surrounded by people her own age dressed in genteel finery. The mercenary presence did not diminish, but the soldiers she saw now wore brightly polished armor, lounged at parade rest and spoke with a gentrified courtliness that was absent in the lower neighborhoods.

Jade spent the first several blocks grumbling to herself or glaring at strangers who sized her up a little too obviously, but eventually, her simmering anger at Risa and at herself grew quiescent. The two of them had both been right about what they'd said, and they'd both had reason to be short with each other, so there was nothing for it now but for Jade to let the matter drop and not go out of her way to keep stirring the antagonism.

That decision didn't make the anger go away, of course, so Jade kept walking, hoping to lose herself for a while until she felt better. She had learned the layout of the main streets fairly well since her arrival, so she just let her feet carry her while her thoughts drifted into some sort of order. This sort of thing had certainly been easier back at the Salmalin compound in the Southern desert. Jade remembered confining herself to her cell for hours on end either meditating or memorizing prayers to the Yozis. If she ever got bored, she could exercise alone or train with her many instructors or the other acolytes like her. There was no time to nurse personal grudges or nagging irritation when she had so much training to do.

And when she wasn't training, she was doing the work the Salmalin had trained her for—namely committing murder in the Yozis' names. She could spend days on end in intensive study of her targets' behaviors and security practices, then spend up to a week crawling around her targets' home cities looking for obscure lines of approach, wide firing lanes and convenient escape routes. As she had been taught, she could focus her mind to her task and allow nothing to infringe. Whenever she finished an assignment, she made her reports to Sahan and any other elders who wanted to hear, then she returned to her cell with no praise or accolades. Such rewards were never granted, as she was only doing what was required of her. She never ended a mission content in her pride or eager to look ahead to the next job—she simply meditated and waited and did as she was told without thinking too hard about any of it. That was the way she had grown up, so she had never been especially creative or prone to distraction.

After leaving the Salmalin and relocating in Chiaroscuro, she had come by this habit of walking alone among crowds of people. The jostling of moving bodies and the economy of personal space she found in a milling throng reminded her of the few comfortable aspects of life in the hidden Salmalin fortress. What's more, the sounds and the sights and the smells of large numbers of people living their lives among one another filled up Jade's senses and distracted her from the persistent questions that nagged at her—or, as now, the irritation that dealing with frustrating, intractable people so often spawned.

Perhaps best of all, she overheard and learned things while she walked that gave her ideas of what normal life in a free city was like. She heard the way people spoke to one another in friendship, in commerce, in reverence and in disdain, and she learned to emulate those patterns when she found herself in similar situations. She watched the way people treated their children, and she wondered how strange her life would have been if her own mother and father had behaved that way rather than selling her into slavery as an infant. Sometimes, as she walked, she paid particular attention to young lovers and old married companions. The affection they showed tended to embarrass her and make her feel guilty for noticing (especially where lovers her own age were concerned), but it provided the best distraction. It inspired her to wonder what it would have been like if Sahan had treated her that way, or if Zeroun had. Or the Disciple of the Seven Forbidden Wisdoms…

In Nexus as in Chiaroscuro, though, there was only so much social immersion Jade could stand. Eventually, the press of the crowds would evolve from a pleasing distraction to an oppressive bother, and she'd have to slip away and take to the rooftops. One of the drawbacks of going among common people and watching how they acted, it turned out, was that you couldn't help but see people at their worst. Every now and then, people proved themselves to be just as petty and insular and obstinate as the Salmalin among whom she had grown up had been. They expected too much from their peers and not enough from themselves, and they took unavoidable inconveniences as personal insults. They leered at each other or treated each other like livestock or did their best to ignore the people standing all around them at arms' length, sometimes alternately within the space of a minute. The more she walked and observed city people living their normal lives, the more she usually became convinced that "normal" life wasn't necessarily any better than the life she'd had growing up. And when she began to think like that, she could hear the insistent voices of her multitude of unanswerable questions growing louder, which brought her full circle to where she began.

Such was the case now, and she could feel her irritation with Dace's lieutenant being subsumed by a greater irritation with humanity in general. That tended to happen regularly when she went on walks to clear her head. The sensation signaled to her that she had been lost in her own thoughts for too long and that she had begun to neglect her larger responsibilities. For instance, she could be returning to Kerrek Deset's Bastion manor right now and completing the job she'd left unfinished last night. She thought she probably ought to do that before she went back into the Undercity to find and finish off Selaine Chaisa. After all, if Chaisa had been working with Kerrek, perhaps the Guildsman could give her some idea of what they two had been working on and what surprises might be in store. Regardless, even if he had fled town in the night or been killed by his own nemissaries as a liability, checking out his estate would at least give her something to do. It didn't always work, but sometimes, that cleared her head more effectively than taking long walks and fantasizing about what might have been.

So, having calmed the worst of her anger at Risa and suppressed the rest, Jade slipped into an alley away from the press of the milling throng and headed for the nearest rooftop to make her way back uphill toward Bastion. Now that night had finally fallen, she was in her element once again, and she felt she could safely get back to work.

Perhaps not unexpectedly, Harmonious Jade found Kerrek Deset's estate even more of an upset anthill than Dace's compound had been that afternoon. A mercenary peacekeeping guard of Hooded Executioners had been posted at the boundary of Kerrek's property to keep anyone inside from getting out, and several detachments of mercenaries were poring over the property. Dozens of civilians ranging in age from fourteen to more than fifty years old had been rounded up outside the manor house in the front courtyard, and none of them looked happy. They were being clapped into shackles and carried away by the wagonload by yet more mercenaries, presumably to interrogate them about what had gone on the previous night. These civilians wore identical liveries—the insignias on which matched those on the flags over the manor's main doors—and Jade remembered them as Kerrek's house staff. Jade assumed that all these people were being arrested on suspicion of being Salmalin cultists like their master, but it was just as likely that they were suspected of discovering their master's involvement in the cult and rising up to murder him. Either way, Jade didn't envy them their upcoming incarceration and questioning. She also winced to see gangs of mercenaries from smaller companies swaggering up and down the block, either chasing unescorted servants back to their homes or banging on doors and dragging people outside to answer questions about Kerrek's behavior and business practices of late. Jade had not seen evidence of this, but she presumed that the same thing was happening to Kerrek's business partners, to his friends and to anyone who shared a connection to Stalwart Mastiff with him. Not to mention what Mastiff's friends and family must be going through as the Council's agents rushed to make up for their preceding laxity...

As Jade sat thinking about these things, a man exited the main door of Kerrek's manor wearing a black outfit with two rows of three red spots each down the front of his chest and red at his cuffs, collar and boot tops. He wore red gloves as well, and as he turned slightly to approach the soldier in charge of crowd control, Jade could see what might have been an eight-rayed red sunburst on his back. That design wasn't actually a sunburst, though, but the company insignia of the Stalking Spiders mercenary company. Jade had heard stories about the Stalking Spiders even as far away as Chiaroscuro. They devoted their time and expertise to tracking down and bringing to justice local murderers, and they collected handsome bounties from the Council of Entities for doing so. Some people claimed that the Spiders could stand blindfolded in the middle of a room where a murder had taken place and deduce characteristics about the perpetrator of the act that even stone-sober witnesses had missed. Others claimed that the Spiders were nothing but ancestor-worshipers who called in favors with their dearly departed to arrange for interviews with the victims' spirits.

Regardless, the Stalking Spiders were well-trained and highly capable inspectors and bounty hunters, and the fact that someone had called on them was an unwelcome inconvenience. It likely meant one of three things. Either Kerrek Deset had used his influence to have them track down the murderer of several of his servants, his Guild associates had called on them to investigate the murders, or the Council's agents had hired the Spiders to summon and interrogate the ghosts of the slain. Watching the scene from high up on the side of a night-shadowed marble aqueduct, Jade gritted her teeth and cursed her luck. She wasn't worried that the Spiders would capture her—or even so much as attribute the crime to her—but she had to get inside the manor house and look around for a while, and doing that was going to be complicated with people snooping around.

Of course, if she'd come straight here instead of Dace's place—or if she'd stayed last night to make sure the job was done in the first place—she wouldn't have this problem. Kerrek would be dead, she would have all his personal files and secret notes, and she could be discussing the results of what she'd found with Dace. Or rather, with Risa, since Dace had decided that honor and civil nobility was better than results and expediency. She bet the old captain wished he could go back to last night and change his mind on that subject right about now. Probably about as much as she wished she could go back to last night and do things right herself.

But no, the past was the past, and it profited a mind nothing to wish otherwise. That was something Sahan had taught her, and although most of what he had said had been half-truths or outright lies, that sentiment still spoke to her sometimes. She took it to heart now as she cloaked herself in shadow and set forth to finish the job she'd come here to finish. She hopped from her high perch to the top of the boundary wall of the estate, well above the heads of the Hooded Executioners who'd been stationed at the perimeter outside. She waited in silence for an inspection patrol to pass under her, then she hopped down behind them and followed them back toward the manor.

When she neared the manor house, she separated from the patrol and scaled the wall to Kerrek Deset's bedroom balcony. She climbed fast, improvising foot- and handholds on ivy, window frames, cornice embellishments and the building's quoins, and she was perched on the balcony rail in seconds. When she reached this vantage, she heard noises coming from inside, so she squatted on her haunches and waited.

Watching through the open bay window, she saw a tall Stalking Spider standing in the center of the disarrayed room and lecturing a smaller, less severely dressed adjutant who was taking notes. The one talking seemed to have a pretty good idea that a fight had taken place in this room and that at least one of the participants had escaped out the window and onto the lawn. Neither he nor his assistant, though, knew what to make of the fact that although at least three other people had been in the room, all traces of them indicated that they had not so much left as disappeared. Even stranger—though less so to Jade than to the Stalking Spiders—was the fact that the day servants reported finding six corpses in a rough heap outside the bedroom doors with no discernable wounds on them. They'd also found another half dozen downstairs who'd been either burned or shot with arrows. Jade recognized those corpses as the discarded shells of the nemissaries she had faced, though there was no particular reason the Stalking Spider would draw that conclusion.

Regardless, Jade credited the Spider's quick deductive wit, even though he obviously had no idea what had really happened. The man had a sharp eye for detail, and he was doing very well simply pointing out the facts and trying to base a theory on them, rather than trying to interpret the facts in light of a pet theory as a less experienced inspector might do. Although he likely knew very little about the abilities of an Exalt—and probably knew even less about deathknights' capabilities than Jade did—he had a decent grasp of what had happened in this room. Yet, there was only so much he could learn from the evidence here, so he and his assistant made to leave the room and continue their investigation. As they did, being very careful to disturb as little of the scene as possible, the Spider said something that made Jade's ears perk up. He asked where Kerrek's body was, to which his assistant responded with the location of the downstairs office.

The fact that Kerrek had been killed intrigued her, and she knew then that she had to get inside to find out more. She appreciated not having to sneak through all these mercenaries and servants to kill Kerrek herself, but she didn't like not having him to interrogate about what the local Salmalin were planning. She hadn't done the deed, and neither Chaisa nor the deathknights had had the opportunity, so that left two options in Jade's mind. The most likely one was that one of the nemissaries she had had such trouble dispatching had come down to where Kerrek was hiding and killed him to keep him from becoming a liability, before returning to the Underworld.

A more tantalizing possibility was that Selaine Chaisa had activated a sleeper Salmalin agent in the city and ordered him to kill Kerrek for secrecy's sake. If that were the case, it meant that not only had Chaisa long since seeded cells of the faithful here in Nexus, but she had arranged for the training of at least one Janissary of the Faithful Elite—the rank Jade herself had held before her Exaltation. If that were the case, the killer might have left clues at the scene that even a rigorous inspection by the local mercenaries would miss, but which an examination by a peer would reveal. Jade knew that if she could find something the Stalking Spiders didn't, she might be able to track down the

Salmalin killer herself and follow him to Chaisa, rather than having to trek down into the Undercity and wait to see if and where the priestess showed back up.

Therefore, she stole in through Kerrek's bedroom window and followed the Stalking Spider inspector down to the basement. The Unconquered Sun's power cloaked her from sight and banished her sound and scent, yet she still took mundane precautions against detection. She stepped only in the Stalking Spider's footprints in the carpet and kept from stepping in any of the blood on the floor in the hallway. She stayed in the shadows and waited until the lesser inspectors crowding the house were not looking her way before she passed close to them. In this manner, she made her way undetected to Kerrek Deset's basement office and slipped in behind the inspector and his assistant. As she followed them, she gleaned from ambient conversation that the inspector's name was Erra Chelis and the adjutant's name was Layton.

The room was more or less as she had left it the night before, except that, where she had left Kerrek alive and cowering and reeking of his own urine, the Guildsman now lay slumped against the wall with a hole through his throat. Another hole had been punched in the wall at neck height, deeply enough and shaped such as to suggest that an arrow had done the damage, though oddly, there was no arrow to be found. There was very little blood on the front of Kerrek's body or on the wall behind him, indicating that the missing projectile had killed him almost instantly. Jade could tell that much from training and experience, but she was interested to see what more the Stalking Spider might make of it.

Erra took a long look around the room, turning in a slow circle, then he began to point out details to his assistant. Layton wrote down what his superior said without question, offering no comment or other distraction.

"Note first, Layton," the Spider said, "although the deceased has voided his bladder, as is to be expected in the moments following death, the urine stain on the carpet is not directly under his body."

"I'm aware of that now, sir," Layton said, as his last step squelched in the wet carpet. His superior's shadow had concealed the puddle until it was too late.

"I see," Erra said. "Stand where you are for the moment, then. Don't track that around any more than it has been already."

"Yes, sir," Layton sighed.

"Furthermore, note these scuffs and the indented tracks in the carpet under this desk," Erra went on. "The desk had been moved around very recently."

"All the locks on all the desk and cabinet drawers are unlocked too," Layton added.

"Yes. You've, no doubt, noticed how the wall safe has been left open as well."

Layton murmured assent, dividing his attention between his notepad and his boots.

"These facts lead me to deduce that the primary crime that was intended here was not murder but robbery. Kerrek probably surprised his attacker in the attempt, which likely frightened the daylights out of him."

"And the juice," Layton murmured under his breath.

"Then," Erra continued, oblivious, "only in the ensuing mayhem and bloodshed was the killer able to escape. This crime escalated in severity very quickly as he, more than likely, found obstacles and resistance at every turn. It smacks of desperation. I doubt very much he expected to be caught or forced to fight his way to temporary freedom."

"Plus, it's Calibration," Layton replied. "That probably didn't help focus the killer's mind any. So, what do you make of him, then? Can you tell anything about him?"

"I'm not certain," he said, which echoed Jade's thoughts on the subject. "The downward angle of the arrow-hole in the wall suggests that the killer was tall, and Kerrek's fear stain on the floor suggests that the attacker was quite an imposing figure. Yet, the only identifiable footprints left in the thick carpet were Kerrek's and a smaller set that could only have belonged to a woman or a teenage boy."

"Strange."

"What's even more strange is the fact that this arrow-hole is different from the others we've seen elsewhere in the house. It was made by a three-pronged, serrated arrowhead, whereas all the others we've retrieved have been flat heads with razor-straight edges."

"And there's the fact that we can't find the arrow that did the deed, while the other kind of arrows are all over the place," Layton added. Jade winced thinking about the litter she'd strewn across the mansion.

"It's possible that more than one robber was at work here, each using a different type of arrow," Erra said, "but that doesn't dovetail with the evidence in the master bedroom. There, one person was taking on three assailants, none of whom were using this type of arrowhead."

"Maybe there was more than one robber and they all turned on each other after they killed Kerrek and his servants," Layton said. "Maybe they went to the bedroom to find a hidden safe and get out while they still could, but the pressure and excitement was all too much for them. They started arguing, then one thing led to another…"

"Stop it, Layton," Erra said, walking away and scrubbing his eyes with his long fingers. "You're speculating when I should be hypothesizing. Don't cloud my judgment with your chatter."

The inspector's adjutant glowered and said, "Sorry, sir. So, what is your hypothesis, then?"

"As yet, I don't have one that encompasses all the facts," Erra admitted. "We should look around the house and talk to the sequestered servants again. I'm missing something here that another round of inspection might rectify."

"I'd be glad to start over again," Layton said, "if it means I don't have to stand in this anymore."

"Stand in… Ah, yes, of course." Erra took a long handkerchief from his pocket and handed it to his adjutant. "Here, clean your sole with this, but don't dispose of it on the premises. You'll contaminate the state of the evidence."

Layton did as Erra asked while the inspector waited then tried to give back the handkerchief. Erra refused with a moue of disgust and told his adjutant to consider it a gift, then he left the room to inspect the higher floors. Grumbling to himself, Layton stuffed the handkerchief into a deep coat pocket and followed Erra.

When they were gone, Jade counted backward and forward to thirty to make sure that no one else was coming right away, then she crossed the room to Kerrek's body. She almost pitied the man as he lay there, undignified in his urine-stained robe, a slack gape of terror forever on his face. If his soul had not gone on to the great cycle of reincarnation, his ghost was likely cowering in shame over the ignominious fate he had suffered. Yet, this fate was better than what Kerrek deserved, Jade had to tell herself. After all, the man was a Yozi-worshiping Salmalin conspirator who'd unrepentantly done the work of the cult and subsidized its activities for gods knew how long. If there was any justice in the afterlife, Kerrek's Yozi masters were using his soul for kite string right now.

As for the physical state of Kerrek's body, Jade could tell no more than the Stalking Spider inspector had. She was fairly certain, however, that the murder hadn't been a Salmalin job. It wasn't the cult's style to sneak all the way into someone's house past all his guards and servants, only to shoot him at point-blank range with an arrow, then *remove* that arrow after the fact. For that sort of personal, upfront killing, the Salmalin were expected to use a knife, a needle, a garrote or their bare hands. They considered the bow a weapon of secrecy or expediency. It was probably just one of the nemissaries, then, who had done this deed, likely digging out some hunting equipment Kerrek had stored on the premises. For that matter, it might have even been a living servant who just wanted revenge for some past slight and had taken the opportunity to exact it before notifying the authorities about the rest of the carnage. Stranger things had happened, and rich people tended to accrue enemies from every station in life.

Regardless, Jade didn't find any professional calling cards that were going to lead her to Chaisa. She remembered that Kerrek had kept records and maps detailing his involvement in various Undercity development projects, but she couldn't find any of those now either. They weren't where she'd left them, and Kerrek's various hiding places had been cleaned out down to the dust. Whoever had killed him had apparently stolen or destroyed his records too. Not that Jade especially needed them, but she would have liked to find something incriminating to give Dace so that he could hand it over to the Council's agents. If he could have used it to prove a connection between Mastiff and the Salmalin, it might have helped him preserve his station in the eyes of the Council somehow if he could use it the right way. It didn't matter now, of course, but it would have been nice.

When the sound of footsteps coming down the stairs reached her through the open door, Jade reluctantly gave up on the room and decided to make her exit. There wasn't anything else she could do in here now, and the longer she lingered, the less time she would have later on to follow her remaining solid lead on Chaisa down into the Undercity. She dodged the inspector coming down the stairs and slipped out into the shadows of the grand foyer on the main level.

Her plan now was to check the rest of the manor as quickly and discreetly as she could for any other caches of records or damning evidence Kerrek might have been squirreling away. She didn't hold out much hope of finding anything especially helpful, but the only other course of action open to her was to make her way back to the forgotten caverns of the Undercity and wait to see what would happen. And while that seemed like the most reasonable course of action from a tactical standpoint, Jade could not force herself to take it right away. She was not consciously stalling, exactly, but in the back of her mind, she knew very well that wandering into those ruins without knowing what waited for her had almost cut short her life once already. What's more, it very likely *had* cost the Disciple of the Seven Forbidden Wisdoms his life, and that only because he had recognized something in her from long ago and had chosen to help her achieve her personal vendetta. They hardly knew each other, yet he'd thrown himself to the lions for her sake so she could carry on her sacred mission. The idea disturbed her in a way she couldn't name. Therefore, she had no intention of going back to the place where that had happened until she had exhausted every other option she could conceive of in the short term.

Not even the Yozis themselves could force her to do that.

CHAPTER FOURTEEN

"So, you destroyed them all?" the Visitor in the Hall of Obsidian Mirrors asked his reluctant watchdog, who now knelt before him. "You destroyed all of Kerrek Deset's secret records and the Undercity maps he made?"

The watchdog glared and said nothing, but he nodded.

"And you killed him, as I asked?"

"I did," the watchdog grumbled.

"And the local authorities? They're still in the dark?"

"They don't know anything," the watchdog said. "My rash, ill-conceived oath to you notwithstanding, I still have certain stylistic standards. I left no clue to my presence or to your involvement. Local inspectors won't be able to separate my one crime from Harmonious Jade's many."

"Yes, Jade," the Visitor said, scratching his neck with a finger. "She's provided a useful screen, hasn't she? All the same, I haven't liked leaving her out there to stray all day. I don't get the impression she has the good sense to go to ground and leave the city after what she's done."

"I wouldn't worry about her," the watchdog offered, perhaps too eagerly. "She has no more leads. Her only connections to what you're planning lay in Stalwart Mastiff and Kerrek Deset, and they're both dead. The only other place she knows to look is the place she last entered and exited the Undercity with me, and if she'd chosen to use it, we would have noticed by now. If you must, you can forestall her further interference by simply collapsing the roof of that tunnel. Then, with no place left to go, she can run around like a mindless child until it's too late to bother you."

The Visitor smiled and held up a finger in mock reproach. "Your words make it easy to trust you, Disciple, though I know I can't. But what you say has some merit nonetheless. That girl does know where we are, and she does know how to reach us, if only by that one route." He paused a moment to think, then said, "I want you to wait out here in the first open cavern off that tunnel. Then, I want you to lay a trap to spring on her when she comes here. As a matter of fact, I want you to keep her well away from where the ritual is taking place and prevent her from interfering any further. Will you do these things?"

The Disciple of the Seven Forbidden Wisdoms glowered. "You know I must do as I'm oathbound. Still, I'm confused about one thing. When you say keep Jade away and prevent her from interfering, does that mean you just want me to stall her? Did you and your partner have something special in mind for her after your ritual is complete? Or does that Yozi-worshiping… *woman?*"

"No, I was merely being tactful."

"So, you're telling me to kill her?" the Disciple said, crestfallen. "You're commanding it."

"Yes," the Visitor said. "You swore to do as I say, so I'm telling you now to kill her."

The Disciple lowered his eyes and looked away. "I'd rather not. I'd rather have let you kill me instead when you had the chance."

"Be that as it may," the Visitor said, "you weren't ready to face Oblivion then, remember? Your faith was too weak. Some day, perhaps, you'll thank me for giving you more time to bolster your waning conviction. Your master certainly will—provided he doesn't destroy you outright for your cowardice in the face of death. And provided, of course, I ever allow you to return to him."

"Of course," the Disciple said, balling his hands into fists and speaking through gritted teeth.

"Now, go do as I've asked," the Visitor said, smiling at the Disciple's obvious discomfort. "Great things are at hand, and I'm needed within. And just to reiterate our earlier bargain, I'll ask you again not to interfere. The Walker in Darkness would take that very poorly indeed, and I know he won't be as merciful with you as I was."

"I understand," the Disciple said. "I won't interfere. Now, if I may be excused…"

"Very well," the Visitor said. "You are dismissed."

The Disciple turned and left, practically trembling with shame and rage, and the Visitor smiled to see it. It pleased him to no end that the brash, young Exalt had brought his current misfortune upon himself. If he had only been firmer in his faith, he could have died with his dignity intact, and his Exalted essence could have gone forward to the next worthier servant. As it was, he would play out his usefulness to a master not his own in a service he obviously found deplorable, and then, he would die anyway. Maybe his Deathlord deserved some of the blame for not vetting out his deathknights more carefully, but ultimately, the Disciple of the Seven Forbidden Wisdoms' cowardice was responsible for his forthcoming ignominious fate. The Visitor in the Hall of Obsidian Mirrors appreciated the justice inherent in that.

Now, having dealt with that trifle, he navigated the dark maze of the Undercity ruins and made his way back to the unearthed temple where the Witness of Lingering Shadows, Selaine Chaisa and the recently arrived Salmalin cultists were waiting. His personal participation in the ritual would not be required until after the stroke of midnight when the Witness of Lingering Shadows breached the barrier between Creation and the Elsewhere of Malfeas, but he felt he shouldn't miss too much of the ceremony leading up to that point. Some might consider that impolite.

After several minutes walking, he approached the lantern-lit area bounded on two sides by stone and rubble, with a mausoleum on one end and a large, ornately decorated temple on the other. The walls of that temple disappeared into the rubble that served still as Nexus' foundation, hinting at just how large the building buried here was, and oil lanterns hung from a pair of sconces on either side of the enormous doors. Two guards stood under the hanging lanterns, both wearing grotesquely demonic porcelain masks and red uniforms chased in green. They stood at rigid attention, each holding a spear in one hand and resting the other hand on a belt-slung, short-hafted ax. They peered intently at the Visitor as he approached, and they lifted their spears out of his way so he could pass.

Beyond that door lay an enormous, dimly lit antechamber decorated in faded frescoes and bas-relief sculptures of figures now lost to time. A set of modern-looking wood and brass double doors led into the main sanctuary chamber, and the sound of chanting was filtering this way from inside. On either end of this room, two darkened portals gave way to stone steps that led up to the mezzanine level above the sanctuary on one side and down to a lower chamber on the other.

In the center of this room was a long table covered in stacks of at least twenty neatly folded outfits. The clothes were all modern and cut in familiar Nexus styles, and they crossed boundaries of class and district. The Visitor had greeted the adherents to the Salmalin faith who had arrived wearing these clothes, and he had been surprised by how broad an appeal Yozi-worship had in Nexus. It seemed the young, old, rich, poor, male, female, healthy and sickly could all be persuaded to worship the demon princes of Malfeas. The Visitor headed for the mezzanine stairway.

A few minutes later, he stood at the edge of an interior balcony in this converted Yozi sanctuary, watching the Salmalin priestess, Selaine Chaisa, perform for her eager audience. The chamber was circular in design with a raised dais in the center and rings of benches radiating back to the walls. Halfway up the inner wall hung a circular balcony with a short stone rail carved in the shape of a vine-wrapped lattice. Four doors, with accompanying stairways, led into this sanctuary—one from each of the cardinal directions.

The ceiling was a dizzying mosaic of either colored glass or precious gems. Every wall the Visitor could see was hung with Southern-style tapestries that Selaine had brought with her, which venerated certain Yozi princes and captured the scenes of carnage that the demon lords would most like to wreak upon Creation once they were set free.

The Visitor watched Selaine Chaisa striding back and forth addressing the acolytes who filled the first two rows of benches. She orbited an object in the center of the dais that was either a water fountain of some sort or a stone brazier—an object she had brought with her from the South along with the tapestries and a trunkload of other objects. As each supplicant had arrived, Chaisa had made him prick one finger and touch a drop of blood to the top of the fountain. It now glowed a bilious yellow-green and illuminated the chamber as much as the oil lanterns that hung from hooks below the balcony. This light washed the color out of the priestess's trailing green and golden robes and brought out the most hideous of the demonic features of the green jade mask she wore over her ruined face. As the priestess walked and spoke, thick smoke wafted from a large wooden-handled pan sitting on top of the brazier-font.

"In the time before time," Selaine was saying, "all creatures bent knee to the Yozis and served them faithfully. It was to the Yozis that every humble man prayed for salvation." This elicited an undignified moan of affirmation from the swaying, undulating acolytes all around the dais. "In the First Age, Creation's faith was broken as the usurper gods gave birth to the Anathema and waged unholy war. Yet, even then, some few faithful still prayed to their true masters for salvation. Then again, when the Great Contagion came and the Fair Folk of the deep Wyld rode their waves of madness in a crusade to conquer Creation, some faithful few remembered their true masters and prayed to them for salvation. They prayed to the Yozis, and in each time of tumult, they were delivered from evil. The Anathema were hunted down and exterminated, the Contagion faded away, and the Fair Folk were driven back beyond the elemental poles once again."

The Visitor rolled his eyes at that liberal reimagining of history, though the crowd seemed to love it. It was sad to think that otherwise reasonable people could be made to believe these lies. The Yozis were powerful beyond measure—only slightly less so than the Deathlords' masters—but ancient oaths bound them far from Creation. Too far to take an active hand in preserving the mere humans who venerated them.

"Now, a new time of tribulation has shaken the Realm and all of Creation," the priestess went on, walking in a tight circle around the smoking pan sitting on top of the strange altar in the center of the room. "Now, the Scarlet Empress, Scion of the Dragons, Mother of the Imperial Dynasty, has disappeared, leaving her empire in ruin. Now, the Celestial Bureaucracy has grown rife with corruption and fallen into disarray. Now, the Anathema are reborn, waging their campaigns of terror against all civilization. There is no hope in this world, but you few—you faithful—have remembered your true masters and offered them your prayers for salvation. And they have heard your prayers. But the Yozis will not simply indulge your whims. They must feel your devotion. They must drink your tears of rapture. You must live every moment in their names, doing their holy work."

This elicited another thrill of moans and exclamations from the worshipers, and the priestess lifted the smoking, wooden-handled pan from its altar and held it aloft. If the Visitor remembered correctly what the Witness had told him earlier of this ceremony, the coals burning in the pan had soaked for days in a mixture of consecrated lantern oil, some of Kerrek's finest qat tea and blood taken from those slaughtered in Ikari Village.

"Lift now your voices," the priestess went on, turning in a slow circle with the smoking pan over her head. "Shake the walls of the demon world with your praise." The crowd responded obediently, rising from bent knees and raising hands skyward. Selaine then bowed her head and lifted the pan in offering toward the North. "Adorjan, Demon Wind, be praised!" The worshipers repeated the cry. The priestess turned toward the East. "Malfeas, Demon Home, be praised!" Again the worshipers responded, jumping in the air or groveling on their faces. The priestess turned to the West. "Cecelyne, Demon Keeper, be praised!" Another ululation of utmost joy, and the priestess turned toward the South, the direction from which the Visitor was watching. She raised her offering and spoke again, "Ligier, Demon Sun, be praised!"

"This goes on for a while," the Witness of Lingering Shadows said softly, coming from the stairwell to the rear and standing at the Visitor's side. "The invocation is the longest part of a summoning ritual. They'll go around the compass rose another dozen times or so naming off the Yozi princes and their most notable souls. They won't be finished for another hour, until just before midnight."

"I thought you'd be downstairs already," the Visitor said as the cycle of exhortation and exultation continued below. "Is anything wrong?"

"Nothing," the Witness said. "It's just going to take a while before Chaisa gets her adherents worked up enough to make it worth my while to wait downstairs. As midnight draws nearer, I'll adjourn below to do my part. You should definitely come with me then."

"Of course," the Visitor said. "And the priestess too. All as our master has commanded." The Witness nodded, and the two of them stood at the balcony rail watching the ceremony progress beneath them. The finer points of ritual were lost on the Visitor, but the Witness never indicated that she'd noted any misstep. After a few minutes, he grew bored with passive observation and began to ask her about the significance of what Selaine Chaisa was doing.

"She's getting the Yozis' attention," the Witness whispered. "It's the first step toward opening a fissure into their world. Most of the time, you just call out to the specific demon or the general class of demon you want to summon and get on with it. Here, however, Chaisa must be a little more circumspect. Not only must she attract and extol the virtues of the demon lord we want, she must also be careful not to displease or insult that lord's peers. Eventually, those she praises least will grow bored and turn away, leaving only our desired subject and his most jealous rivals. Then, we break open our fissure and pour in our sacrifice of essence and souls, making certain that the offering appeals only to the demon we want while repelling those we don't want. Yet, even then, the offering must not be *offensive* to those others. In its way, it's not unlike playing a clever game of politics."

"Is it?" the Visitor said. "So, why wasn't I more involved in the planning of this aspect of the ritual?"

The Witness looked at him frankly. "I'm sorry, did you want to be?"

"Well, not especially. But I could have handled it while you performed this ritual yourself, using the items Walker told us the priestess had in her possession when she arrived. I just don't understand why we need the priestess or any of these pathetic hangers on. Mastiff I understood—he helped screen us from the Council's scrutiny and divert the attention of Ikari Village's neighbors. Kerrek I understood—without his resources, we would never have found this once-holy place and been able to make it suitable. But thus far, Selaine has been more trouble than it seems she's worth."

The Witness smiled and patted the Visitor's shoulder. "It's all a question of expediency," she said. "Chaisa's cult has access to resources we need to carry out Walker's plan. Chaisa knows the denizens and customs of the demon world far better than I do. Her cultists provide the faith that supplements my essence enough to do what I must without burning myself out. As our master's plan calls for quick action in a very limited amount of time, it behooves us just to make use of those resources rather than wasting time and effort suborning them. Besides, Chaisa and her followers assume they're getting what they want out of our bargain, so they're more willing to help us. I've always found that a willing dupe is a better tool than a reluctant slave." She cocked an eyebrow and added, "Haven't you?"

"That hasn't been my experience," he said back with a smirk. "Don't tease me."

"Just making conversation to help pass the time, darling. You seem bored."

"I am. Is there anything useful I could be doing downstairs? Anything to keep me from having to watch this... display."

"Possibly," the Witness said. "Perhaps I'll start my next cycle of preparatory meditations early. I would appreciate your company if you feel like joining me."

"Then, let's go. All this fanaticism is starting to agitate my stomach."

Smiling and taking his arm in hers, the Witness led the Visitor away toward the stairs.

Her one-sided game of hide-and-seek with the Stalking Spiders in Kerrek Deset's manor lasted much longer than Harmonious Jade intended, and when she finally ended it, she felt somewhat guilty for spending so much time inside. She hadn't found anything even remotely useful or germane to her cause, but she did manage to find two drug stashes, a cleverly concealed safe full of silver and jade coins and a cache of... *toys* of dubious lineage and purpose. She'd palmed some of the money but left the drugs and adult novelties where they were. After that, making her way back outside and out into the greater Bastion district had just been a matter of patience and timing. She still took a long, circuitous path to foil any attempt to follow her, but no such attempt was in the offing, so she didn't put in as much effort as she had the night before. In a short time, she was out of Bastion and heading in the general direction of Sentinel's Hill.

As she walked, she saw that ominous clouds had rolled in while she was at Kerrek's, and they now blanketed the sky from horizon to horizon—except over the heart of

Firewander, where the enduring pillar of Wyld energy roiled. The cloud cover blocked out even the starlight of the moonless sky, casting an overbearing pall of claustrophobic darkness across the city. It made the light cast by the street lamps seem like insular islands of false hope in the waxing gloom. It made the "poor man's breath" of Nighthammer nearly impenetrable to sight and lent it an eerie, graveyard aspect. Such a dense coverage of storm clouds seemed strange for this late in the summer, but then again, Jade had come from deep in the South, where dense cloud coverage of any kind was considered strange. Perhaps, lying where three rivers met, Nexus was prone to late-summer pounding rainstorms. Jade couldn't say.

Regardless, the gloom was not enough to keep the Calibration revelers off the streets. They staggered around and danced and sang and drank just as they had done each of the three nights before, generally making a racket and enjoying themselves in hopes of ignoring this inauspicious time of year. A part of Jade wished she could join them and just throw her cares to the wind, but the notion of it made her feel even more guilty. She had work to do—twice as much now that Dace had removed himself from the picture—and she'd already wasted hours and hours dragging her feet. It was probably after midnight already, and she knew exactly where she needed to be going, yet here she stood wishing she could debauch herself with the friendly local drunkards and wondering exactly how a person was supposed to use the toys hidden in Kerrek's bathing room. Such thoughts were disgraceful, really, and she couldn't help but wonder if perhaps they were why the Unconquered Sun hadn't spoken to her since her Exaltation. She certainly hoped not. She didn't know how not to think them.

Such self-flagellation aside, she was through stalling for now. She'd put off what needed doing for long enough, and now, she was headed for the hidden passage into the Undercity that she and the Disciple of the Seven Forbidden Wisdoms had last traversed together. She couldn't think of anything that would prepare her more for whatever might await than she was already prepared, so the moment of truth had come at last. She would go down into the darkness and find the place where she and the Disciple had been separated, and there, she would lie in wait for Selaine Chaisa to reappear whence the deathknights had absconded with her. And this time, she would do the job right. She would let nothing distract her. She would kill Selaine Chaisa.

This time, there would be no escape.

CHAPTER FIFTEEN

Just prior to the stroke of midnight, the Visitor, the Witness and Selaine Chaisa stood in a ring holding hands in a chamber beneath their converted Yozi sanctuary. Black essence seeped from the Witness and swirled about the three of them, and a bilious yellow-green energy lit the chamber from above. That energy emanated from the awl-shaped base of the fountain-cum-brazier Selaine had brought to this place and used as her altar during her sermon to her Salmalin followers. As those followers reveled and raved in ecstatic worship of their demon lords, the altar glowed brighter and collected the essence of their faith. Now, as midnight drew near, it transmitted that faith down to this chamber and into a gaudy pendant Selaine had given to the Witness specifically for this ritual. The Witness wore the pendant against her alabaster skin, and as the altar glowed brighter, her consciousness expanded, and ambient essence began to flow through her as she breathed.

The Visitor in the Hall of Obsidian Mirrors was impressed. The amount of power his partner was putting off dwarfed anything she had shown a capacity for in the time that he'd known her. He had to admit, this wouldn't have been possible without the Yozi priestess's help, and it wouldn't have been this effective without her inspiring sermon to her faithful adherents. Now, if she could just perform this last task, he might have to reconsider his assessment that Selaine was a worthless hindrance to the Walker in Darkness's plan.

"It's time," the Witness said as the sound from upstairs grew to a frenzied climax. "Get ready, and hold on to each other. And to me, of course."

He and Selaine nodded, and the Witness of Lingering Shadows began to speak in an ancient language that throbbed with power. Her words were not those of unwholesome necromancy, but those of pure Exalted sorcery—the power to reshape reality, which the Chosen had stolen from the Primordials long ago. As she spoke, the light from the artifact penetrating the ceiling grew to blinding intensity, and a bonfire of black essence engulfed the room. It spun like a tornado and thrashed like a monsoon, but the Witness reined it in with the power of her will and forced it down to the floor. It crashed like lightning into the summoning circle she had painstakingly carved into the floor, and a tremendous surge of energy radiated from the point of impact. It dove into the earth with such force that it split the fabric of Creation itself, punching a hole into Malfeas, the Yozis' prison. Light blinded everyone in the chamber.

The Visitor was the last to regain his senses, and when he did, he nearly lost his nerve. He began to panic and thrash like a drowning man, but the Witness and Selaine squeezed his hands and held him still.

Don't be afraid, the Witness's voice said in his mind. *You are not in the place you see. But don't let go of us, or you'll surely be lost here.* The voice grew fainter then, as if its source were suddenly a great distance away. *It worked just as you said, Chaisa. Now take us where we need to be. Take us to Jacint.* The Visitor could not hear Selaine Chaisa's reply, but he recognized her presence as a warm grip on his wounded hand and a sensation of both rapturous wonder and stark terror.

Considering the surroundings—illusory or not—the Visitor couldn't fault her for the latter, for this was no less than Hell. They slid between the bones of the demon Malfeas—for whom the realm was named—and passed over the vast living desert Cecelyne. The desert gave way to the disconsolate sea Kimbery, which in turn receded before the metal forests Szoreny, Vitalius and Hrotsvitha. The demon sun, Ligier—the living heart and most notable soul of Malfeas—beat arhythmically and blasted the landscape with its unrelenting green rays.

Feeling as if he were falling from a great height, the Visitor passed through layer upon layer of this gruesome place as he squeezed his companions' hands desperately. In time—the Visitor knew not how long—they saw an enormous, sprawling city on the horizon. This city, too, was Malfeas, and every layer of it quivered with the hatred of the imprisoned demon who gave it form. It was a boundless metropolis of brass and basalt, draped in a webwork of roads that crisscrossed at every level of the city but never touched. Among these roads stood pillars of steel and glass, minarets of salt and flesh, and great towers shaped like nautilus horns. Closer to the ground, vast nests of ichorous needles grew bit by bit from within, and glass libraries protruded from the laps of unmoving clockwork obscenities whose purpose had been lost to time. Lesser demons of the first and second circles carried on their bizarre business among the structures, occasionally pausing to ring a stand of hanging bells, shout into the awful sky or sing in monstrous voices, all in hopes of pushing back the lethal rage of the Silent Wind.

The Visitor let himself be led through this incomprehensible landscape by the urgency of Selaine's will, and before long, they approached the foot of a tower of flawless black stone. They changed course then, shooting straight up. At the top of the tower stood a brass statue of a winged man holding out a house-sized hand. In the palm of that hand stood a pillar of marble, surmounted by a glowing disk. The glow blinded the Visitor once again, but not for nearly long enough. He and his companions came to rest in mid air at the top of that glowing disk, facing the demon who stood there. It looked much like a man, the Visitor thought, save that basalt wings graced its back and its legs bent the wrong way at the knees.

The demon sang in a wordless non-language, ignoring those who sought its attention, and as it sang, more roads appeared in the city beneath them. The Visitor wondered where the other jealous demons were whom Selaine's invocation was supposed to attract then repel, but he did not mourn their absence. In fact, he was somewhat relieved that this demon did not appear to care that they were there. Unfortunately, that state did not persist much longer.

I'll do it, Chaisa, you're only going to scream yourself hoarse, the Visitor distantly heard the Witness say. She then spoke in a voice that actually penetrated into the demon world, loud enough to drown out some of the cacophony below.

"Jacint!" she called, her voice ringing like a thunderclap in the Visitor's ears. "Third-Circle soul of Adorjan! Prince Upon the Tower! Take heed!"

At this, the demon turned his blue and black glittering eyes toward the Witness's voice. The Witness called to him again, and this time, he actually deigned to reply. As he did, he continued to sing.

"Speak, lingering sorceress," he said. "Speak circle of three."

"I command your attendance and obedience!" the Witness replied. "I command a service of you! In the name of your greater self, Lady Adorjan the Silent Wind."

"What do you offer, lingering sorceress? I am not yours to command."

"You are!" the Witness said, and black lightning tore through the sky and enwrapped the demon. Jacint did not seem perturbed by this development. "But I offer payment for your service! I offer blood spilled in secret as cries of hope fell silent! I offer essence, harvested beyond the silence of the grave! I offer lost, restless souls entombed in silence beneath Nexus to preserve a secret! And finally, I offer living souls, pledged to you in secret by those forced to worship in silence!"

The Visitor felt a flash of regret from Selaine, but that singular sensation did not interest the Prince Upon the Tower. The demon's eyes flashed, and he nodded in acceptance of the Witness's offer. He took hold of the black lightning that surrounded him and pulled it to him as energy began to pulse through it from outside the Yozi realm. In the throb and pulse of that energy, the Visitor thought he heard screaming.

"Your offering suits me," Jacint said, languidly caressing the bonds around him. "What service would you beg of me, lingering sorceress?"

"Not beg!" the Witness snapped. "You will to come into Creation and build a path as I command!"

"Alas, I cannot leave this prison realm," Jacint replied with a sly smile.

"You will!"

"Your kind hasn't the power to compel demons of my rank."

"Today, I do!" the Witness barked, and the bands of lightning constricted around Jacint's body. The demon writhed and struggled against this sudden power, but he could not break free.

"If I come," he said instead, "what kind of path would you have me build?"

"A path connecting this place to the heart of the River Province!" the Witness answered. "A path that touches your greater whole and guides her to the city of Nexus! You will unleash the Silent Wind upon that city!"

"Why?"

The Witness did not respond, except to tighten the demon's bonds.

"I must respectfully decline," Jacint said, grimacing in pain. "I cannot free one greater than myself. It is beyond my power."

"*You* will come!" the Witness said. "You will come to Nexus, and when Creation trembles at your presence, you will beckon the Silent Wind to move through you and take your place there! And when she does, the Lady Adorjan will scour that city such that shadowlands erupt and fester over every inch of it! Such a thing is possible in this, the time of Calibration, when the barriers between the realms are thin!"

"I cannot!" Jacint said. "Adorjan is greater than I! I am but a component soul with no—"

"She *will* do this!" the Witness thundered. "She will compel *herself*!"

"Why?" Jacint cried.

The Witness did not respond, for she did not know the answer. She had only repeated what her master, the Walker in Darkness, had told her before sending her here to do this thing. The Visitor knew, however, and it was he who spoke, snapping his awed reverie as the ring-and-circle Moonshadow caste mark on his forehead burned. He spoke a secret that his master had told him, which the Deathlord's own eternal master had passed along to him.

"She is obligated!" he roared, scorching the sky of the demon realm with the power of what he said. "She swore an oath to a lover she allowed to die as her own cowardice preserved her! This thing is the smallest dram of what she owes, but she will pay it! She will do this in the name of—"

The Visitor spoke the ancient verse that the Walker in Darkness had given him, and every demon in Malfeas screeched and recoiled. It was but the first syllable of Walker's master's name—the most even a Deathlord could contain without being subsumed and destroyed—but it was enough. Jacint recognized the power in the Visitor's words, as did Adorjan, whose eighteenth component soul Jacint was. The demon bowed its head in defeat, and a third and final flash of light blinded the Visitor in the Hall of Obsidian Mirrors.

When the Visitor opened his eyes again, he was standing in the chamber beneath the converted Salmalin sanctuary with the Witness and Selaine Chaisa. He and the Witness both glowed with black animas that were bright enough to read by, and in the unhealthy light, they could both see that Selaine's eyes within her demonic mask were filmed over with alabaster cataracts. The priestess moaned and quivered in orgasmic ecstasy, and she wrapped her arms tightly around herself. Of the bilious light from above, there was not so much as a glimmer, and the sounds of revelatory excess upstairs had fallen silent.

"It worked?" the Visitor said, somewhat disappointed that Jacint was not standing in the room with them, crouching in submission.

"It did," the Witness said, in a quavering, exhausted voice. "Jacint has come unto this world. He will open the way. The Silent Wind will scour Nexus. It begins."

The Visitor's brow furrowed. "When?"

The Witness looked at him then, but it was not her eyes that regarded him. Two glittering, blue-black orbs gazed from the Witness's face, and Jacint's voice issued from her mouth. "At once," it said. "The coming of Adorjan is at hand."

The Visitor fell back a step, and the Witness looked up toward the sky. She shuddered and convulsed, and the form of Jacint passed out of her, heading straight up. The ceiling parted before him like oil before water, as did the sanctuary ceiling above that and the tons of stone that buried the Undercity. Jacint opened a path from the sanctuary straight up to the surface streets of Nexus, and when he reached it, the cloud-dimmed light of morning sun shone back down the way he had come. The Visitor hadn't realized how long the contest of wills between the Witness and the demon had gone on.

"It's finished," he breathed. "You did it. Our master will be proud. We should get back to him at—"

"No," the Witness said. She started to sway as if she were hyperventilating, and the Visitor steadied her. When she looked at him, her eyes were still demonic blue-black. "The path must still be opened between the realms. Jacint cannot do this except by the power of the oath you and I represent, so I must remain and see it through. I must anchor and filter his power with my essence. How troublesome. I fear this won't be pleasant…"

"It won't," Selaine murmured, holding her knees and rocking contentedly.

"Then, I'll stay with you," the Visitor said.

"No, please," the Witness said in a wavering voice. "I can't... I don't want you to see me like this."

"What would you rather I do then?"

"Stand watch... stand guard. Just... away... somewhere else. Please."

"Very well," the Visitor grumbled, hurt and confused. "But I won't go far. Call out if you need me."

"I will."

Harmonious Jade stole into lively, middle-class Sentinel's Hill and over the wall into less affluent Firewander without incident, and she located the hidden tunnel entrance into the Undercity with only a little trouble. The neighborhoods looked different at this time of the early, predawn morning, and she was distracted by the absence of the Disciple of the Seven Forbidden Wisdoms, but she eventually found what she was looking for. She recognized it by the morbid nursery rhyme scrawled near the entrance.

Crouching in the shadows behind a refuse bin, she pored over the area for concealed guards, tripwires or other mantraps. When she was convinced the area was clear—at least at this end of the tunnel—she pressed her palms together, blurred, distorted and, finally, disappeared. Thus had she made her way into the Undercity before, and now, she did so again. The way down the tunnel was as she remembered it—a dusty, rubble-choked stairway that forced her to pick her way over, under and between mounds of tumbled rock. She navigated the twisted, broken path with ease, mostly letting muscle memory guide her as she remained on alert for signs of trouble ahead of her. Yet, no guards or hidden traps barred her path, and she reached the bottom of the stairway without incident.

She paused in the antechamber at the bottom of the steps and put her hand on the wall to her right. Where before it had displayed a rack of oil lanterns on iron hooks, it was now bare, which told her that others had come this way and were still within. Chaisa's local Salmalin contacts, no doubt.

Jade wondered how long they'd been inside waiting for their priestess and what fell scheme they were cooking up. Actually, she had a decent idea about that last part already. It was Calibration, when the barriers between realms were thin, and Selaine Chaisa led a cult of demon-worshipers, which meant that the Salmalin were probably trying to summon a demon up out of the prison of Malfeas. The only real question was which demon the cult had targeted and what Chaisa intended to command that demon to do when it showed up. Jade was also curious about what the deathknights who were helping Chaisa intended to get out of such a ritual, but she supposed that didn't really matter. In truth, it didn't even really matter what Chaisa hoped to accomplish, considering what Jade was here to do. The things that really mattered included how many people had already come and where they were. It would also help to know how long those who were here had been here. If they had only just arrived, she might be able to move more quickly and come upon them as they were still settling in.

To answer that last question, Jade performed a quick inspection of the antechamber. She found little dust on the lantern rack or on the opposite wall, which indicated that after everyone had come and gone through this area, dust hadn't had much time to resettle. A smell of lantern oil lingered, though it was not an overpowering aroma. She remembered how strong the odor had been when she was last here, and it was not nearly as strong now, which indicated that it had been at least several hours since any of the lanterns had been in here. That realization especially annoyed Jade, as it drove home just how much time she had wasted at Kerrek Deset's place and in taking her time to get here. She couldn't let herself worry about that now, though—she still had work to do. She turned her inspection to the floor, looking for telltale tracks or some other clue that would indicate how many people had come this way from outside and give her a better idea of how long ago that had been. Yet, instead of helpful clues, she found something there that froze her in place and almost cost her her life.

Had she not attuned and sharpened her senses, she would never have noticed it. As she knelt in the ante-chamber alcove to inspect the floor, she saw a long strip of thin fabric draped across a tumble of rocks at the entrance to the larger underground chamber. It was light scarf woven from tough Southern silk, and it revealed a peculiar bouquet of scents to her heightened senses. The most prominent of them was the smell of blood, which came from the center of the scarf. It seemed that a ring of blood roughly the size of Jade's own caste mark had been soaked into the material. The other most prominent scent was one with which Jade was so familiar that she almost couldn't identify it. It was the smell of her own hair. In the same instant that she realized that, she also realized what it was she had found—this was the scarf she had given the Disciple of the Seven Forbidden Wisdoms to keep blood from running down in his eyes. And as she made that realization, it occurred to her to wonder if she had just taken the bait in a cunning trap.

She did not have to wait long to get her answer.

On the morning of the last day of Calibration, Captain Dace of the Bronze Tigers awoke feeling better than he thought he had a right to. The wounds he had taken standing up to the Emissary had not completely healed, but the aches and the stiffness in his body had worn down to a manageable level. He would probably be completely back to normal in another day or so. As it was, he only felt like a tired old man, rather than a whipped, wounded old hound. That was a refreshing sensation in its way.

"Sorry, sir, did I wake you?" he heard a voice say as he sat up and blinked cobwebs out of his eyes. He looked toward his chamber door and saw Risa standing there holding a roll of papers.

"Morning, Lieutenant," he said. "No, I didn't even hear you come in. What do you need?"

"I just thought I'd sneak in and drop this off, sir," Risa said, gesturing with the roll of papers. "I didn't want to disturb you. You still look like you need some rest."

"What is that? The security report I've been asking you for?"

"Sir? Security… Ah… no, this is the inventory registry. The list of things we'll need to take with us when we start packing."

"Right," Dace rumbled, clearing his throat. "That. Sure, leave it here. I'll get to it."

"Sir, are you feeling any better?" Risa asked, dropping the roll of paper on a table by the door. "You look a little more…"

"I feel better," Dace said, "but I had some pretty surreal nightmares. They felt… I don't know… like something was coming. Did anything big happen last night?"

"Not that I'm aware of, sir. We had some bad storm clouds roll in and clear some of the revelers off the streets, but that's about it. I did find out about your man in Bastion, though. Apparently Beads knocked off about a quarter of his house staff and slaughtered him in his own study. The Guild and the Council both have mercenaries looking all over Nexus for her."

"Great," Dace said unsurprised, as he hauled himself out of bed. "But that isn't what I meant. There's something… wrong going on out there right now. I can't explain it, I can just *feel* it. It's like the city's essence smells funny. If I were a sorcerer, maybe I could explain it better."

Risa frowned and shrugged. "I don't know what to tell you, sir. I don't remember my lessons about the way essence is supposed to smell from back at the academy."

"Very funny, Lieutenant. Look, seriously, I don't like this. Have you got all the men on work details packing up our gear?" Risa nodded. "Call all that off. And get everybody who's not a Bronze Tiger off these premises until further notice. I want the men on alert, armed, mounted and ready to ride out at a moment's notice."

"Sir?"

"You heard me, Lieutenant. It feels like a fight's coming, and I want the men ready to meet it. If we wait, whatever's coming's going to catch us flat-footed, and I don't want that to happen."

"Yes, sir, I understand. Well, no, I don't really, but you're in charge. I'll get the men ready."

She left confused and annoyed, and Dace dug out a clean field uniform to wear under his armor.

CHAPTER SIXTEEN

When the trap first sprung, pure luck saved Jade from a quick death. She had rocked back on her heels with her discarded scarf in her hands, wondering why it was lying here, when an arrow streaked out of the darkness and severed the metal clasp that held her cloak closed. She ducked, both to shrug out of her cloak and to drop her bow down into her hand, and another arrow streaked by, just missing her. This one severed the new scarf with which she had bound her hair, and as she jumped back to her feet and pressed herself flat against the metal lantern rack, her beaded braids swung down around her shoulders.

The fact that her sniper might be able to see her despite magical near-invisibility troubled her, but she did not panic. It was quite possible he had been watching the scarf for signs of movement and had fired as soon as it twitched. Jade tested this theory by reaching out with a foot toward her sloughed cloak. She managed to pull the garment closer, but only the grace of her supernal reflexes allowed her to avoid having her heel tendon slashed by a third arrow. Nonetheless, she had a slight advantage now. Judging from the trajectories of the three arrows that had missed her and based on her rough recall of how the chamber beyond this one had been laid out, she now had an estimation of where the sniper was hiding. And knowing that, she was able to change the balance of power.

After a deep, calming breath, she took her cloak in one hand and threw it ahead of her toward the sniper in such a way that it opened like an unfurled sail and obscured the opening back into the antechamber alcove. As soon as the garment left her hand, she sprinted from behind its cover and darted into the shadowed rubble of a half-buried building to her left. Two arrows punched through the cloak but missed her, and as she leaped from a boulder toward the broken wall of the ruined building, she unleashed a dazzling arrow of burning energy toward where the sniper lay in wait. Shining brilliantly, her arrow roared through the darkness and exploded against a concealing ledge overlooking the antechamber. Exposed and now lacking the element of surprise, the sniper leaped down from his shadowed firing position and alighted on the roof of the building beneath it. He fired another two arrows at the spot where Jade was going to land. Jade rolled and twisted in midair and landed safely, although one of the arrows skated across the back of her armor.

As soon as her feet touched down, she dove into a somersault and started running. She moved deeper into the darkness, firing off an arrow back toward where her sniper had landed. Two more answered it, and as she dodged them, she heard her opponent running now as well, moving to cut her off. She had to leap over some prodigious gaps between half-buried buildings, and each time she landed on one or bounded off another to change directions, she did so just ahead of another ricocheting arrow. She returned fire only once more, hoping to conserve ammunition. The shot caught fire and burned as it flew, with which she hoped at least to distract her opponent and ruin his darkness vision. He dodged the bolt with ophidian grace and celerity, though, then hurled himself through the air amazingly far, trailing a black, necrotic wake of energy. The energy was the same as that of the deathknights Jade had faced, and her stomach turned cold inside.

What was worse, the man's jump put him right in Jade's path. He landed on the stone ledge of a shell of a building with a collapsed roof, just a second before Jade landed on that same building not fifteen feet from him. They both slid to a halt on the dusty ledge, aiming drawn arrows at each other's throats. But before either could fire, the shadows that clung to the sniper melted away and rained down around his feet, revealing the Disciple of the Seven Forbidden Wisdoms. A weeping ring of blood stained the pale flesh of his forehead, and the ghastly eyes of the skull set in his bow shone menacingly. Stunned, Jade almost loosed her arrow accidentally.

"You," she gasped, becoming fully visible again. "I thought…"

"I know," the Disciple said, not letting his aim waver.

"I thought you'd been killed," Jade said. Her aim did not waver either. "I thought you'd sacrificed yourself so I could escape."

"That doesn't surprise me."

"What are you doing here?"

"Alas," the Disciple said, "I'm preventing you from proceeding deeper into this cavern."

"Why?" Jade demanded. "Is Selaine Chaisa down there?"

"She is."

"And the deathknights?"

"They're with her."

"Are they summoning something? They're going to let a demon loose in Nexus, aren't they?"

"That does seem to be what Yozi-worshipers do," the Disciple said with a shrug. "This also seems to be the time of year for it."

"And you're helping them," Jade growled. "You're one of them, aren't you, you bastard? A deathknight."

"I don't think you understand what's—"

Jade took a step forward, her fingers trembling on her bowstring at the point of release. "Don't lie to me. Your caste mark is crying blood instead of glowing like mine does. You know about shadowlands, nemissaries, Deathlords… You even have the same kind of ridiculous name they do. I can't believe I didn't realize it. I know what you are now. Deny it!"

The Disciple took a step back to match Jade's advance. "I never led you to believe otherwise."

"And you're working with them," Jade accused, stepping forward again. "How blind was I? You led me here. You sent me out to that village that led me to Dace. You wanted me to kill him, didn't you? Probably because he found out what you were up to."

"You don't know what you're saying," the Disciple said, watching the trembling hand on Jade's bowstring.

"You wanted me to hunt down Kerrek and Stalwart Mastiff too while I was looking for Chaisa, thinking I was getting revenge for your death. You hoped I'd kill them and Dace before Dace exposed what you were all up to. It all makes sense now!"

"Actually, that doesn't…"

"And then, after you'd stolen my trust and manipulated me into cleaning up after your Salmalin partners, you lay in wait here to complete your betrayal!"

"Jade, listen to me," the Disciple said softly. "I haven't betrayed or manipulated you. I'm not even here to kill you."

The preposterousness of that claim was the last straw for Jade. Her eyes blazed, and she loosed her arrow at a range of less than ten feet. It should have punched into the Disciple's throat, but his Exaltation preserved him. With a flick of his wrist, he knocked the shaft aside with his bow, earning only a shallow nick on the cheek. Jade reached back for a second arrow, but before she had even half drawn it from her quiver, the Disciple loosed his own shaft. The projectile severed Jade's arrow's just below the fletching, and before she could react, he was right in front of her. He stepped in between her feet on the narrow ledge and disengaged her bow hand with his free elbow. Jade tried to draw her knife from her belt sheath and slash the Disciple's throat, but he caught her wrist on his bow, turned it against her own armor breastplate and grabbed her wrist with his other hand. Jade would have tried to wrench the knife away or sweep the Disciple's legs out from under him, but when he touched her, she remembered something…

She was standing at the deck rail of an ocean-going vessel made of glass and gold. The boat was as large as a manor house and encircled by an expansive deck. The entire body of the vessel rested atop an enormous, spinning disk that acted like a river stone and skipped from wave crest to wave crest, with a mind-boggling array of complex mechanisms keeping the passenger decks calm and level.

She stood at the rail, leaning against it and watching the slow rise and fall of the horizon. She was lost in ancient thoughts, and she did not hear the stealthy approach of her lover. He crept up behind her and covered her eyes with his delicate hands. He whispered something dangerous and tantalizing then kissed her ear, and she responded by wrapping her arms around him behind her back. He murmured something else, and she twisted around to face him, never leaving the warm circle of his arms.

Fighting the lure of her former incarnation's life, Jade shook her head violently and pulled back from the Disciple. In her sudden disorientation, however, she stepped awkwardly on the ledge. Her foot went out from under her, and she lurched backward out over empty space. Coming to his senses as well, the Disciple leaned out precariously far and snagged her wrist before she could drop into the darkness. Only essence and sheer will pinned his feet to the roof ledge as he clung like a raiton to a clothesline. He even had the presence of mind to reach out with his bow and catch the crosspiece of her dagger with it as it slipped out of her hand. They both froze like that for a moment, the Disciple leaning out at a precarious angle over the edge of the roof with Harmonious Jade dangling from his outstretched hand. Jade glared at him in contempt but hung motionless just the same.

"Perhaps we should have a discussion," the Disciple said when a beat had passed. "I'll make it as polite a one as I'm able under the circumstances." Jade only scowled. "First of all, I *am* a deathknight—an Abyssal Exalt. I work for a Deathlord who approached me at the point of my death and offered me this lingering mortality. However, my master is *not* the Walker in Darkness. The Visitor and the Witness who are helping your Yozi priestess are not my partners. I told you before that the Yozis are pathetic cowards who begged for their lives while their brothers died in battle. Working with those who could forgive such cowardice would disgust me."

"You're lying," Jade snapped.

"Why, exactly, would I bother?" the Disciple said. "I could just drop you and skewer you with arrows as you fell. For that matter, I can always find you no matter how you hide—I could have killed you the second you picked up your scarf."

Jade frowned at that and was silent for several long moments. Both she and Dace had used this same logic on each other a few days ago, and now, as then, she couldn't find fault with it. "But if that's true and you're not working with those others, what are you doing here? And why didn't you come meet me after we were separated like you said you would? Why did you let me think you'd been killed?"

"I had no choice," the Disciple said. As he spoke, he lifted Jade back to secure footing. He didn't let go of her even after he'd set her down, though. "I wanted to, but I'd been wounded by one too many of the Visitor's damn needles. When you and I separated, I found myself at his mercy, almost completely paralyzed. He would have killed me if I hadn't done what I did."

"Which was?"

"I swore him a hasty oath. It was the only way I could think to distract him long enough for you to get away. And when I swore it, the Visitor sanctified it. Since then, he's been holding it over my head—ordering me around and keeping me too busy to interfere in what they're doing. That's why I didn't get back in contact with you. I simply couldn't."

"I see," Jade said, scowling in confusion and frustration. "But how do I know this isn't just more lies? Maybe you've arranged all this to gain my trust and make it easier to kill me."

"This is easier?"

"You could be leading me into a trap, where the other deathknights intend to kill me."

"I wouldn't do that."

"You might not want to, but you just said you were oath-bound. How do I know you aren't under *orders* to lead me to my fate?"

"Even a sanctified oath is not compulsion," the Disciple said, looking into Jade's eyes in a way that disquieted her. "I would risk calamity to preserve you from harm."

"Oh," Jade said. Only then did it occur to her that the Disciple was still holding her hand. She hesitated a long moment then pulled away, saying, "Are you at least sorry then?"

"Sorry?" the Disciple said, holding back a relieved smile. "Unremittingly. Would that desperation had never inspired me to pledge that oath. But it seemed—"

"I meant for misleading me about what you are."

The Disciple opened him mouth to properly lay the blame for Jade's misapprehension, then thought better of it. "I apologize for giving you the wrong impression," he said instead. "But for what it's worth, not every Abyssal Exalt is a villain. My master, in fact, is quite fond of the living. He's more than willing to be patient as—"

"Let's please not over-examine your master's agenda right now," Jade said. "Now that we're not trying to kill each other… again… let's just figure out what we're going to do."

"About that… Unfortunately, I'm still bound by my oath not to let you interfere. I can't let you go any farther until the ritual your priestess is performing comes to an end."

"So, do you intend to start shooting at me again? That hasn't worked very well thus far."

"I was only trying to get your attention. Now that you're here, I know better ways to keep you safely occupied. Regardless, I can't let you go any further."

"Are you telling me you're willing to keep me here like this until midnight?"

"Midnight?" The Disciple sighed in frustration. "Damnation. I didn't realize it was going to take more than twenty-four hours."

Jade blinked. "More than... What? Does that mean they already started?"

"Yes," the Disciple said. "Just before I returned from Kerrek Deset's manor house last night. You made quite a mess there, by the—"

"If they started last night," Jade said, fear rising in her voice, "then the ritual is already *over*. Breaching the barrier to the demon world only takes from sundown to midnight. It's well past that now. It might even be past dawn already."

"It is," the Disciple said.

"Then, either they're still battling the demon for dominance, or they've already called it up and begun to issue commands. Or worse, they couldn't control it, and it's loose right now. Either way, we can't afford to just stand here!"

"Hmm," the Disciple said, scratching his neck. "All right, since you're the one who grew up among demonworshipers, you must know more about their rituals than I do. If you say they're finished, I believe you."

"Good," Jade said, retrieving her knife from the Disciple and setting an arrow to her bowstring. "Let's get down there, then."

"After you," the Disciple said with a deferential bow. "I presume you remember the way."

As Jade and the Disciple rushed to the hidden Salmalin sanctuary beneath Nexus, the demon Jacint ascended from that subterranean sanctuary to the surface world. He carved a path straight up through the stone, for path-making was his purpose, and rose higher than the tallest imperishable spire of the city. Even through the oppressive clouds, the dawn glare of the hated sun blinded and cowed him. He detested this pure brilliance and this open sky, and he rued the day his greater self, Adorjan, had quit the field of battle and forfeited this harsh realm. Yet, he could not leave it and return to his tower home within Malfeas until he had done the work he was bound to complete. So, he sang his chthonian song into being, fighting the power of oaths sworn to victorious Solar heroes eons ago. Even though this was the time of Calibration and he had the lingering sorceress as his anchor, he still made only slight progress. Were he forging a path anywhere else in Creation or beyond, the path would have appeared immediately, but under these circumstances, he could only breach the barrier infinitesimally and by degrees. Yet, even that slow progress had an effect on the city of Nexus that would not soon be forgotten. As he forced open the path from Malfeas, Jacint felt the spawn of Adorjan begin to stir and claw their way toward Creation.

The first noticeable effect Jacint's song had was to awaken the Things That Dwell in Corners. Barely alive and hardly sentient, they responded to the demonic energy gathering here and began to roil and skitter. They flitted from one corner to another, helping Creation remember the ancient ones who had built it. They did no harm and took no notice of the citizens of Nexus, but they did not go unnoticed themselves.

As the Things That Dwell in Corners awakened, Jacint's children gathered at the tear he had forged back into their prison. The first to arrive was Gumela, the Jeweled Auditor. He longed to be free so that he could search for his lost Mayoigo, but he also wished to join in the passionate revels of Nexus' citizens as they celebrated the passing of Calibration. Jacint's second most eager child was Zsofika, the Kite Flute. She was a celebrant like her brother, but seeing a breach in the demon prison filled her with an overpowering desire to stalk and kill mortal prey in Creation. She fought with Gumela to be the first to break free, and the two of them pushed back Jacint's other offspring.

Yet, their father's work was slow and laborious, and they could not emerge into Creation immediately. Therefore, they called to their own children—demons of the first circle—and urged them to go forth and prepare the way. These lesser spawn existed only to be near their masters, but they could not resist their masters' commands. Many of them crowded at the fissure and forced their way into Creation one by one.

The first to emerge were called hopping puppeteers, and they caused an enormous commotion. They were children of Gumela, and as they materialized, they appeared to be head-sized lumps of hair soaked in bile and phlegm. Yet, when they heard the song of Jacint in the open air, they began to uncoil and rise high into the sky. When they had fully unfolded themselves, their spindly, hair-thin legs stood as high as Sentinel's Hill's watchtowers, and their heads were no larger than a jade obol. They were so tall and thin that they could barely be seen against the cloudy sky, but they made their presence felt in short order. Following their bizarre whims, they moved toward the residential district of Sentinel's Hill, rearranging the landscape and architecture as they went. The puppeteers moved with a twitchy, floating stride, and those of their legs that were not involved in locomotion grabbed objects at random and moved them to more suitable positions. As soon as they were material, two of the things took apart a tenement house and part of an aqueduct built nearby, then carried the pieces two blocks over and refashioned them into a high tower right in the middle of an important intersection. This mad rampage of construction and destruction—which sent waking men running and crushed sleeping ones in their beds—drew attention immediately, especially that of the watchtower sentinels at Firewander's border. The sentinels tore their eyes away from the strangely flickering Wyld-fire at Firewander's heart and hearkened to this odd commotion.

Seeing this, Zsofika grew jealous of her brother, so she swept aside he and his children to make way for some of her own. The ones of which she was most proud were her teodozjia, so she sent two of them side by side to spread their scripture. The teodozjia were great jade lions, and they moved in perfect synchrony to the beat that Zsofika's celebrant legion pounded out. They came into the world and began to march, and as they moved, their scripture took root, overpowering the faith of lesser creatures. The shrines to the little gods of Creation that a portion of Nexus' citizens kept in their homes were defiled and reduced to dust. Newly built Immaculate temples and older ones in which the faith of the congregation was weak cracked and fell in on themselves. Even the unholy clouds that blanketed Nexus grew thicker and darker and hung lower to spite the Unconquered Sun. The scripture of the teodozjia held at bay the morning light of the greatest of gods and turned the day dark as night. They did these things as their scripture commanded, to remind humanity that all things falter and die.

Zsofika was much pleased by her teodozjia, but she did not grow complacent. Her greater self, Jacint, was still struggling to open the way into Creation, and his long effort had finally widened the breach enough to permit a demon of the second circle. The honor of being the first Zsofika took for herself. She took up a sword in each hand and commenced a centuries-old celebration. An ethereal fire sprung up at the point of her entry in Creation, and she turned within it for seventy beats, blocking her brothers' way behind her. As she turned, she took on form and materialized to begin the hunt that was customary to her arrival in this realm. She appeared as an ebony-skinned Southerner with argent clothing and long red hair with bells knotted into it. She wore long braids of her own hair as vambraces, and she held a long black sword in each hand. As she materialized, she clashed her swords together in time to the rhythm that the teodozjia kept. As she turned in the flame, her skin began to smoke, and her eyes blazed. Lesser demonic standardbearers began to appear around her as well, each holding up a kite flute, which howled mournfully in the wind.

When Zsofika's dance was complete, the fire around her went out, and she and her revelers went on the hunt that would inaugurate their stay in Creation. She chose a victim—a mercenary captain whose interference in this holy work had too long gone unpunished—at the urging of the Abyssal Exalt through whom Jacint did his work, for such was her way. Such was her power that she knew exactly where this nuisance was to be found, and she did not intend to do anything else until she had run him down and killed him. She began to march with her lions at her sides, and as she strode forth, clashing her swords, her retinue of standardbearers grew.

In Malfeas, meanwhile, others of Jacint's children clamored to escape as Zsofika had, but a greater force forestalled them. A terrible silence began to swell, snatching up and devouring those hangers on who were slowest to react. The spawn of Jacint recognized this silence as the coming of Adorjan—the greatest of their greater selves—and they made way for her. They could have driven her off with cacophonous outbursts, but such was not their place at this time. Bound by an oath older than that which bound the Yozis here, Adorjan, the Silent Wind, had come to perform a service for a fallen comrade whose name was kept secret in Oblivion. As they could not gainsay the power of that obligation, the lesser demons made way so that when Jacint's work was done—as it would be very soon—the Silent Wind could blow through him into Creation.

CHAPTER SEVENTEEN

"He's dead," Jade said, scowling. "They both are."

She was crouching in the dull lantern light by the door of the converted underground Salmalin sanctuary, inspecting the corpses of two temple wardens who lay sprawled facedown at their posts. Each man had a large black hole scorched in his back, as though a fire had burned within but not entirely consumed him. Jade rolled the men over and pulled off their masks, to find contorted expressions of agony and terror on their faces. Each man also had a pinprick on his right middle finger.

"Yes," the Disciple said. "We might already be too late. What do you suppose killed them?"

Jade shrugged. "If we're lucky, their ritual blew up in their faces. If not… it was whatever the deathknights summoned. The *other* deathknights."

The Disciple ignored the dull gibe and said, "Is it still in there?"

"Maybe. If they could control it, it's wherever they told it to go. But if they couldn't control it, it might have gone back to the demon world. Or…"

"Or it's stuck in there and extremely upset about it." Jade nodded. "I see. Well, in that case, perhaps experience should guide desire." When Jade only frowned, the Disciple bowed courteously and said, "That is, after you."

"Ah."

Jade stood, opened the buried temple's door and preceded the Disciple inside. Just beyond the door, they found the dim antechamber and the table on which the local Salmalin had discarded their civilian clothes. As the Disciple looked at the ancient frescoes on the wall, Jade walked a circuit around the table.

"At least twenty people," she whispered. "But I don't hear anyone inside. Maybe they've all gone."

"Or they're dead. Or this temple is bigger than it seems. Let's find out. Where do you want to start?"

"This door leads to stairs going up," Jade said, crossing the room. "Let's work top to bottom."

The Disciple agreed, and the two of them made their way to the mezzanine above the ancient, circular sanctuary. The guttering lanterns gave the place a grim aspect, and unwholesome shadows crowded all around them. They did not notice the hole in the center of the roof, which Jacint's recent passing had carved there, but they noticed the one in the center of the floor, beneath which a light pulsed. The wan flickering illuminated scores of burnt, black trails radiating out from it in all directions along the floor. Each gruesome channel that led from the hole terminated at the motionless body of a Salmalin cultist, almost threescore of which littered the main sanctuary floor below. Some of the bodies lay strewn on the floor's central dais, others lay sprawled over the encircling pews, and still others lay on the floor at the room's edges, where they'd tried in vain to get to one of the doors.

"Gods…" Jade whispered.

"What a waste," the Disciple sighed. "What do you suppose happened? Shall we take a closer look?"

Jade nodded, unable to speak. The Disciple put a foot up on the guardrail to jump over but looked back at her first.

"Jade?" he said, trying to sound sympathetic. "If this sight disturbs you, perhaps I—"

"Don't worry, I'm coming," Jade snapped. "Seeing all this just reminds me of… Never mind. I'm coming."

So saying, she hopped over the rail and down to the lower level, and the Disciple followed her. They touched down near the dais and examined the bodies there more closely in the stronger lantern light. Up close, they could see that these corpses were burned and terror-wracked like the two guards outside had been. Jade clenched her teeth but gave no other sign of her discomfort.

"You're the expert," the Disciple said, casually strolling among the bodies, occasionally nudging one with a toe. Despite his casual air, he studiously avoided the hole in the center of the dais. "Any idea what did this?"

Jade shook her head. "Could have been a suicide ritual. Their deaths burn a hole into the demon realm, then they consign their souls to their masters. But that would've been quick. They wouldn't have tried to run."

"They might have," the Disciple said. "Confronting death inspires uncustomary behavior."

"As you well know, Disciple," a voice said from the darkness beneath the mezzanine. It was cold and familiar and possessed of a cruel amusement. Jade and the Disciple both turned and saw the Visitor in the Hall of Obsidian Mirrors crouching over a corpse in the shadows. Standing and coming toward them, he appeared to be smiling beneath the brim of his hat.

At Nexus' surface, a panic was spreading. Dawn had broken on this last day of Calibration, and the citizens had largely awakened to attend to their jobs. A large population of middle-class workers and the working poor came from the Sentinel's Hill and Firewander districts, and it was from those regions that the spread of the Things That Dwell in Corners originated. From the Undercity homes to towering tenements, people awoke to find the manifestations playing at the edges of the perceptions, taunting and terrifying them.

Yet, try as they might to ignore, rationalize or wish away the phantasmagoria of the Things That Dwell in

Corners, they could not overlook the rampage of the hopping puppeteers. They scattered in horror as the inscrutable fiends tore down what hard work had built, only to carry it off and reshape it as mad whim dictated. And where the puppeteers encountered terrified citizens, they incorporated the flailing bodies in their designs. Dozens of their hair-thin legs twined around select victims and hauled them away to be foundation blocks or keystones. Where they encountered infants or young children, the puppeteers snatched them up with great care and cradled them, screaming, near their coin-sized hearts.

Being unfamiliar with the denizens of Malfeas, most of the terrified masses assumed that the pyroclastic Wyld energy of Firewander had spilled over into the rest of the city, as happened from time to time. Yet, the sentinels hired by the Council of Entities to watch for such incursions knew better. They could make out the shapes of the hopping puppeteers against the preternaturally dark sky; they could see the dance of Zsofika and hear her dread cadence; they could see Jacint hovering over the city and hear his song of damnation. Taking all this in, the watchers sounded clarion alarums that carried on the wind from Sentinel's Hill to Cinnabar and on to every other district in the waking metropolis, even over the incessant clang of industry in Nighthammer. It was a signal they seldom had occasion to ring out, as it was a cry of direst import. The first part of it commanded the soldiers of every mercenary company with whom the Council had dealings to stand now in defense of their city home, regardless of how else they might be contractually bound. The second part of the call told them that the danger against which they must stand was to be found within the city itself, rather than without. Following parts told where in the city the trouble was, then the entire sequence repeated, urging the fighting men to mobilize.

And mobilize they did, though slowly. Many mercenaries who were new to the city spent precious time deciphering the archaic warning signals and deciding how to react accordingly. Others dragged their feet, unaccustomed as they were to fighting during Calibration—which was a notoriously inauspicious time for armies to do their work. Some were simply too large and unwieldy to deploy with agility, especially for the in-city fighting that the warning signals seemed to call for. Still others held back, resenting their contractual obligations to the Council of Entities.

Yet, many fighting men did respond to the warning from Sentinel's Hill, at first expecting to find Wyld-barbarians overrunning the Undercity or the Fair Folk to be pouring out of Firewander. Hooded Executioners and Iron Wolves swarmed toward that district both to confront the bizarre menace there and to rescue the citizens whose homes were being torn apart. Eagle Striders took to the streets to break up rampaging, panicked mobs and to curtail the widespread looting that threatened to break out at every turn. The Jackal Spears and the Stalking Spiders even took it upon themselves to punish the abuses of those rare mercenaries who took this opportunity to indulge in the tumult.

Most of the mercenaries who deployed earliest and fastest, however, turned their attention toward Zsofika, her jade lions and her growing army of standardbearers. They heard the pounding cadence of her hunting rhythm, as well as the mournful howl of her kite flutes. They heard the shattering of glass and the splintering of wood that occurred every time she clashed her swords together. They marked her progress by the mobs of terrified civilians that stampeded away from her. They marked her progress by the smoke that rose from her as she stalked her prey. They marked her progress by the excitement of the Things That Dwell in Corners, which thrashed in waves of adulation at her every step.

But despite all their ease in finding her, few could resist her dread advance. Many soldiers simply fled, driven mad with terror by Zsofika's music. Others faltered as their blessed weapons or the reliquaries of their patron gods shattered before the might of the teodozjia's scripture. Even those captained by mighty God-Blooded heroes retreated when their commanders quailed and diminished before the jade lions' words. And those few that were driven to attack—either by an excess of bravery or the senseless desperation of mortal terror—did so poorly and with no coordination. The teodozjia scattered their cavalry, Zsofika herself slaughtered their commanders, and the kite flute standardbearers trod their skittish infantry underfoot. And in all this conflict, Zsofika proceeded in a trance, focused solely on the lone mercenary captain who would be her prey. She did not know his name, but she knew where he was and that she must kill him.

What she did not know was that her prey, Captain Dace of the Bronze Tigers, was aware of her progress and was lying in wait for her. Having prepared his men first thing this morning for a danger he could not name, his was the first mercenary company to respond to the warnings from Sentinel's Hill. Yet, instead of rushing into danger as less experienced captains had begun to do, Dace had sent scouts into the city to determine where the Bronze Tigers were most needed. They had all returned in short order, wild-eyed with inconsolable panic, raving about the danger that was on its way. In response, Dace had formed his men up on his compound's parade ground and given them their orders. They would await this growing, oncoming army here on their own home ground. They would let the enemy advance and overextend itself. Then, they would throw open the gates and meet the aggressor head to head, right on the street where the advancing force had no room to maneuver.

Many of the men questioned Dace about what the scouts had reported, while others wondered aloud what doom had befallen Nexus that so much chaos had erupted all at once. When he could give no answer, fearful whispers and murmuring broke out, and the men's courage began to waver. The clash of demonic war drums and the howl of malfeasant pipers unmanned them, and the shrill call of the Sentinel's Hill alarms unsettled their mounts. Yet, Dace was unafraid. He rode out in front of them on his enormous cavalry charger and stood up in the stirrups where all of his men could see him. With his Dragon-Blooded lieutenant by his side, he held aloft his golden sword and let his sunburst caste mark blaze as he exhorted them.

"Gird up your courage men!" he called, riding back and forth before them. "Still your mounts, and hold fast your weapons! You don't know fear! You don't know defeat! You only know victory! You've put down armies twice your size! You've sent barbarians and beastmen sniveling back to the Wyld! You've crushed Fair Folk raiders and sent the walking dead screaming to Oblivion! And why? Because you're the favored army of the Unconquered Sun! You can't be beaten because, wherever you go, the power of the Unconquered Sun goes with you! So, let's show these bastards that power and let it scour them from Creation! Let it burn them back to Hell!"

Those words broke through the fear in Dace's men, and they cheered their devotion to his leadership. Thus it was that the Bronze Tigers were the only ones not to falter or retreat before Zsofika's demon soldiers. When their lookouts atop the walls gave the signal, the heavily armored foot soldiers deployed from the rear of the compound then doubled back on parallel streets to approach Zsofika's force from both flanks. When those men were in position, the wardens threw open the compound's front gates, and Dace's horsemen charged howling into the midst of their enemies without fear. And in the center of the formation were Dace and Risa, brimming with their divine, Exalted power.

Jade recovered from her surprise first and raised her bow to take aim at the Visitor in the Hall of Obsidian Mirrors. She drew, aimed and fired all in one motion, yet even then, she was too slow to gain the advantage. Already, the Visitor held a bone needle in his hand, and as Jade loosed her arrow, he sidestepped and hurled the spike at her. Yet, rather than hitting an eye, her throat or some other soft target, the projectile missed her by inches and bisected her bowstring instead. Her powerbow recoiled and nearly jumped out of her hand, and the snap of the taut wire lashed her above her right eye. Jade lurched backward, and blood blinded her.

To add insult to injury, the Visitor snagged Jade's arrow out of the air and snapped it in half between his fingers as he continued to come toward her. He then held up one half in each hand and imparted to them a portion of his necrotic energy, such that they growled with malignant hunger. He flicked the two missiles at Jade casually, almost within arm's reach of her. Jade maintained the presence of mind to defend herself, swinging her disabled powerbow like a short staff, but the hungry projectiles thwarted her. While she was able to knock one away, the other twisted in mid-flight and plunged into her thigh. She yelped and staggered, stumbling over the outstretched arm of a Salmalin corpse at her feet, and the Visitor closed in. He swept her wounded leg with a short kick, then hammered a flat-palm thrust into her chest, sending her flying backward several feet.

She landed in front of the Disciple, who caught her less than gently but kept her from sprawling over a pew or into more of the scattered bodies. He lifted her with one arm around her midsection so she could get her feet under her, but when she tried to jump back toward the Visitor, the Disciple restrained her. She tried to pull away, but his grip just tightened around her orichalcum-flanged cuirass.

"That's enough, Jade," he hissed.

"Indeed it is," the Visitor said, stopping short and smiling even wider. "For you as well, Disciple. You've forestalled the inevitable long enough. You have an obligation to fulfill, and I expect you to make good on it. In fact, I command it, just as I did last night. Kill her. On your oath, kill her now."

Jade's eyes flared as she realized how, once again, she had been maneuvered, lied to and betrayed by this man her ancient soul wanted so much to trust. She struggled and tried to get a hand on the knife at her belt, but he twisted with her and grabbed her wrist, never releasing his grip around her abdomen. The contact evoked an ill-timed memory of a similar contact shared between them long ago in a hollow beneath a waterfall, but Jade had become accustomed enough to the phenomenon to ignore it now. And if the Disciple experienced the same thing, he showed no sign. As Jade tried to smash his feet with her heels and roll free with her knife in hand, the Disciple hauled her entirely off the ground and took the knife away from her. An instant later, he pressed the blade to her throat, and Jade ceased her struggles, rather than forcing the issue. Seeing this, the Visitor laughed with delight.

"Go ahead then," Jade sneered over her shoulder, trying to blink blood out of her eye. "Do it. It's what I deserve for trusting you."

"Don't panic, Jade," the Disciple murmured. "You can still trust me. I have no intention of doing you harm."

"Your intention pales before your obligation, Disciple," the Visitor said, frowning slightly. "I admire your willpower thus far, but you have no choice. Kill her now or you'll be breaking your oath. It's her blood on your hands or our gods' wrath on your head. You can't avoid them both."

"As a matter of fact," the Disciple said with a grim smile, "I can."

So saying, he took the knife away from Jade's throat and eased her back to the ground. Her eyes danced in confusion and smoldering anger, but she did not take the opportunity to lash out at him. He rewarded this morsel of grudging trust by returning her knife to her and stepping up so that he was between her and the Visitor.

"Kill her!" the Visitor barked, incredulous.

"Jade," the Disciple said, looking her in the eyes, "if this faithless recreant is still loitering here, I suspect his master's work isn't finished. That must mean that his partner and your priestess are still here as well—likely down that hole. Kindly do the honors of dealing with them."

"Disciple, I command you to kill that girl! Immediately!"

"Just a second," the Disciple chided over his shoulder. "Jade?"

"I… I'll take care of it," Jade said, trying to hide how her mind was reeling. "But don't you want some help dealing with him?"

The Disciple looked at the bleeding gash over Jade's eye, the broken arrow shaft sticking out of her thigh and the useless powerbow in her hand, and a smile touched the corner of his mouth. "I'll manage. You just go. I'll be along shortly."

Jade narrowed her eyes warily, but ultimately, she did as the Disciple said. She nodded once, then headed for the door that led back out to the antechamber and the downward stairway—which seemed safer than plunging down the hole in the center of this chamber's floor.

"And you…" the Disciple said, raising his bow and turning toward the Visitor, who was only now breaking his paralyzing stupefaction. "You should sanctify your oaths more carefully."

The Visitor tried to create a bone needle, but the Disciple drew and fired an arrow into his hand. He then began to advance.

"You were too eager to shame me," he said. "You rejoiced in my show of cowardice."

He fired again, his arm a blur, and an obsidian shaft passed under the rim of the Visitor's hat. The Visitor tried to grab it, but that was impossible at this range. The shaft only nicked him, however, cutting his brow above the right eye. The Disciple continued to advance, and the ring of dried blood that marred his forehead began to bleed freely once again. The Visitor began to back away now, cradling his twice-punctured hand against his chest.

"But you didn't listen to what I said. I swore an oath to do anything you asked, and for days I've been marking your words very carefully. Your every polite request has been my command."

The Disciple put his hand to his empty bowstring, and when he drew it back, a portion of his power coalesced into a jagged sliver of black glass. He loosed this relic arrow at almost point-blank range, and it pierced the Visitor's thigh, shattering inside the wound. The Visitor howled and tripped backward over a stone pew. The Disciple jumped up onto that pew before the Visitor could rise, and he held the rival deathknight down with a foot against his throat. He could see the Visitor's eyes beneath his broad hat now, and the Walker in Darkness's undying diplomat looked terrified.

"Yet, your actual *commands*," he said, laying a hand to his empty bowstring once again, "have been nothing to me but the blather of a Yozi sympathizer."

The Visitor opened his mouth to speak, but the Disciple applied gentle pressure to his throat and drew back his bowstring. As he did, an aura of radiant black surrounded him, and a bolt of pure, crackling Oblivion appeared where an arrow should have been. The Disciple shook his head and aimed this splinter of the Void at the Visitor's forehead.

"Silence," he said. "There's only one thing I want to hear from you. First, though, I want you to foreswear the oath I gave you and revoke my obligations. You'll do that with a nod, and you'll sanctify your promise. Are we agreed?"

The Visitor closed his eyes, nodded and sanctified this new oath. Glowing black symbols swirled around him and the Disciple, abolishing the power of the Disciple's earlier oath.

"Good," the grim archer said, breathing somewhat deeper in relief. "Now, I want you to beg. Beg just like the Yozis did in the time before time. Beg me to spare you and let you live."

The fury of the Bronze Tigers' charge shocked and impressed Zsofika, and she almost checked her inexorable progress at the sight of it. Her quarry, it seemed, had come out to face her with honor and dignity, rather than cowering or fleeing from her. She had not expected that. Nor had she expected her quarry to be one of the contemptible and accursed Chosen of the Unconquered Sun. The sight of the mark blazing on his brow and the determination on the face of his Dragon-Blooded lieutenant instilled Zsofika with a deep-seated, instinctive terror that harked back to her masters' defeat at the hands of ones like him. The cadence of her infernal procession faltered, and the trill of her standardbearers' kite flutes warbled off key for just a moment. Even her jade lions hissed in agitation. Yet, despite having reason enough to fear the Solar Exalted, the demons had even more reason to hate them. So, while Zsofika's forces flinched, they did not break rank.

For their part, Dace's men showed no fear whatsoever. Emboldened by their captain's speech and his aura of power, they would have followed him anywhere and done anything he commanded. Most of them would have done as much anyway, especially the riders of his cavalry. Most of them had left the Wolves with him after his Exaltation, and they still carried the broken fang daggers to prove it. Now, at his urging, they charged this slowly growing demon army, howling and roaring in elation with every confidence that their captain would lead them to victory.

The first wave of cavalry crashed into the front rank of demon footmen in the middle of the street, and the battle was joined. The standardbearers lowered their kite flutes to plant them like pikes, but Dace's heavy horsemen trampled them and carved a path into the heart of their formation. Boxed in between walled compounds, the demons could do little but face the charge. Those standardbearers who tried to escape into the side streets met Dace's foot soldiers who penned them in and drove them back into the cavalry. And as the horses rode them down and the soldiers' swords and spears slashed them apart, the demons disintegrated and were drawn inexorably back to Malfeas. The diminishing song of the kite flutes mingled with squeals of anguish, and only the demons' sheer numbers kept the conflict from immediately becoming a rout. Their numbers, that is, and the fearsome power of their command cadre.

As Dace, Risa and a faithful detachment of riders bogged down and were absorbed in the melee, the contingent of cavalrymen who had led the charge cut a path through their opponents right to Zsofika and her jade lions.

The men roared their courage and slashed at every demon in reach, but despite their zeal, they were no match for the demons they faced. Slashing outward with both black swords, Zsofika intercepted this rash charge alone and knocked the riders and horses aside like wind blowing down tall grass. The dead and wounded crashed to the street, unhorsing those of their unharmed fellows who were too close to get out of the way. And where the living fell, the jade lions pounced, crushing armored bodies and tearing flesh all in time with their inexorable rhythm. Demon footmen converged on these downed soldiers as well, making way for their mistress to advance. Another, smaller, group of riders tried to break away and attack Zsofika, but the jade lions intercepted them and tore them down as well. Zsofika ignored those distractions and continued toward Dace.

"Risa!" Dace called, cleaving an air pocket between his horse and hers. "Signal the foot to start closing in, then form whatever's left of your fifty up on me! Wherever this bitch thinks she's going, we're stopping her here!"

Risa nodded sharply, then whistled out the signal Dace had called for. Foot soldiers started pushing their way toward the center street, forcing Zsofika's footmen into tighter quarters. Risa whistled out again, and some twenty mounted riders who'd spread out at random across the width of the street formed back up around her and Dace. Then, at a howl from their Exalted commander, this concentrated force plunged straight to the heart of Zsofika's dissipated procession. Instead of making the first part of his men absorb Zsofika's counterattack, he shouted for a formation change just as the rider's came within range. Rather than throwing themselves headlong into the demon's blades, the riders split up around her and drove back the demon soldiers who tried to rush to their mistress's aid. Risa and a select detachment of canny veterans made a special effort to intercept the rush of Zsofika's jade lions, and the Dragon-Blood's verdant anima flared as her enormous jade-tipped spear hacked into their impossibly malleable jade hides.

That left only Dace at the center of the formation, but he did not turn aside as he'd ordered his men to do. While his brave mounted men cleared him a space, he charged straight at Zsofika, brandishing his glowing orichalcum blade. He no longer felt the pain and fatigue of his confrontation with the Emissary. The power of the Unconquered Sun burned within him and flooded him with strength. When Zsofika raised a sword to block his attack, his daiklave sheared off three of her fingers and sent the black blade flying. Yet, Zsofika was fast and powerful in her own right, and the sword in her other hand slashed the throat of Dace's horse. The beast went out from under him, and he jumped clear, disappearing into a knot of standardbearers, who piled on him. A moment later, these demon footmen flew back in all directions, and only Dace remained, his entire body glowing.

Zsofika smiled to see this, and she leaped through the air at Dace, trailing smoke from her hair and burning eyes. Dace sprang forward to meet her halfway, and when their swords crossed high above the street, lightning flashed in the clouds. They hit the ground unharmed and rushed each other again, and their swords were a ringing, crashing blur between them. Thunder exploded in the sky, and the clouds roiled, mirroring the chaos below. For every hack and slash of Dace's reaver daiklave, Zsofika answered with an up-thrust vambrace or a slash with her own remaining weapon. After a particularly intense exchange, the combatants paused to size each other up. Dace managed to nick and wound her a number of times, but never decisively. He remained unharmed thus far, but his armor was on its last fraying straps.

"I have but to kill you to win my freedom, Sun-Child," Zsofika hissed, attacking anew and marking the rhythm of her words with sword-slashes. "I'll flense your skin. I'll taste your marrow. I'll savor your—"

As the demon spoke, Dace parried and listened, timing the rhythm of her attacks. When he thought he had it, he stepped to the side and caught her last attack low on his blade. Knocking her sword aside, he then twisted in a half circle and brought his blade around in a devastating slash that trailed golden fire. The attack passed through Zsofika's chattering mouth, knocking out half of her teeth, ruining her tongue and laying open her cheek.

"Savor that," he spat as the demon reeled in shock. "And remember that taste in Hell."

The wound enraged Zsofika, who recovered from her surprise quickly and leaped at Dace again, howling incoherently. Her black sword was a blur, and it threw furious orange sparks as it clanged off Dace's blade. Dace had to rush backward on the blood-slicked street, and it was all he could do to remain upright and turn Zsofika's attacks aside. But he maintained his footing and defended himself long enough to realize something important. In her outrage and pain, Zsofika had begun to attack out of synch with her standardbearers and jade lions. She had lost her grounding in the unearthly music that impelled and accompanied her, and as a result, her manic attacks became even more predictable. Attacking into her wild swings, Dace was able to score deeper, more painful hits under the demon's guard—though he paid for two of them with wounds of his own.

The first such wound was a vicious, smoking laceration across his left forearm that almost numbed his hand with shock and cost him his grip on his sword. The second came three swings later and was by far the more dangerous of the two. Risking a slash at Zsofika's knee, Dace got too close to her and overextended his blade. Zsofika punished the move with a sharp pommel-blow to his injured arm and a follow-up slash across his chest. The burning cut was a shallow one that wouldn't even leave a scar once it healed, but it had a much more devastating effect—it sheared through what was left of Dace's lamellar armor, exposing his chest and shoulder to the demon's next attack. Yet, this sudden advantage did not ease Zsofika's desperation. Rather than collecting herself and synchronizing her movements with her infernal song once again, she pressed the advantage immediately. She lunged forward in a long, ungainly stride, trying to skewer Dace through the heart with her long black blade.

Realizing what was coming a beat before it got there, Dace twisted and jerked to the side, trying to dodge the attack. Zsofika's blade cut him again, skating off a rib, but it did not find the purchase Zsofika wanted. Even better, as it glanced aside, it punched into the dangling ruin of Dace's armor, its serrated edge catching in the metal and leather. Before the demon could dislodge the blade, Dace seized the opportunity and grabbed the hilt of her sword, crushing her fingers against it. She tried to pull free, but Dace would not let her go, and he chopped into the back of her wrist with his heavy blade. Her hand popped free, spraying him in black blood, and the demon did exactly what a mortal would have done in response to the exact same injury. She pulled the jagged stump to her chest and grabbed it with her other hand (ruined though it was), trying to back away.

Dace did not let her get away. As soon as his blade cleaved off the demon's hand, he rushed forward and aimed another savage chop at the demon's throat. Too hurt and disoriented to defend herself effectively anymore, the demon could only watch as the blazing orichalcum daiklave arced toward her. An instant later, her head crashed to the ground, and her body collapsed on top of it. Zsofika was no more.

With Zsofika gone, her kite flute standardbearers began to panic and scatter. Dace largely ignored them as they fled the light that emanated from him, but he saw that one major threat remained on the field. That threat took the form of Zsofika's one remaining jade lion, which was wounded but still fighting. It seemed to be largely ignoring the mundane weapons of the cavalrymen and foot soldiers surrounding it, but Risa's jade-tipped spear had opened its slick, glossy flesh in several places. That weapon had also done in the second lion, which had already shattered and vanished. As a result, the survivor focused its attention on trying to unhorse her and drag her down. It succeeded in its first goal, digging its claws into the horse's ribs and hindquarters. The animal went down screaming, and it pinned Risa beneath it on top of the haft of her spear. Yet, before the teodozji could capitalize on its gain, Dace tore Zsofika's blade from his ruined armor and pounced on the beast, hacking into its side with a heavy overhand chop. The impact hurled the demon through the air, and when it hit the street's paving stones, it exploded into a million shards that began to evaporate into green smoke.

"Thank you, sir," Risa said, pulling herself from beneath her mount and accepting the hand Dace offered to help her up.

"No problem, Lieutenant. You got the other one?" Risa nodded. "Good. How many men have we lost?"

"Not many," Risa said, looking around. Cavalry and foot units were closing in now, sweeping up the remaining standardbearers that Zsofika had stranded. "Less than fifty."

"Good, because what we've done here puts me in mind to do something else."

"What's that, sir?"

"Have another talk with the Council of Entities," he said, grinning like an old wolf but breathing heavily like an old man. "Maybe even renegotiate our contract."

Risa opened her mouth to answer that, but she saw something in the sky over Firewander that stole her breath and froze the words on her tongue. Dace only saw her eyes go wide with shock at first, but when he turned to face that way, he understood. The unnatural clouds had turned lighter now and begun to break up, allowing the light of the sun to penetrate. But as it did, it revealed a figure hovering over Nexus under the power of two enormous basalt wings. This figure was Jacint, the Prince Upon the Tower, and his fearsome visage made Zsofika look like the child she was. He glared down at the city, singing an ancient and terrible song that had been drowned out until now by the noise of Zsofika's procession.

As soon as Dace could pick the song out on the wind, though, it suddenly fell silent, and Jacint was no longer alone.

Harmonious Jade paused only long enough to yank the broken shaft out of her thigh before proceeding to the ritual chamber beneath the converted Salmalin sanctuary. The wound throbbed and made her leg wobble, but at least the arrowhead wasn't rattling around between her muscles anymore. She ignored it just as she ignored the blood that ran into her eye, stubbornly refusing to clot on her forehead. She set those distractions aside in her mind and fastened her useless bow to the side of her quiver across her back as she descended. Then, when she reached the basement level, she took her blade in hand and opened the door.

Within, she found the Witness of Lingering Shadows standing in the center of the room over the obliterated remains of a summoning circle. She stood directly beneath the hole in the ceiling with her arms straight up, and the ugly light Jade and the Disciple had noticed before seemed to be emanating from her. As Jade entered, the Witness turned to face her with an expression that was half rapture, half agony. Her caste mark swirled with black and yellow-green energy, and her eyes were infernal blue-black orbs. Jade had seen such eyes before in her dreams, and the sight of them froze her.

"I know you," the Witness said as she drew her blade from a thigh sheath. Her voice sounded strange, as if a deeper, older one were layered on top of it. "I thought you might come."

Jade blinked, gathered her courage and took another step toward the Witness, hefting her knife.

"I don't know what you're doing," she said, "but it's over now."

"I'm afraid not," the Witness replied. "I must fulfill my obligation first."

"Fine," Jade said. "As you wish."

With that, she attacked. She feinted with her knife to draw the Witness's weapon out, then disengaged to slash the deathknight's arm. Yet, the Witness was quick, and although she fell for the feint, she managed to avoid Jade's cut just the same. Jade circled in a crouch and took another few experimental stabs, but each time, the Witness held her at bay.

"I know about you," the Witness said, turning with Jade and keeping a wary eye on her. "Your once-master speaks of you often. Considering your past, it seems you'd *want* this to happen."

"If you think that," Jade snarled, "you obviously don't know a thing about me."

The Witness only shrugged with a faint smile and said, "Perhaps. But in time, even you will come to understand why this is necessary."

Jade doubted that, but she was of no mind to argue the point. Having gauged her opponent's speed and agility thus far, she attacked full out, unwilling to let up or give any ground. The Witness managed to dodge some of the attacks and even counter with a few slashes of her own, but her knife never found purchase. Jade dodged the deathknight's blade with eerily unnatural grace and balance while never forgoing her own offensive. She slipped inside the Witness's reach, trapped the wrist of the deathknight's knife hand under her armpit and stabbed her in the abdomen just beneath the ribs. The deathknight's black blade fell from numb fingers, and her eyes shot open. Just to be on the safe side, Jade twisted her blade before she withdrew it then pulled it across the Witness's pale throat, spilling deep crimson blood. The light leached from the woman's caste mark, and her eyes faded from infernal blue-black to their original shade. The fingers of her free hand clutched the golden lion on the front of Jade's cuirass, and she tried to whisper something, but her words were lost to Oblivion. Finally, her legs went out from under her, and she sank to her knees. Jade shoved the woman down.

Only then did she think to wonder where Selaine Chaisa had hidden herself. As the unwholesome light surrounding the Witness faded, to be replaced with the pure glow of Jade's anima, Jade noticed a figure in green and red

Salmalin robes sitting back in the darkest corner of the room. The figure sat with her knees to her chest and her arms wrapped around her legs, and she wore the ceremonial jade mask of a priestess. Flicking blood from her knife, Jade crossed the chamber and stood over this hunched figure, glowing with the power of the Unconquered Sun. She tore the jade mask away and saw the same mass of bandages she had seen Chaisa wearing at Kerrek Deset's manor house, only Chaisa's eyes were no longer covered.

Now, after all the trouble she had put herself through, Jade had finally found the woman she had originally come to Nexus to kill. She hoisted the priestess to her feet and put the knife to her throat. Chaisa didn't even seem to know that she was there.

In the darkened sky above Nexus, a gleaming silver oval appeared and formed itself into an empty floating mask a few meters from where Jacint hovered. The demon regarded this appearance with distaste, then shielded his eyes briefly as a bright flash lit up the air in front of him. When Jacint lowered his hand, the Emissary stood before him en pointe with his arms crossed. The Council's enforcer wore stark white robes that flapped in the high, skirling winds, and an ancient power burned in the eyes of his perfect silver mask.

"I know you," Jacint said, pausing in his arduous work. His voice sounded strange, as if a deeper, older one were layered on top of it. "I thought you might come."

"Of course," the Emissary said. "You left me little choice, inviting a most disagreeable outcast to my city when you, yourself, are not welcome. Is it possible I could persuade you to leave of your own accord?"

"I'm afraid not," Jacint sighed. "I must fulfill my obligation first."

"You're aware of what and who I represent," the Emissary said. "Surely you realize I can't allow that?"

"I know about you," Jacint said, nodding. "Your once-master speaks of you often. Considering your past, it seems you'd *want* this to happen."

"It isn't your place to speculate about what I want," the Emissary said. "Your forfeited that right long ago. And for your presumption, I've decided to educate you about what your proper place truly is."

Brimming with power and secure in the knowledge that his greater self was at the threshold of Creation, Jacint smiled in contempt for this arrogant "Emissary." He spread his basalt wings and raised his hands to form a crackling ball of luminous energy, which would surely be powerful enough to obliterate the upstart before him.

Before he could do the deed, something changed in the Undercity far below. All at once, the Abyssal anchor through whom he had been filtering his infernal essence to break open a pathway to Malfeas was taken away, and the fissure that he had labored so long to wedge open slammed shut, barring his greater self's way into this world. Jacint cried out in alarm.

At the same time, the Emissary put a delicate hand to his perfect mask and pulled the silver façade aside. So doing, he unleashed an aspect of himself that had never before been revealed in Creation. Green and purple energy exploded from the Emissary, and Jacint recoiled in abject horror from the mysteries he saw revealed within. The energy stained the clouds in the sky such that they later rained bile for the better part of that day. Some of that power even drifted down to the city, and every human and animal child conceived from that moment until the end of Calibration was born at exactly the same time exactly nine months later. When they were born, they were horribly deformed but possessed of a malign intelligence that disturbed their parents and siblings.

This awesome power seized Jacint and consumed him, hurling him back to the demon world with the force of a hundred thunderbolts. And when the Prince Upon the Tower crashed back into his prison dimension, his entire nature was changed. From that point forward, whenever anyone summoned Jacint, he could no longer exist in the demon world and Creation simultaneously as even the least of the first circle demons could do. Such was the Emissary's unbridled power, and such was the nature of the lesson he had chosen to impart.

And when the lesson was finished, the Emissary forced his mask back into place, containing what was left of his prodigious store of power. He was much diminished by what he had done, and it would take time to recoup what he had paid out. So, with a twist of air and space, he vanished from sight and headed for the chamber of the Council of Entities. He would inform the Council of his intention, then retreat to his private place until he had regained his full power. With the worst of the danger past and the city relatively safe again, the Council would just have to enforce its will without him for a while.

The Disciple of the Seven Forbidden Wisdoms dropped into the chamber through the hole in the ceiling and found Harmonious Jade leaning against the far wall restringing her bow. The black glow of his anima mixed with the gold and violet of hers, throwing strange shadows all around them. Jade looked up as the Disciple entered, and the two of them simultaneously wiped a trickle of blood from their brows.

"I see you didn't need my help," the Disciple said, stepping over the prone body of the Witness of Lingering Shadows, who lay in a drying crimson pool. Another body lay in the corner, facing the wall. "Have I kept you waiting long?"

"Not especially," Jade said, glancing away from the embarrassing look in his eyes.

"I take it that's your erstwhile hero in the corner."

"It's Chaisa."

"And you've done what you came all this way to do?"

"I did," Jade sighed. "I killed her. Or rather, I put her out of her misery. After all her lies and betrayals over all the years I've known her, I think I actually did her a kindness at the end. She just looked so wretchedly pathetic and afraid. I pitied her. And to think, I used to look up to her…"

"So, do you feel any different now? More independent, perhaps? More mature?"

"Not especially."

The Disciple smiled. "That doesn't surprise me. All things being equal, of course, you could have saved us both a great deal of trouble if you'd just killed her your first day in the city and gone back home to Chiaroscuro."

"How insightful," Jade said, smiling back at him despite herself. "But I thought it better to wait… until you were satisfied."

The Disciple slung his bow over his shoulder, and his smile turned into a surprised laugh. "Of course, you're right. I remember that."

Jade laughed along with him, then neither one of them said anything for a moment.

"So, what about the other deathknight?" Jade finally asked before an awkward silence could descend. "The one upstairs with you, I mean. The Visitor"

"I dealt with him," the Disciple said. "You'll probably never see or hear from him again."

"And what about you? Will I ever see or hear from you again?"

"I'm sorry?" the Disciple said, taken aback. "Was I going somewhere?"

Jade blinked. "Well, I thought… Your work here is done; my work here is done. I assumed you had some Underworld home you had to get back to. Maybe your Deathlord was expecting you. I didn't think you intended to stay in Nexus."

"I don't," the Disciple said. "Nonetheless, I didn't intend to leave right away. Actually, I was rather hoping you and I could spend some time together first. Time to get to know each other; time to unearth long-buried memories. Perhaps time enough to forge some new ones. If you're amenable…"

"I see," Jade said, and for the first time, she looked into his eyes without drawing away apprehensively. "Yes, I think I'd like that."

EPILOGUE

A week after Calibration ended, life had returned to normal in Nexus. The remaining demons had been hunted down, and the rebuilding of what they had damaged had begun. Peace had largely been restored, and trade flowed as smoothly as it ever did. The Council of Entities was still in control, and the city still stood, so for most of the citizens, life went on much as it always had.

One of those citizens who was particularly enjoying the return of the status quo was Dace. In the wake of the recent unpleasantness and the subsequent withdrawal of the Emissary, he had caught the Council of Entities at an especially vulnerable opportunity and renegotiated his mercenary company's contract on especially favorable terms. The Council was willing to consider him more of a business associate than a servile thug, granting him the respect his actions had earned him. It had returned full control of his men and affairs to him and torn up the lien it had had filed against his property. It had even cancelled more than one of his outstanding debts as a sign of good faith. The Councilors welcomed Dace and his men now, asking only that they help maintain the peace for a little while longer and adhere to the Incunabulum at all times. This arrangement satisfied Dace and relaxed him after so many days of excitement. Therefore, it was with a dizzy, sinking feeling that he greeted Harmonious Jade when she appeared at his office door late in the evening, one week to the day since he'd last seen her. Her arrival didn't tend to bode well for him.

"Captain," Jade said, slipping in and closing the door. "May I come in?"

"Sure," Dace said. "How are you, Jade?"

"Fine. You?"

"Can't complain." When Jade fell silent and started to look pretty much everywhere but at him, Dace finally said, "Is there something I can do for you?"

"Not really, Captain," the girl said. "I just hadn't seen you since before... everything. I heard about what you did, though. They say you faced Zsofika one on one, and she never even touched you."

Dace shrugged. "It wasn't quite that easy, but I've seen worse than the likes of her."

"I know. I heard about you and the Emissary at the Executioners' compound, too. I... I'm glad he didn't kill you for getting in his way."

Dace frowned and scratched the underside of his beard. "Yeah, well..."

"Yeah."

Another period of silence loomed between them, and this time, it was Jade who broke it.

"So, Risa said you all were supposed to move out of here last week. What happened?"

"The power of timely renegotiation," Dace said. "Word's been getting around about what the men and I did for the city, and so is word about what Mastiff and his cohorts could have done to the city. Risa and I sat down with some of the Council members to discuss it, and we got things all worked out."

"That's great. I would've felt bad if... you know."

Dace dismissed that notion with a wave. "Things could have been worse. But enough about that. I've been worried about you this last week. Where have you been?"

"Actually, about that... That's why I'm here. It turns out I'm no longer welcome in Nexus. I'm leaving."

"What? Who says you're not welcome?"

"That would be the Council," Jade said. "They even made it into a city ordinance. 'The woman called Harmonious Jade is hereby exiled from Nexus and must depart by sunset tomorrow, never to return.' They decreed that yesterday."

"Does this have anything to do with what you did at Kerrek Deset's manor? They said you painted the walls red with his servants' blood, robbed the man blind and then murdered him in his bathrobe just for fun."

"That's mostly just a big misunderstanding," Jade said, which earned her an incredulous look. "I did rob Kerrek, a little, but I didn't murder him. And yes, I killed more than a few of his servants, but they were already dead when I got there."

"I see."

"I bet it was one of them who gave my name and description to the Stalking Spiders."

"You know," Dace said, "maybe the less you explain about this the better."

"Sure," Jade said. "Let's just let it suffice to say that enough proof has come out tying Kerrek to Chaisa and those deathknights that the Council sees what I did as a sort of public service. All the same, I'm not really from here, so it's not like exile's going to be any big hardship. It's about time I was heading home anyway."

"And where's that?"

"Chiaroscuro... for now, anyway. You should visit sometime. That is, if you're ever down the coast. If you wanted to. You could tell me about how you found your blade."

"Sure," Dace said. "I'd hate to lose touch so soon after meeting you. I don't get to spend much time with others... like us."

"Me either."

"And when it comes down to it, we made a strangely effective kind of team for a while there, didn't we?"

"I suppose."

"It'd be a shame to lose that, especially with everything so screwed up in the world these days. With people like us working together, like in the old days, there isn't much we couldn't do. But then, I guess that's a discussion for another time. You must be anxious to get back home."

Jade shrugged. "Not really, but sunset's coming, and I don't want to take my chances. Take care, Captain. I'll see you around."

"You too, Jade. And good luck to you."

Jade nodded, and without another word, she was gone.

"So, Nexus still lives and breathes?" the Walker in Darkness said to the deathknight kneeling in shame before him.

"It does, Master," the Visitor in the Hall of Obsidian Mirrors replied.

"And the Witness of Lingering Shadows is no more?"

"Her soul has gone forward, Master. Her body rots in Nexus' Undercity."

"And Adorjan was prevented from fulfilling her obligation?"

"It was not possible to accommodate her, Master," the Visitor said.

"I cannot even articulate my displeasure," the Deathlord said. He turned to his consort, the Green Lady, who stood next to him with a hand on his shoulder. "What reward befits this performance?"

"Let him decide," the Green Lady replied.

"Yes," Walker said, turning once again to his vassal. "What should I do with you? Surely, you have some idea."

"None I would dare voice, Master," the Visitor said, "for fear of disappointing you further."

Walker smiled at that, though he did not let the Visitor see the gesture. The Green Lady, also, was pleased.

"Then, think on it," the Deathlord said. "Excuse yourself to the terrace and wait for me there. When I join you, we will enter the Labyrinth and journey to the Well of the Void.

There, you will explain your incompetence to my master, whom Adorjan also failed in the time before time."

The Visitor visibly trembled, and his voice nearly cracked on his reply. "As you command, Master." He then retreated in haste, leaving the Walker in Darkness alone with the Green Lady.

"Things are not proceeding as you foresaw," the Deathlord said. "Of all the victories you prophesied for this enterprise, only the diminishing of the Emissary of Nexus has actually come to pass."

"I know, my lord, and that disturbs me. But as I warned you at the outset, prophesies and auguries that target the time of Calibration are notoriously suspect. With the added influence of the Yozi princes, even my foresight could not account for every possibility."

"No, it could not, which is why I don't hold you accountable for my deathknights' failure. But if your prophesies and auguries ever prove so unhelpful again, you'll be the one joining me at the Well of the Void."

"Yes, my lord," the Green Lady murmured. "That would only be fitting."

About the Author

Carl Bowen has written two novels, two novellas and more than a dozen short stories for White Wolf's World of Darkness setting, as well as a good chunk of game supplement material. He's also a copyeditor and sometime developer. **A Day Dark as Night** is his first foray into writing for the **Exalted** setting. He lives in Stone Mountain, Georgia, and in his spare time, he runs across clotheslines and practices back flips.

Acknowledgments

As much of a genius as I like to think I am, I couldn't have written this book entirely on my own. I'd like to thank Geoffrey C. Grabowski (**Exalted**'s developer for White Wolf) for double-checking my continuity and setting details. Thanks also to Philippe Boulle (White Wolf Fiction's managing editor) for going over the story with fresh eyes and helping me tighten up the weak bits. And finally, my enduring thanks to my good pal John Chambers (**Exalted**'s copyeditor) for helping me "get" **Exalted**, for untangling some of the setting's tricky hidden background and for suggestions that shaped the writing of this book for the better. (The mask thing, for instance, was all John.)

Credit where it's due: I couldn't have done it without you guys. Thanks.